The yellowbacks... classics of popular fiction

The yellowjackets or yellowbacks were a great series of bestselling adventure and crime thrillers that had its origins in the mid to late 19th century following on from the 'penny dreadfuls'. They virtually began the mass market revolution of the early 20th century with a clear standard format and imprint/series livery (what would today be called branding). Hodder & Stoughton published the yellowjackets in two main series with series run dates of: 1923-1939 and later 1949-1957.

As the tagline ('where thrillers really began') on the back cover implies, the imprint and series focused on thrillers that were the bestsellers of their time. This current reissue or retro revival if you will, brings back many of these masterpieces, now classics in their own way and extends it further by including key titles from that period that were either great crime or thriller or even general commercial fiction (including sub-genres of noir, horror, gothic, romance, westerns etc.) influences of their time. There are some perennial favourites and many rarities either lost or not easily available being revived in the current series. Writers and characters ranged from adventure heroes like Bulldog Drummond, Allan Quatermain, Richard Hannay or the Saint through thriller grandmasters Edgar Wallace and E. Phillips Oppenheim, crime and mystery maestros like Patricia Wentworth, GK Chesterton, Agatha Christie and the Detection club, to western and swashbucklers like Zane Grey, Max Brand, Captain Blood and even romance or general fiction classics like Hermina Black, Denise Robins, Marie Corelli or Stella Morton. These were books that had storytelling at their heart and always entertained.

The yellowbacks had both hardback (with varying design elements) and paperback (which built the series look) versions with the latter still carrying the imprint 'yellowjacket'. The current reissues pay tribute to both and use an amalgam of elements from both editions while retaining the complete yellow (or 'mustard-plaster') livery with the author's name in blue beveled type with a 'simulated emboss' effect and a white outer 'outline', and the book title in black. These reissues retain the distinctive size of the original mass market paperback and follow the three main category variations—the thrillers (crime, westerns, mystery, adventure) had blue lettering for the author's name, while Romance and softer general fiction had red; and other categories like humour had green.

For more detail and a full list of titles visit https://www.hachetteindia.com/home/yellowbacks

ARSÈNE LUPIN
THE TEETH OF THE TIGER

ARSÈNE LUPIN THE TEETH OF THE TIGER

Maurice Marie Émile Leblanc was a French novelist and writer of short stories, known primarily as the creator of the gentleman burglar, adventurer and detective Arsène Lupin, often described as a French counterpart to Arthur Conan Doyle's Sherlock Holmes and E.W. Hornung's Raffles.

Refusing the career that his father had set up for him at a card factory, Leblanc instead went to Paris in 1888, to pursue writing as a journalist. But he soon turned novelist and storyteller. His first novel, Une femme (A Woman), published in 1893 was a success and was followed by other works, such as Des couples (The Couples), Voici des ailes (Here are Wings) and a play La pitié, released in 1902, which was a flop. In 1905, Pierre Lafitte, the director of the monthly Je sais tout, commissioned a short story from Leblanc, with the brief that he was to combine the appeal of A.J Raffles by Ernest William Hornung and Sherlock Holmes. The result was 'L'Arrestation d'Arsène Lupin' ('The Arrest of Arsène Lupin') which was a huge success. Two years later, Arsène Lupin, Gentleman Burglar was released, and the rest was history – with one of the most successful series being born.

ARSÈNE LUPIN
THE TEETH OF THE TIGER

Maurice Leblanc

Arsène Lupin, The Teeth of the Tiger
First published in 1914

This Hodder Yellowback edition © Hachette India 2023
(Registered Name: Hachette Book Publishing India Pvt. Ltd.)
An Hachette UK Company www.hachetteindia.com

1

All rights reserved. No part of the publication may be reproduced, stored in a retrieval system (including but not limited to computers, disks, external drives, electronic or digital devices, e-readers, websites), or transmitted in any form or by any means (including but not limited to cyclostyling, photocopying, docutech or other reprographic reproductions, mechanical, recording, electronic, digital versions) without the prior written permission of the publisher, nor be otherwise circulated in any form of binding or cover other than that in which it is published and without a similar condition being imposed on the subsequent purchaser.

The texts in these editions in most cases have been reprinted as is, with minimal editorial changes and by and large no bowdlerizing for political correctness; though in some editions, a few words and phrases considered archaic, or those considered offensive now, along with archaic punctuation may have been modified in places to make the text more accessible to today's readers. The narratives, language, beliefs, social mores and/or cultural depictions, in these volumes are a reflection of their times and must be viewed as such. They may also contain certain cultural, racial and gender prejudices and stereotypes that may be outdated or clearly wrong then and wrong today; but their removal would be tantamount to claiming these prejudices never existed. The Publisher does not endorse or support those depictions or stereotypes; and these books have been made available for a discerning audience that will read it for entertainment value and a chronicle/record of popular fiction of past times.

Cover design by Priya Singh adapted from the original classic yellowjacket by Hodder & Stoughton.

Cover illustration by Ishan Trivedi.

Series note: Some of the books in the series (unless otherwise credited) may have cover or inside illustrations from the original yellowbacks or early editions, and while full restoration has been attempted, some images may be grainy or faded due to the condition of the original material. The end notes or bonus material or blurb details may have been sourced from the public domain or free use publications such as Wikipedia and attribution is hereby made also allowing similar free use reproduction from here. Sources requiring further specific attribution may write in and further detailing and/or corrections shall be made in subsequent printings/editions.

Reprint specifications may be subject to change including but not limited to finishes, paper, colour sections.

ISBN: 978-93-5731-043-7

Hachette Book Publishing India Pvt. Ltd.
4th & 5th Floors, Corporate Centre,
Plot No. 94, Sector 44, Gurugram - 122 003, India

Typeset in Electra LT STD 10/12.5 pt by Manipal Technologies Limited, Manipal

Printed and bound in India by Manipal Technologies Limited, Manipal

CONTENTS

1.	D'Artagnan, Porthos... and Monte Cristo	1
2.	A Man Dead	23
3.	A Man Doomed	45
4.	The Clouded Turquoise	67
5.	The Iron Curtain	96
6.	The Man with the Ebony Walking-Stick	116
7.	Shakespeare's Works, Volume VIII	138
8.	The Devil's Post-Office	159
9.	Lupin's Anger	175
10.	Gaston Sauverand Explains	192
11.	Routed	214
12.	"Help!"	229
13.	The Explosion	246
14.	The "Hater"	265
15.	The Heir to the Hundred Millions	288
16.	Weber Takes His Revenge	311
17.	Open Sesame!	332
18.	Arsène I Emperor of Mauretania	349
19.	"The Snare is Laid. Beware, Lupin!"	366
20.	Florence's Secret	387
21.	Lupin's Lupins	411

1

D'ARTAGNAN, PORTHOS... AND MONTE CRISTO

It was half-past four; M. Desmalions, the Prefect of Police, was not yet back at the office. His private secretary laid on the desk a bundle of letters and reports which he had annotated for his chief, rang the bell and said to the messenger who entered by the main door:

"Monsieur le Préfet has sent for a number of people to see him at five o'clock. Here are their names. Show them into separate waiting-rooms, so that they can't communicate with one another, and let me have their cards when they come."

The messenger went out. The secretary was turning towards the small door that led to his room, when the main door opened once more and admitted a man who stopped and leaned swaying over the back of a chair.

"Why, it's you, Vérot!" said the secretary. "But what's happened? What's the matter?"

Inspector Vérot was a very stout, powerfully built man, with a big neck and shoulders and a florid complexion. He had obviously been upset by some violent excitement, for his face, streaked with red veins and usually so apoplectic, seemed almost pale.

"Oh, nothing, Monsieur le Secrétaire!" he said.

"Yes, yes; you're not looking your usual self. You're gray in the face... And the way you're perspiring..."

Inspector Vérot wiped his forehead and, pulling himself together, said:

"It's just a little tiredness... I've been overworking myself lately: I was very keen on clearing up a case which Monsieur Desmalions had put in my hands. All the same, I have a funny sort of feeling—"

"Will you have a pick-me-up?"

"No, no; I'm more thirsty."

"A glass of water?"

"No, thank you."

"What then?"

"I should like—I should like—"

His voice faltered. He wore a troubled look, as if he had suddenly lost his power of getting out another word. But he recovered himself with an effort and asked:

"Isn't Monsieur Desmalions here?"

"No; he won't be back till five, when he has an important meeting."

"Yes... I know... most important. That's what I'm here for. But I should have liked to see him first. I should so much have liked to see him!"

The secretary stared at Vérot and said:

"What a state you're in! Is your message so urgent as all that?"

"It's very urgent, indeed. It has to do with a crime that took place a month ago, to the day. And, above all, it's a matter of preventing two murders which are the outcome of that other crime and which are to be committed tonight. Yes, tonight, inevitably, unless we take the necessary steps."

"Sit down, Vérot, won't you?"

"You see, the whole thing has been planned in such an infernal manner! You would never have imagined—"

"Still, Vérot, as you know about it beforehand, and as Monsieur le Préfet is sure to give you full powers—"

"Yes, of course, of course. But, all the same, it's terrible to think that I might miss him. So I wrote him this letter, telling him all I know about the business. I thought it safer."

He handed the secretary a large yellow envelope and added:

"And here's a little box as well; I'll leave it on this table. It contains something that will serve to complete and explain the contents of the letter."

"But why don't you keep all that by you?"

"I'm afraid to. They're watching me. They're trying to get rid of me. I shan't be easy in my mind until someone besides myself knows the secret."

"Have no fear, Vérot. Monsieur le Préfet is bound to be back soon. Meanwhile, I advise you to go to the infirmary and ask for a pick-me-up."

The inspector seemed undecided what to do. Once more he wiped away the perspiration that was trickling down his forehead. Then, drawing himself up, he left the office. When he was gone the secretary slipped the letter into a big bundle of papers that lay on the Prefect's desk and went out by the door leading to his own room.

He had hardly closed it behind him when the other door opened once again and the inspector returned, spluttering:

"Monsieur le Secrétaire... it'd be better if I showed you—"

The unfortunate man was as white as a sheet. His teeth were chattering. When he saw that the secretary was gone, he tried to walk across to his private room. But he was seized with an attack of weakness and sank into a chair, where he remained for some minutes, moaning helplessly:

"What's the matter with me?... Have I been poisoned, too? ...Oh, I don't like this; I don't like the look of this!"

The desk stood within reach of his hand. He took a pencil, drew a writing-pad towards him and began to scribble a few characters. But he next stammered:

"Why, no, it's not worthwhile. The Prefect will be reading my letter... What on earth's the matter with me. I don't like this at all!"

Suddenly he rose to his feet and called out:

"Monsieur le Secrétaire, we've got... we've got to... It's for tonight. Nothing can prevent—"

Stiffening himself with an effort of his whole will, he made for the door of the secretary's room with little short steps, like an automaton. But he reeled on the way—and had to sit down a second time.

A mad terror shook him from head to foot; and he uttered cries which were too faint, unfortunately, to be heard. He realized this and looked round for a bell, for a gong; but he was no longer able to distinguish anything. A veil of darkness seemed to weigh upon his eyes.

Then he dropped on his knees and crawled to the wall, beating the air with one hand, like a blind man, until he ended by touching some woodwork. It was the partition-wall.

He crept along this; but, as ill-luck would have it, his bewildered brain showed him a false picture of the room, so that, instead of turning to the left as he should have done, he followed the wall to the right, behind a screen which concealed a third door.

His fingers touched the handle of this door and he managed to open it. He gasped, "Help! Help!" and fell at his full length in a sort of cupboard or closet which the Prefect of Police used as a dressing-room.

"Tonight!" he moaned, believing that he was making himself heard and that he was in the secretary's room. "Tonight! The job is fixed for tonight! You'll see... The mark of the teeth!... It's awful!... Oh, the pain I'm in!... It's the poison! Save me! Help!"

The voice died away. He repeated several times, as though in a nightmare:

"The teeth! The teeth! They're closing!"

Then his voice grew fainter still; and inarticulate sounds issued from his pallid lips. His mouth munched the air like the mouth of one of those old men who seem to be interminably chewing the cud. His head sank lower and lower on his breast. He heaved two or three sighs; a great shiver passed through his body; and he moved no more.

And the death-rattle began in his throat, very softly and rhythmically, broken only by interruptions in which a last instinctive effort appeared to revive the flickering life of the intelligence, and to rouse fitful gleams of consciousness in the dimmed eyes.

The Prefect of Police entered his office at ten minutes to five. M. Desmalions, who had filled his post for the past three years with an authority that made him generally respected, was a heavily built man of fifty with a shrewd and intelligent face. His dress, consisting of a gray jacket-suit, white spats, and a loosely flowing tie, in no way suggested the public official. His manners were easy, simple, and full of good-natured frankness.

He touched a bell, and when his secretary entered, asked:

"Are the people whom I sent for here?"

"Yes, Monsieur le Préfet, and I gave orders that they were to wait in different rooms."

"Oh, it would not have mattered if they had met! However, perhaps it's better as it is. I hope that the American Ambassador did not trouble to come in person?"

"No, Monsieur le Préfet."

"Have you their cards?"

"Yes."

The Prefect of Police took the five visiting cards which his secretary handed him and read:

"Mr Archibald Bright, First Secretary United States Embassy; Maître Lepertuis, Solicitor; Juan Caceres, Attaché to the Peruvian Legation; Major Comte d'Astrignac, retired."

The fifth card bore merely a name, without address or quality of any kind—

DON LUIS PERENNA

"That's the one I'm curious to see!" said M. Desmalions. "He interests me like the very devil! Did you read the report of the Foreign Legion?"

"Yes, Monsieur le Préfet, and I confess that this gentleman puzzles me, too."

"He does, eh? Did you ever hear of such pluck? A sort of heroic madman, something absolutely wonderful! And then there's that nickname of Arsène Lupin which he earned among his messmates for the way in which he used to boss them and astound them!... How long is it since the death of Arsène Lupin?"

"It happened two years before your appointment, Monsieur le Préfet. His corpse and Mme. Kesselbach's were discovered under the ruins of a little chalet which was burnt down close to the Luxemburg frontier. It was found at the inquest that he had strangled that monster, Mrs Kesselbach, whose crimes came to light afterwards, and that he hanged himself after setting fire to the chalet."

"It was a fitting end for that—rascal," said M. Desmalions, "and I confess that I, for my part, much prefer not having him to fight against. Let's see, where were we? Are the papers of the Mornington inheritance ready for me?"

"On your desk, Monsieur le Préfet."

"Good. But I was forgetting: is Inspector Vérot here?"

"Yes, Monsieur le Préfet. I expect he's in the infirmary getting something to pull him together."

"Why, what's the matter with him?"

"He struck me as being in a queer state—rather ill."

"How do you mean?"

The secretary described his interview with Inspector Vérot.

"And you say he left a letter for me?" said M. Desmalions with a worried air. "Where is it?"

"Among the papers, Monsieur le Préfet."

"Very odd: it's all very odd. Vérot is a first-rate inspector, a very sober-minded fellow; and he doesn't get frightened easily. You might go and fetch him. Meanwhile, I'll look through my letters."

The secretary hurried away. When he returned, five minutes later, he stated, with an air of astonishment, that he had not seen Inspector Vérot.

"And what's more curious still," he added, "is that the messenger who saw him leave this room saw him come in again almost at once and did not see him go out a second time."

"Perhaps he only passed through here to go to you."

"To me, Monsieur le Préfet? I was in my room all the time."

"Then it's incomprehensible."

"Yes... unless we conclude that the messenger's attention was distracted for a second, as Vérot is neither here nor next door."

"That must be it. I expect he's gone to get some air outside; and he'll be back at any moment. For that matter, I shan't want him to start with."

The Prefect looked at his watch.

"Ten past five. You might tell the messenger to show those gentlemen in... Wait, though—"

M. Desmalions hesitated. In turning over the papers he had found Vérot's letter. It was a large, yellow, business envelope, with "Café du Pont-Neuf" printed at the top.

The secretary suggested:

"In view of Vérot's absence, Monsieur le Préfet, and of what he said, it might be as well for you to see what's in the letter first."

M. Desmalions paused to reflect.

"Perhaps you're right."

And, making up his mind, he inserted a paper-knife into the envelope and cut it open. A cry escaped him.

"Oh, I say, this is a little too much!"

"What is it, Monsieur le Préfet?"

"Why, look here, a blank... sheet of paper! That's all the envelope contains!"

"Impossible!"

"See for yourself—a plain sheet folded in four, with not a word on it."

"But Vérot told me in so many words that he had said in that letter all that he knew about the case."

"He told you so, no doubt, but there you are! Upon my word, if I didn't know Inspector Vérot, I should think he was trying to play a game with me."

"It's a piece of carelessness, Monsieur le Préfet, at the worst."

"No doubt, a piece of carelessness, but I'm surprised at him. It doesn't do to be careless when the lives of two people are at stake. For he must have told you that there is a double murder planned for tonight?"

"Yes, Monsieur le Préfet, and under particularly alarming conditions; infernal was the word he used."

M. Desmalions was walking up and down the room, with his hands behind his back. He stopped at a small table.

"What's this little parcel addressed to me? 'Monsieur le Préfet de Police—to be opened in case of accident.'"

"Oh, yes," said the secretary, "I was forgetting! That's from Inspector Vérot, too; something of importance, he said, and serving to complete and explain the contents of the letter."

"Well," said M. Desmalions, who could not help laughing, "the letter certainly needs explaining; and, though there's no question of 'accident,' I may as well open the parcel."

As he spoke, he cut the string and discovered, under the paper, a box, a little cardboard box, which might have come from a druggist, but which was soiled and spoiled by the use to which it had been put.

He raised the lid. Inside the box were a few layers of cotton wool, which were also rather dirty, and in between these layers was half a cake of chocolate.

"What the devil does this mean?" growled the Prefect in surprise.

He took the chocolate, looked at it, and at once perceived what was peculiar about this cake of chocolate, which was also undoubtedly the reason why Inspector Vérot had kept it. Above and below, it bore the prints of teeth, very plainly marked, very plainly separated one from the other, penetrating to a depth of a tenth of an inch or so into the chocolate. Each possessed its individual shape and width, and each was divided from its neighbours by a different interval. The jaws which had started eating the cake of chocolate had dug into it the mark of four upper and five lower teeth.

M. Desmalions remained wrapped in thought and, with his head sunk on his chest, for some minutes resumed his walk up and down the room, muttering:

"This is queer... There's a riddle here to which I should like to know the answer. That sheet of paper, the marks of those teeth: what does it all mean?"

But he was not the man to waste much time over a mystery which was bound to be cleared up presently, as Inspector Vérot must be either at the police office or somewhere just outside; and he said to his secretary:

"I can't keep those five gentlemen waiting any longer. Please have them shown in now. If Inspector Vérot arrives while they are here, as he is sure to do, let me know at once. I want to see him as soon as he comes. Except for that, see that I'm not disturbed on any pretext, won't you?"

***

Two minutes later the messenger showed in Maître Lepertuis, a stout, red-faced man, with whiskers and spectacles, followed by Archibald Bright, the Secretary of Embassy, and Caceres, the Peruvian attaché. M. Desmalions, who knew all three of them, chatted to them until he stepped forward to receive Major Comte d'Astrignac, the hero of La Chouïa, who had been forced into premature retirement by his glorious wounds. The Prefect was complimenting him warmly on his gallant conduct in Morocco when the door opened once more.

"Don Luis Perenna, I believe?" said the Prefect, offering his hand to a man of middle height and rather slender build, wearing the military medal and the red ribbon of the Legion of Honour.

The newcomer's face and expression, his way of holding himself, and his very youthful movements inclined one to look upon him as a man of forty, though there were wrinkles at the corners of the eyes and on the forehead, which perhaps pointed to a few years more. He bowed.

"Yes, Monsieur le Préfet."

"Is that you, Perenna?" cried Comte d'Astrignae. "So you are still among the living?"

"Yes, Major, and delighted to see you again."

"Perenna alive! Why, we had lost all sight of you when I left Morocco! We thought you dead."

"I was a prisoner, that's all."

"A prisoner of the tribesmen; the same thing!"

"Not quite, Major; one can escape from anywhere. The proof stands before you."

The Prefect of Police, yielding to an irresistible attraction to resist, spent some seconds in examining that powerful face, with the smiling glance, the frank and resolute eyes, and the bronzed complexion, which looked as if it had been baked and baked again by the sun.

Then, motioning to his visitors to take chairs around his desk, M. Desmalions himself sat down and made a preliminary statement in clear and deliberate tones:

"The summons, gentlemen, which I addressed to each of you, must have appeared to you rather peremptory and mysterious. And the manner in which I propose to open our conversation is not likely to diminish your surprise. But if you will attach a little credit to my method, you will soon realize that the whole thing is very simple and very natural. I will be as brief as I can."

He spread before him the bundle of documents prepared for him by his secretary and, consulting his notes as he spoke, continued:

"Over fifty years ago, in 1860, three sisters, three orphans, Ermeline, Elizabeth, and Armande Roussel, aged twenty-two, twenty, and eighteen respectively, were living at Saint-Etienne with a cousin named Victor, who was a few years younger. The eldest, Ermeline, was the first to leave Saint-Etienne. She went to London, where she married an Englishman of the name Mornington, by whom she had a son, who was christened Cosmo.

"The family was very poor and went through hard times. Ermeline repeatedly wrote to her sisters to ask for a little assistance. Receiving no reply, she broke off the correspondence altogether. In 1870 Mr and Mrs Mornington left England for America. Five years later they were rich. Mr Mornington died in 1878; but his widow continued to administer the fortune bequeathed to her and, as she had a genius for business and speculation, she increased this fortune until it attained a colossal figure. At her decease, in 1900, she left her son the sum of four hundred million francs."

The amount seemed to make an impression on the Prefect's hearers. He saw the Major and Don Luis Perenna exchange a glance and asked:

"You knew Cosmo Mornington, did you not?"

"Yes, Monsieur le Préfet," replied Comte d'Astrignac. "He was in Morocco when Perenna and I were fighting there."

"Just so," said M. Desmalions. "Cosmo Mornington had begun to travel about the world. He took up the practise of medicine, from what I hear, and, when occasion offered, treated the sick with great skill and, of course, without charge. He lived first in Egypt and then in Algiers and Morocco. Last year he settled down in Paris, where he died four weeks ago as the result of a most stupid accident."

"A carelessly administered hypodermic injection, was it not, Monsieur le Préfet?" asked the secretary of the American Embassy. "It was mentioned in the papers and reported to us at the embassy."

"Yes," said Desmalions. "To assist his recovery from a long attack of influenza which had kept him in bed all the winter, Mr Mornington, by his doctor's orders, used to give himself injections of glycero-phosphate of soda. He must have omitted the necessary precautions on the last occasion when he did so, for the wound was poisoned, inflammation set in with lightning rapidity, and Mr Mornington was dead in a few hours."

The Prefect of Police turned to the solicitor and asked:

"Have I summed up the facts correctly, Maître Lepertuis?"

"Absolutely, Monsieur le Préfet."

M. Desmalions continued:

"The next morning, Maître Lepertuis called here and, for reasons which you will understand when you have heard the document read, showed me Cosmo Mornington's will, which had been placed in his hands."

While the Prefect was looking through the papers, Maître Lepertuis added:

"I may be allowed to say that I saw my client only once before I was summoned to his death-bed; and that was on the day when he sent for me to come to his room in the hotel to hand me the will which he had just made. This was at the beginning of his influenza. In the course of conversation he told me that he had been making some inquiries with a view to tracing his mother's family, and that he intended to pursue these inquiries seriously after his recovery. Circumstances, as it turned out, prevented his fulfilling his purpose."

Meanwhile, the Prefect of Police had taken from among the documents an open envelope containing two sheets of paper. He unfolded the larger of the two and said:

"This is the will. I will ask you to listen attentively while I read it and also the document attached to it."

The others settled themselves in their chairs; and the Prefect read out:

"The last will and testament of me, Cosmo Mornington, eldest son of Hubert Mornington and Ermeline Roussel, his wife, a naturalized citizen of the United States of America. I give and bequeath to my adopted country three fourths of my estate, to be employed on works of charity in accordance with the instructions, written in my hand, which Maître Lepertuis will be good enough to forward to the Ambassador of the United States. The remainder of my property, to the value of about one hundred million francs, consisting of deposits in various Paris and London banks, a list of which is in the keeping of Maître Lepertuis, I give and bequeath, in memory of my dear mother, to her favourite sister Elizabeth Roussel or her direct heirs; or, in default of Elizabeth and her heirs, to her second sister Armande Roussel or her direct heirs; or, in default of both sisters and their heirs, to their cousin Victor Roussel or his direct heirs.

"In the event of my dying without discovering the surviving members of the Roussel family, or of the cousin of the three sisters, I request my friend Don Luis Perenna to make all the necessary investigations. With this object, I hereby appoint him the executor of my will in so far as concerns the European portion of my estate, and I beg him to undertake the conduct of the events that may arise after my death or in consequence of my death to consider himself my representative and to act in all things for the benefit of my memory and the accomplishment of my wishes. In gratitude for this service and in memory of the two occasions on which he saved my life, I give and bequeath to the said Don Luis Perenna the sum of one million francs."

The Prefect stopped for a few seconds. Don Luis murmured:

"Poor Cosmo!... I should not have needed that inducement to carry out his last wishes."

M. Desmalions continued his reading:

"Furthermore, if, within three months of my death, the investigations made by Don Luis Perenna and by Maître Lepertuis have led to no result; if no heir and no survivor of the Roussel family have come forward to receive the bequest, then the whole hundred million francs shall definitely, all later claims notwithstanding, accrue to my friend Don Luis Perenna. I know him well enough to feel assured that he will employ this fortune in a manner which shall accord with the loftiness of his schemes and the greatness of the plans which he described to me so enthusiastically in our tent in Morocco."

M. Desmalions stopped once more and raised his eyes to Don Luis, who remained silent and impassive, though a tear glistened on his lashes. Comte d'Astrignac said:

"My congratulations, Perenna."

"Let me remind you, Major," he answered, "that this legacy is subject to a condition. And I swear that, if it depends on me, the survivors of the Roussel family shall be found."

"I'm sure of it," said the officer. "I know you."

"In any case," asked the Prefect of Police of Don Luis, "you do not refuse this conditional legacy?"

"Well, no," said Perenna, with a laugh. "There are things which one can't refuse."

"My question," said the Prefect, "was prompted by the last paragraph of the will: 'If, for any reason, my friend Perenna should refuse this legacy, or if he should have died before the date fixed for its payment, I request the Ambassador of the United States and the Prefect of Police for the time being to consult as to the means of building and maintaining in Paris a university confined to students and artists of American nationality and to devote the money to this purpose. And I hereby authorize the Prefect of Police in any case to receive a sum of three hundred thousand francs out of my estate for the benefit of the Paris Police Fund.'"

M. Desmalions folded the paper and took up another.

"There is a codicil to the will. It consists of a letter which Mr Mornington wrote to Maître Lepertuis sometime after and which explains certain points with greater precision:

"I request Maître Lepertuis to open my will on the day after my death, in the presence of the Prefect of Police, who will be good enough to keep the matter an entire secret for a month. One month later, to the day, he will have the kindness to summon to his office Maître Lepertuis, Don Luis Perenna, and a prominent member of the United States Embassy. Subsequent to the reading of the will, a cheque for one million francs shall be handed to my friend and legatee Don Luis Perenna, after a simple examination of his papers and a simple verification of his identity. I should wish this verification to be made as regards the personality by Major Comte d'Astrignac, who was his commanding officer in Morocco, and who unfortunately had to retire prematurely from the army; and as regards birth by a member of the Peruvian Legation, as Don Luis Perenna, though retaining his Spanish nationality, was born in Peru.

"Furthermore, I desire that my will be not communicated to the Roussel heirs until two days later, at Maître Lepertuis's office. Finally—and this is the last expression of my wishes as regards the disposal of my estate and the method of proceeding with that disposal—the Prefect of Police will be good enough to summon the persons aforesaid to his office, for a second time, at a date to be selected by himself, not less than sixty nor more than ninety days after the first meeting. Then and not till then will the definite legatee be named and proclaimed according to his rights, nor shall any be so named and proclaimed unless he be present at this meeting, at the conclusion of which Don Luis Perenna, who must also attend it, shall become the definite legatee if, as I have said, no survivor nor heir of the Roussel sisters or of their cousin Victor have come forward to claim the bequest."

Replacing both documents in the envelope the Prefect of Police concluded:

"You have now, gentlemen, heard the will of Mr Cosmo Mornington, which explains your presence here. A sixth person will join us shortly: one of my detectives, whom I instructed to make the first inquiries about the Roussel family and who will give you the result of his investigations. But, for the moment, we must proceed in accordance with the testator's directions.

"Don Luis Perenna's papers, which he sent me, at my request, a fortnight ago, have been examined by myself and are perfectly in order. As regards his birth, I wrote and begged his Excellency the Peruvian minister to collect the most precise information."

"The minister entrusted this mission to me," said Señor Caceres, the Peruvian attaché. "It offered no difficulties. Don Luis Perenna comes of an old Spanish family which emigrated thirty years ago, but which retained its estates and property in Europe. I knew Don Luis's father in America; and he used to speak of his only son with the greatest affection. It was our legation that informed the son, three years ago, of his father's death. I produce a copy of the letter sent to Morocco."

"And I have the original letter here, among the documents forwarded by Don Luis Perenna to the Prefect of Police. Do you, Major, recognize Private Perenna, who fought under your orders in the Foreign Legion?"

"I recognize him," said Comte d'Astrignac.

"Beyond the possibility of a mistake?"

"Beyond the possibility of a mistake and without the least feeling of hesitation."

The Prefect of Police, with a laugh, hinted:

"You recognize Private Perenna, whom the men, carried away by a sort of astounded admiration of his exploits, used to call Arsène Lupin?"

"Yes, Monsieur le Préfet," replied the Major sharply, "the one whom the men called Arsène Lupin, but whom the officers called simply the Hero, the one who we used to say was as brave as d'Artagnan, as strong as Porthos..."

"And as mysterious as Monte Cristo," said the Prefect of Police, laughing. "I have all this in the report which I received from the Fourth Regiment of the Foreign Legion. It is not necessary to read the whole of it; but it contains the unprecedented fact that Private Perenna, in the space of two years' time, received the military medal, received the Legion of Honour for exceptional services, and was mentioned fourteen times in dispatches. I will pick out a detail here and there."

"Monsieur le Préfet, I beg of you," protested Don Luis. "These are trivial matters, of no interest to anybody; and I do not see the reason..."

"There is every reason, on the contrary," declared M. Desmalions. "You gentlemen are here not only to hear a will read, but also to authorize its execution as regards the only one of its clauses that is to be carried out at once, the payment of a legacy of a million francs. It is necessary, therefore, that all of you should know what there is to know of the personality of the legatee. Consequently, I propose to continue..."

"In that case, Monsieur le Préfet," said Perenna, rising and making for the door, "you will allow me..."

"Right about turn! Halt!... Eyes front!" commanded Major d'Astrignac in a jesting tone.

He dragged Don Luis back to the middle of the room and forced him into a chair.

"Monsieur le Préfet," he said, "I plead for mercy for my old comrade-in-arms, whose modesty would really be put to too severe a test if the story of his prowess were read out in front of him. Besides, the report is here; and we can all of us consult it for ourselves. Without having seen it, I second every word of praise that it contains; and I declare that, in the course of my whole military career, I have never met a soldier who could compare with Private Perenna. And yet I saw plenty of fine fellows over there, the sort of demons whom you only find in the Legion and who will get themselves cut to bits for the sheer pleasure of the thing, for the lark of it, as they say, just to astonish one another.

"But not one of them came anywhere near Perenna. The chap whom we nicknamed d'Artagnan, Porthos, and de Bussy deserved to be classed with the most amazing heroes of legend and history. I have seen him perform feats which I should not care to relate, for fear of being treated as an impostor; feats so improbable that today, in my calmer moments, I wonder if I am quite sure that I did see them. One day, at Settat, as we were being pursued—"

"Another word, Major," cried Don Luis, gayly, "and this time I really will go out! I must say you have a nice way of sparing my modesty!"

"My dear Perenna," replied Comte d'Astrignac, "I always told you that you had every good quality and only one fault, which was that you were not a Frenchman."

"And I always answered, Major, that I was French on my mother's side and a Frenchman in heart and temperament. There are things which only a Frenchman can do."

The two men again gripped each other's hands affectionately.

"Come," said the Prefect, "we'll say no more of your feats of prowess, Monsieur, nor of this report. I will mention one thing, however, which is that, after two years, you fell into an ambush of forty Berbers, that you were captured, and that you did not rejoin the Legion until last month."

"Just so, Monsieur le Préfet, in time to receive my discharge, as my five years' service was up."

"But how did Mr Cosmo Mornington come to mention you in his will, when, at the time when he was making it, you had disappeared from view for eighteen months?"

"Cosmo and I used to correspond."

"What!"

"Yes; and I had informed him of my approaching escape and my return to Paris."

"But how did you manage it? Where were you? And how did you find the means?..."

Don Luis smiled without answering.

"Monte Cristo, this time," said M. Desmalions. "The mysterious Monte Cristo."

"Monte Cristo, if you like, Monsieur le Préfet. In point of fact, the mystery of my captivity and escape is a rather strange one. It may be interesting to throw some light upon it one of these days. Meanwhile, I must ask for a little credit."

A silence ensued. M. Desmalions once more inspected this curious individual; and he could not refrain from saying, as though in obedience to an association of ideas for which he himself was unable to account:

"One word more, and one only. What were your comrades' reasons for giving you that rather odd nickname of Arsène Lupin? Was it just an allusion to your pluck, to your physical strength?"

"There was something besides, Monsieur le Préfet: the discovery of a very curious theft, of which certain details, apparently incapable of explanation, had enabled me to name the perpetrator."

"So you have a gift for that sort of thing?"

"Yes, Monsieur le Préfet, a certain knack which I had the opportunity of employing in Africa on more than one occasion. Hence my nickname of Arsène Lupin. It was soon after the death of the man himself, you know, and he was much spoken of at the time."

"Was it a serious theft?"

"It was rather; and it happened to be committed upon Cosmo Mornington, who was then living in the Province of Oran. That was really what started our relations."

There was a fresh silence; and Don Luis added:

"Poor Cosmo! That incident gave him an unshakable confidence in my little detective talents. He was always saying, 'Perenna, if I die murdered'—he had a fixed notion in his head that he would meet with a violent death—'if I die murdered, swear that you will pursue the culprit.'"

"His presentiment was not justified," said the Prefect of Police. "Cosmo Mornington was not murdered."

"That's where you make a mistake, Monsieur le Préfet," said Don Luis.

M. Desmalions gave a start.

"What! What's that? Cosmo Mornington—?"

"I say that Cosmo Mornington did not die, as you think, of a carelessly administered injection, but that he died, as he feared he would, by foul play."

"But, Monsieur, your assertion is based on no evidence whatever!"

"It is based on fact, Monsieur le Préfet."

"Were you there? Do you know anything?"

"I was not there. A month ago I was still with the colours. I even admit that, when I arrived in Paris, not having seen the newspapers regularly, I did not know of Cosmo's death. In fact, I learned it from you just now, Monsieur le Préfet."

"In that case, Monsieur, you cannot know more about it than I do, and you must accept the verdict of the doctor."

"I am sorry, but his verdict fails to satisfy me."

"But look here, Monsieur, what prompts you to make the accusation? Have you any evidence?"

"Yes."

"What evidence?"

"Your own words, Monsieur le Préfet."

"My own words? What do you mean?"

"I will tell you, Monsieur le Préfet. You began by saying that Cosmo Mornington had taken up medicine and practised it with great skill; next, you said that he had given himself an injection which, carelessly administered, set up inflammation and caused his death within a few hours."

"Yes."

"Well, Monsieur le Préfet, I maintain that a man who practises medicine with great skill and who is accustomed to treating sick people, as Cosmo Mornington was, is incapable of giving himself a hypodermic injection without first taking every necessary antiseptic precaution. I have seen Cosmo at work, and I know how he set about things."

"Well?"

"Well, the doctor just wrote a certificate as any doctor will when there is no sort of clue to arouse his suspicions."

"So your opinion is—"

"Maître Lepertuis," asked Perenna, turning to the solicitor, "did you notice nothing unusual when you were summoned to Mr Mornington's deathbed?"

"No, nothing. Mr Mornington was in a state of coma."

"It's a strange thing in itself," observed Don Luis, "that an injection, however badly administered, should produce such rapid results. Were there no signs of suffering?"

"No... or rather, yes... Yes, I remember the face showed brown patches which I did not see on the occasion of my first visit."

"Brown patches? That confirms my supposition Cosmo Mornington was poisoned."

"But how?" exclaimed the Prefect.

"By some substance introduced into one of the phials of glycero-phosphate, or into the syringe which the sick man employed."

"But the doctor?" M. Desmalions objected.

"Maître Lepertuis," Perenna continued, "did you call the doctor's attention to those brown patches?"

"Yes, but he attached no importance to them."

"Was it his ordinary medical adviser?"

"No, his ordinary medical adviser, Doctor Pujol, who happens to be a friend of mine and who had recommended me to him as a solicitor, was ill. The doctor whom I saw at his deathbed must have been a local practitioner."

"I have his name and address here," said the Prefect of Police, who had turned up the certificate. "Doctor Bellavoine, 14 Rue d'Astorg."

"Have you a medical directory, Monsieur le Préfet?"

M. Desmalions opened a directory and turned over the pages. Presently he declared:

"There is no Doctor Bellavoine; and there is no doctor living at 14 Rue d'Astorg."

2

A MAN DEAD

The declaration was followed by a silence of some length. The Secretary of the American Embassy and the Peruvian attaché had followed the conversation with eager interest. Major d'Astrignac nodded his head with an air of approval. To his mind, Perenna could not be mistaken.

The Prefect of Police confessed:

"Certainly, certainly... we have a number of circumstances here... that are fairly ambiguous... Those brown patches; that doctor... It's a case that wants looking into." And, questioning Don Luis Perenna as though in spite of himself, he asked, "No doubt, in your opinion, there is a possible connection between the murder... and Mr Mornington's will?"

"That, Monsieur le Préfet, I cannot tell. If there is, we should have to suppose that the contents of the will were known. Do you think they could have leaked out, Maître Lepertuis?"

"I don't think so, for Mr Mornington seemed to behave with great caution."

"And there's no question, is there, of any indiscretion committed in your office?"

"By whom? No one handled the will except myself; and I alone have the key of the safe in which I put away documents of that importance every evening."

"The safe has not been broken into? There has been no burglary at your office?"

"No."

"You saw Cosmo Mornington in the morning?"

"Yes, on a Friday morning."

"What did you do with the will until the evening, until you locked it away up your safe?"

"I probably put it in the drawer of my desk."

"And the drawer was not forced?"

Maître Lepertuis seemed taken aback and made no reply.

"Well?" asked Perenna.

"Well, yes, I remember... there was something that day... that same Friday."

"Are you sure?"

"Yes. When I came in from lunch I noticed that the drawer was not locked, although I had locked it beyond the least doubt. At the time I attached comparatively little importance to the incident. Today, I understand, I understand—"

Thus, little by little, were all the suppositions conceived by Don Luis verified: suppositions resting, it is true, upon just one or two clues, but yet containing an amount of intuition, of divination, that was really surprising in a man who had been present at none of the events between which he traced the connection so skilfully.

"We will lose no time, Monsieur," said the Prefect of Police, "in checking your statements, which you will confess to be a little venturesome, by the more positive evidence of one of my detectives who has the case in charge... and who ought to be here by now."

"Does his evidence bear upon Cosmo Mornington's heirs?" asked the solicitor.

"Upon the heirs principally, because two days ago he telephoned to me that he had collected all the particulars, and also upon the very points which—But wait: I remember that he spoke to my secretary of a murder committed a month ago today... Now it's a month today since Mr Cosmo Mornington—"

M. Desmalions pressed hard on a bell. His private secretary at once appeared.

"Inspector Vérot?" asked the Prefect sharply.

"He's not back yet."

"Have him fetched! Have him brought here! He must be found at all costs and without delay."

He turned to Don Luis Perenna.

"Inspector Vérot was here an hour ago, feeling rather unwell, very much excited, it seems, and declaring that he was being watched and followed. He said he wanted to make a most important statement to me about the Mornington case and to warn the police of two murders which are to be committed tonight... and which would be a consequence of the murder of Cosmo Mornington."

"And he was unwell, you say?"

"Yes, ill at ease and even very queer and imagining things. By way of being prudent, he left a detailed report on the case for me. Well, the report is simply a blank sheet of letter-paper.

"Here is the paper and the envelope in which I found it, and here is a cardboard box which he also left behind him. It contains a cake of chocolate with the marks of teeth on it."

"May I look at the two things you have mentioned, Monsieur le Préfet?"

"Yes, but they won't tell you anything."

"Perhaps so—"

Don Luis examined at length the cardboard box and the yellow envelope, on which were printed the words, "Café du Pont-Neuf." The others awaited his words as though they were bound to shed an unexpected light. He merely said:

"The handwriting is not the same on the envelope and the box. The writing on the envelope is less plain, a little shaky, obviously imitated."

"Which proves—?"

"Which proves, Monsieur le Préfet, that this yellow envelope does not come from your detective. I presume that, after writing his report at a table in the Café du Pont-Neuf and closing it, he had a moment of inattention during which somebody substituted for his envelope another with the same address, but containing a blank sheet of paper."

"That's a supposition!" said the Prefect.

"Perhaps; but what is certain, Monsieur le Préfet, is that your inspector's presentiments are well-grounded, that he is being closely watched, that the discoveries about the Mornington inheritance which he has succeeded in making are interfering with criminal designs, and that he is in terrible danger."

"Come, come!"

"He must be rescued, Monsieur le Préfet. Ever since the commencement of this meeting I have felt persuaded that we are up against an attempt which has already begun. I hope that it is not too late and that your inspector has not been the first victim."

"My dear sir," exclaimed the Prefect of Police, "you declare all this with a conviction which rouses my admiration, but which is not enough to establish the fact that your fears are justified. Inspector Vérot's return will be the best proof."

"Inspector Vérot will not return."

"But why not?"

"Because he has returned already. The messenger saw him return."

"The messenger was dreaming. If you have no proof but that man's evidence—"

"I have another proof, Monsieur le Préfet, which Inspector Vérot himself has left of his presence here: these few, almost illegible letters which he scribbled on this memorandum pad, which your secretary did not see him write and which have just caught my eye. Look at them. Are they not a proof, a definite proof that he came back?"

The Prefect did not conceal his perturbation. The others all seemed impressed. The secretary's return but increased their apprehensions: nobody had seen Inspector Vérot.

"Monsieur le Préfet," said Don Luis, "I earnestly beg you to have the office messenger in."

And, as soon as the messenger was there, he asked him, without even waiting for M. Desmalions to speak:

"Are you sure that Inspector Vérot entered this room a second time?"

"Absolutely sure."

"And that he did not go out again?"

"Absolutely sure."

"And your attention was not distracted for a moment?"

"Not for a moment."

"There, Monsieur, you see!" cried the Prefect. "If Inspector Vérot were here, we should know it."

"He is here, Monsieur le Préfet."

"What!"

"Excuse my obstinacy, Monsieur le Préfet, but I say that, when someone enters a room and does not go out again, he is still in that room."

"Hiding?" said M. Desmalions, who was growing more and more irritated.

"No, but fainting, ill—dead, perhaps."

"But where, hang it all?"

"Behind that screen."

"There's nothing behind that screen, nothing but a door."

"And that door—?"

"Leads to a dressing-room."

"Well, Monsieur le Préfet, Inspector Vérot, tottering, losing his head, imagining himself to be going from your office to your secretary's room, fell into your dressing-room."

M. Desmalions ran to the door, but, at the moment of opening it, shrank back. Was it apprehension, the wish to withdraw himself from the influence of that astonishing man, who gave his orders with such authority and who seemed to command events themselves?

Don Luis stood waiting imperturbably, in a deferential attitude.

"I cannot believe—" said M. Desmalions.

"Monsieur le Préfet, I would remind you that Inspector Vérot's revelations may save the lives of two persons who are doomed to die tonight. Every minute lost is irreparable."

M. Desmalions shrugged his shoulders. But that man mastered him with the power of his conviction; and the Prefect opened the door.

He did not make a movement, did not utter a cry. He simply muttered:

"Oh, is it possible!—"

By the pale gleam of light that entered through a ground-glass window they saw the body of a man lying on the floor.

"The inspector! Inspector Vérot!" gasped the office messenger, running forward.

He and the secretary raised the body and placed it in an armchair in the Prefect's office.

Inspector Vérot was still alive, but so little alive that they could scarcely hear the beating of his heart. A drop of saliva trickled from the corner of his mouth. His eyes were devoid of all expression. However, certain muscles of the face kept moving, perhaps with the effort of a will that seemed to linger almost beyond life.

Don Luis muttered:

"Look, Monsieur le Préfet—the brown patches!"

The same dread unnerved all. They began to ring bells and open doors and call for help.

"Send for the doctor!" ordered M. Desmalions. "Tell them to bring a doctor, the first that comes—and a priest. We can't let the poor man—"

Don Luis raised his arm to demand silence.

"There is nothing more to be done," he said. "We shall do better to make the most of these last moments. Have I your permission, Monsieur le Préfet?"

He bent over the dying man, laid the swaying head against the back of the chair, and, in a very gentle voice, whispered:

"Vérot, it's Monsieur le Préfet speaking to you. We should like a few particulars about what is to take place tonight. Do you hear me, Vérot? If you hear me, close your eyelids."

The eyelids were lowered. But was it not merely chance? Don Luis went on:

"You have found the heirs of the Roussel sisters, that much we know; and it is two of those heirs who are threatened with death. The double murder is to be committed tonight. But what we do not know is the name of those heirs, who are doubtless not called Roussel. You must tell us the name.

"Listen to me: you wrote on a memorandum pad three letters which seem to form the syllable Fau... Am I right? Is this the first syllable of a name? Which is the next letter after those three? Close your eyes when I mention the right letter. Is it 'b?' Is it 'c?'"

But there was now not a flicker in the inspector's pallid face. The head dropped heavily on the chest. Vérot gave two or three sighs, his frame shook with one great shiver, and he moved no more.

He was dead.

The tragic scene had been enacted so swiftly that the men who were its shuddering spectators remained for a moment confounded. The solicitor made the sign of the cross and went down on his knees. The Prefect murmured:

"Poor Vérot!... He was a good man, who thought only of the service, of his duty. Instead of going and getting himself seen to—and who knows? Perhaps he might have been saved—he came back here in the hope of communicating his secret. Poor Vérot!—"

"Was he married? Are there any children?" asked Don Luis.

"He leaves a wife and three children," replied the Prefect.

"I will look after them," said Don Luis simply.

Then, when they brought a doctor and when M. Desmalions gave orders for the corpse to be carried to another room, Don Luis took the doctor aside and said:

"There is no doubt that Inspector Vérot was poisoned. Look at his wrist: you will see the mark of a puncture with a ring of inflammation round it."

"Then he was pricked in that place?"

"Yes, with a pin or the point of a pen; and not as violently as they may have wished, because death did not ensue until some hours later."

The messengers removed the corpse; and soon there was no one left in the office except the five people whom the Prefect had originally sent for. The American Secretary of Embassy and the Peruvian attaché, considering their continued presence unnecessary, went away, after warmly complimenting Don Luis Perenna on his powers of penetration.

Next came the turn of Major d'Astrignac, who shook his former subordinate by the hand with obvious affection. And Maître Lepertais and Perenna, having fixed an appointment for the payment of the legacy, were themselves on the point of leaving, when M. Desmalions entered briskly.

"Ah, so you're still here, Don Luis Perenna! I'm glad of that. I have an idea: those three letters which you say you made out on the writing-table, are you sure they form the syllable Fau?"

"I think so, Monsieur le Préfet. See for yourself: are not these an 'F,' an 'A' and a 'U'? And observe that the 'F' is a capital, which made me suspect that the letters are the first syllable of a proper name."

"Just so, just so," said M. Desmalions. "Well, curiously enough, that syllable happens to be—But wait, we'll verify our facts—"

M. Desmalions searched hurriedly among the letters which his secretary had handed him on his arrival and which lay on a corner of the table.

"Ah, here we are!" he exclaimed, glancing at the signature of one of the letters. "Here we are! It's as I thought: 'Fauville.'... The first syllable is the same... Look, 'Fauville,' just like that, without Christian name or initials. The letter must have been written in a feverish moment: there is no date nor address... The writing is shaky—"

And M. Desmalions read out:
"MONSIEUR LE PRÉFET:

"A great danger is hanging over my head and over the head of my son. Death is approaching apace. I shall have tonight, or tomorrow morning at the latest, the proofs of the abominable plot that threatens us. I ask leave to bring them to you in the course of the morning. I am in need of protection and I call for your assistance.

"Permit me to be, etc. FAUVILLE."

"No other designation?" asked Perenna. "No letter-heading?"

"None. But there is no mistake. Inspector Vérot's declarations agree too evidently with this despairing appeal. It is clearly M. Fauville and his son who are to be murdered tonight. And the terrible thing is that, as this name of Fauville is a very common one, it is impossible for our inquiries to succeed in time."

"What, Monsieur le Préfet? Surely, by straining every nerve—"

"Certainly, we will strain every nerve; and I shall set all my men to work. But observe that we have not the slightest clue."

"Oh, it would be awful!" cried Don Luis. "Those two creatures doomed to death; and we unable to save them! Monsieur le Préfet, I ask you to authorize me—"

He had not finished speaking when the Prefect's private secretary entered with a visiting-card in his hand.

"Monsieur le Préfet, this caller was so persistent... I hesitated—"

M. Desmalions took the card and uttered an exclamation of mingled surprise and joy.

"Look, Monsieur," he said to Perenna.

And he handed him the card.

Hippolyte Fauville,
Civil Engineer.
14 bis Boulevard Suchet.

"Come," said M. Desmalions, "chance is favouring us. If this M. Fauville is one of the Roussel heirs, our task becomes very much easier."

"In any case, Monsieur le Préfet," the solicitor interposed, "I must remind you that one of the clauses of the will stipulates that it shall not be read until forty-eight hours have elapsed. M. Fauville, therefore, must not be informed—"

The door was pushed open and a man hustled the messenger aside and rushed in.

"Inspector... Inspector Vérot?" he spluttered. "He's dead, isn't he? I was told—"

"Yes, Monsieur, he is dead."

"Too late! I'm too late!" he stammered.

And he sank into a chair, clasping his hands and sobbing:

"Oh, the scoundrels! The scoundrels!"

He was a pale, hollow-cheeked, sickly looking man of about fifty. His head was bald, above a forehead lined with deep wrinkles. A nervous twitching affected his chin and the lobes of his ears. Tears stood in his eyes.

The Prefect asked:

"Whom do you mean, Monsieur? Inspector Vérot's murderers? Are you able to name them, to assist our inquiry?"

Hippolyte Fauville shook his head.

"No, no, it would be useless, for the moment... My proofs would not be sufficient... No, really not."

He had already risen from his chair and stood apologizing:

"Monsieur le Préfet, I have disturbed you unnecessarily, but I wanted to know... I was hoping that Inspector Vérot might have escaped... His evidence, joined to mine, would have been invaluable. But perhaps he was able to tell you?"

"No, he spoke of this evening—of tonight—"

Hippolyte Fauville started.

"This evening! Then the time has come!... But no, it's impossible, they can't do anything to me yet... They are not ready—"

"Inspector Vérot declared, however, that the double murder would be committed tonight."

"No, Monsieur le Préfet, he was wrong there... I know all about it... Tomorrow evening at the earliest... and we will catch them in a trap... Oh, the scoundrels!"

Don Luis went up to him and asked:

"Your mother's name was Ermeline Roussel, was it not?"

"Yes, Ermeline Roussel. She is dead now."

"And she was from Saint-Etienne?"

"Yes. But why these questions?"

"Monsieur le Préfet will tell you tomorrow. One word more." He opened the cardboard box left by Inspector Vérot. "Does this cake of chocolate mean anything to you? These marks?"

"Oh, how awful!" said the civil engineer, in a hoarse tone. "Where did the inspector find it?"

He dropped into his chair again, but only for a moment; then, drawing himself up, he hurried toward the door with a jerky step.

"I'm going, Monsieur le Préfet, I'm going. Tomorrow morning I'll show you... I shall have all the proofs... And the police will protect me... I am ill, I know, but I want to live! I have the right to live... and my son, too... And we will live... Oh, the scoundrels! —"

And he ran, stumbling out, like a drunken man.

M. Desmalions rose hastily.

"I shall have inquiries made about that man's circumstances... I shall have his house watched. I've telephoned to the detective office already. I'm expecting someone in whom I have every confidence."

Don Luis said:

"Monsieur le Préfet, I beg you, with an earnestness which you will understand, to authorize me to pursue the investigation. Cosmo Mornington's will makes it my duty and, allow me to say, gives me the right to do so. M. Fauville's enemies have given proofs of extraordinary cleverness and daring. I want to have the honour of being at the post of danger tonight, at M. Fauville's house, near his person."

The Prefect hesitated. He was bound to reflect how greatly to Don Luis Perenna's interest it was that none of the Mornington heirs should be discovered, or at least be able to come between him and the millions of the inheritance. Was it safe to attribute to a noble sentiment of gratitude, to a lofty conception of friendship and duty, that strange longing to protect Hippolyte Fauville against the death that threatened him?

For some seconds M. Desmalions watched that resolute face, those intelligent eyes, at once innocent and satirical, grave and smiling, eyes through which you could certainly not penetrate their owner's baffling individuality, but which nevertheless looked at you with an expression of absolute frankness and sincerity. Then he called his secretary:

"Has anyone come from the detective office?"

"Yes, Monsieur le Préfet; Sergeant Mazeroux is here."

"Please have him shown in."

And, turning to Perenna:

"Sergeant Mazeroux is one of our smartest detectives. I used to employ him together with that poor Vérot when I wanted anyone more than ordinarily active and sharp. He will be of great use to you."

***

Sergeant Mazeroux entered. He was a short, lean, wiry man, whose drooping moustache, heavy eyelids, watery eyes and long, lank hair gave him a most doleful appearance.

"Mazeroux," said the Prefect, "you will have heard, by this time, of your comrade Vérot's death and of the horrible circumstances attending it. We must now avenge him and prevent further crimes. This gentleman, who knows the case from end to end, will explain all that is necessary. You will work with him and report to me tomorrow morning."

This meant giving a free hand to Don Luis Perenna and relying on his power of initiative and his perspicacity. Don Luis bowed:

"I thank you, Monsieur le Préfet. I hope that you will have no reason to regret the trust which you are good enough to place in me."

And, taking leave of M. Desmalions and Maître Lepertuis, he went out with Sergeant Mazeroux.

As soon as they were outside, he told Mazeroux what he knew. The detective seemed much impressed by his companion's professional gifts and quite ready to be guided by his views.

They decided first to go to the Café du Pont-Neuf. Here they learned that Inspector Vérot, who was a regular customer of the place, had written a long letter there that morning. And the waiter remembered that a man at the next table, who had entered the café at almost the same time as the inspector, had also asked for writing-paper and called twice for yellow envelopes.

"That's it," said Mazeroux to Don Luis. "As you suspected, one letter has been substituted for the other."

The description given by the waiter was pretty explicit: a tall man, with a slight stoop, wearing a reddish-brown beard cut into a point, a tortoise-shell eyeglass with a black silk ribbon, and an ebony walking-stick with a handle shaped like a swan's head.

"That's something for the police to go upon," said Mazeroux.

They were leaving the café when Don Luis stopped his companion.

"One moment."

"What's the matter?"

"We've been followed."

"Followed? What next? And by whom, pray?"

"No one that matters. I know who it is and I may as well settle his business and have done with it. Wait for me. I shall be back; and I'll show you some fun. You shall see one of the 'nuts,' I promise you."

He returned in a minute with a tall, thin man with his face set in whiskers. He introduced him:

"M. Mazeroux, a friend of mine, Señor Caceres, an attaché at the Peruvian Legation. Señor Caceres took part in the interview at the Prefect's just now. It was he who, on the Peruvian Minister's instructions, collected the documents bearing upon my identity." And he added gayly: "So you were looking for me, dear Señor Caceres. Indeed, I expected, when we left the police office—"

The Peruvian attaché made a sign and pointed to Sergeant Mazeroux. Perenna replied:

> "Oh, pray don't mind M. Mazeroux! You can speak before him; he is the soul of discretion. Besides, he knows all about the business."

The attaché was silent. Perenna made him sit down in front of him.

"Speak without beating about the bush, dear Señor Caceres. It's a subject that calls for plain dealing; and I don't mind a blunt word or two. It saves such a lot of time! Come on. You want money, I suppose? Or, rather, more money. How much?"

The Peruvian had a final hesitation, gave a glance at Don Luis's companion, and then, suddenly making up his mind, said in a dull voice:

"Fifty thousand francs!"

"Oh, by Jove, by Jove!" cried Don Luis. "You're greedy, you know! What do you say, M. Mazeroux? Fifty thousand francs is a lot of money. Especially as—Look here, my dear Caceres, let's go over the ground again.

"Three years ago I had the honour of making your acquaintance in Algeria, when you were touring the country. At the same time, I understood the sort of man you were; and I asked you if you could manage, in three years, with my name of Perenna, to fix me up a Spanish-Peruvian identity, furnished with unquestionable papers and respectable ancestors. You said, 'Yes,' We settled the price: twenty thousand francs. Last week, when the Prefect of Police asked me for my papers, I came to see you and learned that you had just been instructed to make inquiries into my antecedents.

"Everything was ready, as it happened. With the papers of a deceased Peruvian nobleman, of the name of Pereira, properly revised, you had faked me up a first-rate civic status. We arranged what you were to say before the Prefect of Police; and I paid up the twenty thousand. We were quits. What more do you want?"

The Pervian attaché did not betray the least embarrassment. He put his two elbows on the table and said, very calmly:

"Monsieur, when treating with you, three years ago, I thought I was dealing with a gentleman who, hiding himself under the uniform of the Foreign Legion, wished to recover the means to live respectably afterward. Today, I have to do with the universal legatee of Cosmo Mornington, with a man who, tomorrow, under a false name, will receive the sum of one million francs and, in a few months, perhaps, the sum of a hundred millions. That's quite a different thing."

The argument seemed to strike Don Luis. Nevertheless, he objected:

"And, if I refuse—?"

"If you refuse, I shall inform the solicitor and the Prefect of Police that I made an error in my inquiry and that there is some mistake about Don Luis Perenna. In consequence of which you will receive nothing at all and very likely find yourself in jail."

"With you, my worthy sir."

"Me?"

"Of course: on a charge of forgery and tampering with registers. For you don't imagine that I should take it lying down."

The attaché did not reply. His nose, which was a very big one, seemed to lengthen out still farther between his two long whiskers.

Don Luis began to laugh.

"Come, Señor Caceres, don't pull such a face! No one's going to hurt you. Only don't think that you can corner me. Better men than you have tried and have broken their backs in the process. And, upon my word, you don't cut much of a figure when you're doing your best to diddle your fellowmen.

"You look a bit of a mug, in fact, Caceres: a bit of a mug is what you look. So it's understood, what? We lay down our arms. No more base designs against our excellent friend Perenna. Capital, Señor Caceres, capital. And now I'll be magnanimous and prove to you that the decent man of us two is—the one whom anyone would have thought!"

He produced a checkbook on the Crédit Lyonnais.

"Here, my dear chap. Here's twenty thousand francs as a present from Cosmo Mornington's legatee. Put it in your pocket and look pleasant. Say thank you to the kind gentleman, and make yourself scarce without turning your head any more than if you were one of old man Lot's daughters. Off you go: hoosh!"

This was said in such a manner that the attaché obeyed Don Luis Perenna's injunctions to the letter. He smiled as he pocketed the check, said thank you twice over, and made off without turning his head.

"The low hound!" muttered Don Luis. "What do you say to that, Sergeant?"

Sergeant Mazeroux was looking at him in stupefaction, with his eyes starting from his head.

"Well, but, Monsieur—"

"What, Sergeant?"

"Well, but, Monsieur, who are you?"

"Who am I?"

"Yes."

"Didn't they tell you? A Peruvian nobleman, or a Spanish nobleman, I don't know which. In short, Don Luis Perenna."

"Bunkum! I've just heard—"

"Don Luis Perenna, late of the Foreign Legion."

"Enough of that, Monsieur—"

"Medalled and decorated with a stripe on every seam."

"Once more, Monsieur, enough of that; and come along with me to the Prefect."

"But, let me finish, hang it! I was saying, late private in the Foreign Legion... Late hero... Late prisoner of the Sureté... Late Russian prince... Late chief of the detective service... Late—"

"But you're mad!" snarled the sergeant. "What's all this story?"

"It's a true story, Sergeant, and quite genuine. You ask me who I am; and I'm telling you categorically. Must I go farther back? I have still more titles to offer you: marquis, baron, duke, archduke, grand-duke, petty-duke, super duke—the whole 'Almanach de Gotha,' by Jingo! If anyone told me that I had been a king, by all that's holy, I shouldn't dare swear to the contrary!"

Sergeant Mazeroux put out his own hands, accustomed to rough work, seized the seemingly frail wrists of the man addressing him and said:

"No nonsense, now. I don't know whom I've got hold of, but I shan't let you go. You can say what you have to say at the Prefect's."

"Don't speak so loud, Alexandre."

The two frail wrists were released with unparalleled ease; the sergeant's powerful hands were caught and rendered useless; and Don Luis grinned:

"Don't you know me, you idiot?"

Sergeant Mazeroux did not utter a word. His eyes started still farther from his head. He tried to understand and remained absolutely dumfounded.

The sound of that voice, that way of jesting, that schoolboy playfulness allied with that audacity, the quizzing expression of those eyes, and lastly that Christian name of Alexandre, which was not his name at all and which only one person used to give him, years ago. Was it possible?

"The chief!" he stammered. "The chief!"

"Why not?"

"No, no, because—"

"Because what?"

"Because you're dead."

"Well, what about it? D'you think it interferes with my living, being dead?"

And, as the other seemed more and more perplexed, he laid his hand on his shoulder and said:

"Who put you into the police office?"

"The Chief Detective, M. Lenormand."

"And who was M. Lenormand?"

"The chief."

"You mean Arsène Lupin, don't you?"

"Yes."

"Well, Alexandre, don't you know that it was much more difficult for Arsène Lupin to be Chief Detective—and a masterly Chief Detective he was—than to be Don Luis Perenna, to be decorated in the Foreign Legion, to be a hero, and even to be alive after he was dead?"

Sergeant Mazeroux examined his companion in silence. Then his lacklustre eyes brightened, his drab features turned scarlet and, suddenly striking the table with his fist, he growled, in an angry voice:

"All right, very well! But I warn you that you mustn't reckon on me. No, not that! I'm in the detective service; and in the detective service I remain. Nothing doing. I've tasted honesty and I mean to eat no other bread. No, no, no, no! No more humbug!"

Perenna shrugged his shoulders:

"Alexandre, you're an ass. Upon my word, the bread of honesty hasn't enlarged your intelligence. Who talked of starting again?"

"But—"

"But what?"

"All your manoeuvres, Chief."

"My manoeuvres! Do you think I have anything to say to this business?"

"Look here, Chief—"

"Why, I'm out of it altogether, my lad! Two hours ago I knew no more about it than you do. It's Providence that chucked this legacy at me, without so much as shouting, 'Heads!' And it's in obedience to the decrees of—"

"Then—?"

"It's my mission in life to avenge Cosmo Mornington, to find his natural heirs, to protect them and to divide among them the hundred millions that belong to them. That's all. Don't you call that the mission of an honest man?"

"Yes, but—"

"Yes, but, if I don't fulfil it as an honest man: is that what you mean?"

"Chief—"

"Well, my lad, if you notice the least thing in my conduct that dissatisfies you, if you discover a speck of black on Don Luis Perenna's conscience, examined under the magnifying glass, don't hesitate: collar me with both hands. I authorize you to do it. I order you to do it. Is that enough for you?"

"It's not enough for it to be enough for me, Chief."

"What are you talking about?"

"There are the others."

"Explain yourself."

"Suppose you're nabbed?"

"How?"

"You can be betrayed."

"By whom?"

"Your old mates."

"Gone away. I've sent them out of France."

"Where to?"

"That's my secret. I left you at the police office, in case I should require your services; and you see that I was right."

"But suppose the police discover your real identity?"

"Well?"

"They'll arrest you."

"Impossible!"

"Why?"

"They can't arrest me."

"For what reason?"

"You've said it yourself, fat-head: a first-class, tremendous, indisputable reason."

"What do you mean?"

"*I'm dead!*"

Mazeroux seemed staggered. The argument struck him fully. He at once perceived it, with all its common sense and all its absurdity. And suddenly he burst into a roar of laughter which bent him in two and convulsed his doleful features in the oddest fashion:

"Oh, Chief, just the same as always!... Lord, how funny!... Will I come along? I should think I would! As often as you like! You're dead and buried and put out of sight!... Oh, what a joke, what a joke!"

***

Hippolyte Fauville, civil engineer, lived on the Boulevard Suchet, near the fortifications, in a fair-sized private house having on its left a small garden in which he had built a large room that served as his study. The garden was thus reduced to a few trees and to a strip of grass along the railings, which were covered with ivy and contained a gate that opened on the Boulevard Suchet.

Don Luis Perenna went with Mazeroux to the commissary's office at Passy, where Mazeroux, on Perenna's instructions, gave his name and asked to have M. Fauville's house watched during the night by two policemen who were to arrest any suspicious person trying to obtain admission. The commissary agreed to the request.

Don Luis and Mazeroux next dined in the neighbourhood. At nine o'clock they reached the front door of the house.

"Alexandre," said Perenna.

"Yes, Chief?"

"You're not afraid?"

"No, Chief. Why should I be?"

"Why? Because, in defending M. Fauville and his son, we are attacking people who have a great interest in doing away with them and because those people seem pretty wide-awake. Your life, my life: a breath, a trifle. You're not afraid?"

"Chief," replied Mazeroux, "I can't say if I shall ever know what it means to be afraid. But there's one case in which I certainly shall never know."

"What case is that, old chap?"

"As long as I'm by your side, Chief."

And firmly he rang the bell.

3

A MAN DOOMED

The door was opened by a manservant. Mazeroux sent in his card.

Hippolyte received the two visitors in his study. The table, on which stood a movable telephone, was littered with books, pamphlets, and papers. There were two tall desks, with diagrams and drawings, and some glass cases containing reduced models, in ivory and steel, of apparatus constructed or invented by the engineer.

A large sofa stood against the wall. In one corner was a winding staircase that led to a circular gallery. An electric chandelier hung from the ceiling.

Mazeroux, after stating his quality and introducing his friend Perenna as also sent by the Prefect of Police, at once expounded the object of their visit.

M. Desmalions, he said, was feeling anxious on the score of very serious indications which he had just received and, without waiting for the next day's interview, begged M. Fauville to take all the precautions which his detectives might advise.

Fauville at first displayed a certain ill humour.

"My precautions are taken, gentlemen, and well taken. And, on the other hand, I am afraid that your interference may do harm."

"In what way?"

"By arousing the attention of my enemies and preventing me, for that reason, from collecting proofs which I need in order to confound them."

"Can you explain—?"

"No, I cannot... Tomorrow, tomorrow morning—not before."

"And if it's too late?" Don Luis interjected.

"Too late? Tomorrow?"

"Inspector Vérot told M. Desmalions's secretary that the two murders would take place tonight. He said it was fatal and irrevocable."

"Tonight?" cried Fauville angrily. "I tell you no! Not tonight. I'm sure of that. There are things which I know, aren't there, which you do not?"

"Yes," retorted Don Luis, "but there may also be things which Inspector Vérot knew and which you don't know. He had perhaps learned more of your enemies' secrets than you did. The proof is that he was suspected, that a man carrying an ebony walking-stick was seen watching his movements, that, lastly, he was killed."

Hippolyte Fauville's self-assurance decreased. Perenna took advantage of this to insist; and he insisted to such good purpose that Fauville, though without withdrawing from his reserve, ended by yielding before a will that was stronger than his own.

"Well, but you surely don't intend to spend the night in here?"

"We do indeed."

"Why, it's ridiculous! It's sheer waste of time! After all, looking at things from the worst—And what do you want besides?"

"Who lives in the house?"

"Who? My wife, to begin with. She has the first floor."

"Mme. Fauville is not threatened?"

"No, not at all. It's I who am threatened with death; I and my son Edmond. That is why, for the past week, instead of sleeping in my regular bedroom, I have locked myself up in this room. I have given my work as a pretext; a quantity of writing which keeps me up very late and for which I need my son's assistance."

"Does he sleep here, then?"

"He sleeps above us, in a little room which I have had arranged for him. The only access to it is by this inner staircase."

"Is he there now?"

"Yes, he's asleep."

"How old is he?"

"Sixteen."

"But the fact that you have changed your room shows that you feared someone would attack you. Whom had you in mind? An enemy living in the house? One of your servants? Or people from the outside? In that case, how could they get in? The whole question lies in that."

"Tomorrow, tomorrow," replied Fauville, obstinately. "I will explain everything tomorrow—"

"Why not tonight?" Perenna persisted.

"Because I want proofs, I tell you; because the mere fact of my talking may have terrible consequences—and I am frightened; yes, I'm frightened—"

He was trembling, in fact, and looked so wretched and terrified that Don Luis insisted no longer.

"Very well," he said, "I will only ask your permission, for my comrade and myself, to spend the night where we can hear you if you call."

"As you please, Monsieur. Perhaps, after all, that will be best."

At that moment one of the servants knocked and came in to say that his mistress wished to see the master before she went out. Madame Fauville entered almost immediately. She bowed pleasantly as Perenna and Mazeroux rose from their chairs.

She was a woman between thirty and thirty-five, a woman of a bright and smiling beauty, which she owed to her blue eyes, to her wavy hair, to all the charm of her rather vapid but amiable and very pretty face. She wore a long, figured-silk cloak over an evening dress that showed her fine shoulders.

Her husband said, in surprise:

"Are you going out tonight?"

"You forget," she said. "The Auverards offered me a seat in their box at the opera; and you yourself asked me to look in at Mme. d'Ersingen's party afterward—"

"So I did, so I did," he said. "It escaped my memory; I am working so hard."

She finished buttoning her gloves and asked:

"Won't you come and fetch me at Mme. d'Ersingen's?"

"What for?"

"They would like it."

"But I shouldn't. Besides, I don't feel well enough."

"Then I'll make your apologies for you."

"Yes, do."

She drew her cloak around her with a graceful gesture, and stood for a few moments, without moving, as though seeking a word of farewell. Then she said:

"Edmond's not here! I thought he was working with you?"

"He was feeling tired."

"Is he asleep?"

"Yes."

"I wanted to kiss him goodnight."

"No, you would only wake him. And here's your car; so go, dear. Amuse yourself."

"Oh, amuse myself!" she said. "There's not much amusement about the opera and an evening party."

"Still, it's better than keeping one's room."

There was some little constraint. It was obviously one of those ill-assorted households in which the husband, suffering in health and not caring for the pleasures of society, stays at home, while the wife seeks the enjoyments to which her age and habits entitle her.

As he said nothing more, she bent over and kissed him on the forehead. Then, once more bowing to the two visitors, she went out. A moment later they heard the sound of the motor driving away.

Hippolyte Fauville at once rose and rang the bell. Then he said:

"No one here has any idea of the danger hanging over me. I have confided in nobody, not even in Silvestre, my own man, though he has been in my service for years and is honesty itself."

The manservant entered.

"I am going to bed, Silvestre," said M. Fauville. "Get everything ready."

Silvestre opened the upper part of the great sofa, which made a comfortable bed, and laid the sheets and blankets. Next, at his master's orders, he brought a jug of water, a glass, a plate of biscuits, and a dish of fruit.

M. Fauville ate a couple of biscuits and then cut a dessert-apple. It was not ripe. He took two others, felt them, and, not thinking them good, put them back as well. Then he peeled a pear and ate it.

"You can leave the fruit dish," he said to his man. "I shall be glad of it, if I am hungry during the night... Oh, I was forgetting! These two gentlemen are staying. Don't mention it to anybody. And, in the morning, don't come until I ring."

The man placed the fruit dish on the table before retiring. Perenna, who was noticing everything, and who was afterwards to remember every smallest detail of that evening, which his memory recorded with a sort of mechanical faithfulness, counted three pears and four apples in the dish.

Meanwhile, Fauville went up the winding staircase, and, going along the gallery, reached the room where his son lay in bed.

"He's fast asleep," he said to Perenna, who had joined him.

The bedroom was a small one. The air was admitted by a special system of ventilation, for the dormer window was hermetically closed by a wooden shutter tightly nailed down.

"I took the precaution last year," Hippolyte Fauville explained. "I used to make my electrical experiments in this room and was afraid of being spied upon, so I closed the aperture opening on the roof."

And he added in a low voice:

"They have been prowling around me for a long time."

The two men went downstairs again.

Fauville looked at his watch.

"A quarter past ten: bedtime, I am exceedingly tired, and you will excuse me—"

It was arranged that Perenna and Mazeroux should make themselves comfortable in a couple of easy chairs which they carried into the passage between the study and the entrance hall. But, before bidding them goodnight, Hippolyte Fauville, who, although greatly excited, had appeared until then to retain his self-control, was seized with a sudden attack of weakness. He uttered a faint cry. Don Luis turned round and saw the sweat pouring like gleaming water down his face and neck, while he shook with fever and anguish.

"What's the matter?" asked Perenna.

"I'm frightened! I'm frightened!" he said.

"This is madness!" cried Don Luis. "Aren't we here, the two of us? We can easily spend the night with you, if you prefer, by your bedside."

Fauville replied by shaking Perenna violently by the shoulder, and, with distorted features, stammering:

"If there were ten of you—if there were twenty of you with me, you need not think that it would spoil their schemes! They can do anything they please, do you hear, anything! They have already killed Inspector Vérot—they will kill me—and they will kill my son. Oh, the blackguards! My God, take pity on me! The awful terror of it! The pain I suffer!"

He had fallen on his knees and was striking his breast and repeating:

"O God, have pity on me! I can't die! I can't let my son die! Have pity on me, I beseech Thee!"

He sprang to his feet and led Perenna to a glass-fronted case, which he rolled back on its brass castors, revealing a small safe built into the wall.

"You will find my whole story here, written up day by day for the past three years. If anything should happen to me, revenge will be easy."

He hurriedly turned the letters of the padlock and, with a key which he took from his pocket, opened the safe.

It was three fourths empty; but on one of the shelves, between some piles of papers, was a diary bound in drab cloth, with a rubber band round it. He took the diary, and, emphasizing his words, said:

"There, look, it's all in here. With this, the hideous business can be reconstructed... There are my suspicions first and then my certainties... Everything, everything... how to trap them and how to do for them... You'll remember, won't you? A diary bound in drab cloth... I'm putting it back in the safe."

Gradually his calmness returned. He pushed back the glass case, tidied a few papers, switched on the electric lamp above his bed, put out the lights in the middle of the ceiling, and asked Don Luis and Mazeroux to leave him.

Don Luis, who was walking round the room and examining the iron shutters of the two windows, noticed a door opposite the entrance door and asked the engineer about it.

"I use it for my regular clients," said Fauville, "and sometimes I go out that way."

"Does it open on the garden?"

"Yes."

"Is it properly closed?"

"You can see for yourself; it's locked and bolted with a safety bolt. Both keys are on my bunch; so is the key of the garden gate."

He placed the bunch of keys on the table with his pocketbook and, after first winding it, his watch.

Don Luis, without troubling to ask permission, took the keys and unfastened the lock and the bolt. A flight of three steps brought him to the garden. He followed the length of the narrow border. Through the ivy he saw and heard the two policemen pacing up and down the boulevard. He tried the lock of the gate. It was fastened.

"Everything's all right," he said when he returned, "and you can be easy. Goodnight."

"Goodnight," said the engineer, seeing Perenna and Mazeroux out.

Between his study and the passage were two doors, one of which was padded and covered with oilcloth. On the other side, the passage was separated from the hall by a heavy curtain.

"You can go to sleep," said Perenna to his companion. "I'll sit up."

"But surely, Chief, you don't think that anything's going to happen!"

"I don't think so, seeing the precautions which we've taken. But, knowing Inspector Vérot as you did, do you think he was the man to imagine things?"

"No, Chief."

"Well, you know what he prophesied. That means that he had his reasons for doing so. And therefore I shall keep my eyes open."

"We'll take it in turns, Chief; wake me when it's my time to watch."

Seated motionlessly, side by side, they exchanged an occasional remark. Soon after, Mazeroux fell asleep. Don Luis remained in his chair without moving, his ears pricked up. Everything was quiet in the house. Outside, from time to time, the sound of a motor car or of a cab rolled by. He could also hear the late trains on the Auteuil line.

He rose several times and went up to the door. Not a sound. Hippolyte Fauville was evidently asleep.

"Capital!" said Perenna to himself. "The boulevard is watched. No one can enter the room except by this way. So there is nothing to fear."

At two o'clock in the morning a car stopped outside the house, and one of the manservants, who must have been waiting in the kitchen, hastened to the front door. Perenna switched off the light in the passage, and, drawing the curtain slightly aside, saw Mme. Fauville enter, followed by Silvestre.

She went up. The lights on the staircase were put out. For half an hour or so there was a sound overhead of voices and of chairs moving. Then all was silence.

And, amid this silence, Perenna felt an unspeakable anguish arise within him, he could not tell why. But it was so violent, the impression became so acute, that he muttered:

"I shall go and see if he's asleep. I don't expect that he has bolted the doors."

He had only to push both doors to open them; and, with his electric lantern in his hand, he went up to the bed. Hippolyte Fauville was sleeping with his face turned to the wall.

Perenna gave a smile of relief. He returned to the passage and, shaking Mazeroux:

"Your turn, Alexandre."

"No news, Chief?"

"No, none; he's asleep."

"How do you know?"

"I've had a look at him."

"That's funny; I never heard you. It's true, though, I've slept like a pig."

He followed Perenna into the study, and Perenna said:

"Sit down and don't wake him. I shall take forty winks."

He had one more turn at sentry duty. But, even while dozing, he remained conscious of all that happened around him. A clock struck the hours with a low chime; and each time Perenna counted the strokes. Then came the life outside awakening, the rattle of the milk-carts, the whistle of the early suburban trains.

People began to stir inside the house. The daylight trickled in through the crannies of the shutters, and the room gradually became filled with light.

"Let's go away," said Sergeant Mazeroux. "It would be better for him not to find us here."

"Hold your tongue!" said Don Luis, with an imperious gesture.

"Why?"

"You'll wake him up."

"But you can see I'm not waking him," said Mazeroux, without lowering his tone.

"That's true, that's true," whispered Don Luis, astonished that the sound of that voice had not disturbed the sleeper.

And he felt himself overcome with the same anguish that had seized upon him in the middle of the night, a more clearly defined anguish, although he would not, although he dared not, try to realize the reason of it.

"What's the matter with you, Chief? You're looking like nothing on earth. What is it?"

"Nothing—nothing. I'm frightened—"

Mazeroux shuddered.

"Frightened of what? You say that just as he did last night."

"Yes... yes... and for the same reason."

"But—?"

"Don't you understand? Don't you understand that I'm wondering—?"

A MAN DOOMED

"No; what?"

"If he's not dead!"

"But you're mad, Chief!"

"No... I don't know... Only, only... I have an impression of death—"

Lantern in hand, he stood as one paralyzed, opposite the bed; and he who was afraid of nothing in the world had not the courage to throw the light on Hippolyte Fauville's face. A terrifying silence rose and filled the room.

"Oh, Chief, he's not moving!"

"I know... I know... and I now see that he has not moved once during the night. And that's what frightens me."

He had to make a real effort in order to step forward. He was now almost touching the bed.

The engineer did not appear to breathe.

This time, Perenna resolutely took hold of his hand.

It was icy cold.

Don Luis at once recovered all his self-possession.

"The window! Open the window!" he cried.

And, when the light flooded the room, he saw the face of Hippolyte Fauville all swollen, stained with brown patches.

"Oh," he said, under his breath, "he's dead!"

"Dash it all! Dash it all!" spluttered the detective sergeant.

For two or three minutes they stood petrified, stupefied, staggered at the sight of this most astonishing and mysterious phenomenon. Then a sudden idea made Perenna start. He flew up the winding staircase, rushed along the gallery, and darted into the attic.

Edmond, Hippolyte Fauville's son, lay stiff and stark on his bed, with a cadaverous face, dead, too.

"Dash it all! Dash it all!" repeated Mazeroux.

Never, perhaps, in the course of his adventurous career, had Perenna experienced such a knockdown blow. It gave him a feeling of extreme lassitude, depriving him of all power of speech or movement. Father and son were dead! They had been killed during that night! A few hours earlier, though the house was watched and every outlet hermetically closed, both had been poisoned by an infernal puncture, even as Inspector Vérot was poisoned, even as Cosmo Mornington was poisoned.

"Dash it all!" said Mazeroux once more. "It was not worth troubling about the poor devils and performing such miracles to save them!"

The exclamation conveyed a reproach. Perenna grasped it and admitted:

"You are right, Mazeroux; I was not equal to the job."

"Nor I, Chief."

"You... you have only been in this business since yesterday evening—"

"Well, so have you, Chief!"

"Yes, I know, since yesterday evening, whereas the others have been working at it for weeks and weeks. But, all the same, these two are dead; and I was there, I, Lupin, was there! The thing has been done under my eyes; and I saw nothing! I saw nothing! How is it possible?"

He uncovered the poor boy's shoulders, showing the mark of a puncture at the top of the arm.

"The same mark—the same mark obviously that we shall find on the father... The lad does not seem to have suffered, either... Poor little chap! He did not look very strong... Never mind, it's a nice face; what a terrible blow for his mother when she learns!"

The detective sergeant wept with anger and pity, while he kept on mumbling:

"Dash it all!... Dash it all!"

"We shall avenge them, eh, Mazeroux?"

"Rather, Chief! Twice over!"

"Once will do, Mazeroux. But it shall be done with a will."

"That I swear it shall!"

"You're right; let's swear. Let us swear that this dead pair shall be avenged. Let us swear not to lay down our arms until the murderers of Hippolyte Fauville and his son are punished as they deserve."

"I swear it as I hope to be saved, Chief."

"Good!" said Perenna. "And now to work. You go and telephone at once to the police office. I am sure that M. Desmalions will approve of your informing him without delay. He takes an immense interest in the case."

"And if the servants come? If Mme. Fauville—?"

"No one will come till we open the doors; and we shan't open them except to the Prefect of Police. It will be for him, afterward, to tell Mme. Fauville that she is a widow and that she has no son. Go! Hurry!"

"One moment, Chief; we are forgetting something that will help us enormously."

"What's that?"

"The little drab-cloth diary in the safe, in which M. Fauville describes the plot against him."

"Why, of course!" said Perenna. "You're right... especially as he omitted to mix up the letters of the lock last night, and the key is on the bunch which he left lying on the table."

They ran down the stairs.

"Leave this to me," said Mazeroux. "It's more regular that you shouldn't touch the safe."

He took the bunch, moved the glass case, and inserted the key with a feverish emotion which Don Luis felt even more acutely than he did. They were at last about to know the details of the mysterious story. The dead man himself would betray the secret of his murderers.

"Lord, what a time you take!" growled Don Luis.

Mazeroux plunged both hands into the crowd of papers that encumbered the iron shelf.

"Well, Mazeroux, hand it over."

"What?"

"The diary."

"I can't Chief."

"What's that?"

"It's gone."

Don Luis stifled an oath. The drab-cloth diary, which the engineer had placed in the safe before their eyes, had disappeared.

Mazeroux shook his head.

"Dash it all! So they knew about that diary!"

"Of course they did; and they knew plenty of other things besides. We've not seen the end of it with those fellows. There's no time to lose. Ring up!"

Mazeroux did so and soon received the answer that M. Desmalions was coming to the telephone. He waited.

In a few minutes Perenna, who had been walking up and down, examining different objects in the room, came and sat down beside Mazeroux. He seemed thoughtful. He reflected for some time. But then, his eyes falling on the fruit dish, he muttered:

"Hullo! There are only three apples instead of four. Then he ate the fourth."

"Yes," said Mazeroux, "he must have eaten it."

"That's funny," replied Perenna, "for he didn't think them ripe."

He was silent once more, sat leaning his elbows on the table, visibly preoccupied; then, raising his head, he let fall these words:

"The murder was committed before we entered the room, at half-past twelve exactly."

"How do you know, Chief?"

"M. Fauville's murderer or murderers, in touching the things on the table, knocked down the watch which M. Fauville had placed there. They put it back; but the fall had stopped it. And it stopped at half-past twelve."

"Then, Chief, when we settled ourselves here, at two in the morning, it was a corpse that was lying beside us and another over our heads?"

"Yes."

"But how did those devils get in?"

"Through this door, which opens on the garden, and through the gate that opens on the Boulevard Suchet."

"Then they had keys to the locks and bolts?"

"False keys, yes."

"But the policemen watching the house outside?"

"They are still watching it, as that sort watch a house, walking from point to point without thinking that people can slip into a garden while they have their backs turned. That's what took place in coming and going."

Sergeant Mazeroux seemed flabbergasted. The criminals' daring, their skill, the precision of their acts bewildered him.

"They're deuced clever," he said.

"Deuced clever, Mazeroux, as you say; and I foresee a tremendous battle. By Jupiter, with what a vim they set to work!"

The telephone bell rang. Don Luis left Mazeroux to his conversation with the Prefect, and, taking the bunch of keys, easily unfastened the lock and the bolt of the door and went out into the garden, in the hope of there finding some trace that should facilitate his quest.

As on the day before, he saw, through the ivy, two policemen walking between one lamp-post and the next. They did not see him. Moreover, anything that might happen inside the house appeared to be to them a matter of total indifference.

"That's my great mistake," said Perenna to himself. "It doesn't do to entrust a job to people who do not suspect its importance."

His investigations led to the discovery of some traces of footsteps on the gravel, traces not sufficiently plain to enable him to distinguish the shape of the shoes that had left them, yet distinct enough to confirm his supposition. The scoundrels had been that way.

Suddenly he gave a movement of delight. Against the border of the path, among the leaves of a little clump of rhododendrons, he saw something red, the shape of which at once struck him. He stooped. It was an apple, the fourth apple, the one whose absence from the fruit dish he had noticed.

"Excellent!" he said. "Hippolyte Fauville did not eat it. One of them must have carried it away—a fit of appetite, a sudden hunger—and it must have rolled from his hand without his having time to look for it and pick it up."

He took up the fruit and examined it.

"What!" he exclaimed, with a start. "Can it be possible?"

He stood dumfounded, a prey to real excitement, refusing to admit the inadmissible thing which nevertheless presented itself to his eyes with the direct evidence of actuality. Someone had bitten into the apple; into the apple which was too sour to eat. And the teeth had left their mark!

"Is it possible?" repeated Don Luis. "Is it possible that one of them can have been guilty of such an imprudence! The apple must have fallen without his knowing... or he must have been unable to find it in the dark."

He could not get over his surprise. He cast about for plausible explanations. But the fact was there before him. Two rows of teeth, cutting through the thin red peel, had left their regular, semi-circular bite clearly in the pulp of the fruit. They were clearly marked on the top, while the lower row had melted into a single curved line.

"The teeth of the tiger!" murmured Perenna, who could not remove his eyes from that double imprint. "The teeth of the tiger! The teeth that had already left their mark on Inspector

Vérot's piece of chocolate! What a coincidence! It can hardly be fortuitous. Must we not take it as certain that the same person bit into this apple and into that cake of chocolate which Inspector Vérot brought to the police office as an incontestable piece of evidence?"

He hesitated a second. Should he keep this evidence for himself, for the personal inquiry which he meant to conduct? Or should he surrender it to the investigations of the police? But the touch of the object filled him with such repugnance, with such a sense of physical discomfort, that he flung away the apple and sent it rolling under the leaves of the shrubs.

And he repeated to himself:

"The teeth of the tiger! The teeth of the wild beast!"

He locked the garden door behind him, bolted it, put back the keys on the table and said to Mazeroux:

"Have you spoken to the Chief of Police?"

"Yes."

"Is he coming?"

"Yes."

"Didn't he order you to telephone for the commissary of police?"

"No."

"That means that he wants to see everything by himself. So much the better. But the detective office? The public prosecutor?"

"He's told them."

"What's the matter with you, Alexandre? I have to drag your answers out of you. Well, what is it? You're looking at me very queerly. What's up?"

"Nothing."

"That's all right. I expect this business has turned your head. And no wonder... The Prefect won't enjoy himself, either,... especially as he put his faith in me a bit light-heartedly and will be called upon to give an explanation of my presence here. By the way, it's much better that you should take upon yourself the responsibility for all that we have done. Don't you agree? Besides, it'll do you all the good in the world.

"Put yourself forward, flatly; suppress me as much as you can; and, above all—I don't suppose that you will have any objection to this little detail—don't be such a fool as to say that you went to sleep for a single second, last night, in the passage. First of all, you'd only be blamed for it. And then... well, that's understood, eh? So we have only to say goodbye.

"If the Prefect wants me, as I expect he will, telephone to my address, Place du Palais-Bourbon. I shall be there. Goodbye. It is not necessary for me to assist at the inquiry; my presence would be out of place. Goodbye, old chap."

He turned toward the door of the passage.

"Half a moment!" cried Mazeroux.

"Half a moment?... What do you mean?"

The detective sergeant had flung himself between him and the door and was blocking his way.

"Yes, half a moment... I am not of your opinion. It's far better that you should wait until the Prefect comes."

"But I don't care a hang about your opinion!"

"May be; but you shan't pass."

"What! Why, Alexandre, you must be ill!"

"Look here, Chief," said Mazeroux feebly. "What can it matter to you? It's only natural that the Prefect should wish to speak to you."

"Ah, it's the Prefect who wishes, is it?... Well, my lad, you can tell him that I am not at his orders, that I am at nobody's orders, and that, if the President of the Republic, if Napoleon I himself were to bar my way... Besides, rats! Enough said. Get out of the road!"

"You shall not pass!" declared Mazeroux, in a resolute tone, extending his arms.

"Well, I like that!"

"You shall not pass."

"Alexandre, just count ten."

"A hundred, if you like, but you shall not..."

"Oh, blow your catchwords! Get out of this."

He seized Mazeroux by both shoulders, made him spin round on his heels and, with a push, sent him floundering over the sofa. Then he opened the door.

"Halt, or I fire!"

It was Mazeroux, who had scrambled to his feet and now stood with his revolver in his hand and a determined expression on his face.

Don Luis stopped in amazement. The threat was absolutely indifferent to him, and the barrel of that revolver aimed at him left him as cold as could be. But by what prodigy did Mazeroux, his former accomplice, his ardent disciple, his devoted servant, by what prodigy did Mazeroux dare to act as he was doing?

Perenna went up to him and pressed gently on the detective's outstretched arm.

"Prefect's orders?" he asked.

"Yes," muttered the sergeant, uncomfortably.

"Orders to keep me here until he comes?"

"Yes."

"And if I betrayed an intention of leaving, to prevent me?"

"Yes."

"By every means?"

"Yes."

"Even by putting a bullet through my skin?"

"Yes."

Perenna reflected; and then, in a serious voice:

"Would you have fired, Mazeroux?"

The sergeant lowered his head and said faintly:

"Yes, Chief."

Perenna looked at him without anger, with a glance of affectionate sympathy; and it was an absorbing sight for him to see his former companion dominated by such a sense of discipline and duty. Nothing was able to prevail against that sense, not even the fierce admiration, the almost animal attachment which Mazeroux retained for his master.

"I'm not angry, Mazeroux. In fact, I approve. Only you must tell me the reason why the Prefect of Police—"

The detective did not reply, but his eyes wore an expression of such sadness that Don Luis started, suddenly understanding.

"No," he cried, "no!... It's absurd... he can't have thought that!... And you, Mazeroux, do you believe me guilty?"

"Oh, I, Chief, am as sure of you as I am of myself!... You don't take life!... But, all the same, there are things... coincidences—"

"Things... coincidences..." repeated Don Luis slowly.

He remained pensive; and, in a low voice, he said:

"Yes, after all, there's truth in what you say... Yes, it all fits in... Why didn't I think of it?... My relations with Cosmo Mornington, my arrival in Paris in time for the reading of the will, my insisting on spending the night here, the fact that the death of the two Fauvilles undoubtedly gives me the millions... And then... and then... why, he's absolutely right, your Prefect of Police!... All the more so as... Well, there, I'm a goner!"

"Come, come, Chief!"

"A dead-goner, old chap; you just get that into your head. Not as Arsène Lupin, ex-burglar, ex-convict, ex-anything you please—I'm unattackable on that ground—but as Don Luis Perenna, respectable man, residuary legatee, and the rest of it. And it's too stupid! For, after all, who will find the murderers of Cosmo, Vérot, and the two Fauvilles, if they go clapping me into jail?"

"Come, come, Chief—"

"Shut up!... Listen!"

A motor car was stopping on the boulevard, followed by another. It was evidently the Prefect and the magistrates from the public prosecutor's office.

Don Luis took Mazeroux by the arm.

"There's only one way out of it, Alexandre! Don't say you went to sleep."

"I must, Chief."

"You silly ass!" growled Don Luis. "How is it possible to be such an ass! It's enough to disgust one with honesty. What am I to do, then?"

"Discover the culprit, Chief."

"What!... What are you talking about?"

Mazeroux, in his turn, took him by the arm and, clutching him with a sort of despair, said, in a voice choked with tears:

"Discover the culprit, Chief. If not, you're done for... that's certain... the Prefect told me so... The police want a culprit... they want him this evening... One has got to be found... It's up to you to find him."

"What you have, Alexandre, is a merry wit."

"It's child's play for you, Chief. You have only to set your mind to it."

"But there's not the least clue, you ass!"

"You'll find one... you must... I entreat you, hand them over somebody... It would be more than I could bear if you were arrested. You, the chief, accused of murder! No, no... I entreat you, discover the criminal and hand him over... You have the whole day to do it in... and Lupin has done greater things than that!"

He was stammering, weeping, wringing his hands, grimacing with every feature of his comic face. And it was really touching, this grief, this dismay at the approach of the danger that threatened his master.

M. Desmalions's voice was heard in the hall, through the curtain that closed the passage. A third motor car stopped on the boulevard, and a fourth, both doubtless laden with policemen.

The house was surrounded, besieged.

Perenna was silent.

Beside him, anxious-faced, Mazeroux seemed to be imploring him.

A few seconds elapsed.

Then Perenna declared, deliberately:

"Looking at things all round, Alexandre, I admit that you have seen the position clearly and that your fears are fully justified. If I do not manage to hand over the murderer or murderers of Hippolyte Fauville and his son to the police in a few hours from now, it is I, Don Luis Perenna, who will be lodged in durance vile on the evening of this Thursday, the first of April."

4

THE CLOUDED TURQUOISE

It was about nine o'clock in the morning when the Prefect of Police entered the study in which the incomprehensible tragedy of that double murder had been enacted.

He did not even bow to Don Luis; and the magistrates who accompanied him might have thought that Don Luis was merely an assistant of Sergeant Mazeroux, if the chief detective had not made it his business to tell them, in a few words, the part played by the stranger.

M. Desmalions briefly examined the two corpses and received a rapid explanation from Mazeroux. Then, returning to the hall, he went up to a drawing-room on the first floor, where Mme. Fauville, who had been informed of his visit, joined him almost at once.

Perenna, who had not stirred from the passage, slipped into the hall himself. The servants of the house, who by this time had heard of the murder, were crossing it in every direction. He went down the few stairs leading to a ground-floor landing, on which the front door opened.

There were two men there, of whom one said:

"You can't pass."

"But—"

"You can't pass: those are our orders."

"Your orders? Who gave them?"

"The Prefect himself."

"No luck," said Perenna, laughing. "I have been up all night and I am starving. Is there no way of getting something to eat?"

The two policemen exchanged glances and one of them beckoned to Silvestre and spoke to him. Silvestre went towards the dining-room, and returned with a horseshoe roll.

"Good," thought Don Luis, after thanking him. "This settles it. I'm nabbed. That's what I wanted to know. But M. Desmalions is deficient in logic. For, if it's Arsène Lupin whom he means to detain here, all these worthy plain-clothesmen are hardly enough; and, if it's Don Luis Perenna, they are superfluous, because the flight of Master Perenna would deprive Master Perenna of every chance of seeing the colour of my poor Cosmo's shekels. Having said which, I will take a chair."

He resumed his seat in the passage and awaited events.

Through the open door of the study he saw the magistrates pursuing their investigations. The divisional surgeon made a first examination of the two bodies and at once recognized the same symptoms of poisoning which he himself had perceived, the evening before, on the corpse of Inspector Vérot.

Next, the detectives took up the bodies and carried them to the adjoining bedrooms which the father and son formerly occupied on the second floor of the house.

The Prefect of Police then came downstairs; and Don Luis heard him say to the magistrates:

"Poor woman! She refused to understand... When at last she understood, she fell to the ground in a dead faint. Only think, her husband and her son at one blow!... Poor thing!"

From that moment Perenna heard and saw nothing. The door was shut. The Prefect must afterward have given some order through the outside, through the communication with the front door offered by the garden, for the two detectives

THE CLOUDED TURQUOISE

came and took up their positions in the hall, at the entrance to the passage, on the right and left of the dividing curtain.

"One thing's certain," thought Don Luis. "My shares are not booming. What a state Alexandre must be in! Oh, what a state!"

At twelve o'clock Silvestre brought him some food on a tray.

And the long and painful wait began anew.

In the study and in the house, the inquiry, which had been adjourned for lunch, was resumed. Perenna heard footsteps and the sound of voices on every side. At last, feeling tired and bored, he leaned back in his chair and fell asleep.

***

It was four o'clock when Sergeant Mazeroux came and woke him. As he led him to the study, Mazeroux whispered:

"Well, have you discovered him?"

"Whom?"

"The murderer."

"Of course!" said Perenna. "It's as easy as shelling peas!"

"That's a good thing!" said Mazeroux, greatly relieved and failing to see the joke. "But for that, as you saw for yourself, you would have been done for."

Don Luis entered. In the room were the public prosecutor, the examining magistrate, the chief detective, the local commissary of police, two inspectors, and three constables in uniform.

Outside, on the Boulevard Suchet, shouts were raised; and, when the commissary and his three policemen went out, by the Prefect's orders, to listen to the crowd, the hoarse voice of a newsboy was heard shouting:

"The double murder on the Boulevard Suchet! Full particulars of the death of Inspector Vérot! The police at a loss!—"

Then, when the door was closed, all was silent.

"Mazeroux was quite right," thought Don Luis. "It's I or the other one: that's clear. Unless the words that will be spoken and the facts that will come to light in the course of this examination supply me with some clue that will enable me to give them the name of that mysterious X, they'll surrender me this evening for the people to batten on. Attention, Lupin, old chap, the great game is about to commence!"

He felt that thrill of delight which always ran through him at the approach of the great struggles. This one, indeed, might be numbered among the most terrible that he had yet sustained.

He knew the Prefect's reputation, his experience, his tenacity, and the keen pleasure which he took in conducting important inquiries and in personally pushing them to a conclusion before placing them in the magistrate's hands; and he also knew all the professional qualities of the chief detective, and all the subtlety, all the penetrating logic possessed by the examining magistrate.

The Prefect of Police himself directed the attack. He did so in a straightforward fashion, without beating about the bush, and in a rather harsh voice, which had lost its former tone of sympathy for Don Luis. His attitude also was more formal and lacked that geniality which had struck Don Luis on the previous day.

"Monsieur," he said, "circumstances having brought about that, as the residuary legatee and representative of Mr Cosmo Mornington, you spent the night on this ground floor while a double murder was being committed here, we wish to receive your detailed evidence as to the different incidents that occurred last night."

"In other words, Monsieur le Préfet," said Perenna, replying directly to the attack, "in other words, circumstances having brought about that you authorized me to spend the night here, you would like to know if my evidence corresponds at all points with that of Sergeant Mazeroux?"

"Yes."

"Meaning that the part played by myself strikes you as suspicious?"

M. Desmalions hesitated. His eyes met Don Luis's eyes; and he was visibly impressed by the other's frank glance. Nevertheless he replied, plainly and bluntly:

"It is not for you to ask me questions, Monsieur."

Don Luis bowed.

"I am at your orders, Monsieur le Préfet."

"Please tell us what you know."

Don Luis thereupon gave a minute account of events, after which M. Desmalions reflected for a few moments and said:

"There is one point on which we want to be informed. When you entered this room at half-past two this morning and sat down beside M. Fauville, was there nothing to tell you that he was dead?"

"Nothing, Monsieur le Préfet. Otherwise, Sergeant Mazeroux and I would have given the alarm."

"Was the garden door shut?"

"It must have been, as we had to unlock it at seven o'clock."

"With what?"

"With the key on the bunch."

"But how could the murderers, coming from the outside, have opened it?"

"With false keys."

"Have you a proof which allows you to suppose that it was opened with false keys?"

"No, Monsieur le Préfet."

"Therefore, until we have proofs to the contrary, we are bound to believe that it was not opened from the outside, and that the criminal was inside the house."

"But, Monsieur le Préfet, there was no one here but Sergeant Mazeroux and myself!"

There was a silence, a pause whose meaning admitted of no doubt. M. Desmalions's next words gave it an even more precise value.

"You did not sleep during the night?"

"Yes, toward the end."

"You did not sleep before, while you were in the passage?"

"No."

"And Sergeant Mazeroux?"

Don Luis remained undecided for a moment; but how could he hope that the honest and scrupulous Mazeroux had disobeyed the dictates of his conscience?

He replied:

"Sergeant Mazeroux went to sleep in his chair and did not wake until Mme. Fauville returned, two hours later."

There was a fresh silence, which evidently meant:

"So, during the two hours when Sergeant Mazeroux was asleep, it was physically possible for you to open the door and kill the two Fauvilles."

The examination was taking the course which Perenna had foreseen; and the circle was drawing closer and closer around him. His adversary was conducting the contest with a logic and vigour which he admired without reserve.

"By Jove!" he thought. "How difficult it is to defend one's self when one is innocent. There's my right wing and my left wing driven in. Will my centre be able to stand the assault?"

M. Desmalions, after a whispered colloquy with the examining magistrate, resumed his questions in these terms:

"Yesterday evening, when M. Fauville opened his safe in your presence and the sergeant's, what was in the safe?"

"A heap of papers, on one of the shelves; and, among those papers, the diary in drab cloth which has since disappeared."

"You did not touch those papers?"

"Neither the papers nor the safe, Monsieur le Préfet. Sergeant Mazeroux must have told you that he made me stand aside, to insure the regularity of the inquiry."

THE CLOUDED TURQUOISE 73

"So you never came into the slightest contact with the safe?"

"Not the slightest."

M. Desmalions looked at the examining magistrate and nodded his head. Had Perenna been able to doubt that a trap was being laid for him, a glance at Mazeroux would have told him all about it. Mazeroux was ashen gray.

Meanwhile, M. Desmalions continued:

"You have taken part in inquiries, Monsieur, in police inquiries. Therefore, in putting my next question to you, I consider that I am addressing it to a tried detective."

"I will answer your question, Monsieur le Préfet, to the best of my ability."

"Here it is, then: Supposing that there were at this moment in the safe an object of some kind, a jewel, let us say, a diamond out of a tie pin, and that this diamond had come from a tie pin which belonged to somebody whom we knew, somebody who had spent the night in this house, what would you think of the coincidence?"

"There we are," said Perenna to himself. "There's the trap. It's clear that they've found something in the safe, and next, that they imagine that this something belongs to me. Good! But, in that case, we must presume, as I have not touched the safe, that the thing was taken from me and put in the safe to compromise me. But I did not have a finger in this pie until yesterday, and it is impossible that, during last night, when I saw nobody, anyone can have had time to prepare and contrive such a determined plot against me. So—"

The Prefect of Police interrupted this silent monologue by repeating:

"What would be your opinion?"

"There would be an undeniable connection between that person's presence in the house and the two crimes that had been committed."

"Consequently, we should have the right at least to suspect the person?"

"Yes."

"That is your view?"

"Decidedly."

M. Desmalions produced a piece of tissue paper from his pocket and took from it a little blue stone, which he displayed.

"Here is a turquoise which we found in the safe. It belongs, without a shadow of a doubt, to the ring which you are wearing on your finger."

Don Luis was seized with a fit of rage. He half grated, through his clenched teeth:

"Oh, the rascals! How clever they are! But no, I can't believe—"

He looked at his ring, which was formed of a large, clouded, dead turquoise, surrounded by a circle of small, irregular turquoises, also of a very pale blue. One of these was missing; and the one which M. Desmalions had in his hand fitted the place exactly.

"What do you say?" asked M. Desmalions.

"I say that this turquoise belongs to my ring, which was given me by Cosmo Mornington on the first occasion that I saved his life."

"So we are agreed?"

"Yes, Monsieur le Préfet, we are agreed."

Don Luis Perenna began to walk across the room, reflecting. The movement which the two detectives made toward the two doors told him that his arrest was provided for. A word from M. Desmalions, and Sergeant Mazeroux would be forced to take his chief by the collar.

Don Luis once more gave a glance toward his former accomplice. Mazeroux made a gesture of entreaty, as though to say:

"Well, what are you waiting for? Why don't you give up the criminal? Quick, it's time!"

Don Luis smiled.

"What's the matter?" asked the Prefect, in a tone that now entirely lacked the sort of involuntary politeness which he had shown since the commencement of the examination.

"The matter? The matter?—"

Perenna seized a chair by the back, spun it round and sat down upon it, with the simple remark:

"Let's talk!"

And this was said in such a way and the movement executed with so much decision that the Prefect muttered, as though wavering:

"I don't quite see—"

"You soon will, Monsieur le Préfet."

And, speaking in a slow voice, laying stress on every syllable that he uttered, he began:

"Monsieur le Préfet, the position is as clear as daylight. Yesterday evening you gave me an authorization which involves your responsibility most gravely. The result is that what you now want, at all costs and without delay, is a culprit. And that culprit is to be myself. By way of incriminating evidence, you have the fact of my presence here, the fact the door was locked on the inside, the fact that Sergeant Mazeroux was asleep while the crime was committed, and the fact of the discovery of the turquoise in the safe. All this is crushing, I admit. Added to it," he continued, "we have the terrible presumption that I had every interest in the removal of M. Fauville and his son, inasmuch as, if there is no heir of Cosmo Mornington's in existence, I come into a hundred million francs. Exactly. There is therefore nothing for me to do, Monsieur le Préfet, but to go with you to the lockup or else—"

"Or else what?"

"Or else hand over to you the criminal, the real criminal."

The Prefect of Police smiled and took out his watch.

"I'm waiting," he said.

"It will take me just an hour, Monsieur le Préfet, and no more, if you give me every latitude. And the search of the truth, it seems to me, is worth a little patience."

"I'm waiting," repeated M. Desmalions.

"Sergeant Mazeroux, please tell Silvestre, the manservant, that Monsieur le Préfet wishes to see him."

Upon a sign from M. Desmalions, Mazeroux went out.

Don Luis explained his motive.

"Monsieur le Préfet, whereas the discovery of the turquoise constitutes in your eyes an extremely serious proof against me, to me it is a revelation of the highest importance. I will tell you why. That turquoise must have fallen from my ring last evening and rolled on the carpet.

"Now there are only four persons," he continued, "who can have noticed this fall when it happened, picked up the turquoise and, in order to compromise the new adversary that I was, slipped it into the safe. The first of those four persons is one of your detectives, Sergeant Mazeroux, of whom we will not speak. The second is dead: I refer to M. Fauville. We will not speak of him. The third is Silvestre, the manservant. I should like to say a few words to him. I shall not take long."

Silvestre's examination, in fact, was soon over. He was able to prove that, pending the return of Mme. Fauville, for whom he had to open the door, he had not left the kitchen, where he was playing at cards with the lady's maid and another manservant.

"Very well," said Perenna. "One word more. You must have read in this morning's papers of the death of Inspector Vérot and seen his portrait."

"Yes."

"Do you know Inspector Vérot?"

"No."

"Still, it is probable that he came here yesterday, during the day."

"I can't say," replied the servant. "M. Fauville used to receive many visitors through the garden and let them in himself."

"You have no more evidence to give?"

"No."

"Please tell Mme. Fauville that Monsieur le Préfet would be very much obliged if he could have a word with her."

Silvestre left the room.

The examining magistrate and the public prosecutor had drawn nearer in astonishment.

The Prefect exclaimed:

"What, Monsieur! You don't mean to pretend that Mme. Fauville is mixed up—"

"Monsieur le Préfet, Mme. Fauville is the fourth person who may have seen the turquoise drop out of my ring."

"And what then? Have we the right, in the absence of any real proof, to suppose that a woman can kill her husband, that a mother can poison her son?"

"I am supposing nothing, Monsieur le Préfet."

"Then—?"

Don Luis made no reply. M. Desmalions did not conceal his irritation. However, he said:

"Very well; but I order you most positively to remain silent. What questions am I to put to Mme. Fauville?"

"One only, Monsieur le Préfet: ask Mme. Fauville if she knows anyone, apart from her husband, who is descended from the sisters Roussel."

"Why that question?"

"Because, if that descendant exists, it is not I who will inherit the millions, but he; and then it will be he and not I who would be interested in the removal of M. Fauville and his son."

"Of course, of course," muttered M. Desmalions. "But even so, this new trail—"

Mme. Fauville entered as he was speaking. Her face remained charming and pretty in spite of the tears that had reddened her eyelids and impaired the freshness of her cheeks. But her eyes expressed the scare of terror; and the obsession of the tragedy imparted to all her attractive personality, to her gait and to her movements, something feverish and spasmodic that was painful to look upon.

"Pray sit down, Madame," said the Prefect, speaking with the height of deference, "and forgive me for inflicting any additional emotion upon you. But time is precious; and we must do everything to make sure that the two victims whose loss you are mourning shall be avenged without delay."

Tears were still streaming from her beautiful eyes; and, with a sob, she stammered:

"If the police need me, Monsieur le Préfet—"

"Yes, it is a question of obtaining a few particulars. Your husband's mother is dead, is she not?"

"Yes, Monsieur le Préfet."

"Am I correct in saying that she came from Saint-Etienne and that her maiden name was Roussel?"

"Yes."

"Elizabeth Roussel?"

"Yes."

"Had your husband any brothers or sisters?"

"No."

"Therefore there is no descendant of Elizabeth Roussel living?"

"No."

"Very well. But Elizabeth Roussel had two sisters, did she not?"

"Yes."

"Ermeline Roussel, the elder, went abroad and was not heard of again. The other, the younger—"

"The other was called Armande Roussel. She was my mother."

"Eh? What do you say?"

"I said my mother's maiden name was Armande Roussel, and I married my cousin, the son of Elizabeth Roussel."

The statement had the effect of a thunderclap. So, upon the death of Hippolyte Fauville and his son Edmond, the direct descendants of the eldest sister, Cosmo Mornington's inheritance passed to the other branch, that of Armande Roussel; and this branch was represented so far by Mme. Fauville!

The Prefect of Police and the examining magistrate exchanged glances and both instinctively turned toward Don Luis Perenna, who did not move a muscle.

"Have you no brother or sister, Madame?" asked the Prefect.

"No, Monsieur le Préfet, I am the only one."

The only one! In other words, now that her husband and son were dead, Cosmo Mornington's millions reverted absolutely and undeniably to her, to her alone.

Meanwhile, a hideous idea weighed like a nightmare upon the magistrates and they could not rid themselves of it: the woman sitting before them was the mother of Edmond Fauville. M. Desmalions had his eyes on Don Luis Perenna, who wrote a few words on a card and handed it to the Prefect.

M. Desmalions, who was gradually resuming toward Don Luis his courteous attitude of the day before, read it, reflected a moment, and put this question to Mme. Fauville:

"What was your son Edmond's age?"

"Seventeen."

"You look so young—"

"Edmond was not my son, but my stepson, the son of my husband by his first wife, who died,"

"Ah! So Edmond Fauville—" muttered the Prefect, without finishing his sentence.

In two minutes the whole situation had changed. In the eyes of the magistrates, Mme. Fauville was no longer the widow and mother who must on no account be attacked. She had suddenly become a woman whom circumstances compelled them to cross-examine. However prejudiced they might be in her favour, however charmed by the seductive qualities of her beauty, they were inevitably bound to ask themselves, whether for some reason or other, for instance, in order to be alone in the enjoyment of the enormous fortune, she had not had the madness to kill her husband and to kill the boy who was only her husband's son. In any case, the question was there, calling for a solution.

The Prefect of Police continued:

"Do you know this turquoise?"

She took the stone which he held out to her and examined it without the least sign of confusion.

"No," she said. "I have an old-fashioned turquoise necklace, which I never wear, but the stones are larger and none of them have this irregular shape."

"We found this one in the safe," said M. Desmalions. "It forms part of a ring belonging to a person whom we know."

"Well," she said eagerly, "you must find that person."

"He is here," said the Prefect, pointing to Don Luis, who had been standing some way off and who had not been noticed by Mme. Fauville.

She started at the sight of Perenna and cried, very excitedly:

"But that gentleman was here yesterday evening! He was talking to my husband—and so was that other gentleman," she said, referring to Sergeant Mazeroux. "You must question them, find out why they were here. You understand that, if the turquoise belonged to one of them—"

The insinuation was direct, but clumsy; and it lent the greatest weight to Perenna's unspoken argument:

"The turquoise was picked up by someone who saw me yesterday and who wishes to compromise me. Apart from M. Fauville and the detective sergeant, only two people saw me: Silvestre, the manservant, and Mme. Fauville. Consequently, as Silvestre is outside the question, I accuse Mme. Fauville of putting the turquoise in the safe."

M. Desmalions asked:

"Will you let me see the necklace, Madame?"

"Certainly. It is with my other jewels, in my wardrobe. I will go for it."

"Pray don't trouble, Madame. Does your maid know the necklace?"

"Quite well."

"In that case, Sergeant Mazeroux will tell her what is wanted."

***

Not a word was spoken during the few minutes for which Mazeroux was absent. Mme. Fauville seemed absorbed in her grief. M. Desmalions kept his eyes fixed on her.

The sergeant returned, carrying a very large box containing a number of jewel-cases and loose ornaments.

M. Desmalions found the necklace, examined it, and realized, in fact, that the stones did not resemble the turquoise and that none of them was missing. But, on separating two jewel cases in order to take out a tiara which also contained blue stones, he made a gesture of surprise.

"What are these two keys?" he asked, pointing to two keys identical in shape and size with those which opened the lock and the bolt of the garden door.

Mme. Fauville remained very calm. Not a muscle of her face moved. Nothing pointed to the least perturbation on account of this discovery. She merely said:

"I don't know. They have been there a long time."

"Mazeroux," said M. Desmalions, "try them on that door."

Mazeroux did so. The door opened.

"Yes," said Mme. Fauville. "I remember now, my husband gave them to me. They were duplicates of his own keys—"

The words were uttered in the most natural tone and as though the speaker did not even suspect the terrible charge that was forming against her.

And nothing was more agonizing than this tranquillity. Was it a sign of absolute innocence, or the infernal craft of a criminal whom nothing is able to stir? Did she realize nothing of the tragedy which was taking place and of which she was the unconscious heroine? Or did she guess the terrible accusation which was gradually closing in upon her on every side and which threatened her with the most awful danger? But, in that case, how could she have been guilty of the extraordinary blunder of keeping those two keys?

A series of questions suggested itself to the minds of all those present. The Prefect of Police put them as follows:

"You were out, Madame, were you not, when the murders were committed?"

"Yes."

"You were at the opera?"

"Yes; and I went on to a party at the house of one of my friends, Mme. d'Ersingen."

"Did your chauffeur drive you?"

"To the opera, yes. But I sent him back to his garage; and he came to fetch me at the party."

"I see," said M. Desmalions. "But how did you go from the opera to Mme. d'Ersingen's?"

For the first time, Mme. Fauville seemed to understand that she was the victim of a regular cross-examination; and her look and attitude betrayed a certain uneasiness. She replied:

"I took a motor cab."

"In the street?"

"On the Place de l'Opéra."

"At twelve o'clock, therefore?"

"No, at half-past eleven: I left before the opera was over."

"You were in a hurry to get to your friend's?"

"Yes... or rather—"

She stopped; her cheeks were scarlet; her lips and chin trembled; and she asked:

"Why do you ask me all these questions?"

"They are necessary, Madame. They may throw a light on what we want to know. I beg you, therefore, to answer them. At what time did you reach your friend's house?"

"I hardly know. I did not notice the time."

"Did you go straight there?"

"Almost."

"How do you mean, almost?"

"I had a little headache and told the driver to go up the Champs Elysées and the Avenue du Bois—very slowly—and then down the Champs Elysées again—"

She was becoming more and more embarrassed. Her voice grew indistinct. She lowered her head and was silent.

Certainly her silence contained no confession, and there was nothing entitling anyone to believe that her dejection was other than a consequence of her grief. But yet she seemed so weary as to give the impression that, feeling herself lost, she was giving up the fight. And it was almost a feeling of pity that was entertained for this woman against whom all the circumstances seemed to be conspiring, and who defended herself so badly that her cross-examiner hesitated to press her yet further.

M. Desmalions, in fact, wore an irresolute air, as if the victory had been too easy, and as if he had some scruple about pursuing it.

Mechanically he observed Perenna, who passed him a slip of paper, saying:

"Mme. d'Ersingen's telephone number."

M. Desmalions murmured:

"Yes, true, they may know—"

And, taking down the receiver, he asked for number 325.04. He was connected at once and continued:

"Who is that speaking?... The butler? Ah! Is Mme. d'Ersingen at home?... No?... Or Monsieur?... Not he, either?... Never mind, you can tell me what I want to know. I am M. Desmalions, the Prefect of Police, and I need certain information. At what time did Mme. Fauville come last night?... What do you say?... Are you sure?... At two o'clock in the morning?... Not before?... And she went away?... In ten minutes time?... Good... But you're certain you are not mistaken about the time when she arrived? I must know this positively: it is most important... You say it was two o'clock in the morning? Two o'clock in the morning?... Very well... Thank you."

When M. Desmalions turned round, he saw Mme. Fauville standing beside him and looking at him with an expression of mad anguish. And one and the same idea occurred to the mind of all the onlookers. They were in the presence either of an absolutely innocent woman or else of an exceptional actress whose face lent itself to the most perfect simulation of innocence.

"What do you want?" she stammered. "What does this mean? Explain yourself!"

Then M. Desmalions asked simply.

"What were you doing last night between half-past eleven in the evening and two o'clock in the morning?"

It was a terrifying question at the stage which the examination had reached, a fatal question implying:

"If you cannot give us an exact and strict account of the way in which you employed your time while the crime was being committed, we have the right to conclude that you were not alien to the murder of your husband and stepson—"

She understood it in this sense and staggered on her feet, moaning:

"It's horrible!... Horrible!"

The Prefect repeated:

"What were you doing? The question must be quite easy to answer."

"Oh," she cried, in the same piteous tone, "how can you believe!... Oh, no, no, it's not possible! How can you believe!"

"I believe nothing yet," he said. "Besides, you can establish the truth with a single word."

It seemed, from the movement of her lips and the sudden gesture of resolution that shook her frame, as though she were about to speak that word. But all at once she appeared stupefied and dumbfounded, pronounced a few unintelligible syllables, and fell huddled into a chair, sobbing convulsively and uttering cries of despair.

It was tantamount to a confession. At the very least, it was a confession of her inability to supply the plausible explanation which would have put an end to the discussion.

The Prefect of Police moved away from her and spoke in a low voice to the examining magistrate and the public prosecutor. Perenna and Sergeant Mazeroux were left alone together, side by side.

Mazeroux whispered:

"What did I tell you? I knew you would find out! Oh, what a man you are! The way you managed!"

He was beaming at the thought that the chief was clear of the matter and that he had no more crows to pluck with his, Mazeroux's, superiors, whom he revered almost as much as he did the chief. Everybody was now agreed; they were "friends all round"; and Mazeroux was choking with delight.

"They'll lock her up, eh?"

"No," said Perenna. "There's not enough 'hold' on her for them to issue a warrant."

"What!" growled Mazeroux indignantly. "Not enough hold? I hope, in any case, that you won't let her go. She made no bones, you know, about attacking you! Come, Chief, polish her off, a she-devil like that!"

Don Luis remained pensive. He was thinking of the unheard-of coincidences, the accumulation of facts that bore down on Mme. Fauville from every side. And the decisive proof which would join all these different facts together and give to the accusation the grounds which it still lacked was one which Perenna was able to supply. This was the marks of the teeth in the apple hidden among the shrubs in the garden. To the police these would be as good as any fingerprint, all the more as they could compare the marks with those on the cake of chocolate.

Nevertheless, he hesitated; and, concentrating his anxious attention, he watched, with mingled feelings of pity and repulsion, that woman who, to all seeming, had killed her husband and her husband's son. Was he to give her the finishing stroke? Had he the right to play the part of judge? And supposing he were wrong?

***

Meantime, M. Desmalions had walked up to him and, while pretending to speak to Mazeroux, was really asking Perenna:

"What do you think of it?"

Mazeroux shook his head. Perenna replied:

"I think, Monsieur le Préfet, that, if this woman is guilty, she is defending herself, for all her cleverness, with inconceivable lack of skill."

"Meaning—?"

"Meaning that she was doubtless only a tool in the hands of an accomplice."

"An accomplice?"

"Remember, Monsieur le Préfet, her husband's exclamation in your office yesterday: 'Oh, the scoundrels! The scoundrels!' There is, therefore, at least one accomplice, who perhaps is the same as the man who was present, as Sergeant Mazeroux must have told you, in the Café du Pont-Neuf when Inspector Vérot was last there: a man with a reddish-brown beard, carrying an ebony walking-stick with a silver handle. So that—"

"So that," said M. Desmalions, completing the sentence, "by arresting Mme. Fauville today, merely on suspicion, we have a chance of laying our hands on the accomplice."

Perenna did not reply. The Prefect continued, thoughtfully:

"Arrest her... arrest her... We should need a proof for that... Did you receive no clue?"

"None at all, Monsieur le Préfet. True, my search was only summary."

"But ours was most minute. We have been through every corner of the room."

"And the garden, Monsieur le Préfet?"

"The garden also."

"With the same care?"

"Perhaps not... But I think—"

"I think, on the contrary, Monsieur le Préfet, that, as the murderers passed through the garden in coming and going, there might be a chance—"

"Mazeroux," said M. Desmalions, "go outside and make a more thorough inspection."

The sergeant went out. Perenna, who was once more standing at one side, heard the Prefect of Police repeating to the examining magistrate:

"Ah, if we only had a proof, just one! The woman is evidently guilty. The presumption against her is too great!... And then there are Cosmo Mornington's millions... But, on the other hand, look at her... look at all the honesty in that pretty face of hers, look at all the sincerity of her grief."

She was still crying, with fitful sobs and starts of indignant protest that made her clench her fists. At one moment she took her tear-soaked handkerchief, bit it with her teeth and tore it, after the manner of certain actresses.

Perenna saw those beautiful white teeth, a little wide, moist and gleaming, rending the dainty cambric. And he thought of the marks of teeth on the apple. And he was seized with an extreme longing to know the truth. Was it the same pair of jaws that had left its impress in the pulp of the fruit?

Mazeroux returned. M. Desmalions moved briskly toward the sergeant, who showed him the apple which he had found under the ivy. And Perenna at once realized the supreme importance which the Prefect of Police attached to Mazeroux's explanations and to his unexpected discovery.

A conversation of some length took place between the magistrates and ended in the decision which Don Luis foresaw. M. Desmalions walked across the room to Mme. Fauville. It was the catastrophe. He reflected for a second on the manner in which he should open this final contest, and then he asked:

"Are you still unable, Madame, to tell us how you employed your time last night?"

She made an effort and whispered:

"Yes, yes... I took a taxi and drove about... I also walked a little—"

"That is a fact which we can easily verify when we have found the driver of the taxi. Meanwhile, there is an opportunity of removing the somewhat... grievous impression which your silence has left on our minds."

"I am quite ready—"

"It is this: the person or one of the persons who took part in the crime appears to have bitten into an apple which was afterward thrown away in the garden and which has just been found. To put an end to any suppositions concerning yourself, we should like you to perform the same action."

"Oh, certainly!" she cried, eagerly. "If this is all you need to convince you—"

She took one of the three apples which Desmalions handed her from the dish and lifted it to her mouth.

It was a decisive act. If the two marks resembled each other, the proof existed, assured and undeniable.

Before completing her movement, she stopped short, as though seized with a sudden fear... Fear of what? Fear of the monstrous chance that might be her undoing? Or fear rather of the dread weapon which she was about to deliver against herself? In any case nothing accused her with greater directness than this last hesitation, which was incomprehensible if she was innocent, but clear as day if she was guilty!

"What are you afraid of, Madame?" asked M. Desmalions.

"Nothing, nothing," she said, shuddering. "I don't know... I am afraid of everything... It is all so horrible—"

"But, Madame, I assure you that what we are asking of you has no sort of importance and, I am persuaded, can only have a fortunate result for you. If you don't mind, therefore—"

She raised her hand higher and yet higher, with a slowness that betrayed her uneasiness. And really, in the fashion in which things were happening, the scene was marked by a certain solemnity and tragedy that wrung every heart.

"And, if I refuse?" she asked, suddenly.

"You are absolutely entitled to refuse," said the Prefect of Police. "But is it worthwhile, Madame? I am sure that your counsel would be the first to advise you—"

"My counsel?" she stammered, understanding the formidable meaning conveyed by that reply.

And, suddenly, with a fierce resolve and the almost ferocious air that contorts the face when great dangers threaten, she made the movement which they were pressing her to make. She opened her mouth. They saw the gleam of the white teeth. At one bite, the white teeth dug into the fruit.

"There you are, Monsieur," she said.

M. Desmalions turned to the examining magistrate.

"Have you the apple found in the garden?"

"Here, Monsieur le Préfet."

M. Desmalions put the two apples side by side.

And those who crowded round him, anxiously looking on, all uttered one exclamation.

The two marks of teeth were identical.

Identical! Certainly, before declaring the identity of every detail, the absolute analogy of the marks of each tooth, they must wait for the results of the expert's report. But there was one thing which there was no mistaking and that was the complete similarity of the two curves.

In either fruit the rounded arch was bent according to the same inflection. The two semicircles could have fitted one into the other, both very narrow, both a little long-shaped and oval and of a restricted radius which was the very character of the jaw.

The men did not speak a word. M. Desmalions raised his head. Mme. Fauville did not move, stood livid and mad with terror. But all the sentiments of terror, stupor and indignation that she might simulate with her mobile face and her immense gifts as an actress, did not prevail against the compelling proof that presented itself to every eye.

The two imprints were identical! The same teeth had bitten into both apples!

"Madame—" the Prefect of Police began.

"No, no," she cried, seized with a fit of fury, "no, it's not true... This is all just a nightmare... No, you are never going to arrest me? I in prison! Why, it's horrible!... What have I done? Oh, I swear that you are mistaken—"

She took her head between her hands.

"Oh, my brain is throbbing as if it would burst! What does all this mean? I have done no wrong... I knew nothing. It was you who told me this morning... Could I have suspected? My poor husband... and that dear Edmond who loved me... and whom I loved! Why should I have killed them? Tell me that! Why don't you answer?" she demanded. "People don't commit murder without a motive... Well?... Well?... Answer me, can't you?"

And once more convulsed with anger, standing in an aggressive attitude, with her clenched hands outstretched at the group of magistrates, she screamed:

"You're no better than butchers... you have no right to torture a woman like this... Oh, how horrible! To accuse me... to arrest me... for nothing!... Oh, it's abominable!... What butchers you all are!... And it's you in particular," addressing Perenna, "it's you—yes, I know—it's you who are the enemy.

"Oh, I understand! You had your reasons, you were here last night... Then why don't they arrest you? Why not you, as you were here and I was not and know nothing, absolutely nothing of what happened... Why isn't it you?"

The last words were pronounced in a hardly intelligible fashion. She had no strength left. She had to sit down, with her head bent over her knees, and she wept once more, abundantly.

Perenna went up to her and, raising her forehead and uncovering the tear-stained face, said:

"The imprints of teeth in both apples are absolutely identical. There is therefore no doubt whatever but that the first comes from you as well as the second."

"No!" she said.

"Yes," he affirmed. "That is a fact which it is materially impossible to deny. But the first impression may have been left by you before last night, that is to say, you may have bitten that apple yesterday, for instance—"

She stammered:

"Do you think so? Yes, perhaps, I seem to remember—yesterday morning—"

But the Prefect of Police interrupted her.

"It is useless, Madame; I have just questioned your servant, Silvestre. He bought the fruit himself at eight o'clock last evening. When M. Fauville went to bed, there were four apples in the dish. At eight o'clock this morning there were only three. Therefore the one found in the garden is incontestably the fourth; and this fourth apple was marked last night. And the mark is the mark of your teeth."

She stammered:

"It was not I... it was not I... that mark is not mine."

"But—"

"That mark is not mine... I swear it as I hope to be saved... And I also swear that I shall die, yes, die... I prefer death to prison... I shall kill myself... I shall kill myself—"

Her eyes were staring before her. She stiffened her muscles and made a supreme effort to rise from her chair. But, once on her feet, she tottered and fell fainting on the floor.

While she was being seen to, Mazeroux beckoned to Don Luis and whispered:

"Clear out, Chief."

"Ah, so the orders are revoked? I'm free?"

"Chief, take a look at the beggar who came in ten minutes ago and who's talking to the Prefect. Do you know him?"

"Hang it all!" said Perenna, after glancing at a large red-faced man who did not take his eyes off him. "Hang it, it's Weber, the deputy chief!"

"Andhe's recognized you, Chief! He recognized Lupinat first sight. There's no fake that he can't see through. He's got the knack of it. Well, Chief, just think of all the tricks you've played on him and ask yourself if he'll stick at anything to have his revenge!"

"And you think he has told the Prefect?"

"Of course he has; and the Prefect has ordered my mates to keep you in view. If you make the least show of trying to escape them, they'll collar you."

"In that case, there's nothing to be done?"

"Nothing to be done? Why, it's a question of putting them off your scent and mighty quickly!"

"What good would that do me, as I'm going home and they know where I live?"

"Eh, what? Can you have the cheek to go home after what's happened?"

"Where do you expect me to sleep? Under the bridges?"

"But, dash it all, don't you understand that, after this job, there will be the most infernal stir, that you're compromised up to the neck as it is, and that everybody will turn against you?"

"Well?"

"Drop the business."

"And the murderers of Cosmo Mornington and the Fauvilles?"

"The police will see to that."

"Alexandre, you're an ass."

"Then become Lupin again, the invisible, impregnable Lupin, and do your own fighting, as you used to. But in Heaven's name don't remain Perenna! It is too dangerous. And don't occupy yourself officially with a business in which you are not interested."

"The things you say, Alexandre! I am interested in it to the tune of a hundred million. If Perenna does not stick to his post, the hundred million will be snatched from under his nose. And, on the one occasion when I can earn a few honest centimes, that would be most annoying."

"And, if they arrest you?"

"No go! I'm dead!"

"Lupin is dead. But Perenna is alive."

"As they haven't arrested me today, I'm easy in my mind."

"It's only put off. And the orders are strict from this moment onward. They mean to surround your house and to keep watch day and night."

"Capital. I always was frightened at night."

"But, good Lord! What are you hoping for?"

"I hope for nothing, Alexandre. I am sure. I am sure now that they will not dare arrest me."

"Do you imagine that Weber will stand on ceremony?"

"I don't care a hang about Weber. Without orders, Weber can do nothing."

"But they'll give him his orders."

"The order to shadow me, yes; to arrest me, no. The Prefect of Police has committed himself about me to such an extent that he will be obliged to back me up. And then there's this: the whole affair is so absurd, so complicated, that you people will never find your way out of it alone. Sooner or later, you will come and fetch me. For there is no one but myself able to fight such adversaries as these: not you nor Weber, nor any of your pals at the detective office. I shall expect your visit, Alexandre."

On the next day an expert examination identified the tooth prints on the two apples and likewise established the fact that the print on the cake of chocolate was similar to the others.

Also, the driver of a taxicab came and gave evidence that a lady engaged him as she left the opera, told him to drive her straight to the end of the Avenue Henri Martin, and left the cab on reaching that spot.

Now the end of the Avenue Henri Martin was within five minutes' walk of the Fauvilles' house.

The man was brought into Mme. Fauville's presence and recognized her at once.

What had she done in that neighbourhood for over an hour?

Marie Fauville was taken to the central lockup, was entered on the register, and slept, that night, at the Saint-Lazare prison.

That same day, when the reporters were beginning to publish details of the investigation, such as the discovery of the tooth prints, but when they did not yet know to whom to attribute them, two of the leading dailies used as a headline for their article the very words which Don Luis Perenna had employed to describe the marks on the apple, the sinister words which so well suggested the fierce, savage, and so to speak, brutal character of the incident:

"THE TEETH OF THE TIGER."

5

THE IRON CURTAIN

It is sometimes an ungrateful task to tell the story of Arsène Lupin's life, for the reason that each of his adventures is partly known to the public, having at the time formed the subject of much eager comment, whereas his biographer is obliged, if he would throw light upon what is not known, to begin at the beginning and to relate in full detail all that which is already public property.

It is because of this necessity that I am compelled to speak once more of the extreme excitement which the news of that shocking series of crimes created in France, in Europe and throughout the civilized world. The public heard of four murders practically all at once, for the particulars of Cosmo Mornington's will were published two days later.

There was no doubt that the same person had killed Cosmo Mornington, Inspector Vérot, Fauville the engineer, and his son Edmond. The same person had made the identical sinister bite, leaving against himself or herself, with a heedlessness that seemed to show the avenging hand of fate, a most impressive and incriminating proof, a proof which made people shudder as they would have shuddered at the awful reality: the marks of his or her teeth, the teeth of the tiger!

And, in the midst of all this bloodshed, at the most tragic moment of the dismal tragedy, behold the strangest of figures emerging from the darkness!

An heroic adventurer, endowed with astounding intelligence and insight, had in a few hours partly unravelled the tangled skeins of the plot, divined the murder of Cosmo Mornington, proclaimed the murder of Inspector Vérot, taken the conduct of the investigation into his own hands, delivered to justice the inhuman creature whose beautiful white teeth fitted the marks as precious stones fit their settings, received a cheque for a million francs on the day after these exploits and, finally, found himself the probable heir to an immense fortune.

And here was Arsène Lupin coming to life again!

For the public made no mistake about that, and, with wonderful intuition, proclaimed aloud that Don Luis Perenna was Arsène Lupin, before a close examination of the facts had more or less confirmed the supposition.

"But he's dead!" objected the doubters.

To which the others replied:

"Yes, Dolores Kesselbach's corpse was recovered under the still smoking ruins of a little chalet near the Luxemburg frontier and, with it, the corpse of a man whom the police identified as Arsène Lupin. But everything goes to show that the whole scene was contrived by Lupin, who, for reasons of his own, wanted to be thought dead. And everything shows that the police accepted and legalized the theory of his death only because they wished to be rid of their everlasting adversary.

"As a proof, we have the confidences made by Valenglay, who was Prime Minister at the time and whom the chances of politics have just replaced at the head of the government. And there is the mysterious incident on the island of Capri when the German Emperor, just as he was about to be buried under a landslip, was saved by a hermit who, according to the German version, was none other than Arsène Lupin."

To this came a fresh objection:

"Very well; but read the newspapers of the time: ten minutes afterward, the hermit flung himself into the sea from Tiberius' Leap." And the answer:

"Yes, but the body was never found. And, as it happens, we know that a steamer picked up a man who was making signals to her and that this steamer was on her way to Algiers. Well, a few days later, Don Luis Perenna enlisted in the Foreign Legion at Sidi-bel-Abbes."

Of course, the controversy upon which the newspapers embarked on this subject was carried on discreetly. Everybody was afraid of Lupin; and the journalists maintained a certain reserve in their articles, confined themselves to comparing dates and pointing out coincidences, and refrained from speaking too positively of any Lupin that might lie hidden under the mask of Perenna.

But, as regards the private in the Foreign Legion and his stay in Morocco, they took their revenge and let themselves go freely.

Major d'Astrignac had spoken. Other officers, other comrades of Perenna's, related what they had seen. The reports and daily orders concerning him were published. And what became known as "The Hero's Idyll" began to take the form of a sort of record each page of which described the maddest and unlikeliest of facts.

At Médiouna, on the twenty-fourth of March, the adjutant, Captain Pollex, awarded Private Perenna four days' cells on a charge of having broken out of camp past two sentries after evening roll call, contrary to orders, and being absent without leave until noon on the following day. Perenna, the report went on to say, brought back the body of his sergeant, killed in ambush. And in the margin was this note, in the colonel's hand:

"The colonel commanding doubles Private Perenna's award, but mentions his name in orders and congratulates and thanks him."

After the fight of Ber-Réchid, Lieutenant Fardet's detachment being obliged to retreat before a band of four hundred Moors, Private Perenna asked leave to cover the retreat by installing himself in a *kasbah*.

"How many men do you want, Perenna?"

"None, sir."

"What! Surely you don't propose to cover a retreat all by yourself?"

"What pleasure would there be in dying, sir, if others were to die as well as I?"

At his request, they left him a dozen rifles, and divided with him the cartridges that remained. His share came to seventy-five.

The detachment got away without being further molested. Next day, when they were able to return with reinforcements, they surprised the Moors lying in wait around the *kasbah*, but afraid to approach. The ground was covered with seventy-five of their killed.

Our men drove them off. They found Private Perenna stretched on the floor of the *kasbah*. They thought him dead. He was asleep!

He had not a single cartridge left. But each of his seventy-five bullets had gone home.

What struck the imagination of the public most, however, was Major Comte d'Astrignac's story of the battle of Dar-Dbibarh. The major confessed that this battle, which relieved Fez at the moment when we thought that all was lost and which created such a sensation in France, was won before it was fought and that it was won by Perenna, alone!

At daybreak, when the Moorish tribes were preparing for the attack, Private Perenna lassoed an Arab horse that was galloping across the plain, sprang on the animal, which had no saddle, bridle, nor any sort of harness, and without jacket, cap, or arms, with his white shirt bulging out and a cigarette between his teeth, charged, with his hands in his trousers-pockets!

He charged straight toward the enemy, galloped through their camp, riding in and out among the tents, and then left it by the same place by which he had gone in.

This quite inconceivable death ride spread such consternation among the Moors that their attack was half-hearted and the battle was won without resistance.

This, together with numberless other feats of bravado, went to make up the heroic legend of Perenna. It threw into relief the superhuman energy, the marvellous recklessness, the bewildering fancy, the spirit of adventure, the physical dexterity, and the coolness of a singularly mysterious individual whom it was impossible not to take for Arsène Lupin, but a new and greater Arsène Lupin, dignified, idealized, and ennobled by his exploits.

One morning, a fortnight after the double murder in the Boulevard Suchet, this extraordinary man, who aroused such eager interest and who was spoken of on every side as a fabulous and more or less impossible being: one morning, Don Luis Perenna dressed himself and went the rounds of his house.

It was a comfortable and roomy eighteenth-century mansion, situated at the entrance to the Faubourg Saint-Germain, on the little Place du Palais-Bourbon. He had bought it, furnished, from a rich Hungarian, Count Malonyi, keeping for his own use the horses, carriages, motor cars, and taking over the eight servants and even the count's secretary, Mlle. Levasseur, who undertook to manage the household and to receive and get rid of the visitors—journalists, bores and curiosity-dealers—attracted by the luxury of the house and the reputation of its new owner.

After finishing his inspection of the stables and garage, he walked across the courtyard and went up to his study, pushed open one of the windows and raised his head. Above him was a slanting mirror; and this mirror reflected, beyond the courtyard and its surrounding wall, one whole side of the Place du Palais-Bourbon.

"Bother!" he said. "Those confounded detectives are still there. And this has been going on for a fortnight. I'm getting tired of this spying."

He sat down, in a bad temper, to look through his letters, tearing up, after he had read them, those which concerned him personally and making notes on the others, such as applications for assistance and requests for interviews. When he had finished, he rang the bell.

"Ask Mlle. Levasseur to bring me the newspapers."

She had been the Hungarian count's reader as well as his secretary; and Perenna had trained her to pick out in the newspapers anything that referred to him, and to give him each morning an exact account of the proceedings that were being taken against Mme. Fauville.

Always dressed in black, with a very elegant and graceful figure, she had attracted him from the first. She had an air of great dignity and a grave and thoughtful face which made it impossible to penetrate the secret of her soul, and which would have seemed austere had it not been framed in a cloud of fair curls, resisting all attempts at discipline and setting a halo of light and gayety around her.

Her voice had a soft and musical tone which Perenna loved to hear; and, himself a little perplexed by Mlle. Levasseur's attitude of reserve, he wondered what she could think of him, of his mode of life, and of all that the newspapers had to tell of his mysterious past.

"Nothing new?" he asked, as he glanced at the headings of the articles.

She read the reports relating to Mme. Fauville; and Don Luis could see that the police investigations were making no headway. Marie Fauville still kept to her first method, that of weeping, making a show of indignation, and assuming entire ignorance of the facts upon which she was being examined.

"It's ridiculous," he said, aloud. "I have never seen anyone defend herself so clumsily."

"Still, if she's innocent?"

It was the first time that Mlle. Levasseur had uttered an opinion or rather a remark upon the case. Don Luis looked at her in great surprise.

"So you think her innocent, Mademoiselle?"

She seemed ready to reply and to explain the meaning of her interruption. It was as though she were removing her impassive mask and about to allow her face to adopt a more animated expression under the impulse of her inner feelings. But she restrained herself with a visible effort, and murmured:

"I don't know. I have no views."

"Possibly," he said, watching her with curiosity, "but you have a doubt: a doubt which would be permissible if it were not for the marks left by Mme. Fauville's own teeth. Those marks, you see, are something more than a signature, more than a confession of guilt. And, as long as she is unable to give a satisfactory explanation of this point—"

But Marie Fauville vouchsafed not the slightest explanation of this or of anything else. She remained impenetrable. On the other hand, the police failed to discover her accomplice or accomplices, or the man with the ebony walking-stick and the tortoise-shell glasses whom the waiter at the Café du Pont-Neuf had described to Mazeroux and who seemed to have played a singularly suspicious part. In short, there was not a ray of light thrown upon the subject.

Equally vain was all search for the traces of Victor, the Roussel sisters' first cousin, who would have inherited the Mornington bequest in the absence of any direct heirs.

"Is that all?" asked Perenna.

"No," said Mlle. Levasseur, "there is an article in the *Echo de France*—"

"Relating to me?"

"I presume so, Monsieur. It is called, 'Why Don't They Arrest Him?'"

"That concerns me," he said, with a laugh.

He took the newspaper and read:

"Why do they not arrest him? Why go against logic and prolong an unnatural situation which no decent man can understand? This is the question which everybody is asking and to which our investigations enable us to furnish a precise reply.

"Two years ago, in other words, three years after the pretended death of Arsène Lupin, the police, having discovered or believing they had discovered that Arsène Lupin was really none other than one Floriani, born at Blois and since lost to sight, caused the register to be inscribed, on the page relating to this Floriani, with the word 'Deceased,' followed by the words 'Under the alias of Arsène Lupin.'

"Consequently, to bring Arsène Lupin back to life, there would be wanted something more than the undeniable proof of his existence, which would not be impossible. The most complicated wheels in the administrative machine would have to be set in motion, and a decree obtained from the Council of State.

"Now it would seem that M. Valenglay, the Prime Minister, together with the Prefect of Police, is opposed to making any too minute inquiries capable of opening up a scandal which the authorities are anxious to avoid. Bring Arsène Lupin back to life? Recommence the struggle with that accursed scoundrel? Risk a fresh defeat and fresh ridicule? No, no, and again no!

"And thus is brought about this unprecedented, inadmissible, inconceivable, disgraceful situation, that Arsène Lupin, the hardened thief, the impenitent criminal, the robber-king, the emperor of burglars and swindlers, is able today, not clandestinely, but in the sight and hearing of the whole world, to pursue the most formidable task that he has yet undertaken, to live publicly under a name which is not his own, but which he has incontestably made his own, to destroy with impunity four persons who stood in his way, to cause the imprisonment of an innocent woman against whom he himself has accumulated false evidence, and at the end of all, despite the protests of common sense and thanks to an unavowed complicity, to receive the hundred millions of the Mornington legacy.

"There is the ignominious truth in a nutshell. It is well that it should be stated. Let us hope, now that it stands revealed, that it will influence the future conduct of events."

"At any rate, it will influence the conduct of the idiot who wrote that article," said Lupin, with a grin.

He dismissed Mlle. Levasseur and rang up Major d'Astrignac on the telephone.

"Is that you, Major? Perenna speaking."

"Yes, what is it?"

"Have you read the article in the *Echo de France?*"

"Yes."

"Would it bore you very much to call on that gentleman and ask for satisfaction in my name?"

"Oh! A duel!"

"It's got to be, Major. All these sportsmen are wearying me with their lucubrations. They must be gagged. This fellow will pay for the rest."

"Well, of course, if you're bent on it—"

"I am, very much."

The preliminaries were entered upon without delay. The editor of the *Echo de France* declared that the article had been sent in without a signature, typewritten, and that it had been published without his knowledge; but he accepted the entire responsibility.

That same day, at three o'clock, Don Luis Perenna, accompanied by Major d'Astrignac, another officer, and a doctor, left the house in the Place du Palais-Bourbon in his car, and, followed by a taxi crammed with the detectives engaged in watching him, drove to the Parc des Princes.

While waiting for the arrival of the adversary, the Comte d'Astrignac took Don Luis aside.

"My dear Perenna, I ask you no questions. I don't want to know how much truth there is in all that is being written about you, or what your real name is. To me, you are Perenna of the Legion, and that is all I care about. Your past began in Morocco. As for the future, I know that, whatever happens and however great the temptation, your only aim will be to revenge Cosmo Mornington and protect his heirs. But there's one thing that worries me."

"Speak out, Major."

"Give me your word that you won't kill this man."

"Two months in bed, Major; will that suit you?"

"Too long. A fortnight."

"Done."

The two adversaries took up their positions. At the second encounter, the editor of the *Echo de France* fell, wounded in the chest.

"Oh, that's too bad of you, Perenna!" growled the Comte d'Astrignac. "You promised me—"

"And I've kept my promise, Major."

The doctors were examining the injured man. Presently one of them rose and said:

"It's nothing. Three weeks' rest, at most. Only a third of an inch more, and he would have been done for."

"Yes, but that third of an inch isn't there," murmured Perenna.

Still followed by the detectives' motor cab, Don Luis returned to the Faubourg Saint-Germain; and it was then that an incident occurred which was to puzzle him greatly and throw a most extraordinary light on the article in the *Echo de France*.

In the courtyard of his house he saw two little puppies which belonged to the coachman and which were generally confined to the stables. They were playing with a twist of red string which kept catching on to things, to the railings of the steps, to the flower vases. In the end, the paper round which the string was wound, appeared. Don Luis happened to pass at that moment. His eyes noticed marks of writing on the paper, and he mechanically picked it up and unfolded it.

He gave a start. He had at once recognized the opening lines of the article printed in the *Echo de France*. And the whole article was there, written in ink, on ruled paper, with erasures, and with sentences added, struck out, and begun anew.

He called the coachman and asked him:

"Where does this ball of string come from?"

"The string, sir? Why, from the harness-room, I think. It must have been that little she-devil of a Mirza who—"

"And when did you wind the string round the paper?"

"Yesterday evening, Monsieur."

"Yesterday evening. I see. And where is the paper from?"

"Upon my word, Monsieur, I can't say. I wanted something to wind my string on. I picked this bit up behind the coach-house where they fling all the rubbish of the house to be taken into the street at night."

Don Luis pursued his investigations. He questioned or asked Mlle. Levasseur to question the other servants. He discovered nothing; but one fact remained: the article in the *Echo de France* had been written, as the rough draft which he had picked up proved, by somebody who lived in the house or who was in touch with one of the people in the house.

The enemy was inside the fortress.

But what enemy? And what did he want? Merely Perenna's arrest?

All the remainder of the afternoon Don Luis continued anxious, annoyed by the mystery that surrounded him, incensed at his own inaction, and especially at that threatened arrest, which certainly caused him no uneasiness, but which hampered his movements.

Accordingly, when he was told at about ten o'clock that a man who gave the name of Alexandre insisted on seeing him, he had the man shown in; and when he found himself face to face with Mazeroux, but Mazeroux disguised beyond recognition and huddled in an old cloak, he flung himself on him as on a prey, hustling and shaking him.

"So it's you, at last?" he cried. "Well, what did I tell you? You can't make head or tail of things at the police office and you've come for me! Confess it, you numskull! You've come to fetch me! Oh, how funny it all is! Gad, I knew that you would never have the cheek to arrest me, and that the Prefect of Police would manage to calm the untimely ardour of that confounded Weber! To begin with, one doesn't arrest a man whom one has need of. Come, out with it! Lord, how stupid you look! Why don't you answer? How far have you got at the office? Quick, speak! I'll settle the thing in five seconds. Just tell me about your inquiry in two words, and I'll finish it for you in the twinkling of a bed-post, in two minutes by my watch. Well, you were saying—"

"But, Chief," spluttered Mazeroux, utterly nonplussed.

"What! Must I drag the words out of you? Come on! I'll make a start. It has to do with the man with the ebony walking-stick, hasn't it? The one we saw at the Café du Pont-Neuf on the day when Inspector Vérot was murdered?"

"Yes, it has."

"Have you found his traces?"

"Yes."

"Well, come along, find your tongue!"

"It's like this, Chief. Someone else noticed him besides the waiter. There was another customer in the cafe; and this other customer, whom I ended by discovering, went out at the same time as our man and heard him ask somebody in the street which was the nearest underground station for Neuilly."

"Capital, that. And, in Neuilly, by asking questions on every side, you ferreted him out?"

"And even learnt his name, Chief: Hubert Lautier, of the Avenue du Roule. Only he decamped from there six months ago, leaving his furniture behind him and taking nothing but two trunks."

"What about the post-office?"

"We have been to the post-office. One of the clerks recognized the description which we supplied. Our man calls once every eight or ten days to fetch his mail, which never amounts to much: just one or two letters. He has not been there for some time."

"Is the correspondence in his name?"

"No, initials."

"Were they able to remember them?"

"Yes: B.R.W.8."

"Is that all?"

"That is absolutely all that I have discovered. But one of my fellow officers succeeded in proving, from the evidence of two detectives, that a man carrying a silver-handled ebony walking-stick and a pair of tortoise-shell glasses walked out of the Gare d'Auteuil on the evening of the double murder and went toward Renelagh. Remember the presence of Mme. Fauville in that neighbourhood at the same hour. And remember that the crime was committed round about midnight. I conclude from this—"

"That will do; be off!"

"But—"

"Get!"

"Then I don't see you again?"

"Meet me in half an hour outside our man's place."

"What man?"

"Marie Fauville's accomplice."

"But you don't know—"

"The address? Why, you gave it to me yourself: Boulevard Richard-Wallace, No. 8. Go! And don't look such a fool."

He made him spin round on his heels, took him by the shoulders, pushed him to the door, and handed him over, quite flabbergasted, to a footman.

He himself went out a few minutes later, dragging in his wake the detectives attached to his person, left them posted on sentry duty outside a block of flats with a double entrance, and took a motor cab to Neuilly.

He went along the Avenue de Madrid on foot and turned down the Boulevard Richard-Wallace, opposite the Bois de Boulogne. Mazeroux was waiting for him in front of a small three-storied house standing at the back of a courtyard contained within the very high walls of the adjoining property.

"Is this number eight?"

"Yes, Chief, but tell me how—"

"One moment, old chap; give me time to recover my breath."

He gave two or three great gasps.

"Lord, how good it is to be up and doing!" he said. "Upon my word, I was getting rusty. And what a pleasure to pursue those scoundrels! So you want me to tell you?"

He passed his arm through the sergeant's.

"Listen, Alexandre, and profit by my words. Remember this: when a person is choosing initials for his address at a *poste restante* he doesn't pick them at random, but always in such a way that the letters convey a meaning to the person corresponding with him, a meaning which will enable that other person easily to remember the address."

"And in this case?"

"In this case, Mazeroux, a man like myself, who knows Neuilly and the neighbourhood of the Bois, is at once struck by those three letters, 'B.R.W.,' and especially by the 'W.', a foreign letter, an English letter. So that in my mind's eye, instantly, as in a flash, I saw the three letters in their logical place as initials at the head of the words for which they stand. I saw the 'B' of 'boulevard,' and the 'R' and the English 'W' of Richard-Wallace. And so I came to the Boulevard Richard-Wallace. And that, my dear sir, explains the milk in the cocoanut."

Mazeroux seemed a little doubtful.

"And what do you think, Chief?"

"I think nothing. I am looking about. I am building up a theory on the first basis that offers a probable theory. And I say to myself... I say to myself... I say to myself, Mazeroux, that this is a devilish mysterious little hole and that this house—Hush! Listen—"

He pushed Mazeroux into a dark corner. They had heard a noise, the slamming of a door.

Footsteps crossed the courtyard in front of the house. The lock of the outer gate grated. Someone appeared, and the light of a street lamp fell full on his face.

"Dash it all," muttered Mazeroux, "it's he!"

"I believe you're right."

"It's he, Chief. Look at the black stick and the bright handle. And did you see the eyeglasses—and the beard? What a oner you are, Chief!"

"Calm yourself and let's go after him."

The man had crossed the Boulevard Richard-Wallace and was turning into the Boulevard Maillot. He was walking pretty fast, with his head up, gayly twirling his stick. He lit a cigarette.

At the end of the Boulevard Maillot, the man passed the octroi and entered Paris. The railway station of the outer circle was close by. He went to it and, still followed by the others, stepped into a train that took them to Auteuil.

"That's funny," said Mazeroux. "He's doing exactly what he did a fortnight ago. This is where he was seen."

The man now went along the fortifications. In a quarter of an hour he reached the Boulevard Suchet and almost immediately afterward the house in which M. Fauville and his son had been murdered.

He climbed the fortifications opposite the house and stayed there for some minutes, motionless, with his face to the front of the house. Then continuing his road he went to La Muette and plunged into the dusk of the Bois de Boulogne.

"To work and boldly!" said Don Luis, quickening his pace.

Mazeroux stopped him.

"What do you mean, Chief?"

"Well, catch him by the throat! There are two of us; we couldn't hope for a better moment."

"What! Why, it's impossible!"

"Impossible? Are you afraid? Very well, I'll do it by myself."

"Look here, Chief, you're not serious!"

"Why shouldn't I be serious?"

"Because one can't arrest a man without a reason."

"Without a reason? A scoundrel like this? A murderer? What more do you want?"

"In the absence of compulsion, of catching him in the act, I want something that I haven't got."

"What's that?"

"A warrant. I haven't a warrant."

Mazeroux's accent was so full of conviction, and the answer struck Don Luis Perenna as so comical, that he burst out laughing.

"You have no warrant? Poor little chap! Well, I'll soon show you if I need a warrant!"

"You'll show me nothing," cried Mazeroux, hanging on to his companion's arm. "You shan't touch the man."

"One would think he was your mother!"

"Come, Chief."

"But, you stick-in-the-mud of an honest man," shouted Don Luis, angrily, "if we let this opportunity slip shall we ever find another?"

"Easily. He's going home. I'll inform the commissary of police. He will telephone to headquarters; and tomorrow morning—"

"And suppose the bird has flown?"

"I have no warrant."

"Do you want me to sign you one, idiot?"

But Don Luis mastered his rage. He felt that all his arguments would be shattered to pieces against the sergeant's obstinacy, and that, if necessary, Mazeroux would go to the length of defending the enemy against him. He simply said in a sententious tone:

"One ass and you make a pair of asses; and there are as many asses as there are people who try to do police work with bits of paper, signatures, warrants, and other gammon. Police work, my lad, is done with one's fists. When you come upon the enemy, hit him. Otherwise, you stand a chance of hitting the air. With that, goodnight. I'm going to bed. Telephone to me when the job is done."

He went home, furious, sick of an adventure in which he had not had elbow room, and in which he had had to submit to the will, or, rather, to the weakness of others.

But next morning when he woke up his longing to see the police lay hold of the man with the ebony stick, and especially the feeling that his assistance would be of use, impelled him to dress as quickly as he could.

"If I don't come to the rescue," he thought, "they'll let themselves be done in the eye. They're not equal to a contest of this kind."

Just then Mazeroux rang up and asked to speak to him. He rushed to a little telephone box which his predecessor had fitted up on the first floor, in a dark recess that communicated only with his study, and switched on the electric light.

"Is that you, Alexandre?"

"Yes, Chief. I'm speaking from a wine shop near the house on the Boulevard Richard-Wallace."

"What about our man?"

"The bird's still in the nest. But we're only just in time."

"Really?"

"Yes, he's packed his trunk. He's going away this morning."

"How do they know?"

"Through the woman who manages for him. She's just come to the house and will let us in."

"Does he live alone?"

"Yes, the woman cooks his meals and goes away in the evening. No one ever calls except a veiled lady who has paid him three visits since he's been here. The housekeeper was not able to see what she was like. As for him, she says he's a scholar, who spends his time reading and working."

"And have you a warrant?"

"Yes, we're going to use it."

"I'll come at once."

"You can't! We've got Weber at our head. Oh, by the way, have you heard the news about Mme. Fauville?"

"About Mme. Fauville?"

"Yes, she tried to commit suicide last night."

"What! Tried to commit suicide!"

Perenna had uttered an exclamation of astonishment and was very much surprised to hear, almost at the same time, another cry, like an echo, at his elbow. Without letting go the receiver, he turned round and saw that Mlle. Levasseur was in the study a few yards away from him, standing with a distorted and livid face. Their eyes met. He was on the point of speaking to her, but she moved away, without leaving the room, however.

"What the devil was she listening for?" Don Luis wondered. "And why that look of dismay?"

Meanwhile, Mazeroux continued:

"She said, you know, that she would try to kill herself. But it must have taken a goodish amount of pluck."

"But how did she do it?" Perenna asked.

"I'll tell you another time. They're calling me. Whatever you do, Chief, don't come."

"Yes," he replied, firmly, "I'm coming. After all, the least I can do is to be in at the death, seeing that it was I who found the scent. But don't be afraid. I shall keep in the background."

"Then hurry, Chief. We're delivering the attack in ten minutes."

"I'll be with you before that."

He quickly hung up the receiver and turned on his heel to leave the telephone box. The next moment he had flung himself against the farther wall. Just as he was about to pass out he had heard something click above his head and he but barely had the time to leap back and escape being struck by an iron curtain which fell in front of him with a terrible thud.

Another second and the huge mass would have crushed him. He could feel it whizzing by his head. And he had never before experienced the anguish of danger so intensely.

After a moment of genuine fright, in which he stood as though petrified, with his brain in a whirl, he recovered his coolness and threw himself upon the obstacle. But it at once appeared to him that the obstacle was unsurmountable.

It was a heavy metal panel, not made of plates or lathes fastened one to the other, but formed of a solid slab, massive, firm, and strong, and covered with the sheen of time darkened here and there with patches of rust. On either side and at the top and bottom the edges of the panel fitted in a narrow groove which covered them hermetically.

He was a prisoner. In a sudden fit of rage he banged at the metal with his fists. He remembered that Mlle. Levasseur was in the study. If she had not yet left the room—and surely she could not have left it when the thing happened—she would hear the noise. She was bound to hear it. She would be sure to come back, give the alarm, and rescue him.

He listened. He shouted. No reply. His voice died away against the walls and ceiling of the box in which he was shut up, and he felt that the whole house—drawing-rooms, staircases, and passages—remained deaf to his appeal.

And yet... and yet... Mlle. Levasseur—

"What does it mean?" he muttered. "What can it all mean?"

And motionless now and silent, he thought once more of the girl's strange attitude, of her distraught face, of her haggard eyes. And he also began to wonder what accident had released the mechanism which had hurled the formidable iron curtain upon him, craftily and ruthlessly.

6

THE MAN WITH THE EBONY WALKING-STICK

A group consisting of Deputy Chief Detective Weber, Chief Inspector Ancenis, Sergeant Mazeroux, three inspectors, and the Neuilly commissary of police stood outside the gate of No. 8 Boulevard Richard-Wallace.

Mazeroux was watching the Avenue de Madrid, by which Don Luis would have to come, and began to wonder what had happened; for half an hour had passed since they telephoned to each other, and Mazeroux could find no further pretext for delaying the work.

"It's time to make a move," said Weber. "The housekeeper is making signals to us from the window: the joker's dressing."

"Why not nab him when he comes out?" objected Mazeroux. "We shall capture him in a moment."

"And if he cuts off by another outlet which we don't know of?" said the deputy chief. "You have to be careful with these beggars. No, let's beard him in his den. It's more certain."

"Still—"

"What's the matter with you, Mazeroux?" asked the deputy chief, taking him on one side. "Don't you see that our men are getting restive? They're afraid of this sportsman. There's only one way, which is to set them on him as if he were a wild beast.

Besides, the business must be finished by the time the Prefect comes,"

"Is he coming?"

"Yes. He wants to see things for himself. The whole affair interests him enormously. So, forward! Are you ready, men? I'm going to ring."

The bell sounded; and the housekeeper at once came and half opened the gate.

Although the orders were to observe great quiet, so as not to alarm the enemy too soon, the fear which he inspired was so intense that there was a general rush; and all the detectives crowded into the courtyard, ready for the fight. But a window opened and someone cried from the second floor:

"What's happening?"

The deputy chief did not reply. Two detectives, the chief inspector, the commissary, and himself entered the house, while the others remained in the courtyard and made any attempt at flight impossible.

The meeting took place on the first floor. The man had come down, fully dressed, with his hat on his head; and the deputy chief roared:

"Stop! Hands up! Are you Hubert Lautier?"

The man seemed disconcerted. Five revolvers were levelled at him. And yet no sign of fear showed in his face; and he simply said:

"What do you want, Monsieur? What are you here for?"

"We are here in the name of the law, with a warrant for your arrest."

"A warrant for my arrest?"

"A warrant for the arrest of Hubert Lautier, residing at 8 Boulevard Richard-Wallace."

"But it's absurd!" said the man. "It's incredible! What does it mean? What for?"

They took him by both arms, without his offering the least resistance, pushed him into a fairly large room containing no furniture but three rush-bottomed chairs, an armchair, and a table covered with big books.

"There," said the deputy chief. "Don't stir. If you attempt to move, so much the worse for you."

The man made no protest. While the two detectives held him by the collar, he seemed to be reflecting, as though he were trying to understand the secret causes of an arrest for which he was totally unprepared. He had an intelligent face, a reddish-brown beard, and a pair of blue-gray eyes which now and again showed a certain hardness of expression behind his glasses. His broad shoulders and powerful neck pointed to physical strength.

"Shall we tie his wrists?" Mazeroux asked the deputy chief.

"One second. The Prefect's coming; I can hear him. Have you searched the man's pockets? Any weapons?"

"No."

"No flask, no phial? Nothing suspicious?"

"No, nothing."

M. Desmalions arrived and, while watching the prisoner's face, talked in a low voice with the deputy chief and received the particulars of the arrest.

"This is good business," he said. "We wanted this. Now that both accomplices are in custody, they will have to speak; and everything will be cleared up. So there was no resistance?"

"None at all, Monsieur le Préfet."

"No matter, we will remain on our guard."

The prisoner had not uttered a word, but still wore a thoughtful look, as though trying to understand the inexplicable events of the last few minutes. Nevertheless, when he realized that the newcomer was none other than the Prefect of Police, he raised his head and looked at M. Desmalions, who asked him:

"It is unnecessary to tell you the cause of your arrest, I presume?" He replied, in a deferential tone:

"Excuse me, Monsieur le Préfet, but I must ask you, on the contrary, to inform me. I have not the least idea of the reason. Your detectives have made a grave mistake which a word, no doubt, will be enough to set right. That word I wish for, I insist upon—"

The Prefect shrugged his shoulders and said:

"You are suspected of taking part in the murder of Fauville, the civil engineer, and his son Edmond."

"Is Hippolyte dead?"

The cry was spontaneous, almost unconscious; a bewildered cry of dismay from a man moved to the depths of his being. And his dismay was supremely strange, his question, trying to make them believe in his ignorance, supremely unexpected.

"Is Hippolyte dead?"

He repeated the question in a hoarse voice, trembling all over as he spoke.

"Is Hippolyte dead? What are you saying? Is it possible that he can be dead? And how? Murdered? Edmond, too?"

The Prefect once more shrugged his shoulders.

"The mere fact of your calling M. Fauville by his Christian name shows that you knew him intimately. And, even if you were not concerned in his murder, it has been mentioned often enough in the newspapers during the last fortnight for you to know of it."

"I never read a newspaper, Monsieur le Préfet."

"What! You mean to tell me—?"

"It may sound improbable, but it is quite true. I lead an industrious life, occupying myself solely with scientific research, in view of a popular work which I am preparing, and I do not take the least part or the least interest in outside things. I defy anyone to prove that I have read a newspaper for months and months past. And that is why I am entitled to say that I did not know of Hippolyte Fauville's murder."

"Still, you knew M. Fauville."

"I used to know him, but we quarrelled."

"For what reason?"

"Family affairs."

"Family affairs! Were you related, then?"

"Yes. Hippolyte was my cousin."

"Your cousin! M. Fauville was your cousin! But... but then... Come, let us have the rights of the matter. M. Fauville and his wife were the children of two sisters, Elizabeth and Armande Roussel. Those two sisters had been brought up with a first cousin called Victor."

"Yes, Victor Sauverand, whose grandfather was a Roussel. Victor Sauverand married abroad and had two sons. One of them died fifteen years ago; the other is myself."

M. Desmalions gave a start. His excitement was manifest. If that man was telling the truth, if he was really the son of that Victor whose record the police had not yet been able to trace, then, owing to this very fact, since M. Fauville and his son were dead and Mme. Fauville, so to speak, convicted of murder and forfeiting her rights, they had arrested the final heir to Cosmo Mornington. But why, in a moment of madness, had he voluntarily brought this crushing indictment against himself?

He continued:

"My statements seem to surprise you, Monsieur le Préfet. Perhaps they throw a light on the mistake of which I am a victim?"

He expressed himself calmly, with great politeness and in a remarkably well-bred voice; and he did not for a moment seem to suspect that his revelations, on the contrary, were justifying the measures taken against him.

Without replying to the question, the Prefect of Police asked him:

"So your real name is—"

"Gaston Sauverand."

"Why do you call yourself Hubert Lautier?"

The man had a second of indecision which did not escape so clear-sighted an observer as M. Desmalions. He swayed from side to side, his eyes flickered and he said:

"That does not concern the police; it concerns no one but myself."

M. Desmalions smiled:

"That is a poor argument. Will you use the same when I ask you why you live in hiding, why you left the Avenue du Roule, where you used to live, without leaving an address behind you, and why you receive your letters at the post-office under initials?"

"Yes, Monsieur le Préfet, those are matters of a private character, which affect only my conscience. You have no right to question me about them."

"That is the exact reply which we are constantly receiving at every moment from your accomplice."

"My accomplice?"

"Yes, Mme. Fauville."

"Mme. Fauville!"

Gaston Sauverand had uttered the same cry as when he heard of the death of the engineer; and his stupefaction seemed even greater, combined as it was with an anguish that distorted his features beyond recognition.

"What?... What?... What do you say? Marie!... No, you don't mean it! It's not true!"

M. Desmalions considered it useless to reply, so absurd and childish was this affectation of knowing nothing about the tragedy on the Boulevard Suchet.

Gaston Sauverand, beside himself, with his eyes starting from his head, muttered:

"Is it true? Is Marie the victim of the same mistake as myself? Perhaps they have arrested her? She, she in prison!"

He raised his clenched fists in a threatening manner against all the unknown enemies by whom he was surrounded, against those who were persecuting him, those who had murdered Hippolyte Fauville and delivered Marie Fauville to the police.

Mazeroux and Chief Inspector Ancenis took hold of him roughly. He made a movement of resistance, as though he intended to thrust back his aggressors. But it was only momentary; and he sank into a chair and covered his face with his hands:

"What a mystery!" he stammered. "I don't understand! I don't understand—"

Weber, who had gone out a few minutes before, returned. M. Desmalions asked:

"Is everything ready?"

"Yes, Monsieur le Préfet, I have had the taxi brought up to the gate beside your car."

"How many of you are there?"

"Eight. Two detectives have just arrived from the commissary's."

"Have you searched the house?"

"Yes. It's almost empty, however. There's nothing but the indispensable articles of furniture and some bundles of papers in the bedroom."

"Very well. Take him away and keep a sharp lookout."

Gaston Sauvrand walked off quietly between the deputy chief and Mazeroux. He turned round in the doorway.

"Monsieur le Préfet, as you are making a search, I entreat you to take care of the papers on the table in my bedroom. They are notes that have cost me a great deal of labour in the small hours of the night. Also—"

He hesitated, obviously embarrassed.

"Well?"

"Well, Monsieur le Préfet, I must tell you—something—"

He was looking for his words and seemed to fear the consequences of them at the same time that he uttered them. But he suddenly made up his mind.

"Monsieur le Préfet, there is in this house—somewhere—a packet of letters which I value more than my life. It is possible that those letters, if misinterpreted, will furnish a weapon against me; but no matter. The great thing is that they should be safe. You will see. They include documents of extreme importance. I entrust them to your keeping—to yours alone, Monsieur le Préfet."

"Where are they?"

"The hiding-place is easily found. All you have to do is to go to the garret above my bedroom and press on a nail to the right of the window. It is an apparently useless nail, but it controls a hiding-place outside, under the slates of the roof, along the gutter."

He moved away between the two men. The Prefect called them back.

"One second. Mazeroux, go up to the garret and bring me the letters."

Mazeroux went out and returned in a few minutes. He had been unable to work the spring.

The Prefect ordered Chief Inspector Ancenis to go up with Mazeroux and to take the prisoner, who would show them how to open the hiding-place. He himself remained in the room with Weber, awaiting the result of the search, and began to read the titles of the volumes piled upon the table.

They were scientific books, among which he noticed works on chemistry: "Organic Chemistry" and "Chemistry Considered in Its Relations with Electricity." They were all covered with notes in the margins. He was turning over the pages of one of them, when he seemed to hear shouts.

The Prefect rushed to the door, but had not crossed the threshold when a pistol shot echoed down the staircase and there was a yell of pain.

Immediately after came two more shots, accompanied by cries, the sound of a struggle, and yet another shot.

Tearing upstairs, four steps at a time, with an agility not to be expected from a man of his build, the Prefect of Police, followed by the deputy chief, covered the second flight and came to a third, which was narrower and steeper. When he reached the bend, a man's body, staggering above him, fell into his arms: it was Mazeroux, wounded.

On the stairs lay another body, lifeless, that of Chief Inspector Ancenis.

Above them, in the frame of a small doorway, stood Gaston Sauverand, with a savage look on his face and his arm outstretched. He fired a fifth shot at random. Then, seeing the Prefect of Police, he took deliberate aim.

The Prefect stared at that terrifying barrel levelled at his face and gave himself up for lost. But, at that exact second, a shot was discharged from behind him, Sauverand's weapon fell from his hand before he was able to fire, and the Prefect saw, as in a dream, a man, the man who had saved his life, striding across the chief inspector's body, propping Mazeroux against the wall, and darting ahead, followed by the detectives. He recognized the man: it was Don Luis Perenna.

Don Luis stepped briskly into the garret where Sauverand had retreated, but had time only to catch sight of him standing on the window ledge and leaping into space from the third floor.

"Has he jumped from there?" cried the Prefect, hastening up. "We shall never capture him alive!"

"Neither alive nor dead, Monsieur le Préfet. See, he's picking himself up. There's a providence which looks after that sort. He's making for the gate. He's hardly limping."

"But where are my men?"

"Why, they're all on the staircase, in the house, brought here by the shots, seeing to the wounded—"

"Oh, the demon!" muttered the Prefect. "He's played a masterly game!"

Gaston Sauverand, in fact, was escaping unmolested.

"Stop him! Stop him!" roared M. Desmalions.

There were two motors standing beside the pavement, which is very wide at this spot: the Prefect's own car, and the cab which the deputy chief had provided for the prisoner. The two chauffeurs, sitting on their seats, had noticed nothing of the fight. But they saw Gaston Sauverand's leap into space; and the Prefect's chauffeur, on whose seat a certain number of incriminating articles had been placed, taking out of the heap the first weapon that offered, the ebony walking-stick, bravely rushed at the fugitive.

"Stop him! Stop him!" shouted M. Desmalions.

The encounter took place at the exit from the courtyard. It did not last long. Sauverand flung himself upon his assailant, snatched the stick from him, and broke it across his face. Then, without dropping the handle, he ran away, pursued by the other chauffeur and by three detectives who at last appeared from the house. He had thirty yards' start of the detectives, one of whom fired several shots at him without effect.

When M. Desmalions and Weber went downstairs again, they found the chief inspector lying on the bed in Gaston Sauverand's room on the second floor, gray in the face. He had been hit on the head and was dying. A few minutes later he was dead.

Sergeant Mazeroux, whose wound was only slight, said, while it was being dressed, that Sauverand had taken the chief inspector and himself up to the garret, and that, outside the door, he had dipped his hand quickly into an old satchel hanging on the wall among some servants' worn-out aprons and jackets. He drew out a revolver and fired point-blank at the chief inspector, who dropped like a log. When seized by Mazeroux, the murderer released himself and fired three bullets, the third of which hit the sergeant in the shoulder.

And so, in a fight in which the police had a band of experienced detectives at their disposal, while the enemy, a prisoner, seemed to possess not the remotest chance of safety, this enemy, by a stratagem of unprecedented daring, had led two of his adversaries aside, disabled both of them, drawn the others into the house and, finding the coast clear, escaped.

M. Desmalions was white with anger and despair. He exclaimed:

"He's tricked us! His letters, his hiding-place, the movable nail, were all shams. Oh, the scoundrel!"

He went down to the ground floor and into the courtyard. On the boulevard he met one of the detectives who had given chase to the murderer and who was returning quite out of breath.

"Well?" he asked anxiously,

"Monsieur le Préfet, he turned down the first street, where there was a motor waiting for him. The engine must have been working, for our man outdistanced us at once."

"But what about my car?"

"You see, Monsieur le Préfet, by the time it was started—"

"Was the motor that picked him up a hired one?"

"Yes, a taxi."

"Then we shall find it. The driver will come of his own accord when he has seen the newspapers."

Weber shook his head.

"Unless the driver is himself a confederate, Monsieur le Préfet. Besides, even if we find the cab, aren't we bound to suppose that Gaston Sauverand will know how to front the scent? We shall have trouble, Monsieur le Préfet."

"Yes," whispered Don Luis, who had been present at the first investigation and who was left alone for a moment with Mazeroux. "Yes, you will have trouble, especially if you let the people you capture take to their heels. Eh, Mazeroux, what did I tell you last night? But, still, what a scoundrel! And he's not alone, Alexandre. I'll answer for it that he has accomplices— and not a hundred yards from my house—do you understand? From my house."

After questioning Mazeroux upon Sauverand's attitude and the other incidents of the arrest, Don Luis went back to the Place du Palais-Bourbon.

***

The inquiry which he had to make related to events that were certainly quite as strange as those which he had just witnessed; and while the part played by Gaston Sauverand in the pursuit of the Mornington inheritance deserved all his attention, the behaviour of Mlle. Levasseur puzzled him no less.

He could not forget the cry of terror that escaped the girl while he was telephoning to Mazeroux, nor the scared expression of her face. Now it was impossible to attribute that cry and that expression to anything other than the words which he had uttered in reply to Mazeroux:

"What! Mme. Fauville tried to commit suicide!"

The fact was certain; and the connection between the announcement of the attempt and Mlle. Levasseur's extreme emotion was too obvious for Perenna not to try to draw conclusions.

He went straight to his study and at once examined the arch leading to the telephone box. This arch, which was about six feet wide and very low, had no door, but merely a velvet hanging, which was nearly always drawn up, leaving the arch uncovered. Under the hanging, among the mouldings of the cornice, was a button that had only to be pressed to bring down the iron curtain against which he had thrown himself two hours before.

He worked the catch two or three times over, and his experiments proved to him in the most explicit fashion that the mechanism was in perfect order and unable to act without outside intervention. Was he then to conclude that the girl had wanted to kill him? But what could be her motive?

He was on the point of ringing and sending for her, so as to receive the explanation which he was resolved to demand from her. However, the minutes passed and he did not ring. He saw her through the window as she walked slowly across the yard, her body swinging gracefully from her hips. A ray of sunshine lit up the gold of her hair.

All the rest of the morning he lay on a sofa, smoking cigars. He was ill at ease, dissatisfied with himself and with the course of events, not one of which brought him the least glimmer of truth; in fact, all of them seemed to deepen the darkness in which he was battling. Eager to act, the moment he did so he encountered fresh obstacles that paralyzed his powers of action and left him in utter ignorance of the nature of his adversaries.

But, at twelve o'clock, just as he had rung for lunch, his butler entered the study with a tray in his hand, and exclaimed, with an agitation which showed that the household was aware of Don Luis's ambiguous position:

"Sir, it's the Prefect of Police!"

"Eh?" said Perenna. "Where is he?"

"Downstairs, sir. I did not know what to do, at first... and I thought of telling Mlle. Levasseur. But—"

"Are you sure?"

"Here is his card, sir."

Perenna took the card from the tray and read M. Desmalions's name. He went to the window, opened it and, with the aid of the overhead mirror, looked into the Place du Palais-Bourbon.

Half a dozen men were walking about. He recognized them. They were his usual watchers, those whom he had got rid of on the evening before and who had come to resume their observation.

"No others?" he said to himself. "Come, we have nothing to fear, and the Prefect of Police has none but the best intentions toward me. It was what I expected; and I think that I was well advised to save his life."

M. Desmalions entered without a word. All that he did was to bend his head slightly, with a movement that might be taken for a bow. As for Weber, who was with him, he did not even give himself the trouble to disguise his feelings toward such a man as Perenna.

Don Luis took no direct notice of this attitude, but, in revenge, ostentatiously omitted to push forward more than one chair. M. Desmalions, however, preferred to walk about the room, with his hands behind his back, as if to continue his reflections before speaking.

The silence was prolonged. Don Luis waited patiently. Then, suddenly, the Prefect stopped and said:

"When you left the Boulevard Richard-Wallace, Monsieur, did you go straight home?"

Don Luis did not demur to this cross-examining manner and answered:

"Yes, Monsieur le Préfet."

"Here, to your study?"

"Here, to my study."

M. Desmalions paused and then went on:

"I left thirty or forty minutes after you and drove to the police office in my car. There I received this express letter. Read it. You will see that it was handed in at the Bourse at half-past nine."

Don Luis took the letter and read the following words, written in capital letters:

This is to inform you that Gaston Sauverand, after making his escape, rejoined his accomplice Perenna, who, as you know, is none other than Arsène Lupin. Arsène Lupin gave you Sauverand's address in order to get rid of him and to receive the Mornington inheritance. They were reconciled this morning, and Arsène Lupin suggested a safe hiding-place to Sauverand. It is easy to prove their meeting and their complicity. Sauverand handed Lupin the half of the walking-stick which he had carried away unawares. You will find it under the cushions of a sofa standing between the two windows of Perenna's study.

Don Luis shrugged his shoulders. The letter was absurd; for he had not once left his study. He folded it up quietly and handed it to the Prefect of Police without comment. He was resolved to let M. Desmalions take the initiative in the conversation.

The Prefect asked:

"What is your reply to the accusation?"

"None, Monsieur le Préfet."

"Still, it is quite plain and easy to prove or disprove."

"Very easy, indeed, Monsieur le Préfet; the sofa is there, between the windows."

M. Desmalions waited two or three seconds and then walked to the sofa and moved the cushions. Under one of them lay the handle end of the walking-stick.

Don Luis could not repress a gesture of amazement and anger. He had not for a second contemplated the possibility of such a miracle; and it took him unawares. However, he mastered himself. After all, there was nothing to prove that this half of a walking-stick was really that which had been seen in Gaston Sauverand's hands and which Sauverand had carried away by mistake.

"I have the other half on me," said the Prefect of Police, replying to the unspoken objection. "Deputy Chief Weber himself picked it up on the Boulevard Richard-Wallace. Here it is."

He produced it from the inside pocket of his overcoat and tried it. The ends of the two pieces fitted exactly.

There was a fresh pause. Perenna was confused, as were those, invariably, upon whom he himself used to inflict this kind of defeat and humiliation. He could not get over it. By what prodigy had Gaston Sauverand managed, in that short space of twenty minutes, to enter the house and make his way into this room? Even the theory of an accomplice living in the house did not do much to make the phenomenon easier to understand.

"It upsets all my calculations," he thought, "and I shall have to go through the mill this time. I was able to baffle Mme. Fauville's accusation and to foil the trick of the turquoise. But M. Desmalions will never admit that this is a similar attempt and that Gaston Sauverand has tried, as Marie Fauville did, to get me out of the way by compromising me and procuring my arrest."

"Well," exclaimed M. Desmalions impatiently, "answer! Defend yourself!"

"No, Monsieur le Préfet, it is not for me to defend myself,"

M. Desmalions stamped his foot and growled:

"In that case... in that case... since you confess... since—"

He put his hand on the latch of the window, ready to open it. A whistle, and the detectives would burst in and all would be over.

"Shall I have your inspectors called, Monsieur le Préfet?" asked Don Luis.

M. Desmalions did not reply. He let go the window latch and started walking about the room again. And, suddenly, while Perenna was wondering why he still hesitated, for the second time the Prefect planted himself in front of him, and said:

"And suppose I looked upon the incident of the walking-stick as not having occurred, or, rather, as an incident which, while doubtless proving the treachery of your servants, is not able to compromise yourself? Suppose I took only the services which you have already rendered us into consideration? In a word, suppose I left you free?"

Perenna could not help smiling. Notwithstanding the affair of the walking-stick and though appearances were all against him, at the moment when everything seemed to be going wrong, things were taking the course which he had prophesied from the start, and which he had mentioned to Mazeroux during the inquiry on the Boulevard Suchet. They wanted him.

"Free?" he asked. "No more supervision? Nobody shadowing my movements?"

"Nobody."

"And what if the press campaign around my name continues, if the papers succeed, by means of certain pieces of tittle-tattle, of certain coincidences, in creating a public outcry, if they call for measures against me?"

"Those measures shall not be taken."

"Then I have nothing to fear?"

"Nothing."

"Will M. Weber abandon his prejudices against me?"

"At any rate, he will act as though he did, won't you, Weber?"

The deputy chief uttered a few grunts which might be taken as an expression of assent; and Don Luis at once exclaimed:

"In that case, Monsieur le Préfet, I am sure of gaining the victory and of gaining it in accordance with the wishes and requirements of the authorities."

And so, by a sudden change in the situation, after a series of exceptional circumstances, the police themselves, bowing before Don Luis Perenna's superior qualities of mind, acknowledging all that he had already done and foreseeing all that he would be able to do, decided to back him up, begging for his assistance, and offering him, so to speak, the command of affairs.

It was a flattering compliment. Was it addressed only to Don Luis Perenna? And had Lupin, the terrible, undaunted Lupin, no right to claim his share? Was it possible to believe that M. Desmalions, in his heart of hearts, did not admit the identity of the two persons?

Nothing in the Prefect's attitude gave any clue to his secret thoughts. He was suggesting to Don Luis Perenna one of those compacts which the police are often obliged to conclude in order to gain their ends. The compact was concluded, and no more was said upon the subject.

"Do you want any particulars of me?" asked the Prefect of Police.

"Yes, Monsieur le Préfet. The papers spoke of a notebook found in poor Inspector Vérot's pocket. Did the notebook contain a clue of any kind?"

"No. Personal notes, lists of disbursements, that's all. Wait, I was forgetting, there was a photograph of a woman, about which I have not yet been able to obtain the least information. Besides, I don't suppose that it bears upon the case and I have not sent it to the newspapers. Look, here it is."

Perenna took the photograph which the Prefect handed him and gave a start that did not escape M. Desmalions's eye.

"Do you know the lady?"

"No. No, Monsieur le Préfet. I thought I did; but no, there's merely a resemblance—a family likeness, which I will verify if you can leave the photograph with me till this evening."

"Till this evening, yes. When you have done with it, give it back to Sergeant Mazeroux, whom I will order to work in concert with you in everything that relates to the Mornington case."

The interview was now over. The Prefect went away. Don Luis saw him to the door. As M. Desmalions was about to go down the steps, he turned and said simply:

"You saved my life this morning. But for you, that scoundrel Sauverand—"

"Oh, Monsieur le Préfet!" said Don Luis, modestly protesting.

"Yes, I know, you are in the habit of doing that sort of thing. All the same, you must accept my thanks."

And the Prefect of Police made a bow such as he would really have made to Don Luis Perenna, the Spanish noble, the hero of the Foreign Legion. As for Weber, he put his two hands in his pockets, walked past with the look of a muzzled mastiff, and gave his enemy a glance of fierce hatred.

"By Jupiter!" thought Don Luis. "There's a fellow who won't miss me when he gets the chance to shoot!"

Looking through a window, he saw M. Desmalions's motor car drive off. The detectives fell in behind the deputy chief and left the Place du Palais-Bourbon. The siege was raised.

"And now to work!" said Don Luis. "My hands are free, and we shall make things hum."

He called the butler.

"Serve lunch; and ask Mlle. Levasseur to come and speak to me immediately after."

He went to the dining-room and sat down, placing on the table the photograph which M. Desmalions had left behind; and, bending over it, he examined it attentively. It was a little faded, a little worn, as photographs have a tendency to become when they lie about in pocketbooks or among papers; but the picture was quite clear. It was the radiant picture of a young woman in evening dress, with bare arms and shoulders, with flowers and leaves in her hair and a smile upon her face.

"Mlle. Levasseur, Mlle. Levasseur," he said. "Is it possible!"

In a corner was a half-obliterated and hardly visible signature. He made out, "Florence," the girl's name, no doubt. And he repeated:

"Mlle. Levasseur, Florence Levasseur. How did her photograph come to be in Inspector Vérot's pocketbook? And what is the connection between this adventure and the reader of the Hungarian count from whom I took over the house?"

He remembered the incident of the iron curtain. He remembered the article in the *Echo de France*, an article aimed against him, of which he had found the rough draft in his own courtyard. And, above all, he thought of the problem of that broken walking-stick conveyed into his study.

And, while his mind was striving to read these events clearly, while he tried to settle the part played by Mlle. Levasseur, his eyes remained fixed upon the photograph and he gazed absent-mindedly at the pretty lines of the mouth, the charming smile, the graceful curve of the neck, the admirable sweep of the shoulders.

The door opened suddenly and Mlle. Levasseur burst into the room. Perenna, who had dismissed the butler, was raising to his lips a glass of water which he had just filled for himself. She sprang forward, seized his arm, snatched the glass from him and flung it on the carpet, where it smashed to pieces.

"Have you drunk any of it? Have you drunk any of it?" she gasped, in a choking voice.

He replied:

"No, not yet. Why?"

She stammered:

"The water in that bottle... the water in that bottle—"

"Well?"

"It's poisoned!"

He leapt from his chair and, in his turn, gripped her arm fiercely:

"What's that? Poisoned! Are you certain? Speak!"

In spite of his usual self-control, he was this time thoroughly alarmed. Knowing the terrible effects of the poison employed by the miscreants whom he was attacking, recalling the corpse of Inspector Vérot, the corpses of Hippolyte Fauville and his son, he knew that, trained though he was to resist comparatively large doses of poison, he could not have escaped the deadly action of this. It was a poison that did not forgive, that killed, surely and fatally.

The girl was silent. He raised his voice in command:

"Answer me! Are you certain?"

"No... it was an idea that entered my head—a presentiment... certain coincidences—"

It was as though she regretted her words and now tried to withdraw them.

"Come, come," he cried, "I want to know the truth: You're not certain that the water in this bottle is poisoned?"

"No... it's possible—"

"Still, just now—"

"I thought so. But no... no!"

"It's easy to make sure," said Perenna, putting out his hand for the water bottle.

She was quicker than he, seized it and, with one blow, broke it against the table.

"What are you doing?" he said angrily.

"I made a mistake. And so there is no need to attach any importance—"

Don Luis hurriedly left the dining-room. By his orders, the water which he drank was drawn from a filter that stood in a pantry at the end of the passage leading from the dining-room to the kitchens and beyond. He ran to it and took from a shelf a bowl which he filled with water from the filter. Then, continuing to follow the passage, which at this spot branched off toward the yard, he called Mirza, the puppy, who was playing by the stables.

"Here," he said, putting the bowl in front of her.

The puppy began to drink. But she stopped almost at once and stood motionless, with her paws tense and stiff. A shiver passed through the little body. The dog gave a hoarse groan, spun round two or three times, and fell.

"She's dead," he said, after touching the animal.

Mlle. Levasseur had joined him. He turned to her and rapped out:

"You were right about the poison—and you knew it. How did you know it?"

All out of breath, she checked the beating of her heart and answered:

"I saw the other puppy drinking in the pantry. She's dead. I told the coachman and the chauffeur. They're over there, in the stable. And I ran to warn you."

"In that case, there was no doubt about it. Why did you say that you were not certain that the water was poisoned, when—"

The chauffeur and the coachman were coming out of the stables. Leading the girl away, Perenna said:

"We must talk about this. We'll go to your rooms."

They went back to the bend in the passage. Near the pantry where the filter was, another passage ran, ending in a flight of three steps, with a door at the top of the steps. Perenna opened this door. It was the entrance to the rooms occupied by Mlle. Levasseur. They went into a sitting-room.

Don Luis closed the entrance door and the door of the sitting-room.

"And now," he said, in a resolute tone, "you and I will have an explanation."

7

SHAKESPEARE'S WORKS, VOLUME VIII

Two lodges, belonging to the same old-time period as the house itself, stood at the extreme right and left of the low wall that separated the front courtyard from the Place du Palais-Bourbon. These lodges were joined to the main building, situated at the back of the courtyard, by a series of outhouses. On one side were the coach-houses, stables, harness-rooms, and garage, with the porter's lodge at the end; on the other side, the wash-houses, kitchens, and offices, ending in the lodge occupied by Mlle. Levasseur.

This lodge had only a ground floor, consisting of a dark entrance hall and one large room, most of which served as a sitting-room, while the rest, arranged as a bedroom, was really only a sort of alcove. A curtain hid the bed and wash-hand-stand. There were two windows looking out on the Place du Palais-Bourbon.

It was the first time that Don Luis had set foot in Mlle. Levasseur's room. Engrossed though he was with other matters, he felt its charm. It was very simply furnished: some old mahogany chairs and armchairs, a plain, Empire writing-table, a round table with one heavy, massive leg, and some bookshelves. But the bright colour of the linen curtains enlivened the room. On the walls hung reproductions of famous pictures, drawings of sunny buildings and landscapes, Italian villas, Sicilian temples...

The girl remained standing. She had resumed her composure, and her face had taken on the enigmatical expression so difficult to fathom, especially as she had assumed a deliberate air of dejection, which Perenna guessed was intended to hide her excitement and alertness, together with the tumultuous feelings which even she had great difficulty in controlling.

Her eyes looked neither timorous nor defiant. It really seemed as though she had nothing to fear from the explanation.

Don Luis kept silent for some little time. It was strange and it annoyed him to feel it, but he experienced a certain embarrassment in the presence of this woman, against whom he was inwardly bringing the most serious charges. And, not daring to put them into words, not daring to say plainly what he thought, he began:

"You know what happened in this house this morning?"

"This morning?"

"Yes, when I had finished speaking on the telephone."

"I know now. I heard it from the servants, from the butler."

"Not before?"

"How could I have known earlier?"

She was lying. It was impossible that she should be speaking the truth. And yet in what a calm voice she had replied!

He went on:

"I will tell you, in a few words, what happened. I was leaving the telephone box, when the iron curtain, concealed in the upper part of the wall, fell in front of me. After making sure that there was nothing to be done, I simply resolved, as I had the telephone by me, to call in the assistance of one of my friends. I rang up Major d'Astrignac. He came at once and, with the help of the butler, let me out. Is that what you heard?"

"Yes, Monsieur. I had gone to my room, which explains why I knew nothing of the incident or of Major d'Astrignac's visit."

"Very well. It appears, however, from what I learned when I was released, that the butler and, for that matter, everybody in the house, including yourself, knew of the existence of that iron curtain."

"Certainly."

"And how did you know it?"

"Through Baron Malonyi. He told me that, during the Revolution, his great-grandmother, on the mother's side, who then occupied this house and whose husband was guillotined, remained hidden in that recess for thirteen months. At that time the curtain was covered with woodwork similar to that of the room."

"It's a pity that I wasn't informed of it, for, after all, I was very nearly crushed to death."

This possibility did not seem to move the girl. She said:

"It would be a good thing to look at the mechanism and see why it became unfastened. It's all very old and works badly."

"The mechanism works perfectly. I tested it. An accident is not enough to account for it."

"Who could have done it, if it was not an accident?"

"Some enemy whom I am unable to name."

"He would have been seen."

"There was only one person who could have seen him— yourself. You happened to pass through my study as I was telephoning and I heard your exclamation of fright at the news about Mme. Fauville."

"Yes, it gave me a shock. I pity the woman so very much, whether she is guilty or not."

"And, as you were close to the arch, with your hand within reach of the spring, the presence of an evildoer would not have escaped your notice."

She did not lower her eyes. A slight flush overspread her face, and she said:

"Yes, I should at least have met him, for, from what I gather, I went out a few seconds before the accident."

"Quite so," he said. "But what is so curious and unlikely is that you did not hear the loud noise of the curtain falling, nor my shouts and all the uproar I created."

"I must have closed the door of the study by that time. I heard nothing."

"Then I am bound to presume that there was someone hidden in my study at that moment, and that this person is a confederate of the ruffians who committed the two murders on the Boulevard Suchet; for the Prefect of Police has just discovered under the cushions of my sofa the half of a walking-stick belonging to one of those ruffians."

She wore an air of great surprise. This new incident seemed really to be quite unknown to her. He came nearer and, looking her straight in the eyes, said:

"You must at least admit that it's strange."

"What's strange?"

"This series of events, all directed against me. Yesterday, that draft of a letter which I found in the courtyard—the draft of the article published in the *Echo de France*. This morning, first the crash of the iron curtain just as I was passing under it, next, the discovery of that walking-stick, and then, a moment ago, the poisoned water bottle—"

She nodded her head and murmured:

"Yes, yes—there is an array of facts—"

"An array of facts so significant," he said, completing her sentence meaningly, "as to remove the least shadow of doubt. I can feel absolutely certain of the immediate intervention of my most ruthless and daring enemy. His presence here is proved. He is ready to act at any moment. His object is plain," explained Don Luis. "By means of the anonymous article, by means of that half of the walking-stick, he meant to compromise me and have me arrested. By the fall of the curtain he meant to kill me or at least to keep me imprisoned for some hours. And now it's poison, the cowardly poison which kills by stealth, which they put in my water today and which they will put in my food tomorrow. And next it will be the dagger and then the revolver and then the rope, no matter which, so long as I disappear; for that is what they want: to get rid of me.

"I am the adversary, I am the man they're afraid of, the man who will discover the secret one day and pocket the millions which they're after. I am the interloper. I stand mounting guard over the Mornington inheritance. It's my turn to suffer. Four victims are dead already. I shall be the fifth. So Gaston Sauverand has decided: Gaston Sauverand or someone else who's managing the business."

Perenna's eyes narrowed.

"The accomplice is here, in this house, in the midst of everything, by my side. He is lying in wait for me. He is following every step I take. He is living in my shadow. He is waiting for the time and place to strike me. Well, I have had enough of it. I want to know, I will know, and I shall know. Who is he?"

The girl had moved back a little way and was leaning against the round table. He took another step forward and, with his eyes still fixed on hers, looking in that immobile face for a quivering sign of fear or anxiety, he repeated, with greater violence:

"Who is the accomplice? Who in the house has sworn to take my life?"

"I don't know," she said, "I don't know. Perhaps there is no plot, as you think, but just a series of chance coincidences—"

He felt inclined to say to her, with his habit of adopting a familiar tone toward those whom he regarded as his adversaries:

"You're lying, dearie, you're lying. The accomplice is yourself, my beauty. You alone overheard my conversation on the telephone with Mazeroux, you alone can have gone to Gaston Sauverand's assistance, waited for him in a motor at the corner of the boulevard, and arranged with him to bring the top half of the walking-stick here. You're the beauty that wants to kill me, for some reason which I do not know. The hand that strikes me in the dark is yours, sweetheart."

But it was impossible for him to treat her in this fashion; and he was so much exasperated at not being able to proclaim his certainty in words of anger and indignation that he took her fingers and twisted them violently, while his look and his whole attitude accused the girl even more forcibly than the bitterest words.

He mastered himself and released his grip. The girl freed herself with a quick movement, indicating repulsion and hatred. Don Luis said:

"Very well. I will question the servants. If necessary I shall dismiss any whom I suspect."

"No, don't do that," she said eagerly. "You mustn't. I know them all."

Was she going to defend them? Was she yielding to a scruple of conscience at the moment when her obstinacy and duplicity were on the point of causing her to sacrifice a set of servants whose conduct she knew to be beyond reproach? Don Luis received the impression that the glance which she threw at him contained an appeal for pity. But pity for whom? For the others? Or for herself?

They were silent for a long time. Don Luis, standing a few steps away from her, thought of the photograph, and was surprised to find in the real woman all the beauty of the portrait, all that beauty which he had not observed hitherto, but which now struck him as a revelation. The golden hair shone with a brilliancy unknown to him. The mouth wore a less happy expression, perhaps, a rather bitter expression, but one which nevertheless retained the shape of the smile. The curve of the chin, the grace of the neck revealed above the dip of the linen collar, the line of the shoulders, the position of the arms, and of the hands resting on her knees: all this was charming and very gentle and, in a manner, very seemly and reassuring. Was it possible that this woman should be a murderess, a poisoner?

He said:

"I forget what you told me that your Christian name was. But the name you gave me was not the right one."

"Yes, it was," she said.

"Your name is Florence: Florence Levasseur."

She started.

"What! Who told you? Florence? How do you know?"

"Here is your photograph, with your name on it almost illegible."

"Oh!" she said, amazed at seeing the picture. "I can't believe it! Where does it come from? Where did you get it from?" And, suddenly, "It was the Prefect of Police who gave it to you, was it not? Yes, it was he, I'm sure of it. I am sure that this photograph is to identify me and that they are looking for me, for me, too. And it's you again, it's you again—"

"Have no fear," he said. "The print only wants a few touches to alter the face beyond recognition. I will make them. Have no fear."

She was no longer listening to him. She gazed at the photograph with all her concentrated attention and murmured:

"I was twenty years old... I was living in Italy. Dear me, how happy I was on the day when it was taken! And how happy I was when I saw my portrait!... I used to think myself pretty in those days... And then it disappeared... It was stolen from me like other things that had already been stolen from me, at that time—"

And, sinking her voice still lower, speaking her name as if she were addressing some other woman, some unhappy friend, she repeated:

"Florence... Florence—"

Tears streamed down her cheeks.

"She is not one of those who kill," thought Don Luis. "I can't believe that she is an accomplice. And yet—and yet—"

He moved away from her and walked across the room from the window to the door. The drawings of Italian landscapes on the wall attracted his attention. Next, he read the titles of the books on the shelves. They represented French and foreign works, novels, plays, essays, volumes of poetry, pointing to a really cultivated and varied taste.

He saw Racine next to Dante, Stendhal near Edgar Allan Poe, Montaigne between Goethe and Virgil. And suddenly, with that extraordinary faculty which enabled him, in any collection of objects, to perceive details which he did not at once take in, he noticed that one of the volumes of an English edition of Shakespeare's works did not look exactly like the others. There was something peculiar about the red morocco back, something stiff, without the cracks and creases which show that a book has been used.

It was the eighth volume. He took it out, taking care not to be heard.

He was not mistaken. The volume was a sham, a mere set of boards surrounding a hollow space that formed a box and thus provided a regular hiding-place; and, inside this book, he caught sight of plain note-paper, envelopes of different kinds, and some sheets of ordinary ruled paper, all of the same size and looking as if they had been taken from a writing-pad.

And the appearance of these ruled sheets struck him at once. He remembered the look of the paper on which the article for the *Echo de France* had been drafted. The ruling was identical, and the shape and size appeared to be the same.

On lifting the sheets one after the other, he saw, on the last but one, a series of lines consisting of words and figures in pencil, like notes hurriedly jotted down.

He read:

"House on the Boulevard Suchet. "First letter. Night of 15 April. "Second. Night of 25th. "Third and fourth. Nights of 5 and 15 May. "Fifth and explosion. Night of 25 May."

And, while noting first that the date of the first night was that of the actual day, and next that all these dates followed one another at intervals of ten days, he remarked the resemblance between the writing and the writing of the rough draft.

The draft was in a notebook in his pocket. He was therefore in a position to verify the similarity of the two handwritings and of the two ruled sheets of paper. He took his notebook and opened it. The draft was not there.

"Gad," he snarled, "but this is a bit too thick!"

And, at the same time, he remembered clearly that, when he was telephoning to Mazeroux in the morning, the notebook was in the pocket of his overcoat and that he had left his overcoat on a chair near the telephone box. Now, at that moment, Mlle. Levasseur, for no reason, was roaming about the study. What was she doing there?

"Oh, the play-actress!" thought Perenna, raging within himself. "She was humbugging me. Her tears, her air of frankness, her tender memories: all bunkum! She belongs to the same stock and the same gang as Marie Fauville and Gaston Sauverand. Like them, she is an accomplished liar and actress from her slightest gesture down to the least inflection of her innocent voice."

He was on the point of having it all out with her and confounding her. This time, the proof was undeniable. Dreading an inquiry which might have brought the facts home to her, she had been unwilling to leave the draft of the article in the adversary's hands.

How could he doubt, from this moment, that she was the accomplice employed by the people who were working the Mornington affair and trying to get rid of him? Had he not every right to suppose that she was directing the sinister gang, and that, commanding the others with her audacity and her intelligence, she was leading them toward the obscure goal at which they were aiming?

For, after all, she was free, entirely free in her actions and movements. The windows opening on the Place du Palais-Bourbon gave her every facility for leaving the house under cover of the darkness and coming in again unknown to anybody.

It was therefore quite possible that, on the night of the double crime, she was among the murderers of Hippolyte Fauville and his son. It was quite possible that she had taken part in the murders, and even that the poison had been injected into the victims by her hand, by that little, white, slender hand which he saw resting against the golden hair.

A shudder passed through him. He had softly put back the paper in the book, restored the book in its place, and moved nearer to the girl.

All of a sudden, he caught himself studying the lower part of her face, the shape of her jaw! Yes, that was what he was making every effort to guess, under the curve of the cheeks and behind the veil of the lips. Almost against his will, with personal anguish mingled with torturing curiosity, he stared and stared, ready to force open those closed lips and to seek the reply to the terrifying problem that suggested itself to him.

Those teeth, those teeth which he did not see, were not they the teeth that had left the incriminating marks in the fruit? Which were the teeth of the tiger, the teeth of the wild beast: these, or the other woman's?

It was an absurd supposition, because the marks had been recognized as made by Marie Fauville. But was the absurdity of a supposition a sufficient reason for discarding it?

Himself astonished at the feelings that agitated him, fearing lest he should betray himself, he preferred to cut short the interview and, going up to the girl, he said to her, in an imperious and aggressive tone:

"I wish all the servants in the house to be discharged. You will give them their wages, pay them such compensation as they ask for, and see that they leave today, definitely. Another staff of servants will arrive this evening. You will be here to receive them."

She made no reply. He went away, taking with him the uncomfortable impression that had lately marked his relations with Florence. The atmosphere between them always remained heavy and oppressive. Their words never seemed to express the private thoughts of either of them; and their actions did not correspond with the words spoken. Did not the circumstances logically demand the immediate dismissal of Florence Levasseur as well? Yet Don Luis did not so much as think of it.

Returning to his study, he at once rang up Mazeroux and, lowering his voice so as not to let it reach the next room, he said:

"Is that you, Mazeroux?"

"Yes."

"Has the Prefect placed you at my disposal?"

"Yes."

"Well, tell him that I have sacked all my servants and that I have given you their names and instructed you to have an active watch kept on them. We must look among them for Sauverand's accomplice. Another thing: ask the Prefect to give you and me permission to spend the night at Hippolyte Fauville's house."

"Nonsense! At the house on the Boulevard Suchet?"

"Yes, I have every reason to believe that something's going to happen there."

"What sort of thing?"

"I don't know. But something is bound to take place. And I insist on being at it. Is it arranged?"

"Right, Chief. Unless you hear to the contrary, I'll meet you at nine o'clock this evening on the Boulevard Suchet."

Perenna did not see Mlle. Levasseur again that day. He went out in the course of the afternoon, and called at the registry office, where he chose some servants: a chauffeur, a coachman, a footman, a cook, and so on. Then he went to a photographer, who made a new copy of Mlle. Levasseur's photograph. Don Luis had this touched up and faked it himself, so that the Prefect of Police should not perceive the substitution of one set of features for another.

He dined at a restaurant and, at nine o'clock, joined Mazeroux on the Boulevard Suchet.

Since the Fauville murders the house had been left in the charge of the porter. All the rooms and all the locks had been sealed up, except the inner door of the workroom, of which the police kept the keys for the purposes of the inquiry.

The big study looked as it did before, though the papers had been removed and put away and there were no books and pamphlets left on the writing-table. A layer of dust, clearly visible by the electric light, covered its black leather and the surrounding mahogany.

"Well, Alexandre, old man," cried Don Luis, when they had made themselves comfortable, "what do you say to this? It's rather impressive, being here again, what? But, this time, no barricading of doors, no bolts, eh? If anything's going to happen, on this night of the fifteenth of April, we'll put nothing in our friends' way. They shall have full and entire liberty. It's up to them, this time."

Though joking, Don Luis was nevertheless singularly impressed, as he himself said, by the terrible recollection of the two crimes which he had been unable to prevent and by the haunting vision of the two dead bodies. And he also remembered with real emotion the implacable duel which he had fought with Mme. Fauville, the woman's despair and her arrest.

"Tell me about her," he said to Mazeroux. "So she tried to kill herself?"

"Yes," said Mazeroux, "a thoroughgoing attempt, though she had to make it in a manner which she must have hated. She hanged herself in strips of linen torn from her sheets and underclothing and twisted together. She had to be restored by artificial respiration. She is out of danger now, I believe, but she is never left alone, for she swore she would do it again."

"She has made no confession?"

"No. She persists in proclaiming her innocence."

"And what do they think at the public prosecutor's? At the Prefect's?"

"Why should they change their opinion, Chief? The inquiries confirm every one of the charges brought against her; and, in particular, it has been proved beyond the possibility of dispute that she alone can have touched the apple and that she can have touched it only between eleven o'clock at night and seven o'clock in the morning. Now the apple bears the undeniable marks of her teeth. Would you admit that there are two sets of jaws in the world that leave the same identical imprint?"

"No, no," said Don Luis, who was thinking of Florence Levasseur. "No, the argument allows of no discussion. We have here a fact that is clear as daylight; and the imprint is almost tantamount to a discovery in the act. But then how, in the midst of all this, are we to explain the presence of—"

"Whom, Chief?"

"Nobody. I had an idea worrying me. Besides, you see, in all this there are so many unnatural things, such queer coincidences and inconsistencies, that I dare not count on a certainty which the reality of tomorrow may destroy."

They went on talking for some time, in a low voice, studying the question in all its bearings.

At midnight they switched off the electric light in the chandelier and arranged that each should go to sleep in turn.

And the hours went by as they had done when the two sat up before, with the same sounds of belated carriages and motor cars; the same railway whistles; the same silence.

The night passed without alarm or incident of any kind. At daybreak the life out of doors was resumed; and Don Luis, during his waking hours, had not heard a sound in the room except the monotonous snoring of his companion.

"Can I have been mistaken?" he wondered. "Did the clue in that volume of Shakespeare mean something else? Or did it refer to events of last year, events that took place on the dates set down?"

In spite of everything, he felt overcome by a strange uneasiness as the dawn began to glimmer through the half-closed shutters. A fortnight before, nothing had happened either to warn him; and yet there were two victims lying near him when he woke.

At seven o'clock he called out:

"Alexandre!"

"Eh? What is it, Chief?"

"You're not dead?"

"What's that? Dead? No, Chief; why should I be?"

"Quite sure?"

"Well, that's a good 'un! Why not you?"

"Oh, it'll be my turn soon! Considering the intelligence of those scoundrels, there's no reason why they should go on missing me."

They waited an hour longer. Then Perenna opened a window and threw back the shutter.

"I say, Alexandre, perhaps you're not dead, but you're certainly very green."

Mazeroux gave a wry laugh:

"Upon my word, Chief, I confess that I had a bad time of it when I was keeping watch while you were asleep."

"Were you afraid?"

"To the roots of my hair. I kept on thinking that something was going to happen. But you, too, Chief, don't look as if you had been enjoying yourself. Were you also—"

He interrupted himself, on seeing an expression of unbounded astonishment on Don Luis's face.

"What's the matter, Chief?"

"Look!... on the table... that letter—"

He looked. There was a letter on the writing-table, or, rather, a letter-card, the edges of which had been torn along the perforation marks; and they saw the outside of it, with the address, the stamp, and the postmarks.

"Did you put that there, Alexandre?"

"You're joking, Chief. You know it can only have been you."

"It can only have been I... and yet it was not I."

"But then—"

Don Luis took the letter-card and, on examining it, found that the address and the postmarks had been scratched out so as to make it impossible to read the name of the addressee or where he lived, but that the place of posting was quite clear, as was the date: Paris, 4 January, 19—.

"So the letter is three and a half months old," said Don Luis.

He turned to the inside of the letter. It contained a dozen lines and he at once exclaimed:

"Hippolyte Fauville's signature!"

"And his handwriting," observed Mazeroux. "I can tell it at a glance. There's no mistake about that. What does it all mean? A letter written by Hippolyte Fauville three months before his death?"

Perenna read aloud:

"MY DEAR OLD FRIEND:

"I can only, alas, confirm what I wrote to you the other day: the plot is thickening around me! I do not yet know what their plan is and still less how they mean to put it into execution; but everything warns me that the end is at hand. I can see it in her eyes. How strangely she looks at me sometimes!

"Oh, the shame of it! Who would ever have thought her capable of it?

"I am a very unhappy man, my dear friend."

"And it's signed Hippolyte Fauville," Mazeroux continued, "and I declare to you that it's actually in his hand... written on the fourth of January of this year to a friend whose name we don't know, though we shall dig him out somehow, that I'll swear. And this friend will certainly give us the proofs we want."

Mazeroux was becoming excited.

"Proofs? Why, we don't need them! They're here. M. Fauville himself supplies them: 'The end is at hand. I can see it in her eyes. ' 'Her' refers to his wife, to Marie Fauville, and the husband's evidence confirms all that we knew against her. What do you say, Chief?"

"You're right," replied Perenna, absent-mindedly, "you're right; the letter is final. Only—"

"Only what?"

"Who the devil can have brought it? Somebody must have entered the room last night while we were here. Is it possible? For, after all, we should have heard. That's what astounds me."

"It certainly looks like it."

"Just so. It was a queer enough job a fortnight ago. But, still, we were in the passage outside, while they were at work in here, whereas, this time, we were here, both of us, close to this very table. And, on this table, which had not the least scrap of paper on it last night, we find this letter in the morning."

A careful inspection of the place gave them no clue to put them on the track. They went through the house from top to bottom and ascertained for certain that there was no one there in hiding. Besides, supposing that any one was hiding there, how could he have made his way into the room without attracting their attention? There was no solving the problem.

"We won't look anymore," said Perenna, "it's no use. In matters of this sort, some day or other the light enters by an unseen cranny and everything gradually becomes clear. Take the letter to the Prefect of Police, tell him how we spent the night, and ask his permission for both of us to come back on the night of the twenty-fifth of April. There's to be another surprise that night; and I'm dying to know if we shall receive a second letter through the agency of some Mahatma."

They closed the doors and left the house.

While they were walking to the right, toward La Muette, in order to take a taxi, Don Luis chanced to turn his head to the road as they reached the end of the Boulevard Suchet. A man rode past them on a bicycle. Don Luis just had time to see his clean-shaven face and his glittering eyes fixed upon himself.

"Look out!" he shouted, pushing Mazeroux so suddenly that the sergeant lost his balance.

The man had stretched out his hand, armed with a revolver. A shot rang out. The bullet whistled past the ears of Don Luis, who had bobbed his head.

"After him!" he roared. "You're not hurt, Mazeroux?"

"No, Chief."

They both rushed in pursuit, shouting for assistance. But, at that early hour, there are never many people in the wide avenues of this part of the town. The man, who was making off swiftly, increased his distance, turned down the Rue Octave-Feuillet, and disappeared.

"All right, you scoundrel, I'll catch you yet!" snarled Don Luis, abandoning a vain pursuit.

"But you don't even know who he is, Chief."

"Yes, I do: it's he."

"Who?"

"The man with the ebony stick. He's cut off his beard and shaved his face, but I knew him for all that. It was the man who was taking pot-shots at us yesterday morning, from the top of his stairs on the Boulevard Richard-Wallace, the one who killed Inspector Ancenis. The blackguard! How did he know that I had spent the night at Fauville's? Have I been followed then and spied on? But by whom? And why? And how?"

Mazeroux reflected and said:

"Remember, Chief, you telephoned to me in the afternoon to give me an appointment. For all you know, in spite of lowering your voice, you may have been heard by somebody at your place."

Don Luis did not answer. He thought of Florence.

That morning Don Luis's letters were not brought to him by Mlle. Levasseur, nor did he send for her. He caught sight of her several times giving orders to the new servants. She must afterward have gone back to her room, for he did not see her again.

In the afternoon he rang for his car and drove to the house on the Boulevard Suchet, to pursue with Mazeroux, by the Prefect's instructions, a search that led to no result whatever.

It was ten o'clock when he came in. The detective sergeant and he had some dinner together. Afterwards, wishing also to examine the home of the man with the ebony stick, he got into his car again, still accompanied by Mazeroux, and told the man to drive to the Boulevard Richard-Wallace.

The car crossed the Seine and followed the right bank.

"Faster," he said to his new chauffeur, through the speaking-tube. "I'm accustomed to go at a good pace."

"You'll have an upset one fine day, Chief," said Mazeroux.

"No fear," replied Don Luis. "Motor accidents are reserved for fools."

They reached the Place de l'Alma. The car turned to the left.

"Straight ahead!" cried Don Luis. "Go up by the Trocadero."

The car veered back again. But suddenly it gave three or four lurches in the road, took the pavement, ran into a tree and fell over on its side.

In a few seconds a dozen people were standing round. They broke one of the windows and opened the door. Don Luis was the first.

"It's nothing," he said. "I'm all right. And you, Alexandre?"

They helped the sergeant out. He had a few bruises and a little pain, but no serious injury.

Only the chauffeur had been thrown from his seat and lay motionless on the pavement, bleeding from the head. He was carried into a chemist's shop and died in ten minutes.

Mazeroux had gone in with the poor victim and, feeling pretty well stunned, had himself been given a pick-me-up. When he went back to the motor car he found two policemen entering particulars of the accident in their notebooks and taking evidence from the bystanders; but the chief was not there.

Perenna in fact had jumped into a taxicab and driven home as fast as he could. He got out in the square, ran through the gateway, crossed the courtyard, and went down the passage that led to Mlle. Levasseur's quarters. He leaped up the steps, knocked, and entered without waiting for an answer.

The door of the room that served as a sitting-room was opened and Florence appeared. He pushed her back into the room, and said, in a tone furious with indignation:

"It's done. The accident has occurred. And yet none of the old servants can have prepared it, because they were not there and because I was out with the car this afternoon. Therefore, it must have been late in the day between six and nine o'clock, that somebody went to the garage and filed the steering-rod three quarters through."

"I don't understand. I don't understand," she said, with a scared look.

"You understand perfectly well that the accomplice of the ruffians cannot be one of the new servants, and you understand perfectly well that the job was bound to succeed and that it did succeed, beyond their hopes. There is a victim, who suffers instead of myself."

"But tell me what has happened, Monsieur! You frighten me! What accident? What was it?"

"The motor car was overturned. The chauffeur is dead."

"Oh," she said, "how horrible! And you think that I can have—Oh, dead, how horrible! Poor man!"

Her voice grew fainter. She was standing opposite to Perenna, close up against him. Pale and swooning, she closed her eyes, staggered.

He caught her in his arms as she fell. She tried to release herself, but had not the strength; and he laid her in a chair, while she moaned, repeatedly:

"Poor man! Poor man!"

Keeping one of his arms under the girl's head, he took a handkerchief in the other hand and wiped her forehead, which was wet with perspiration, and her pallid cheeks, down which the tears streamed.

She must have lost consciousness entirely, for she surrendered herself to Perenna's cares without the least resistance. And he, making no further movement, began anxiously to examine the mouth before his eyes, the mouth with the lips usually so red, now bloodless and discoloured.

Gently passing one of his fingers over each of them, with a continuous pressure, he separated them, as one separates the petals of a flower; and the two rows of teeth appeared.

They were charming, beautifully shaped, and beautifully white; a little smaller perhaps than Mme. Fauville's, perhaps also arranged in a wider curve. But what did he know? Who could say that their bite would not leave the same imprint? It was an improbable supposition, an impossible miracle, he knew. And yet the circumstances were all against the girl and pointed to her as the most daring, cruel, implacable, and terrible of criminals.

Her breathing became regular. He perceived the cool fragrance of her mouth, intoxicating as the scent of a rose. In spite of himself, he bent down, came so close, so close that he was seized with giddiness and had to make a great effort to lay the girl's head on the back of the chair and to take his eyes from the fair face with the half-parted lips.

He rose to his feet and went.

8

THE DEVIL'S POST-OFFICE

Of all these events the public knew only of the attempted suicide of Mme. Fauville, the capture and escape of Gaston Sauverand, the murder of Chief Inspector Ancenis, and the discovery of a letter written by Hippolyte Fauville. This was enough, however, to reawaken their curiosity, as they were already singularly puzzled by the Mornington case and took the greatest interest in all the movements, however slight, of the mysterious Don Luis Perenna, whom they insisted on confusing with Arsène Lupin.

He was, of course, credited with the brief capture of the man with the ebony walking-stick. It was also known that he had saved the life of the Prefect of Police, and that, finally, having at his own request spent the night in the house on the Boulevard Suchet, he had become the recipient of Hippolyte Fauville's famous letter. And all this added immensely to the excitement of the aforesaid public.

But how much more complicated and disconcerting were the problems set to Don Luis Perenna himself! Not to mention the denunciation in the anonymous article, there had been, in the short space of forty-eight hours, no fewer than four separate attempts to kill him: by the iron curtain, by poison, by the shooting on the Boulevard Suchet, and by the deliberately prepared motor accident.

Florence's share in this series of attempts was not to be denied. And, now, behold her relations with the Fauvilles' murderers duly established by the little note found in the eighth volume of Shakespeare's plays, while two more deaths were added to the melancholy list: the deaths of Chief Inspector Ancenis and of the chauffeur. How to describe and how to explain the part played, in the midst of all these catastrophes, by that enigmatical girl?

Strangely enough, life went on as usual at the house in the Place du Palais-Bourbon, as though nothing out of the way had happened there. Every morning Florence Levasseur sorted Don Luis's post in his presence and read out the newspaper articles referring to himself or bearing upon the Mornington case.

Not a single allusion was made to the fierce fight that had been waged against him for two days. It was as though a truce had been proclaimed between them; and the enemy appeared to have ceased his attacks for the moment. Don Luis felt easy, out of the reach of danger; and he talked to the girl with an indifferent air, as he might have talked to anybody.

But with what a feverish interest he studied her unobserved! He watched the expression of her face, at once calm and eager, and a painful sensitiveness which showed under the placid mask and which, difficult to control, revealed itself in the frequent quivering of the lips and nostrils.

"Who are you? Who are you?" he felt inclined to exclaim. "Will nothing content you, you she-devil, but to deal out murder all round? And do you want my death also, in order to attain your object? Where do you come from and where are you making for?"

On reflection, he was convinced of a certainty that solved a problem which had preoccupied him for a long time — namely, the mysterious connection between his own presence in the mansion in the Place du Palais-Bourbon and the presence of a woman who was manifestly wreaking her hatred on him.

He now understood that he had not bought the house by accident. In making the purchase he had been persuaded by an anonymous offer that reached him in the form of a typewritten prospectus. Whence did this offer come, if not from Florence, who wished to have him near her in order to spy upon him and wage war upon him?

"Yes," he thought, "that is where the truth lies. As the possible heir of Cosmo Mornington and a prominent figure in the case, I am the enemy, and they are trying to do away with me as they did with the others. And it is Florence who is acting against me. And it is she who has committed murder.

"Everything tells against her; nothing speaks in her defence. Her innocent eyes? The accent of sincerity in her voice? Her serene dignity? And then? Yes, what then? Have I never seen women with that frank look who have committed murder for no reason, almost for pleasure's sake?"

He started with terror at the memory of Dolores Kesselbach. What was it that made him connect these two women at every moment in his mind? He had loved one of them, that monster Dolores, and had strangled her with his own hands. Was fate now leading him toward a like love and a similar murder?

When Florence left him he would experience a sense of satisfaction and breathe more easily, as though released from an oppressive weight, but he would run to the window and see her crossing the courtyard and be still waiting when the girl whose scented breath he had felt upon his face passed to and fro.

One morning she said to him:

"The papers say that it will be tonight."

"Tonight?"

"Yes," she said, showing him an article in one of the newspapers. "This is the twenty-fifth; and, according to the information of the police, supplied, they say, by you, there should be a letter delivered in the house on the Boulevard Suchet every tenth day, and the house is to be destroyed by an explosion on the day when the fifth and last letter appears."

Was she defying him? Did she wish to make him understand that, whatever happened, whatever the obstacles, the letters would appear, those mysterious letters prophesied on the list which he had found in the eighth volume of Shakespeare's plays?

He looked at her steadily. She did not flinch. He answered:

"Yes, this is the night. I shall be there. Nothing in the world will prevent me."

She was on the point of replying, but once more controlled her feelings.

That day Don Luis was on his guard. He lunched and dined out and arranged with Mazeroux to have the Place du Palais-Bourbon watched.

Mlle. Levasseur did not leave the house during the afternoon. In the evening Don Luis ordered Mazeroux's men to follow anyone who might go out at that time.

At ten o'clock the sergeant joined Don Luis in Hippolyte Fauville's workroom. Deputy Chief Detective Weber and two plain-clothesmen were with him.

Don Luis took Mazeroux aside:

"They distrust me. Own up to it."

"No. As long as M. Desmalions is there, they can do nothing against you. Only, M. Weber maintains—and he is not the only one—that you fake up all these occurrences yourself."

"With what object?"

"With the object of furnishing proof against Marie Fauville and getting her condemned. So I asked for the attendance of the deputy chief and two men. There will be four of us to bear witness to your honesty."

They all took up their posts. Two detectives were to sit up in turns.

This time, after making a minute search of the little room in which Fauville's son used to sleep, they locked and bolted the doors and shutters. At eleven o'clock they switched off the electric chandelier.

Don Luis and Weber hardly slept at all.

The night passed without incident of any kind.

But, at seven o'clock, when the shutters were opened, they saw that there was a letter on the table. Just as on the last occasion, there was a letter on the table!

When the first moment of stupefaction was over, the deputy chief took the letter. His orders were not to read it and not to let anyone else read it.

Here is the letter, published by the newspapers, which also published the declarations of the experts certifying that the handwriting was Hippolyte Fauville's:

"I have seen him! You understand, don't you, my dear friend? I have seen him! He was walking along a path in the Bois, with his coat collar turned up and his hat pulled over his ears. I don't think that he saw me. It was almost dark. But I knew him at once. I knew the silver handle of his ebony stick. It was he beyond a doubt, the scoundrel!

"So he is in Paris, in spite of his promise. Gaston Sauverand is in Paris! Do you understand the terrible significance of that fact? If he is in Paris, it means that he intends to act. If he is in Paris, it means certain death to me. Oh, the harm which I shall have suffered at that man's hands! He has already robbed me of my happiness; and now he wants my life. I am terrified."

So Fauville knew that the man with the ebony walking-stick, that Gaston Sauverand, was designing to kill him. Fauville declared it most positively, by evidence written in his own hand; and the letter, moreover, corroborating the words that had escaped Gaston Sauverand at his arrest, showed that the two men had at one time had relations with each other, that they were no longer friends, and that Gaston Sauverand had promised never to come to Paris.

A little light was therefore being shed on the darkness of the Mornington case. But, on the other hand, how inconceivable was the mystery of that letter found on the table in the workroom!

Five men had kept watch, five of the smartest men obtainable; and yet, on that night, as on the night of the fifteenth of April, an unknown hand had delivered the letter in a room with barricaded doors and windows, without their hearing a sound or discovering any signs that the fastenings of the doors or windows had been tampered with.

The theory of a secret outlet was at once raised, but had to be abandoned after a careful examination of the walls and after an interview with the contractor who had built the house, from Fauville's own plans, some years ago.

It is unnecessary once more to recall what I may describe as the flurry of the public. The deed, in the circumstances, assumed the appearance of a sleight-of-hand trick. People felt tempted to look upon it as the recreation of some wonderfully skilful conjurer rather than as the act of a person employing unknown methods.

Nevertheless, Don Luis Perenna's intelligence was justified at all points, for the expected incident had taken place on the twenty-fifth of April, as on the fifteenth. Would the series be continued on the fifth of May? No one doubted it, because Don Luis had said so and because everybody felt that Don Luis could not be mistaken. All through the night of the fifth of May there was a crowd on the Boulevard Suchet; and quidnuncs and night birds of every kind came trooping up to hear the latest news.

THE DEVIL'S POST-OFFICE

The Prefect of Police, greatly impressed by the first two miracles, had determined to see the next one for himself, and was present in person on the third night.

He came accompanied by several inspectors, whom he left in the garden, in the passage, and in the attic on the upper story. He himself took up his post on the ground floor with Weber, Mazeroux, and Don Luis Perenna.

Their expectations were disappointed; and this was M. Desmalions's fault. In spite of the express opinion of Don Luis, who deprecated the experiment as useless, the Prefect had decided not to turn off the electric light, so that he might see if the light would prevent the miracle. Under these conditions no letter could appear, and no letter did appear. The miracle, whether a conjuring trick or a criminal's device, needed the kindly aid of the darkness.

There were therefore ten days lost, always presuming that the diabolical postman would dare to repeat his attempt and produce the third mysterious letter.

***

On the fifteenth of May the wait was renewed, while the same crowd gathered outside, an anxious, breathless crowd, stirred by the least sound and keeping an impressive silence, with eyes gazing upon the Fauvilles' house.

This time the light was put out, but the Prefect of Police kept his hand on the electric switch. Ten times, twenty times, he unexpectedly turned on the light. There was nothing on the table. What had aroused his attention was the creaking of a piece of furniture or a movement made by one of the men with him.

Suddenly they all uttered an exclamation. Something unusual, a rustling noise, had interrupted the silence.

M. Desmalions at once switched on the light. He gave a cry. A letter lay not on the table, but beside it, on the floor, on the carpet.

Mazeroux made the sign of the cross. The inspectors were as pale as death.

M. Desmalions looked at Don Luis, who nodded his head without a word.

They inspected the condition of the locks and bolts. Nothing had moved.

That day again, the contents of the letter made some amends for the really extraordinary manner of its delivery. It completely dispelled all the doubts that still enshrouded the double murder on the Boulevard Suchet.

Again signed by the engineer, written throughout by himself, on the eighth of February, with no visible address, it said:

"No, my dear friend, I will not allow myself to be killed like a sheep led to the slaughter. I shall defend myself, I shall fight to the last moment. Things have changed lately. I have proofs now, undeniable proofs. I possess letters that have passed between them. And I know that they still love each other as they did at the start, that they want to marry, and that they will let nothing stand in their way. It is written, understand what I say, it is written in Marie's own hand; 'Have patience, my own Gaston. My courage increases day by day. So much the worse for him who stands between us. He shall disappear.'

"My dear friend, if I succumb in the struggle you will find those letters (and all the evidence which I have collected against the wretched creature) in the safe hidden behind the small glass case: Then revenge me. Au revoir. Perhaps goodbye."

Thus ran the third missive. Hippolyte Fauville from his grave named and accused his guilty wife. From his grave he supplied the solution to the riddle and explained the reason why the crimes had been committed: Marie Fauville and Gaston Sauverand were lovers.

Certainly they knew of the existence of Cosmo Mornington's will, for they had begun by doing away with Cosmo Mornington; and their eagerness to come into the enormous fortune had hastened the catastrophe. But the first idea of the murder rose from an older and deep-rooted passion: Marie Fauville and Gaston Sauverand were lovers.

One problem remained to be solved: who was the unknown correspondent to whom Hippolyte Fauville had bequeathed the task of avenging his murder, and who, instead of simply handing over the letters to the police, was exercising his ingenuity to deliver them by means of the most Machiavellian contrivances? Was it to his interest also to remain in the background?

To all these questions Marie Fauville replied in the most unexpected manner, though it was one that fully accorded with her threats. A week later, after a long cross-examination at which she was pressed for the name of her husband's old friend and at which she maintained the most stubborn silence, together with a sort of stupid inertia, she returned to her cell in the evening and opened the veins of her wrist with a piece of glass which she had managed to hide.

Don Luis heard the news from Mazeroux, who came to tell him of it before eight o'clock the next morning, just as he was getting out of bed. The sergeant had a travelling bag in his hand and was on his way to catch a train.

Don Luis was greatly upset.

"Is she dead?" he exclaimed.

"No. It seems that she has had one more let-off. But what's the good?"

"How do you mean, what's the good?"

"She'll do it again, of course. She's set her mind upon it. And, one day or another—"

"Did she volunteer no confession, this time either, before making the attempt on her life?"

"No. She wrote a few words on a scrap of paper, saying that, on thinking it over, she advised us to ask a certain M. Langernault about the mysterious letters. He was the only friend that she had known her husband to possess, or at any rate the only one whom he would have called, 'My dear fellow,' or, 'My dear friend,' This M. Langernault could do no more than prove her innocence and explain the terrible misunderstanding of which she was the victim."

"But," said Don Luis, "if there is anyone to prove her innocence, why does she begin by opening her veins?"

"She doesn't care, she says. Her life is done for; and what she wants is rest and death."

"Rest? Rest? There are other ways in which she can find it besides in death. If the discovery of the truth is to spell her safety, perhaps the truth is not impossible to discover."

"What are you saying, Chief? Have you guessed anything? Are you beginning to understand?"

"Yes, very vaguely, but, all the same, the really unnatural accuracy of those letters just seems to me a sign—"

He reflected for a moment and continued:

"Have they re-examined the erased addresses of the three letters?"

"Yes; and they managed to make out the name of Langernault."

"Where does this Langernault live?"

"According to Mme. Fauville, at the village of Damigni, in the Orme."

"Have they deciphered the word Damigni on one of the letters?"

"No, but they have the name of the nearest town."

"What town is that?"

"Alençon."

"And is that where you're going?"

"Yes, the Prefect of Police told me to go straightaway. I shall take the train at the Invalides."

"You mean you will come with me in my motor."

"Eh?"

"We will both of us go, my lad. I want to be doing something; the atmosphere of this house is deadly for me."

"What are you talking about, Chief?"

"Nothing. I know."

Half an hour later they were flying along the Versailles Road. Perenna himself was driving his open car and driving it in such a way that Mazeroux, almost stifling, kept blurting out, at intervals:

"Lord, what a pace! Dash it all, how you're letting her go, Chief! Aren't you afraid of a smash? Remember the other day—"

They reached Alençon in time for lunch. When they had done, they went to the chief post-office Nobody knew the name of Langernault there. Besides, Damigni had its own post-office, though the presumption was that M. Langernault had his letters addressed *poste restante* at Alençon.

Don Luis and Mazeroux went on to the village of Damigni. Here again the postmaster knew no one of the name of Langernault; and this in spite of the fact that Damigni contained only about a thousand inhabitants.

"Let's go and call on the mayor," said Perenna.

At the mayor's Mazeroux stated who he was and mentioned the object of his visit. The mayor nodded his head.

"Old Langernault? I should think so. A decent fellow: used to run a business in the town."

"And accustomed, I suppose, to fetch his letters at Alençon post-office?"

"That's it, every day, for the sake of the walk."

"And his house?"

"Is at the end of the village. You passed it as you came along."

"Can we see it?"

"Well, of course... only—"

"Perhaps he's not at home?"

"Certainly not! The poor, dear man hasn't even set foot in the house since he left it the last time, four years ago!"

"How is that?"

"Why, he's been dead these four years!"

Don Luis and Mazeroux exchanged a glance of amazement.

"So he's dead?" said Don Luis.

"Yes, a gunshot."

"What's that!" cried Perenna. "Was he murdered?"

"No, no. They thought so at first, when they picked him up on the floor of his room; but the inquest proved that it was an accident. He was cleaning his gun, and it went off and sent a load of shot into his stomach. All the same, we thought it very queer in the village. Daddy Langernault, an old hunter before the Lord, was not the man to commit an act of carelessness."

"Had he money?"

"Yes; and that's just what clinched the matter: they couldn't find a penny of it!"

Don Luis remained thinking for some time and then asked:

"Did he leave any children, any relations of the same name?"

"Nobody, not even a cousin. The proof is that his property — it's called the Old Castle, because of the ruins on it — has reverted to the State. The authorities have had the doors of the house sealed up, and locked the gate of the park. They are waiting for the legal period to expire in order to take possession."

"And don't sightseers go walking in the park, in spite of the walls?"

"Not they. In the first place, the walls are very high. And then — and then the Old Castle has had a bad reputation in the neighbourhood ever since I can remember. There has always been a talk of ghosts: a pack of silly tales. But still — "

Perenna and his companion could not get over their surprise.

"This is a funny affair," exclaimed Don Luis, when they had left the mayor's. "Here we have Fauville writing his letters to a dead man — and to a dead man, by the way, who looks to me very much as if he had been murdered."

"Someone must have intercepted the letters."

"Obviously. But that does not do away with the fact that he wrote them to a dead man and made his confidences to a dead man and told him of his wife's criminal intentions."

Mazeroux was silent. He, too, seemed greatly perplexed.

They spent part of the afternoon in asking about old Langernault's habits, hoping to receive some useful clue from the people who had known him. But their efforts led to nothing.

At six o'clock, as they were about to start, Don Luis found that the car had run out of petrol and sent Mazeroux in a trap to the outskirts of Alençon to fetch some. He employed the delay in going to look at the Old Castle outside the village.

He had to follow a hedged road leading to an open space, planted with lime trees, where a massive wooden gate stood in the middle of a wall. The gate was locked. Don Luis walked along the wall, which was, in fact, very high and presented no opening. Nevertheless, he managed to climb over by means of the branches of a tree.

The park consisted of unkept lawns, overgrown with large wild flowers, and grass-covered avenues leading on the right to a distant mound, thickly dotted with ruins, and, on the left, to a small, tumbledown house with ill-fitting shutters.

He was turning in this direction, when he was much surprised to perceive fresh footprints on a border which had been soaked with the recent rain. And he could see that these footprints had been made by a woman's boots, a pair of elegant and dainty boots.

"Who the devil comes walking here?" he thought.

He found more footprints a little farther, on another border which the owner of the boots had crossed, and they led him away from the house, toward a series of clumps of trees where he saw them twice more. Then he lost sight of them for good.

He was standing near a large, half-ruined barn, built against a very tall bank. Its worm-eaten doors seemed merely balanced on their hinges. He went up and looked through a crack in the wood. Inside the windowless barn was in semi-darkness, for but little light came through the openings stopped up with straw, especially as the day was beginning to wane. He was able to distinguish a heap of barrels, broken wine-presses, old ploughs, and scrap-iron of all kinds.

"This is certainly not where my fair stroller turned her steps," thought Don Luis. "Let's look somewhere else."

Nevertheless, he did not move. He had noticed a noise in the barn.

He listened and heard nothing. But as he wanted to get to the bottom of things he forced out a couple of planks with his shoulder and stepped in.

The breach which he had thus contrived admitted a little light. He could see enough to make his way between two casks, over some broken window frames, to an empty space on the far side.

His eyes grew accustomed to the darkness as he went on. For all that, he knocked his head against something which he had not perceived, something hanging up above, something rather hard which, when set in motion, swung to and fro with a curious grating sound.

It was too dark to see. Don Luis took an electric lantern from his pocket and pressed the spring.

"Damn it all!" he swore, falling back aghast.

Above him hung a skeleton!

And the next moment he uttered another oath. A second skeleton hung beside the first!

They were both fastened by stout ropes to rings fixed in the rafters of the barn. Their heads dangled from the slip-knots. The one against which Perenna had struck was still moving slightly and the bones clicked together with a gruesome sound.

He dragged forward a rickety table, propped it up as best he could, and climbed onto it to examine the two skeletons more closely. They were turned toward each other, face to face. The first was considerably bigger than the second. They were obviously the skeletons of a man and a woman. Even when they were not moved by a jolt of any kind, the wind blowing through the crevices in the barn set them lightly swinging to and fro, in a sort of very slow, rhythmical dance.

But what perhaps was most impressive in this ghastly spectacle was the fact that each of the skeletons, though deprived of every rag of clothing, still wore a gold ring, too wide now that the flesh had disappeared, but held, as in hooks, by the bent joints of the fingers.

He slipped off the rings with a shiver of disgust, and found that they were wedding rings. Each bore a date inside, the same date, 12 August, 1887, and two names: "Alfred—Victorine."

"Husband and wife," he murmured. "Is it a double suicide? Or a murder? But how is it possible that the two skeletons have not yet been discovered? Can one conceive that they have been here since the death of old Langernault, since the government has taken possession of the estate and made it impossible for anybody to walk in?"

He paused to reflect.

"Anybody? I don't know about that, considering that I saw footprints in the garden, and that a woman has been there this very day!"

The thought of the unknown visitor engrossed him once more, and he got down from the table. In spite of the noise which he had heard, it was hardly to be supposed that she had entered the barn. And, after a few minutes' search, he was about to go out, when there came, from the left, a clash of things falling about and some hoops dropped to the ground not far from where he stood.

They came from above, from a loft likewise crammed with various objects and implements and reached by a ladder. Was he to believe that the visitor, surprised by his arrival, had taken refuge in that hiding-place and made a movement that caused the fall of the hoops?

Don Luis placed his electric lantern on a cask in such a way as to send the light right up to the loft. Seeing nothing suspicious, nothing but an arsenal of old pickaxes, rakes, and disused scythes, he attributed what had happened so some animal, to some stray cat; and, to make sure, he walked quickly to the ladder and went up.

Suddenly, at the very moment when he reached the level of the floor, there was a fresh noise, a fresh clatter of things falling: and a form rose from the heap of rubbish with a terrible gesture.

It was swift as lightning. Don Luis saw the great blade of a scythe cleaving the air at the height of his head. Had he hesitated for a second, for the tenth of a second, the awful weapon would have beheaded him. As it was, he just had time to flatten himself against the ladder. The scythe whistled past him, grazing his jacket. He slid down to the floor below.

But he had seen.

He had seen the dreadful face of Gaston Sauverand, and, behind the man of the ebony walking-stick, wan and livid in the rays of the electric light, the distorted features of Florence Levasseur!

9

LUPIN'S ANGER

He remained for one moment motionless and speechless. Above was a perfect clatter of things being pushed about, as though the besieged were building themselves a barricade. But to the right of the electric rays, diffused daylight entered through an opening that was suddenly exposed; and he saw, in front of this opening, first one form and then another stooping in order to escape over the roofs.

He levelled his revolver and fired, but badly, for he was thinking of Florence and his hand trembled. Three more shots rang out. The bullets rattled against the old scrap-iron in the loft. The fifth shot was followed by a cry of pain. Don Luis once more rushed up the ladder.

Slowly making his way through the tangle of farm implements and over some cases of dried rape seed forming a regular rampart, he at last, after bruising and barking his shins, succeeded in reaching the opening, and was greatly surprised, on passing through it, to find himself on level ground. It was the top of the sloping bank against which the barn stood.

He descended the slope at haphazard, to the left of the barn, and passed in front of the building, but saw nobody. He then went up again on the right; and although the flat part was very narrow, he searched it carefully for, in the growing darkness of the twilight, he had every reason to fear renewed attacks from the enemy.

He now became aware of something which he had not perceived before. The bank ran along the top of the wall, which at this spot was quite sixteen feet high. Gaston Sauverand and Florence had, beyond a doubt, escaped this way.

Perenna followed the wall, which was fairly wide, till he came to a lower part, and here he jumped into a ploughed field skirting a little wood toward which the fugitives must have run. He started exploring it, but, realizing its denseness, he at once saw that it was waste of time to linger in pursuit.

He therefore returned to the village, while thinking over this, his latest exploit. Once again Florence and her accomplice had tried to get rid of him. Once again Florence figured prominently in this network of criminal plots.

At the moment when chance informed Don Luis that old Langernault had probably died by foul play, at the moment when chance, by leading him to Hanged Man's Barn, as he christened it, brought him into the presence of two skeletons, Florence appeared as a murderous vision, as an evil genius who was seen wherever death had passed with its trail of blood and corpses.

"Oh, the loathsome creature!" he muttered, with a shudder. "How can she have so fair a face, and eyes of such haunting beauty, so grave, sincere, and almost guileless?"

In the church square, outside the inn, Mazeroux, who had returned, was filling the petrol tank of the motor and lighting the lamps. Don Luis saw the mayor of Damigni crossing the square. He took him aside.

"By the way, Monsieur le Maire, did you ever hear any talk in the district, perhaps two years ago, of the disappearance of a couple forty or fifty years of age? The husband's name was Alfred—"

"And the wife's Victorine, eh?" the mayor broke in. "I should think so! The affair created some stir. They lived at Alengon on a small, private income; they disappeared between one day and the next; and no one has since discovered what became of them, any more than a little hoard, some twenty thousand francs or so, which they had realized the day before by the sale of their house. I remember them well. Dedessuslamare their name was."

"Thank you, Monsieur le Maire," said Perenna, who had learned all that he wanted to know.

The car was ready. A minute after he was rushing toward Alençon with Mazeroux.

"Where are we going, Chief?" asked the sergeant.

"To the station. I have every reason to believe, first, that Sauverand was informed this morning—in what way remains to be seen—of the revelations made last night by Mme. Fauville relating to old Langernault; and, secondly, that he has been prowling around and inside old Langernault's property today for reasons that also remain to be seen. And I presume that he came by train and that he will go back by train."

Perenna's supposition was confirmed without delay. He was told at the railway station that a gentleman and a lady had arrived from Paris at two o'clock, that they had hired a trap at the hotel next door, and that, having finished their business, they had gone back a few minutes ago, by the 7:40 express. The description of the lady and gentleman corresponded exactly with that of Florence and Sauverand.

"Off we go!" said Perenna, after consulting the timetable. "We are an hour behind. We may catch up with the scoundrel at Le Mans."

"We'll do that, Chief, and we'll collar him, I swear: him and his lady, since there are two of them."

"There are two of them, as you say. Only—"

"Only what?"

Don Luis waited to reply until they were seated and the engine started, when he said:

"Only, my boy, you will keep your hands off the lady."

"Why should I?"

"Do you know who she is? Have you a warrant against her?"

"No."

"Then shut up."

"But—"

"One word more, Alexandre, and I'll set you down beside the road. Then you can make as many arrests as you please."

Mazeroux did not breathe another word. For that matter the speed at which they at once began to go hardly left him time to raise a protest. Not a little anxious, he thought only of watching the horizon and keeping a lookout for obstacles.

The trees vanished on either side almost unseen. Their foliage overhead made a rhythmical sound as of moaning waves. Night insects dashed themselves to death against the lamps.

"We shall get there right enough," Mazeroux ventured to observe. "There's no need to put on the pace."

The speed increased and he said no more.

Villages, plains, hills; and then, suddenly in the midst of the darkness, the lights of a large town, Le Mans.

"Do you know the way to the station, Alexandre?"

"Yes, Chief, to the right and then straight on."

Of course they ought to have gone to the left. They wasted seven or eight minutes in wandering through the streets and receiving contradictory instructions. When the motor pulled up at the station the train was whistling.

Don Luis jumped out, rushed through the waiting-room, found the doors shut, jostled the railway officials who tried to stop him, and reached the platform.

A train was about to start on the farther line. The last door was banged to. He ran along the carriages, holding on to the brass rails.

"Your ticket, sir! Where's your ticket?" shouted an angry collector.

Don Luis continued to fly along the footboards, giving a swift glance through the panes, thrusting aside the persons whose presence at the windows prevented him from seeing, prepared at any moment to burst into the compartment containing the two accomplices.

He did not see them in the end carriages. The train started. And suddenly he gave a shout: they were there, the two of them, by themselves! He had seen them! They were there: Florence, lying on the seat, with her head on Sauverand's shoulder, and he, leaning over her, with his arms around her!

Mad with rage he flung back the bottom latch and seized the handle of the carriage door. At the same moment he lost his balance and was pulled off by the furious ticket collector and by Mazeroux, who bellowed:

"Why, you're mad, Chief! You'll kill yourself!"

"Let go, you ass!" roared Don Luis. "It's they! Let me be, can't you!"

The carriages filed past. He tried to jump on to another footboard. But the two men were clinging to him, some railway porters came to their assistance, the station-master ran up. The train moved out of the station.

"Idiots!" he shouted. "Boobies! Pack of asses that you are, couldn't you leave me alone? Oh, I swear to Heaven—!"

With a blow of his left fist he knocked the ticket collector down; with a blow of his right he sent Mazeroux spinning; and shaking off the porters and the station-master, he rushed along the platform to the luggage-room, where he took flying leaps over several batches of trunks, packing-cases, and portmanteaux.

"Oh, the perfect fool!" he mumbled, on seeing that Mazeroux had let the power down in the car. "Trust him, if there's any blunder going!"

Don Luis had driven his car at a fine rate during the day; but that night the pace became vertiginous. A very meteor flashed through the suburbs of Le Mans and hurled itself along the highroad. Perenna had but one thought in his head: to reach the next station, which was Chartres, before the two accomplices, and to fly at Sauverand's throat. He saw nothing but that: the savage grip of his two hands that would set Florence Levasseur's lover gasping in his agony.

"Her lover! Her lover!" he muttered, gnashing his teeth. "Why, of course, that explains everything! They have combined against their accomplice, Marie Fauville; and it is she alone, poor devil, who will pay for the horrible series of crimes!"

"Is she their accomplice even?" he wondered. "Who knows? Who knows if that pair of demons are not capable, after killing Hippolyte and his son, of having plotted the ruin of Marie Fauville, the last obstacle that stood between them and the Mornington inheritance? Doesn't everything point to that conclusion? Didn't I find the list of dates in a book belonging to Florence? Don't the facts prove that the letters were communicated by Florence?...

"Those letters accuse Gaston Sauverand as well. But how does that affect things? He no longer loves Marie, but Florence. And Florence loves him. She is his accomplice, his counsellor, the woman who will live by his side and benefit by his fortune... True, she sometimes pretends to be defending Marie Fauville. Play-acting! Or perhaps remorse, fright at the thought of all that she has done against her rival, and of the fate that awaits the unhappy woman!

"But she is in love with Sauverand. And she continues to carry on the struggle without pity and without respite. And that is why she wanted to kill me, the interloper whose insight she dreaded. And she hates me and loathes me—"

To the hum of the engine and the sighing of the trees, which bent down at the approach, he murmured incoherent words. The recollection of the two lovers clasped in each other's arms made him cry aloud with jealousy. He wanted to be revenged.

For the first time in his life, the longing, the feverish craving to kill set his brain boiling.

"Hang it all!" he growled suddenly. "The engine's misfiring! Mazeroux! Mazeroux!"

"What, Chief! Did you know that I was here?" exclaimed Mazeroux, emerging from the shadow in which he sat hidden.

"You jackass! Do you think that the first idiot who comes along can hang on to the footboard of my car without my knowing it? You must be feeling comfortable down there!"

"I'm suffering agonies, and I'm shivering with cold."

"That's right, it'll teach you. Tell me, where did you buy your petrol?"

"At the grocer's."

"At a thief's, you mean. It's muck. The plugs are getting sooted up."

"Are you sure?"

"Can't you hear the misfiring, you fool?"

The motor, indeed, at moments seemed to hesitate. Then everything became normal again. Don Luis forced the pace. Going downhill they appeared to be hurling themselves into space. One of the lamps went out. The other was not as bright as usual. But nothing diminished Don Luis's ardour.

There was more misfiring, fresh hesitations, followed by efforts, as though the engine was pluckily striving to do its duty. And then suddenly came the final failure, a dead stop at the side of the road, a stupid breakdown.

"Confound it!" roared Don Luis. "We're stuck! Oh, this is the last straw!"

"Come, Chief, we'll put it right. And we'll pick up Sauverand at Paris instead of Chartres, that's all."

"You infernal ass! The repairs will take an hour! And then she'll break down again. It's not petrol, it's filth they've foisted on you."

The country stretched around them to endless distances, with no other lights than the stars that riddled the darkness of the sky.

Don Luis was stamping with fury. He would have liked to kick the motor to pieces. He would have liked—

It was Mazeroux who "caught it," in the hapless sergeant's own words. Don Luis took him by the shoulders, shook him, loaded him with insults and abuse and, finally, pushing him against the roadside bank and holding him there, said, in a broken voice of mingled hatred and sorrow.

"It's she, do you hear, Mazeroux? It's Sauverand's companion who has done everything. I'm telling you now, because I'm afraid of relenting. Yes, I am a weak coward. She has such a grave face, with the eyes of a child. But it's she, Mazeroux. She lives in my house. Remember her name: Florence Levasseur. You'll arrest her, won't you? I might not be able to. My courage fails me when I look at her. The fact is that I have never loved before.

"There have been other women—but no, those were fleeting fancies—not even that: I don't even remember the past! Whereas Florence—! You must arrest her, Mazeroux. You must deliver me from her eyes. They burn into me like poison. If you don't deliver me I shall kill her as I killed Dolores—or else they will kill me—or—Oh, I don't know all the ideas that are driving me wild—!

"You see, there's another man," he explained. "There's Sauverand, whom she loves. Oh, the infamous pair! They have killed Fauville and the boy and old Langernault and those two in the barn and others besides: Cosmo Mornington, Verot, and more still. They are monsters, she most of all—And if you saw her eyes—"

He spoke so low that Mazeroux could hardly hear him. He had let go his hold of Mazeroux and seemed utterly cast down with despair, a surprising symptom in a man of his amazing vigour and authority.

"Come, Chief," said the sergeant, helping him up. "This is all stuff and nonsense. Trouble with women: I've had it like everybody else. Mme. Mazeroux—yes, I got married while you were away—Mme. Mazeroux turned out badly herself, gave me the devil of a time, Mme. Mazeroux did. I'll tell you all about it, Chief, how Mme. Mazeroux rewarded my kindness."

He led Don Luis gently to the car and settled him on the front seat.

"Take a rest, Chief. It's not very cold and there are plenty of furs. The first peasant that comes along at daybreak, I'll send him to the next town for what we want—and for food, too, for I'm starving. And everything will come right; it always does with women. All you have to do is to kick them out of your life—except when they anticipate you and kick themselves out... I was going to tell you: Mme. Mazeroux—"

Don Luis was never to learn what had happened with Mme. Mazeroux. The most violent catastrophes had no effect upon the peacefulness of his slumbers. He was asleep almost at once.

It was late in the morning when he woke up. Mazeroux had had to wait till seven o'clock before he could hail a cyclist on his way to Chartres.

They made a start at nine o'clock. Don Luis had recovered all his coolness. He turned to his sergeant.

"I said a lot last night that I did not mean to say. However, I don't regret it. Yes, it is my duty to do everything to save Mme. Fauville and to catch the real culprit. Only the task falls upon myself; and I swear that I shan't fail in it. This evening Florence Levasseur shall sleep in the lockup!"

"I'll help you, Chief," replied Mazeroux, in a queer tone of voice.

"I need nobody's help. If you touch a single hair of her head, I'll do for you. Do you understand?"

"Yes, Chief."

"Then hold your tongue."

His anger was slowly returning and expressed itself in an increase of speed, which seemed to Mazeroux a revenge executed upon himself. They raced over the cobblestones of Chartres. Rambouillet, Chevreuse, and Versailles received the terrifying vision of a thunderbolt tearing across them from end to end.

Saint-Cloud. The Bois de Boulogne...

On the Place de la Concorde, as the motor was turning toward the Tuileries, Mazeroux objected:

"Aren't you going home, Chief?"

"No. There's something more urgent first: we must relieve Marie Fauville of her suicidal obsession by letting her know that we have discovered the criminals."

"And then?"

"Then I want to see the Prefect of Police."

"M. Desmalions is away and won't be back till this afternoon."

"In that case the examining magistrate."

"He doesn't get to the law courts till twelve; and it's only eleven now."

"We'll see."

Mazeroux was right: there was no one at the law courts.

Don Luis lunched somewhere close by; and Mazeroux, after calling at the detective office, came to fetch him and took him to the magistrate's corridor. Don Luis's excitement, his extraordinary restlessness, did not fail to strike Mazeroux, who asked:

"Are you still of the same mind, Chief?"

"More than ever. I looked through the newspapers at lunch. Marie Fauville, who was sent to the infirmary after her second attempt, has again tried to kill herself by banging her head against the wall of the room. They have put a straitjacket on her. But she is refusing all food. It is my duty to save her."

"How?"

"By handing over the real criminal. I shall inform the magistrate in charge of the case; and this evening I shall bring you Florence Levasseur dead or alive."

"And Sauverand?"

"Sauverand? That won't take long. Unless—"

"Unless what?"

"Unless I settle his business myself, the miscreant!"

"Chief!"

"Oh, dry up!"

There were some reporters near them waiting for particulars. He recognized them and went up to them.

"You can say, gentlemen, that from today I am taking up the defence of Marie Fauville and devoting myself entirely to her cause."

They all protested: was it not he who had had Mme. Fauville arrested? Was it not he who had collected a heap of convicting proofs against her?

"I shall demolish those proofs one by one," he said. "Marie Fauville is the victim of wretches who have hatched the most diabolical plot against her, and whom I am about to deliver up to justice."

"But the teeth! The marks of the teeth!"

"A coincidence! An unparalleled coincidence, but one which now strikes me as a most powerful proof of innocence. I tell you that, if Marie Fauville had been clever enough to commit all those murders, she would also have been clever enough not to leave behind her a fruit bearing the marks of her two rows of teeth."

"But still—"

"She is innocent! And that is what I am going to tell the examining magistrate. She must be informed of the efforts that are being made in her favour. She must be given hope at once. If not, the poor thing will kill herself and her death will be on the conscience of all who accused an innocent woman. She must—"

At that moment he interrupted himself. His eyes were fixed on one of the journalists who was standing a little way off listening to him and taking notes.

He whispered to Mazeroux:

"Could you manage to find out that beggar's name? I can't remember where on earth I've seen him before."

But an usher now opened the door of the examining magistrate, who, on receiving Don Perenna's card, had asked to see him at once. He stepped forward and was about to enter the room with Mazeroux, when he suddenly turned to his companion with a cry of rage:

"It's he! It was Sauverand in disguise. Stop him! He's made off. Run, can't you?"

He himself darted away followed by Mazeroux and a number of warders and journalists, He soon outdistanced them, so that, three minutes later, he heard no one more behind him. He had rushed down the staircase of the "Mousetrap," and through the subway leading from one courtyard to the other. Here two people told him that they had met a man walking at a smart pace.

The track was a false one. He became aware of this, hunted about, lost a good deal of time, and managed to discover that Sauverand had left by the Boulevard du Palais and joined a very pretty, fair-haired woman—Florence Levasseur, obviously—on the Quai de l'Horloge. They had both got into the motor bus that runs from the Place Saint-Michel to the Gare Saint-Lazare.

Don Luis went back to a lonely little street where he had left his car in the charge of a boy. He set the engine going and drove at full speed to the Gare Saint-Lazare, From the omnibus shelter he went off on a fresh track which also proved to be wrong, lost quite another hour, returned to the terminus, and ended by learning for certain that Florence had stepped by herself into a motor bus which would take her toward the Place du Palais-Bourbon. Contrary to all his expectations, therefore, the girl must have gone home.

The thought of seeing her again roused his anger to its highest pitch. All the way down the Rue Royale and across the Place de la Concorde he kept blurting out words of revenge and threats which he was itching to carry out. He would abuse Florence. He would sting her with his insults. He felt a bitter and painful need to hurt the odious creature.

But on reaching the Place du Palais-Bourbon he pulled up short. His practised eye had counted at a glance, on the right and left, a half-dozen men whose professional look there was no mistaking. And Mazeroux, who had caught sight of him, had spun round on his heel and was hiding under a gateway.

He called him:

"Mazeroux!"

The sergeant appeared greatly surprised to hear his name and came up to the car.

"Hullo, the Chief!"

His face expressed such embarrassment that Don Luis felt his fears taking definite shape.

"Look here, is it for me that you and your men are hanging about outside my house?"

"There's a notion, Chief," replied Mazeroux, looking very uncomfortable. "You know that you're in favour all right!"

Don Luis gave a start. He understood. Mazeroux had betrayed his confidence. To obey his scruples of conscience as well as to rescue the chief from the dangers of a fatal passion, Mazeroux had denounced Florence Levasseur.

Perenna clenched his fists in an effort of his whole being to stifle his boiling rage. It was a terrible blow. He received a sudden intuition of all the blunders which his mad jealousy had made him commit since the day before, and a presentiment of the irreparable disasters that might result from them. The conduct of events was slipping from him.

"Have you the warrant?" he asked.

Mazeroux spluttered:

"It was quite by accident. I met the Prefect, who was back. We spoke of the young lady's business. And, as it happened, they had discovered that the photograph—you know, the photograph of Florence Levasseur which the Prefect lent you—well, they have discovered that you faked it. And then when I mentioned the name of Florence, the Prefect remembered that that was the name."

"Have you the warrant?" Don Luis repeated, in a harsher tone.

"Well, you see, I couldn't help it... M. Desmalions, the magistrate—"

If the Place du Palais Bourbon had been deserted at that moment, Don Luis would certainly have relieved himself by a swinging blow administered to Mazeroux's chin according to the most scientific rules of the noble art. And Mazeroux foresaw this contingency, for he prudently kept as far away as possible and, to appease the chief's anger, intended a whole litany of excuses:

"It was for your good, Chief... I had to do it... Only think! You yourself told me: 'Rid me of the creature!' said you. I'm too weak. You'll arrest her, won't you? Her eyes burn into me—like poison! Well, Chief, could I help it? No, I couldn't, could I? Especially as the deputy chief—"

"Ah! So Weber knows?"

"Why, yes! The Prefect is a little suspicious of you since he understood about the faking of the portrait. So M. Weber is coming back in an hour, perhaps, with reinforcements. Well, I was saying, the deputy chief had learnt that the woman who used to go to Gaston Sauverand's at Neuilly—you know, the house on the Boulevard Richard-Wallace—was fair and very good looking, and that her name was Florence. She even used to stay the night sometimes."

"You lie! You lie!" hissed Perenna.

All his spite was reviving. He had been pursuing Florence with intentions which it would have been difficult for him to put into words. And now suddenly he again wanted to destroy her; and this time consciously. In reality he no longer knew what he was doing. He was acting at haphazard, tossed about in turns by the most diverse passions, a prey to that inordinate love which impels us as readily to kill the object of our affections as to die in an attempt to save her.

A newsboy passed with a special edition of the *Paris-Midi*, showing in great black letters:

"SENSATIONAL DECLARATION BY DON LUIS PERENNA
"MME. FAUVILLE IS INNOCENT.
"IMMINENT ARREST OF THE TWO CRIMINALS"

"Yes, yes," he said aloud. "The drama is drawing to an end. Florence is about to pay her debt to society. So much the worse for her."

He started his car again and drove through the gate. In the courtyard he said to his chauffeur, who came up:

"Turn her around and don't put her up. I may be starting again at any moment."

He sprang out and asked the butler:

"Is Mlle. Levasseur in?"

"Yes, sir, she's in her room."

"She was away yesterday, wasn't she?"

"Yes, sir, she received a telegram asking her to go to the country to see a relation who was ill. She came back last night."

"I want to speak to her. Send her to me. At once."

"In the study, sir?"

"No, upstairs, in the boudoir next to my bedroom."

This was a small room on the second floor which had once been a lady's boudoir, and he preferred it to his study since the attempt at murder of which he had been the object. He was quieter up there, farther away; and he kept his important papers there. He always carried the key with him: a special key with three grooves to it and an inner spring.

Mazeroux had followed him into the courtyard and was keeping close behind him, apparently unobserved by Perenna, who having so far appeared not to notice it. He now, however, took the sergeant by the arm and led him to the front steps.

"All is going well. I was afraid that Florence, suspecting something, might not have come back. But she probably doesn't know that I saw her yesterday. She can't escape us now."

They went across the hall and up the stairs to the first floor. Mazeroux rubbed his hands.

"So you've come to your senses, Chief?"

"At any rate I've made up my mind. I will not, do you hear, I will not have Mme. Fauville kill herself; and, as there is no other way of preventing that catastrophe, I shall sacrifice Florence."

"Without regret?"

"Without remorse."

"Then you forgive me?"

"I thank you."

And he struck him a clean, powerful blow under the chin. Mazeroux fell without a moan, in a dead faint on the steps of the second flight.

Halfway up the stairs was a dark recess that served as a lumber room where the servants kept their pails and brooms and the soiled household linen. Don Luis carried Mazeroux to it, and, seating him comfortably on the floor, with his back to a housemaid's box, he stuffed his handkerchief into his mouth, gagged him with a towel, and bound his wrists and ankles with two tablecloths. The other ends of these he fastened to a couple of strong nails. As Mazeroux was slowly coming to himself, Don Luis said:

"I think you have all you want. Tablecloths—napkins—something in your mouth in case you're hungry. Eat at your ease. And then take a little nap, and you'll wake up as fresh as paint."

He locked him in and glanced at his watch.

"I have an hour before me. Capital!"

At that moment his intention was to insult Florence, to throw up all her scandalous crimes in her face, and, in this way, to force a written and signed confession from her. Afterward, when Marie Fauville's safety was insured, he would see. Perhaps he would put Florence in his motor and carry her off to some refuge from which, with the girl for a hostage, he would be able to influence the police. Perhaps—But he did not seek to anticipate events. What he wanted was an immediate, violent explanation.

He ran up to his bedroom on the second floor and dipped his face into cold water. Never had he experienced such a stimulation of his whole being, such an unbridling of his blind instincts.

"It's she!" he spluttered. "I hear her! She is at the bottom of the stairs. At last! Oh, the joy of having her in front of me! Face to face! She and I alone!"

He returned to the landing outside the boudoir. He took the key from his pocket. The door opened.

He uttered a great shout: Gaston Sauverand was there! In that locked room Gaston Sauverand was waiting for him, standing with folded arms.

10

GASTON SAUVERAND EXPLAINS

Gaston Sauverand!

Instinctively, Don Luis took a step back, drew his revolver, and aimed it at the criminal:

"Hands up!" he commanded. "Hands up, or I fire!"

Sauverand did not appear to be put out. He nodded toward two revolvers which he had laid on a table beyond his reach and said:

"There are my arms. I have come here not to fight, but to talk."

"How did you get in?" roared Don Luis, exasperated by this display of calmness. "A false key, I suppose? But how did you get hold of the key? How did you manage it?"

The other did not reply. Don Luis stamped his foot:

"Speak, will you? Speak! If not—"

But Florence ran into the room. She passed him by without his trying to stop her, flung herself upon Gaston Sauverand, and, taking no heed of Perenna's presence, said:

"Why did you come? You promised me that you wouldn't. You swore it to me. Go!"

Sauverand released himself and forced her into a chair.

"Let me be, Florence. I promised only so as to reassure you. Let me be."

"No, I will not!" exclaimed the girl eagerly. "It's madness! I won't have you say a single word. Oh, please, please stop!"

He bent over her and smoothed her forehead, separating her mass of golden hair.

"Let me do things my own way, Florence," he said softly.

She was silent, as though disarmed by the gentleness of his voice; and he whispered more words which Don Luis could not hear and which seemed to convince her.

Perenna had not moved. He stood opposite them with his arm outstretched and his finger on the trigger, aiming at the enemy. When Sauverand addressed Florence by her Christian name, he started from head to foot and his finger trembled. What miracle kept him from shooting? By what supreme effort of will did he stifle the jealous hatred that burnt him like fire? And here was Sauverand daring to stroke Florence's hair!

He lowered his arm. He would kill them later, do with them what he pleased, since they were in his power, and since nothing henceforth could snatch them from his vengeance.

He took Sauverand's two revolvers and laid them in a drawer. Then he went back to the door, intending to lock it. But hearing a sound on the first-floor landing, he leant over the balusters. The butler was coming upstairs with a tray in his hand.

"What is it now?"

"An urgent letter, sir, for Sergeant Mazeroux."

"Sergeant Mazeroux is with me. Give me the letter and don't let me be disturbed again."

He tore open the envelope. The letter, hurriedly written in pencil and signed by one of the inspectors on duty outside the house, contained these words:

"Look out, Sergeant. Gaston Sauverand is in the house. Two people living opposite say that the girl who is known hereabouts as the lady housekeeper came in at half-past one, before we took up our posts. She was next seen at the window of her lodge.

"A few moments after, a small, low door, used for the cellars and situated under the lodge, was opened, evidently by her. Almost at the same time a man entered the square, came along the wall, and slipped in through the cellar door. According to the description it was Gaston Sauverand. So look out, Sergeant. At the least alarm, at the first signal from you, we shall come in."

Don Luis reflected. He now understood how the scoundrel had access to his house, and how, hidden in the safest of retreats, he was able to escape every attempt to find him. He was living under the roof of the very man who had declared himself his most formidable adversary.

"Come on," he said to himself. "The fellow's score is settled—and so is his young lady's. They can choose between the bullets in my revolver and the handcuffs of the police."

He had ceased to think of his motor standing ready below. He no longer dreamt of flight with Florence. If he did not kill the two of them, the law would lay its hand upon them, the hand that does not let go. And perhaps it was better so, that society itself should punish the two criminals whom he was about to hand over to it.

He shut the door, pushed the bolt, faced his two prisoners again and, taking a chair, said to Sauverand:

"Let us talk."

Owing to the narrow dimensions of the room they were all so close together that Don Luis felt as if he were almost touching the man whom he loathed from the very bottom of his heart. Their two chairs were hardly a yard asunder. A long table, covered with books, stood between them and the windows, which, hollowed out of the very thick wall, formed a recess, as is usual in old houses.

Florence had turned her chair away from the light, and Don Luis could not see her face clearly. But he looked straight into Gaston Sauverand's face and watched it with eager curiosity;

and his anger was heightened by the sight of the still youthful features, the expressive mouth, and the intelligent eyes, which were fine in spite of their hardness.

"Well? Speak!" said Don Luis, in a commanding tone. "I have agreed to a truce, but a momentary truce, just long enough to say what is necessary. Are you afraid now that the time has arrived? Do you regret the step which you have taken?"

The man smiled calmly and said:

"I am afraid of nothing, and I do not regret coming, for I have a very strong intuition that we can, that we are bound to, come to an understanding."

"An understanding!" protested Don Luis with a start.

"Why not?"

"A compact! An alliance between you and me!"

"Why not? It is a thought which I had already entertained more than once, which took a more precise shape in the magistrates' corridor, and which finally decided me when I read the announcement which you caused to be made in the special edition of this paper: 'Sensational declaration by Don Luis Perenna. Mme. Fauville is innocent!'"

Gaston Sauverand half rose from his chair and, carefully picking his words, emphasizing them with sharp gestures, he whispered:

"Everything lies, Monsieur, in those four words. Do those four words which you have written, which you have uttered publicly and solemnly—'Mme. Fauville is innocent'—do they express your real mind? Do you now absolutely believe in Marie Fauville's innocence?"

Don Luis shrugged his shoulders.

"Mme. Fauville's innocence has nothing to do with the case. It is a question not of her, but of you, of you two and myself. So come straight to the point and as quickly as you can. It is to your interest even more than to mine."

"To our interest?"

"You forget the third heading to the article," cried Don Luis. "I did more than proclaim Marie Fauville's innocence. I also announced—read for yourself—The 'imminent arrest of the criminals.'"

Sauverand and Florence rose together, with the same unguarded movement.

"And, in your view, the criminals are—?" asked Sauverand.

"Why, you know as well as I do: they are the man with the ebony walking-stick, who at any rate cannot deny having murdered Chief Inspector Ancenis, and the woman who is his accomplice in all his crimes. Both of them must remember their attempts to assassinate me: the revolver shot on the Boulevard Suchet; the motor smash causing the death of my chauffeur; and yesterday again, in the barn—you know where—the barn with the two skeletons hanging from the rafters: yesterday—you remember—the scythe, the relentless scythe, which nearly beheaded me."

"And then?"

"Well, then, the game is lost. You must pay up; and all the more so as you have foolishly put your heads into the lion's mouth."

"I don't understand. What does all this mean?"

"It simply means that they know Florence Levasseur, that they know you are both here, that the house is surrounded, and that Weber, the deputy chief detective, is on his way."

Sauverand appeared disconcerted by this unexpected threat. Florence, standing beside him, had turned livid. A mad anguish distorted her features. She stammered:

"Oh, it is awful! No, no, I can't endure it!"

And, rushing at Don Luis:

"Coward! Coward! It's you who are betraying us! Coward! Oh, I knew that you were capable of the meanest treachery! There you stand like an executioner! Oh, you villain, you coward!"

She fell into her chair, exhausted and sobbing, with her hand to her face.

Don Luis turned away. Strange to say, he experienced no sense of pity; and Florence's tears affected him no more than her insults had done, no more than if he had never loved the girl. He was glad of this release. The horror with which she filled him had killed his love.

But, when he once more stood in front of them after taking a few steps across the room, he saw that they were holding each other's hands, like two friends in distress, trying to give each other courage; and, again yielding to a sudden impulse of hatred, for a moment beside himself, he gripped the man's arm:

"I forbid you—By what right—? Is she your wife? Your mistress? Then—"

His voice became perplexed. He himself felt the strangeness of that fit of anger which suddenly revealed, in all its force and all its blindness, a passion which he thought dead. And he blushed, for Gaston Sauverand was looking at him in amazement; and he did not doubt that the enemy had penetrated his secret.

A long pause followed, during which he met Florence's eyes, hostile eyes, full of rebellion and disdain. Had she, too, guessed?

He dared not speak another word. He waited for Sauverand's explanation. And, while waiting, he gave not a thought to the coming revelations, nor to the tremendous problems of which he was at last about to know the solution, nor to the tragic events at hand.

He thought of one thing only, thought of it with the fevered throbbing of his whole being, thought of what he was on the point of learning about Florence, about the girl's affections, about her past, about her love for Sauverand. That alone interested him.

"Very well," said Sauverand. "I am caught in a trap. Fate must take its course. Nevertheless, can I speak to you? It is the only wish that remains to me."

"Speak," replied Don Luis. "The door is locked. I shall not open it until I think fit. Speak."

"I shall be brief," said Gaston Sauverand. "For one thing, what I can tell you is not much. I do not ask you to believe it, but to listen to it as if I were possibly telling the truth, the whole truth."

And he expressed himself in the following words:

"I never met Hippolyte and Marie Fauville, though I used to correspond with them—you will remember that we were all cousins—until five years ago, when chance brought us together at Palmero. They were passing the winter there while their new house on the Boulevard Suchet was being built.

"We spent five months at Palmero, seeing one another daily. Hippolyte and Marie were not on the best of terms. One evening after they had been quarrelling more violently than usual I found her crying. Her tears upset me and I could no longer conceal my secret. I had loved Marie from the first moment when we met. I was to love her always and to love her more and more."

"You lie!" cried Don Luis, losing his self-restraint. "I saw the two of you yesterday in the train that brought you back from Alençon—"

Gaston Sauverand looked at Florence. She sat silent, with her hands to her face and her elbows on her knees. Without replying to Don Luis's exclamation, he went on:

"Marie also loved me. She admitted it, but made me swear that I would never try to obtain from her more than the purest friendship would allow. I kept my oath. We enjoyed a few weeks of incomparable happiness. Hippolyte Fauville, who had become enamoured of a music-hall singer, was often away.

"I took a good deal of trouble with the physical training of the little boy Edmond, whose health was not what it should be. And we also had with us, between us, the best of friends, the most devoted and affectionate counsellor, who staunched our wounds, kept up our courage, restored our gayety, and bestowed some of her own strength and dignity upon our love. Florence was there."

Don Luis felt his heart beating faster. Not that he attached the least credit to Gaston Sauverand's words; but he had every hope of arriving, through those words, at the real truth. Perhaps, also, he was unconsciously undergoing the influence of Gaston Sauverand, whose apparent frankness and sincerity of tone caused him a certain surprise.

Sauverand continued:

"Fifteen years before, my elder brother, Raoul Sauverand, had picked up at Buenos Aires, where he had gone to live, a little girl, the orphan daughter of some friends. At his death he entrusted the child, who was then fourteen, to an old nurse who had brought me up and who had accompanied my brother to South America. The old nurse brought the child to me and herself died of an accident a few days after her arrival in France... I took the little girl to Italy to friends, where she worked and studied and became—what she is.

"Wishing to live by her own resources, she accepted a position as teacher in a family. Later I recommended her to my Fauville cousins with whom I found her at Palmero as governess to the boy Edmond and especially as the friend, the dear and devoted friend, of Marie Fauville... She was mine, also, at that happy time, which was so sunny and all too short. Our happiness, in fact—the happiness of all three of us—was to be wrecked in the most sudden and tantalizing fashion.

"Every evening I used to write in a diary the daily life of my love, an uneventful life, without hope or future before it, but eager and radiant. Marie Fauville was extolled in it as a goddess.

Kneeling down to write, I sang litanies of her beauty, and I also used to invent, as a poor compensation, wholly imaginary scenes, in which she said all the things which she might have said but did not, and promised me all the happiness which we had voluntarily renounced.

"Hippolyte Fauville found the diary... His anger was something terrible. His first impulse was to get rid of Marie. But in the face of his wife's attitude, of the proofs of her innocence which she supplied, of her inflexible refusal to consent to a divorce, and of her promise never to see me again, he recovered his calmness... I left, with death in my soul. Florence left, too, dismissed. And never, mark me, never, since that fatal hour, did I exchange a single word with Marie. But an indestructible love united us, a love which neither absence nor time was to weaken."

He stopped for a moment, as though to read in Don Luis's face the effect produced by his story. Don Luis did not conceal his anxious attention. What astonished him most was Gaston Sauverand's extraordinary calmness, the peaceful expression of his eyes, the quiet ease with which he set forth, without hurrying, almost slowly and so very simply, the story of that family tragedy.

"What an actor!" he thought.

And as he thought it, he remembered that Marie Fauville had given him the same impression. Was he then to hark back to his first conviction and believe Marie guilty, a dissembler like her accomplice, a dissembler like Florence? Or was he to attribute a certain honesty to that man?

He asked:

"And afterwards?"

"Afterwards I travelled about. I resumed my life of work and pursued my studies wherever I went, in my bedroom at the hotels, and in the public laboratories of the big towns."

"And Mme. Fauville?"

"She lived in Paris in her new house. Neither she nor her husband ever referred to the past."

"How do you know? Did she write to you?"

"No. Marie is a woman who does not do her duty by halves; and her sense of duty is strict to excess. She never wrote to me. But Florence, who had accepted a place as secretary and reader to Count Malonyi, your predecessor in this house, used often to receive Marie's visits in her lodge downstairs.

"They did not speak of me once, did they, Florence? Marie would not have allowed it. But all her life and all her soul were nothing but love and passionate memories. Isn't that so, Florence?

"At last," he went on slowly, "weary of being so far away from her, I returned to Paris. That was our undoing... It was about a year ago. I took a flat in the Avenue du Roule and went to it in the greatest secrecy, so that Hippolyte Fauville might not know of my return. I was afraid of disturbing Marie's peace of mind. Florence alone knew, and came to see me from time to time. I went out little, only after dark, and in the most secluded parts of the Bois. But it happened—for our most heroic resolutions sometimes fail us—one Wednesday night, at about eleven o'clock, my steps led me to the Boulevard Suchet, without my noticing it, and I went past Marie's house.

"It was a warm and fine night and, as luck would have it, Marie was at her window. She saw me, I was sure of it, and knew me; and my happiness was so great that my legs shook under me as I walked away.

"After that I passed in front of her house every Wednesday evening; and Marie was nearly always there, giving me this unhoped-for and ever-new delight, in spite of the fact that her social duties, her quite natural love of amusement, and her husband's position obliged her to go out a great deal."

"Quick! Why can't you hurry?" said Don Luis, urged by his longing to know more. "Look sharp and come to the facts Speak!"

He had become suddenly afraid lest he should not hear the remainder of the explanation; and he suddenly perceived that Gaston Sauverand's words were making their way into his mind as words that were perhaps not untrue. Though he strove to fight against them, they were stronger than his prejudices and triumphed over his arguments.

The fact is, that deep down in his soul, tortured with love and jealousy, there was something that disposed him to believe this man in whom hitherto he had seen only a hated rival, and who was so loudly proclaiming, in Florence's very presence, his love for Marie.

"Hurry!" he repeated. "Every minute is precious!"

Sauverand shook his head.

"I shall not hurry. All my words were carefully thought out before I decided to speak. Every one of them is essential. Not one of them can be omitted, for you will find the solution of the problem not in facts presented anyhow, separated one from the other, but in the concatenation of the facts, and in a story told as faithfully as possible."

"Why? I don't understand."

"Because the truth lies hidden in that story."

"But that truth is your innocence, isn't it?"

"It is Marie's innocence."

"But I don't dispute it!"

"What is the use of that if you can't prove it?"

"Exactly! It's for you to give me proofs."

"I have none."

"What!"

"I tell you, I have no proof of what I am asking you to believe."

"Then I shall not believe it!" cried Don Luis angrily. "No, and again no! Unless you supply me with the most convincing proofs, I shall refuse to believe a single word of what you are going to tell me."

"You have believed everything that I have told you so far," Sauverand retorted very simply.

Don Luis offered no denial. He turned his eyes to Florence Levasseur; and it seemed to him that she was looking at him with less aversion, and as though she were wishing with all her might that he would not resist the impressions that were forcing themselves upon him. He muttered:

"Go on with your story."

And there was something really strange about the attitude of those two men, one making his explanation in precise terms and in such a way as to give every word its full value, the other listening attentively and weighing every one of those words; both controlling their excitement; both as calm in appearance as though they were seeking the philosophical solution in a case of conscience. What was going on outside did not matter. What was to happen presently did not count.

Before all, whatever the consequences of their inactivity at this moment when the circle of the police was closing in around them, before all it was necessary that one should speak and the other listen.

"We are coming," said Sauverand, in his grave voice, "we are coming to the most important events, to those of which the interpretation, which is new to you, but strictly true, will make you believe in our good faith. Ill luck having brought me across Hippolyte Fauville's path in the course of one of my walks in the Bois, I took the precaution of changing my abode and went to live in the little house on the Boulevard Richard-Wallace, where Florence came to see me several times.

"I was even careful to keep her visits a secret and, moreover, to refrain from corresponding with her except through the *poste restante*. I was therefore quite easy in my mind.

"I worked in perfect solitude and in complete security. I expected nothing. No danger, no possibility of danger, threatened us. And, I may say, to use a commonplace but very accurate expression, that what happened came as an absolute bolt from the blue. I heard at the same time, when the Prefect of Police and his men broke into my house and proceeded to arrest me, I heard at the same time and for the first time of the murder of Hippolyte Fauville, the murder of Edmond, and the arrest of my adored Marie."

"Impossible!" cried Don Luis, in a renewed tone of aggressive wrath. "Impossible! Those facts were a fortnight old. I cannot allow that you had not heard of them."

"Through whom?"

"Through the papers," exclaimed Don Luis. "And, more certainly still, through Mlle. Levasseur."

"Through the papers?" said Sauverand. "I never used to read them. What! Is that incredible? Are we under an obligation, an inevitable necessity, to waste half an hour a day in skimming through the futilities of politics and the piffle of the news columns? Is your imagination incapable of conceiving a man who reads nothing but reviews and scientific publications?

"The fact is rare, I admit," he continued. "But the rarity of a fact is no proof against it. On the other hand, on the very morning of the crime I had written to Florence saying that I was going away for three weeks and bidding her goodbye. I changed my mind at the last moment; but this she did not know; and, thinking that I had gone, not knowing where I was, she was unable to inform me of the crime, of Marie's arrest, or, later, when an accusation was brought against the man with the ebony walking-stick, of the search that was being made for me."

"Exactly!" declared Don Luis. "You cannot pretend that the man with the ebony walking-stick, the man who followed Inspector Vérot to the Café du Pont-Neuf and purloined his letter—"

"I am not the man," Sauverand interrupted.

And, when Don Luis shrugged his shoulders, he insisted, in a more forcible tone of voice:

"I am not that man. There is some inexplicable mistake in all this, but I have never set foot in the Café du Pont-Neuf. I swear it. You must accept this statement as positively true. Besides, it agrees entirely with the retired life which I was leading from necessity and from choice. And, I repeat, I knew nothing.

"The thunderbolt was unexpected. And it was precisely for this reason, you must understand, that the shock produced in me an equally unexpected reaction, a state of mind diametrically opposed to my real nature, an outburst of my most savage and primitive instincts. Remember, Monsieur, that they had laid hands upon what to me was the most sacred thing on earth. Marie was in prison. Marie was accused of committing two murders!... I went mad.

"At first controlling myself, playing a part with the Prefect of Police, then overthrowing every obstacle, shooting Chief Inspector Ancenis, shaking off Sergeant Mazeroux, jumping from the window, I had only one thought in my head—that of escape. Once free, I should save Marie. Were there people in my way? So much the worse for them.

"By what right did those people dare to attack the most blameless of women? I killed only one man that day! I would have killed ten! I would have killed twenty! What was Chief Inspector Ancenis's life to me? What cared I for the lives of any of those wretches? They stood between Marie and myself; and Marie was in prison!"

Gaston Sauverand made an effort which contracted every muscle of his face to recover the coolness that was gradually leaving him. He succeeded in doing so, but his voice, nevertheless, remained tremulous, and the fever with which he was consumed shook his frame in a manner which he was unable to conceal.

He continued:

"At the corner of the street down which I turned after outdistancing the Prefect's men on the Boulevard Richard-Wallace, Florence saved me just as I believed that all was lost. Florence had known everything for a fortnight past. She learnt the news of the double murder from the papers, those papers which she used to read out to you, and which you discussed with her. And it was by being with you, by listening to you, that she acquired the opinion which everything that happened tended to confirm: the opinion that Marie's enemy, her only enemy, was yourself."

"But why? Why?"

"Because she saw you at work," exclaimed Sauverand, "because it was more to your interest than to that of anyone else that first Marie and then I should not come between you and the Mornington inheritance, and lastly—"

"What?"

Gaston Sauverand hesitated and then said, plainly.

"Lastly, because she knew your real name beyond a doubt, and because she felt that Arsène Lupin was capable of anything."

They were both silent; and their silence, at such a moment, was impressive to a degree. Florence remained impassive under Don Luis Perenna's gaze; and he was unable to discern on her sealed face any of the feelings with which she must needs be stirred.

Gaston Sauverand continued:

"It was against Arsène Lupin, therefore, that Florence, Marie's terrified friend, engaged in the struggle. It was to unmask Lupin that she wrote or rather inspired the article of which you found the original in a ball of string. It was Lupin whom she spied upon, day by day, in this house. It was Lupin whom she heard one morning telephoning to Sergeant Mazeroux and rejoicing in my imminent arrest. It was to save me from Lupin that she let down the iron curtain in front of him, at the risk of an accident, and took a taxi to the corner of the Boulevard Richard-Wallace, where she arrived too late to warn me, as the detectives had already entered my house, but in time to screen me from their pursuit.

"Her mistrust and terror-stricken hatred of you were told to me in an instant," Sauverand declared. "During the twenty minutes which we employed in throwing our assailants off the scent, she hurriedly sketched the main lines of the business and described to me in a few words the leading part which you were playing in it; and we then and there prepared a counter-attack upon you, so that you might be suspected of complicity.

"While I was sending a message to the Prefect of Police, Florence went home and hid under the cushions of your sofa the end of the stick which I had kept in my hand without thinking. It was an ineffective parry and missed its aim. But the fight had begun; and I threw myself into it headlong.

"Monsieur, to understand my actions thoroughly, you must remember that I was a student, a man leading a solitary life, but also an ardent lover. I would have spent all my life in work, asking no more from fate than to see Marie at her window from time to time at night. But, once she was being persecuted, another man arose within me, a man of action, bungling, certainly, and inexperienced, but a man who was ready to stick at nothing, and who, not knowing how to save Marie Fauville, had no other object before him than to do away with that enemy of Marie's to whom he was entitled to ascribe all the misfortunes that had befallen the woman he loved... This started the series of my attempts upon your life. Brought into your house, concealed in Florence's own rooms, I tried—unknown to her: that I swear—to poison you."

He paused for an instant to mark the effect of his words, then went on:

"Her reproaches, her abhorrence of such an act, would perhaps have moved me, but, I repeat, I was mad, quite mad;

and your death seemed to me to imply Marie's safety. And, one morning, on the Boulevard Suchet, where I had followed you, I fired a revolver at you.

"The same evening your motor car, tampered with by myself—remember, Florence's rooms are close to the garage—carried you, I hoped, to your death, together with Sergeant Mazeroux, your confederate... That time again you escaped my vengeance. But an innocent man, the chauffeur who drove you, paid for you with his life; and Florence's despair was such that I had to yield to her entreaties and lay down my arms.

"I myself, terrified by what I had done, shattered by the remembrance of my two victims, changed my plans and thought only of saving Marie by contriving her escape from prison...

"I am a rich man. I lavished money upon Marie's warders, without, however, revealing my intentions. I entered into relations with the prison tradesmen and the staff of the infirmary. And every day, having procured a card of admission as a law reporter, I went to the law courts, to the examining magistrates' corridor, where I hoped to meet Marie, to encourage her with a look, a gesture, perhaps to slip a few words of comfort into her hand..."

Sauverand moved closer to Don Luis.

"Her martyrdom continued. You struck her a most terrible blow with that mysterious business of Hippolyte Fauville's letters. What did those letters mean? Where did they come from? Were we not entitled to attribute the whole plot to you, to you who introduced them into the horrible struggle?

"Florence watched you, I may say, night and day. We sought for a clue, a glimmer of light in the darkness... Well, yesterday morning, Florence saw Sergeant Mazeroux arrive. She could not overhear what he said to you, but she caught the name of a certain Langernault and the name of Damigni, the village where Langernault lived. She remembered that old friend of

Hippolyte Fauville's. Were the letters not addressed to him and was it not in search of him that you were going off in the motor with Sergeant Mazeroux?...

"Half an hour later we were in the train for Alençon. A carriage took us from the station to just outside Damigni, where we made our inquiries with every possible precaution. On learning what you must also know, that Langernault was dead, we resolved to visit his place, and we had succeeded in effecting an entrance when Florence saw you in the grounds. Wishing at all costs to avoid a meeting between you and myself, she dragged me across the lawn and behind the bushes. You followed us, however, and when a barn appeared in sight she pushed one of the doors which half opened and let us through. We managed to slip quickly through the lumber in the dark and knocked up against a ladder. This we climbed and reached a loft in which we took shelter. You entered at that moment...

"You know the rest: how you discovered the two hanging skeletons; how your attention was drawn to us by an imprudent movement of Florence; your attack, to which I replied by brandishing the first weapon with which chance provided me; lastly, our flight through the window in the roof, under the fire of your revolver. We were free. But in the evening, in the train, Florence fainted. While bringing her to I perceived that one of your bullets had wounded her in the shoulder. The wound was slight and did not hurt her, but it was enough to increase the extreme tension of her nerves. When you saw us—at Le Mans station wasn't it?—she was asleep, with her head on my shoulder."

Don Luis had not once interrupted the latter part of this narrative, which was told in a more and more agitated voice and quickened by an accent of profound truth. Thanks to a superhuman effort of attention, he noted Sauverand's least words and actions in his mind. And as these words were uttered and these actions performed, he received the impression of another woman who rose up beside the real Florence, a woman unspotted and innocent of all the shame which he had attributed to her on the strength of events.

Nevertheless, he did not yet give in. How could Florence possibly be innocent? No, no, the evidence of his eyes, which had seen, and the evidence of his reason, which had judged, both rebelled against any such contention.

He would not admit that Florence could suddenly be different from what she really was to him: a crafty, cunning, cruel, bloodthirsty monster. No, no, the man was lying with infernal cleverness. He put things with a skill amounting to genius, until it was no longer possible to differentiate between the false and the true, or to distinguish the light from the darkness.

He was lying! He was lying! And yet how sweet were the lies he told! How beautiful was that imaginary Florence, the Florence compelled by destiny to commit acts which she loathed, but free of all crime, free of remorse, humane and pitiful, with her clear eyes and her snow-white hands! And how good it was to yield to this fantastic dream!

Gaston Sauverand was watching the face of his former enemy. Standing close to Don Luis, his features lit up with the expression of feelings and passions which he no longer strove to check, he asked, in a low voice:

"You believe me, don't you?"

"No, I don't," said Perenna, hardening himself to resist the man's influence.

"You must!" cried Sauverand, with a fierce outburst of violence. "You must believe in the strength of my love. It is the cause of everything. My hatred for you comes only from my love. Marie is my life. If she were dead, there would be nothing for me to do but die. Oh, this morning, when I read in the papers that the poor woman had opened her veins—and through your fault, after Hippolyte's letters accusing her—I did not want to kill you so much as to inflict upon you the most barbarous tortures! My poor Marie, what a martyrdom she must be enduring!...

"As you were not back, Florence and I wandered about all morning to have news of her: first around the prison, next to the police office and the law courts. And it was there, in the magistrates' corridor, that I saw you. At that moment you were mentioning Marie Fauville's name to a number of journalists; and you told them that Marie Fauville was innocent; and you informed them of the evidence which you possessed in Marie's favour!

"My hatred ceased then and there, Monsieur. In one second the enemy had become the ally, the master to whom one kneels. So you had had the wonderful courage to repudiate all your work and to devote yourself to Marie's rescue! I ran off, trembling with joy and hope, and, as I joined Florence, I shouted, 'Marie is saved! He proclaims her innocent! I must see him and speak to him!'...

"We came back here. Florence refused to lay down her arms and begged me not to carry out my plan before your new attitude in the case was confirmed by deeds. I promised everything that she asked. But my mind was made up. And my will was still further strengthened when I had read your declaration in the newspaper. I would place Marie's fate in your hands whatever happened and without an hour's delay, I waited for your return and came up here."

He was no longer the same man who had displayed such coolness at the commencement of the interview. Exhausted by his efforts and by a struggle that had lasted for weeks, costing him so much fruitless energy, he was now trembling; and clinging to Don Luis, with one of his knees on the chair beside which Don Luis was standing, he stammered:

"Save her, I implore you! You have it in your power. Yes, you can do anything. I learnt to know you in fighting you. There was more than your genius defending you against me; there is a luck that protects you. You are different from other men. Why, the mere fact of your not killing me at once, though I had pursued you so savagely, the fact of your listening to the inconceivable truth of the innocence of all three of us and accepting it as admissible, surely these constitute an unprecedented miracle.

"While I was waiting for you and preparing to speak to you, I received an intuition of it all!" he exclaimed. "I saw clearly that the man who was proclaiming Marie's innocence with nothing to guide him but his reason, I saw that this man alone could save her and that he would save her. Ah, I beseech you, save her — and save her at once. Otherwise it will be too late.

"In a few days Marie will have ended her life. She cannot go on living in prison. You see, she means to die. No obstacle can prevent her. Can anyone be prevented from committing suicide? And how horrible if she were to die!... Oh, if the law requires a criminal I will confess anything that I am asked to. I will joyfully accept every charge and pay every penalty, provided that Marie is free! Save her!... I did not know, I do not yet know the best thing to be done! Save her from prison and death, save her, for God's sake, save her!"

Tears flowed down his anguish-stricken face. Florence also was crying, bowed down with sorrow. And Perenna suddenly felt the most terrible dread steal over him.

Although, ever since the beginning of the interview, a fresh conviction had gradually been mastering him, it was only as it were a glance that he became aware of it. Suddenly he perceived that his belief in Sauverand's words was unrestricted, and that Florence was perhaps not the loathsome creature that he had had the right to think, but a woman whose eyes did not lie and whose face and soul were alike beautiful.

Suddenly he learnt that the two people before him, as well as Marie Fauville, for love of whom they had fought so unskilful a fight, were imprisoned in an iron circle which their efforts would not succeed in breaking. And that circle traced by an unknown hand he, Perenna, had drawn tighter around them with the most ruthless determination.

"If only it is not too late!" he muttered.

He staggered under the shock of the sensations and ideas that crowded upon him. Everything clashed in his brain with tragic violence: certainty, joy, dismay, despair, fury. He was struggling in the clutches of the most hideous nightmare; and he already seemed to see a detective's heavy hand descending on Florence's shoulder.

"Come away! Come away!" he cried, starting up in alarm. "It is madness to remain!"

"But the house is surrounded," Sauverand objected.

"And then? Do you think that I will allow for a second—? No, no, come! We must fight side by side. I shall still entertain some doubts, that is certain. You must destroy them; and we will save Mme. Fauville."

"But the detectives round the house?"

"We'll manage them."

"Weber, the deputy chief?"

"He's not here. And as long as he's not here I'll take everything on myself. Come, follow me, but at some little distance. When I give the signal and not till then—"

He drew the bolt and turned the handle of the door. At that moment someone knocked. It was the butler.

"Well?" asked Don Luis. "Why am I disturbed?"

"The deputy chief detective, M. Weber, is here, sir."

11

ROUTED

Don Luis had certainly expected this formidable blow; and yet it appeared to take him unawares, and he repeated more than once:

"Ah, Weber is here! Weber is here!"

All his buoyancy left him, and he felt like a retreating army which, after almost making good its escape, suddenly finds itself brought to a stop by a steep mountain. Weber was there — that is to say, the chief leader of the enemies, the man who would be sure to plan the attack and the resistance in such a manner as to dash Perenna's hopes to the ground. With Weber at the head of the detectives, any attempt to force a way out would have been absurd.

"Did you let him in?" he asked.

"You did not tell me not to, sir."

"Is he alone?"

"No, sir, the deputy chief has six men with him. He has left them in the courtyard."

"And where is he?"

"He asked me to take him to the first floor. He expected to find you in your study, sir."

"Does he know now that I am with Sergeant Mazeroux and Mlle. Levasseur?"

"Yes, sir."

Perenna thought for a moment and then said:

"Tell him that you have not found me and that you are going to look for me in Mlle. Levasseur's rooms. Perhaps he will go with you. All the better if he does."

And he locked the door again.

The struggle through which he had just passed did not show itself on his face; and, now that all was lost, now that he was called upon to act, he recovered that wonderful composure which never abandoned him at decisive moments. He went up to Florence. She was very pale and was silently weeping. He said:

"You must not be frightened, Mademoiselle. If you obey me implicitly, you will have nothing to fear."

She did not reply and he saw that she still mistrusted him. And he almost rejoiced at the thought that he would compel her to believe in him.

"Listen to me," he said to Sauverand. "In case I should not succeed after all, there are still several things which you must explain."

"What are they?" asked Sauverand, who had lost none of his coolness.

Then, collecting all his riotous thoughts, resolved to omit nothing, but at the same time to speak only what was essential, Don Luis asked, in a calm voice:

"Where were you on the morning before the murder, when a man carrying an ebony walking-stick and answering to your description entered the Café du Pont-Neuf immediately after Inspector Vérot?"

"At home."

"Are you sure that you did not go out?"

"Absolutely sure. And I am also sure that I have never been to the Café du Pont-Neuf, of which I had never even heard."

"Good. Next question. Why, when you learned all about this business, did you not go to the Prefect of Police or the examining magistrate? It would have been simpler for you to give yourself up and tell the exact truth than to engage in this unequal fight."

"I was thinking of doing so. But I at once realized that the plot hatched against me was so clever that no bare statement of the truth would have been enough to convince the authorities. They would never have believed me. What proof could I supply? None at all—whereas, on the other hand, the proofs against us were overwhelming and undeniable. Were not the marks of the teeth evidence of Marie's undoubted guilt? And were not my silence, my flight, the shooting of Chief Inspector Ancenis so many crimes? No, if I would rescue Marie, I must remain free."

"But she could have spoken herself?"

"And confessed our love? Apart from the fact that her womanly modesty would have prevented her, what good would it have done? On the contrary, it meant lending greater weight to the accusation. That was just what happened when Hippolyte Fauville's letters, appearing one by one, revealed to the police the as yet unknown motives of the crimes imputed to us. We loved each other."

"How do you explain the letters?"

"I can't explain them. We did not know of Fauville's jealousy. He kept it to himself. And then, again, why did he suspect us? What can have put it into his head that we meant to kill him? Where did his fears, his nightmares, come from? It is a mystery. He wrote that he had letters of ours in his possession: what letters?"

"And the marks of the teeth, those marks which were undoubtedly made by Mme. Fauville?"

"I don't know. It is all incomprehensible."

"You don't know either what she can have done after leaving the opera between twelve and two in the morning?"

"No. She was evidently lured into a trap. But how and by whom? And why does she not say what she was doing? More mystery."

"You were seen that evening, the evening of the murders, at Auteuil station. What were you doing there?"

"I was going to the Boulevard Suchet and I passed under Marie's windows. Remember that it was a Wednesday. I came back on the following Wednesday, and, still knowing nothing of the tragedy or of Marie's arrest, I came back again on the second Wednesday, which was the evening on which you found out where I lived and informed Sergeant Mazeroux against me."

"Another thing. Did you know of the Mornington inheritance?"

"No, nor Florence either; and we have every reason to think that Marie and her husband knew no more about it than we did."

"That barn at Damigni: was it the first time that you had entered it?"

"Yes; and our astonishment at the sight of the two skeletons hanging from the rafters equalled yours."

Don Luis was silent. He cast about for a few seconds longer to see if he had any more questions to ask. Then he said:

"That is all I wanted to know. Are you, on your side, certain that everything that is necessary has been said?"

"Yes."

"This is a serious moment. It is possible that we may not meet again. Now you have not given me a single proof of your statements."

"I have told you the truth. To a man like yourself, the truth is enough. As for me, I am beaten. I give up the struggle, or, rather, I place myself under your orders. Save Marie."

"I will save the three of you," said Perenna. "The fourth of the mysterious letters is to make its appearance tomorrow: that leaves ample time for us to lay our heads together and study the matter fully. And tomorrow evening I shall go there and, with the help of all that you have told me, I shall prove the innocence of you all. The essential thing is to be present at the meeting on the twenty-fifth of May."

"Please think only of Marie. Sacrifice me, if necessary. Sacrifice Florence even. I am speaking in her name as well as my own when I tell you that it is better to desert us than to jeopardize the slightest chance of success."

"I will save the three of you," Perenna repeated.

He pushed the door ajar and, after listening outside, said:

"Don't move. And don't open the door to anybody, on any pretext whatever, before I come to fetch you. I shall not be long."

He locked the door behind him and went down to the first floor. He did not feel those high spirits which usually cheered him on the eve of his great battles. This time, Florence Levasseur's life and liberty were at stake; and the consequences of a defeat seemed to him worse than death.

Through the window on the landing he saw the detectives guarding the courtyard. He counted six of them. And he also saw the deputy chief at one of the windows of his study, watching the courtyard and keeping in touch with his detectives.

"By Jove!" he thought. "He's sticking to his post. It will be a tough job. He suspects something. However, let's make a start!"

He went through the drawing-room and entered his study. Weber saw him. The two enemies were face to face.

There was a few seconds' silence before the duel opened, the duel which was bound to be swift and vigorous, without the least sign of weakness or distraction on either side. It could not last longer than three minutes.

The deputy chief's face bore an expression of mingled joy and anxiety. For the first time he had permission, he had orders, to fight that accursed Don Luis, against whom he had never yet been able to satisfy his hatred. And his delight was all the greater because he held every trump, whereas Don Luis had put himself in the wrong by defending Florence Levasseur and tampering with the girl's portrait. On the other hand, Weber did not forget that Don Luis was identical with Arsène Lupin; and this consideration caused him a certain uneasiness. He was obviously thinking:

"The least blunder, and I'm done for."

He crossed swords with a jest.

"I see that you were not in Mlle. Levasseur's lodge, as your man pretended."

"My man spoke in accordance with my instructions, I was in my bedroom, upstairs. But I wanted to finish the job before I came down."

"And is it done?"

"It's done. Florence Levasseur and Gaston Sauverand are in my room, gagged and bound. You have only to accept delivery of the goods."

"Gaston Sauverand!" cried Weber. "Then it was he who was seen coming in?"

"Yes. He was simply living with Florence Levasseur, whose lover he is."

"Oho!" said the deputy chief, in a bantering tone. "Her lover!"

"Yes; and when Sergeant Mazeroux brought Florence Levasseur to my room, to question her out of hearing of the servants, Sauverand, foreseeing the arrest of his mistress, had the audacity to join us. He tried to rescue her from our hands."

"And you checkmated him?"

"Yes."

It was clear that the deputy chief did not believe one word of the story. He knew through M. Desmalions and Mazeroux that Don Luis was in love with Florence; and Don Luis was not the man even through jealousy to hand over a woman whom he loved. He increased his attention.

"Good business!" he said. "Take me up to your room. Was it a hard struggle?"

"Not very. I managed to disarm the scoundrel. All the same, Mazeroux got stabbed in the thumb."

"Nothing serious?"

"Oh, dear, no; but he has gone to have his wound dressed at the chemist's."

The deputy chief stopped, greatly surprised.

"What! Isn't Mazeroux in your room with the two prisoners?"

"I never told you that he was."

"No, but your butler—"

"The butler made a mistake. Mazeroux went out a few minutes before you came."

"It's funny," said Weber, watching Don Luis closely, "but my men all think he's here. They haven't seen him go out."

"They haven't seen him go out?" echoed Don Luis, pretending to feel anxious. "But, then, where can he be? He told me he wanted to have his thumb seen to."

The deputy chief was growing more and more suspicious. Evidently Perenna was trying to get rid of him by sending him in search of the sergeant.

"I will send one of my men," he said. "Is the chemist's near?"

"Just around the corner, in the Rue de Bourgogne. Besides, we can telephone."

"Oh, we can telephone!" muttered Weber.

He was quite at a loss and looked like a man who does not know what is going to happen next. He moved slowly toward the instrument, while barring the way to Don Luis to prevent his escaping. Don Luis therefore retreated to the telephone box, as if forced to do so, took down the receiver with one hand, and, calling, "Hullo! Hullo! Saxe, 2409," with the other hand, which was resting against the wall, he cut one of the wires with a pair of pliers which he had taken off the table as he passed.

"Hullo! Are you there? Is that 2409? Are you the chemist?... Hullo!... Sergeant Mazeroux of the detective service is with you, isn't he? Eh? What? What do you say? But it's too awful! Are you sure? Do you mean to say the wound is poisoned?"

Without thinking what he was doing, the deputy chief pushed Don Luis aside and took hold of the receiver. The thought of the poisoned wound was too much for him.

"Are you there?" he cried, keeping an eye on Don Luis and motioning to him not to go away. "Are you there?... Eh?... It's Deputy Chief Weber, of the detective office, speaking... Hullo! Are you there?... I want to know about Sergeant Mazeroux... Are you there?... Oh, hang it, why don't you answer!"

Suddenly he let go the instrument, looked at the wires, perceived that they had been cut, and turned round, showing a face that clearly expressed the thought in his mind.

"That's done it. I've been tricked!"

Perenna was standing a couple of yards behind him, leaning carelessly against the woodwork of the arch, with his left hand passed between his back and the woodwork. He was smiling, smiling pleasantly, kindly, and genially:

"Don't move!" he said, with a gesture of his right hand.

Weber, more frightened by that smile than he would have been by threats, took good care not to move.

"Don't move," repeated Don Luis, in a very queer voice. "And, whatever you do, don't be alarmed. You shan't be hurt, I promise you. Just five minutes in a dark cell for a naughty little boy. Are you ready? One two, three! Bang!"

He stood aside and pressed the button that worked the iron curtain. The heavy panel came crashing to the floor. The deputy chief was a prisoner.

"That's a hundred million gone to Jericho," grinned Don Luis. "A pretty trick, but a bit expensive. Goodbye, Mornington inheritance! Goodbye, Don Luis Perenna! And now, my dear Lupin, if you don't want Weber to take his revenge, beat a retreat and in good order. One, two; left, right; left, right!"

As he spoke, he locked, on the inside, the folding doors between the drawing-room and the first-floor anteroom; then, returning to his study, he locked the door between this room and the drawing-room.

The deputy chief was banging at the iron curtain with all his might and shouting so loud that they were bound to hear him outside through the open window.

"You're not making half enough noise, deputy!" cried Don Luis. "Let's see what we can do."

He took his revolver and fired off three bullets, one of which broke a pane. Then he quickly left his study by a small, massive door, which he carefully closed behind him. He was now in a secret passage which ran round both rooms and ended at another door leading to the anteroom. He opened this door wide and was thus able to hide behind it.

Attracted by the shots and the noise, the detectives were already rushing through the hall and up the staircase. When they reached the first floor and had gone through the anteroom, as the drawing-room doors were locked, the only outlet open to them was the passage, at the end of which they could hear the deputy shouting. They all six darted down it.

When the last of them had vanished round the bend in the passage, Don Luis softly pushed back the door that concealed him and locked it like the rest. The six detectives were as safely imprisoned as the deputy chief.

"Bottled!" muttered Don Luis. "It will take them quite five minutes to realize the situation, to bang at the locked doors, and to break down one of them. In five minutes we shall be far away."

He met two of his servants running up with scared faces, the chauffeur and the butler. He flung each of them a thousand-franc note and said to the chauffeur:

"Set the engine going, there's a sportsman, and let no one near the machine to block my way. Two thousand francs more for each of you if I get off in the motor. Don't stand staring at me like that: I mean what I say. Two thousand francs apiece: it's for you to earn it. Look sharp!"

He himself went up the second flight without undue haste, remaining master of himself. But, on the last stair, he was seized with such a feeling of elation that he shouted:

"Victory! The road is clear!"

The boudoir door was opposite. He opened it and repeated:

"Victory! But there's not a second to lose. Follow me."

He entered. A stifled oath escaped his lips.

The room was empty.

"What!" he stammered. "What does this mean? They're gone... Florence—"

Certainly, unlikely though it seemed, he had hitherto supposed that Sauverand possessed a false key to the lock. But how could they both have escaped, in the midst of the detectives? He looked around him. And then he understood.

In the recess containing the window, the lower part of the wall, which formed a very wide box underneath the casement, had the top of its woodwork raised and resting against the panes, exactly like the lid of a chest. And inside the open chest he saw the upper rungs of a narrow descending ladder.

In a second, Don Luis conjured up the whole story of the past: Count Malonyi's ancestress hiding in the old family mansion, escaping the search of the perquisitors, and in this way living throughout the revolutionary troubles. Everything was explained. A passage contrived in the thickness of the wall led to some distant outlet. And this was how Florence used to come and go through the house; this was how Gaston went in and out in all security; and this also was how both of them were able to enter his room and surprise his secrets.

"Why not have told me?" he wondered. "A lingering suspicion, I suppose—"

But his eyes were attracted by a sheet of paper on the table. With a feverish hand, Gaston Sauverand had scribbled the following lines in pencil:

"We are trying to escape so as not to compromise you. If we are caught, it can't be helped. The great thing is that you should be free. All our hopes are centred in you."

Below were two words written by Florence: "Save Marie."

"Ah," he murmured, disconcerted by the turn of events and not knowing what to decide, "why, oh, why did they not obey my instructions? We are separated now—"

Downstairs the detectives were battering at the door of the passage in which they were imprisoned. Perhaps he would still have time to reach his motor before they succeeded in breaking down the door. Nevertheless, he preferred to take the same road as Florence and Sauverand, which gave him the hope of saving them and of rescuing them in case of danger.

He therefore stepped over the side of the chest, placed his foot on the top rung and went down. Some twenty bars brought him to the middle of the first floor. Here, by the light of his electric lantern, he entered a sort of low, vaulted tunnel, dug, as he thought, in the wall, and so narrow that he could only walk along it sideways.

Thirty yards farther there was a bend, at right angles; and next, at the end of another tunnel of the same length, a trapdoor, which stood open, revealing the rungs of a second ladder. He did not doubt that the fugitives had gone this way.

It was quite light at the bottom. Here he found himself in a cupboard which was also open and which, on ordinary occasions, must have been covered by curtains that were now drawn. This cupboard faced a bed that filled almost the whole space of an alcove. On passing through the alcove and reaching a room from which it was separated only by a slender partition, to his great surprise, he recognized Florence's sitting-room.

This time, he knew where he was. The exit, which was not secret, as it led to the Place du Palais-Bourbon, but nevertheless very safe, was that which Sauverand generally used when Florence admitted him.

Don Luis therefore went through the entrance hall and down the steps and, a little way before the pantry, came upon the cellar stairs. He ran down these and soon recognized the low door that served to admit the wine-casks. The daylight filtered in through a small, grated spy-hole. He groped till he found the lock. Glad to have come to the end of his expedition, he opened the door.

"Hang it all!" he growled, leaping back and clutching at the lock, which he managed to fasten again.

Two policemen in uniform were guarding the exit, two policemen who had tried to seize him as he appeared.

Where did those two men come from? Had they prevented the escape of Sauverand and Florence? But in that case Don Luis would have met the two fugitives, as he had come by exactly the same road as they.

"No," he thought, "they effected their flight before the exit was watched. But, by Jove! It's my turn to clear out; and that's not easy. Shall I let myself be caught in my burrow like a rabbit?"

He went up the cellar stairs again, intending to hasten matters, to slip into the courtyard through the outhouses, to jump into his motor, and to clear a way for himself. But, when he was just reaching the yard, near the coach-house, he saw four detectives, four of those whom he had imprisoned, come up waving their arms and shouting. And he also became aware of a regular uproar near the main gate and the porter's lodge. A number of men were all talking together, raising their voices in violent discussion.

Perhaps he might profit by this opportunity to steal outside under cover of the disorder. At the risk of being seen, he put out his head. And what he saw astounded him.

Gaston Sauverand stood with his back to the wall of the lodge, surrounded by policemen and detectives who pushed and insulted him. The handcuffs were on his wrists.

Gaston Sauverand a prisoner! What had happened between the two fugitives and the police?

His heart wrung with anguish, he leaned out still farther. But he did not see Florence. The girl had no doubt succeeded in escaping.

Weber's appearance on the steps and the deputy chief's first words confirmed his hopes. Weber was mad with rage. His recent captivity and the humiliation of his defeat exasperated him.

"Ah!" he roared, as he saw the prisoner. "There's one of them, at any rate! Gaston Sauverand! Choice game, that!... Where did you catch him?"

"On the Place du Palais-Bourbon," said one of the inspectors. "We saw him slinking out through the cellar door."

"And his accomplice, the Levasseur girl?"

"We missed her, Deputy Chief. She was the first out."

"And Don Luis? You haven't let him leave the house, I hope? I gave orders."

"He tried to get out through the cellar door five minutes after."

"Who said so?"

"One of the men in uniform posted outside the door."

"Well?"

"The beggar went back into the cellar."

Weber gave a shout of delight.

"We've got him! And it's a nasty business for him! Charge of resisting the police!... Complicity... We shall be able to unmask him at last. Tally-ho, my lads, tally-ho! Two men to guard

Sauverand, four men on the Place du Palais-Bourbon, revolver in hand. Two men on the roof. The rest stick to me. We'll begin with the Levasseur girl's room and we'll take his room next. Hark, forward, my lads!"

Don Luis did not wait for the enemies' attack. Knowing their intentions, he beat a retreat, unseen, toward Florence's rooms. Here, as Weber did not yet know the short cut through the outhouses, he had time to make sure that the trapdoor was in perfect working order, and that there was no reason why they should discover the existence of a secret cupboard at the back of the alcove, behind the curtains of the bed.

Once inside the passage, he went up the first staircase, followed the long corridor contrived in the wall, climbed the ladder leading to the boudoir, and, perceiving that this second trapdoor fitted the woodwork so closely that no one could suspect anything, he closed it over him. A few minutes later he heard the noise of men making a search above his head.

And so, on the twenty-fourth of May, at five o'clock in the afternoon, the position was as follows: Florence Levasseur with a warrant out against her, Gaston Sauverand in prison, Marie Fauville in prison and refusing all food, and Don Luis, who believed in their innocence and who alone could have saved them, Don Luis was being blockaded in his own house and hunted down by a score of detectives.

As for the Mornington inheritance, there could be no more question of that, because the legatee, in his turn, had set himself in open rebellion against society.

"Capital!" said Don Luis, with a grin. "This is life as I understand it. The question is a simple one and may be put in different ways. How can a wretched, unwashed beggar, with not a penny in his pocket, make a fortune in twenty-four hours without setting foot outside his hovel? How can a general, with no soldiers and no ammunition left, win a battle which he has lost? In short, how shall I, Arsène Lupin, manage to be present tomorrow evening at the meeting which will be held on the Boulevard Suchet and to behave in such a way as to save Marie Fauville, Florence Levasseur, Gaston Sauverand, and my excellent friend Don Luis Perenna in the bargain?"

Dull blows came from somewhere. The men must be hunting the roofs and sounding the walls.

Don Luis stretched himself flat on the floor, hid his face in his folded arms and, shutting his eyes, murmured:

"Let's think."

12

"HELP!"

When Lupin afterward told me this episode of the tragic story, he said, not without a certain self-complacency:

"What astonished me then, and what astonishes me still, as one of the most amazing victories on which I am entitled to pride myself, is that I was able to admit Sauverand and Marie Fauville's innocence on the spot, as a problem solved once and for all. It was a first-class performance, I swear, and surpassed the most famous deductions of the most famous investigators both in psychological value and in detective merit.

"After all, taking everything into account, there was not the shadow of a fresh fact to enable me to alter the verdict. The charges accumulated against the two prisoners were the same, and were so grave that no examining magistrate would have hesitated for a second to commit them for trial, nor any jury to bring them in guilty. I will not speak of Marie Fauville: you had only to think of the marks of her teeth to be absolutely certain. But Gaston Sauverand, the son of Victor Sauverand and consequently the heir of Cosmo Mornington—Gaston Sauverand, the man with the ebony walking-stick and the murderer of Chief Inspector Ancenis—was he not just as guilty as Marie Fauville, incriminated with her by the mysterious letters, incriminated by the very revelation of the husband whom they had killed?

"And yet why did that sudden change take place in me?" he asked. "Why did I go against the evidence? Why did I credit an incredible fact? Why did I admit the inadmissible? Why? Well, no doubt, because truth has an accent that rings in the ears in a manner all its own. On the one side, every proof, every fact, every reality, every certainty; on the other, a story, a story told by one of the three criminals, and therefore, presumptively, absurd and untrue from start to finish. But a story told in a frank voice, a clear, dispassionate, closely woven story, free from complications or improbabilities, a story which supplied no positive solution, but which, by its very honesty, obliged any impartial mind to reconsider the solution arrived at. I believed the story."

The explanation which Lupin gave me was not complete. I asked:

"And Florence Levasseur?"

"Florence?"

"Yes, you don't tell me what you thought. What was your opinion about her? Everything tended to incriminate her not only in your eyes, because, logically speaking, she had taken part in all the attempts to murder you, but also in the eyes of the police. They knew that she used to pay Sauverand clandestine visits at his house on the Boulevard Richard-Wallace. They had found her photograph in Inspector Vérot's memorandum-book, and then—and then all the rest: your accusations, your certainties. Was all that modified by Sauverand's story? To your mind, was Florence innocent or guilty?"

He hesitated, seemed on the point of replying directly and frankly to my question, but could not bring himself to do so, and said:

"I wished to have confidence. In order to act, I must have full and entire confidence, whatever doubts might still assail me, whatever darkness might still enshroud this or that part of the adventure. I therefore believed. And, believing, I acted according to my belief."

Acting, to Don Luis Perenna, during those hours of forced inactivity, consisted solely in perpetually repeating to himself Gaston Sauverand's account of the events. He tried to reconstitute it in all its details, to remember the very least sentences, the apparently most insignificant phrases. And he examined those sentences, scrutinized those phrases one by one, in order to extract such particle of the truth as they contained.

For the truth was there. Sauverand had said so and Perenna did not doubt it. The whole sinister affair, all that constituted the case of the Mornington inheritance and the tragedy of the Boulevard Suchet, all that could throw light upon the plot hatched against Marie Fauville, all that could explain the undoing of Sauverand and Florence—all this lay in Sauverand's story. Don Luis had only to understand, and the truth would appear like the moral which we draw from some obscure fable.

Don Luis did not once deviate from his method. If any objection suggested itself to his mind, he at once replied:

"Very well. It may be that I am wrong and that Sauverand's story will not enlighten me on any point capable of guiding me. It may be that the truth lies outside it. But am I in a position to get at the truth in any other way? All that I possess as an instrument of research, without attaching undue importance to certain gleams of light which the regular appearance of the mysterious letters has shed upon the case, all that I possess is Gaston Sauverand's story. Must I not make use of it?"

And, once again, as when one follows a path by another person's tracks, he began to live through the adventure which Sauverand had been through. He compared it with the picture of it which he had imagined until then. The two were in opposition; but could not the very clash of their opposition be made to produce a spark of light?

"Here is what he said," he thought, "and there is what I believed. What does the difference mean? Here is the thing that was, and there is the thing that appeared to be. Why did the criminal wish the thing that was to appear under that particular aspect? To remove all suspicion from him? But, in that case, was it necessary that suspicion should fall precisely on those on whom it did?"

The questions came crowding one upon the other. He sometimes answered them at random, mentioning names and uttering words in succession, as though the name mentioned might be just that of the criminal, and the words uttered those which contained the unseen reality.

Then at once he would take up the story again, as schoolboys do when parsing and analysing a passage, in which each expression is carefully sifted, each period discussed, each sentence reduced to its essential value.

***

Hours and hours passed. Suddenly, in the middle of the night, he gave a start. He took out his watch. By the light of his electric lamp he saw that it was seventeen minutes to twelve.

"So at seventeen minutes to twelve at night," he said, "I fathomed the mystery."

He tried to control his emotion, but it was too great; and his nerves were so immensely staggered by the trial that he began to shed tears. He had caught sight of the appalling truth, all of a sudden, as when at night one half sees a landscape under a lightning-flash.

There is nothing more unnerving than this sudden illumination when we have been groping and struggling in the dark. Already exhausted by his physical efforts and by the want of food, from which he was beginning to suffer, he felt the shock so intensely that, without caring to think a moment longer, he managed to go to sleep, or, rather, to sink into sleep, as one sinks into the healing waters of a bath.

When he woke, in the small hours, alert and well despite the discomfort of his couch, he shuddered on thinking of the theory which he had accepted; and his first instinct was to doubt it. He had, so to speak, no time.

All the proofs came rushing to his mind of their own accord and at once transformed the theory into one of those certainties which it would be madness to deny. It was that and nothing else. As he had foreseen, the truth lay recorded in Sauverand's story. And he had not been mistaken, either, in saying to Mazeroux that the manner in which the mysterious letters appeared had put him on the track of the truth.

And the truth was terrible. He felt, at the thought of it, the same fears that had maddened Inspector Vérot when, already tortured by the poison, he stammered:

"Oh, I don't like this, I don't like the look of this!... The whole thing has been planned in such an infernal manner!"

Infernal was the word! And Don Luis remained stupefied at the revelation of a crime which looked as if no human brain could have conceived it.

For two hours more he devoted all his mental powers to examining the situation from every point of view. He was not much disturbed about the result, because, being now in possession of the terrible secret, he had nothing more to do but make his escape and go that evening to the meeting on the Boulevard Suchet, where he would show them all how the murder was committed.

But when, wishing to try his chance of escaping, he went up through the underground passage and climbed to the top of the upper ladder—that is to say, to the level of the boudoir—he heard through the trapdoor the voices of men in the room.

"By Jove!" he said to himself. "The thing is not so simple as I thought! In order to escape the minions of the law I must first leave my prison; and here is at least one of the exits blocked. Let's look at the other."

He went down to Florence's apartments and worked the mechanism, which consisted of a counterweight. The panel of the cupboard moved in the groove.

Driven by horror and hoping to find some provisions which enable him to withstand a siege without being reduced to famine, he was about to pass through the alcove, behind the curtains, when he was stopped short by a sound of footsteps. Someone had entered the room.

"Well, Mazeroux, have you spent the night here? Nothing new!"

Don Luis recognized the Prefect of Police by his voice; and the question put by the Prefect told him, first, that Mazeroux had been released from the dark closet where he had bound him up, and, secondly, that the sergeant was in the next room. Fortunately, the sliding panel had worked without the least sound; and Don Luis was able to overhear the conversation between the two men.

"No, nothing new, Monsieur le Préfet," replied Mazeroux.

"That's funny. The confounded fellow must be somewhere. Or can he have got away over the roof?"

"Impossible, Monsieur le Préfet," said a third voice, which Don Luis recognized as that of Weber, the deputy chief detective. "Impossible. We made certain yesterday, that unless he has wings—"

"Then what do you think, Weber?"

"I think, Monsieur le Préfet, that he is concealed in the house. This is an old house and probably contains some safe hidingplace—"

"Of course, of course," said M. Desmalions, whom Don Luis, peeping through the curtains, saw walking to and fro in front of the alcove. "You're right; and we shall catch him in his burrow. Only, is it really necessary?"

"Monsieur le Préfet!"

"Well, you know my opinion on the subject, which is also the Prime Minister's opinion. Unearthing Lupin would be a blunder which we should end by regretting. After all, he's become an honest man, you know; he's useful to us and he does no harm—"

"No harm, Monsieur le Préfet? Do you think so?" said Weber stiffly.

M. Desmalions burst out laughing.

"Oh, of course, yesterday's trick, the telephone trick! You must admit it was funny. The Premier had to hold his sides when I told him of it."

"Upon my word, I see nothing to laugh at!"

"No, but, all the same, the rascal is never at a loss. Funny or not, the trick was extraordinarily daring. To cut the telephone wire before your eyes and then blockade you behind that iron curtain! By the way, Mazeroux, you must get the telephone repaired this morning, so as to keep in touch with the office. Have you begun your search in these two rooms?"

"As you ordered, Monsieur le Préfet. The deputy chief and I have been hunting round for the last hour."

"Yes," said M. Desmalions, "that Florence Levasseur strikes me as a troublesome creature. She is certainly an accomplice. But what were her relations with Sauverand and what was her connection with Don Luis Perenna? That's what I should like to know. Have you discovered nothing in her papers?"

"No, Monsieur le Préfet," said Mazeroux. "Nothing but bills and tradesmen's letters."

"And you, Weber?"

"I've found something very interesting, Monsieur le Préfet."

Weber spoke in a triumphant tone, and, in answer to M. Desmalions's question, went on:

"This is a volume of Shakespeare, Monsieur le Préfet, Volume VIII. You will see that, contrary to the other volumes, the inside is empty and the binding forms a secret receptacle for hiding documents."

"Yes. What sort of documents?"

"Here they are: sheets of paper, blank sheets, all but three. One of them gives a list of the dates on which the mysterious letters were to appear."

"Oho!" said M. Desmalions. "That's a crushing piece of evidence against Florence Levasseur. And also it tells us where Don Luis got his list from."

Perenna listened with surprise: he had utterly forgotten this particular; and Gaston Sauverand had made no reference to it in his narrative. And yet it was a strange and serious detail. From whom had Florence received that list of dates?

"And what's on the other two sheets?" asked M. Desmalions.

Don Luis pricked up his ears. Those two other sheets had escaped his attention on the day of his interview with Florence in this room.

"Here is one of them," said Weber.

M. Desmalions took the paper and read:

"Bear in mind that the explosion is independent of the letters, and that it will take place at three o'clock in the morning."

"Yes," he said, "the famous explosion which Don Luis foretold and which is to accompany the fifth letter, as announced on the list of dates. Tush! We have plenty of time, as there have been only three letters and the fourth is due tonight. Besides, blowing up that house on the Boulevard Suchet would be no easy job, by Jove! Is that all?"

"Monsieur le Préfet," said Weber, producing the third sheet, "would you mind looking at these lines drawn in pencil and enclosed in a large square containing some other smaller squares and rectangles of all sizes? Wouldn't you say that it was the plan of a house?"

"Yes, I should."

"It is the plan of the house in which we are," declared Weber solemnly. "Here you see the front courtyard, the main building, the porter's lodge, and, over there, Mlle. Levasseur's lodge. From this lodge, a dotted line, in red pencil, starts zigzagging toward the main building. The commencement of this line is marked by a little red cross which stands for the room in which we are, or, to be more correct, the alcove. You will see here something like the design of a chimney, or, rather, a cupboard—a cupboard recessed behind the bed and probably hidden by the curtains."

"But, in that case, Weber," said M. Desmalions, "this dotted line must represent a passage leading from this lodge to the main building. Look, there is also a little red cross at the other end of the line."

"Yes, Monsieur le Préfet, there is another cross. We shall discover later for certain what position it marks. But, meanwhile, and acting on a mere guess, I have posted some men in a small room on the second floor where the last secret meeting between Don Luis, Florence Levasseur, and Gaston Sauverand was held yesterday. And, meanwhile, at any rate, we hold one end of the line and, through that very fact, we know Don Luis Perenna's retreat."

There was a pause, after which the deputy chief resumed in a more and more solemn voice:

"Monsieur le Préfet, yesterday I suffered a cruel outrage at the hands of that man. It was witnessed by our subordinates. The servants must be aware of it. The public will know of it before long. This man has brought about the escape of Florence Levasseur. He tried to bring about the escape of Gaston Sauverand. He is a ruffian of the most dangerous type. Monsieur le Préfet, I am sure that you will not refuse me leave to dig him out of his hole. Otherwise—otherwise, Monsieur le Préfet, I shall feel obliged to hand in my resignation."

"With good reasons to back it up!" said the Prefect, laughing. "There's no doubt about it; you can't stomach the trick of the iron curtain. Well, go ahead! It's Don Luis's own lookout; he's brought it on himself. Mazeroux, ring me up at the office as soon as the telephone is put right. And both of you meet me at the Fauvilles' house this evening. Don't forget it's the night for the fourth letter."

"There won't be any fourth letter, Monsieur le Préfet," said Weber.

"Why not?"

"Because between this and then Don Luis will be under lock and key."

"Oh, so you accuse Don Luis also of—"

Don Luis did not wait to hear more. He softly retreated to the cupboard, took hold of the panel and pushed it back without a sound.

So his hiding-place was known!

"By Jingo," he growled, "this is a bit awkward! I'm in a nice plight!"

He had run halfway along the underground passage, with the intention of reaching the other exit. But he stopped.

"It's not worthwhile, as the exit's watched. Well, let's see; am I to let myself be collared? Wait a bit, let's see—"

Already there came from the alcove below a noise of blows striking on the panel, the hollow sound of which had probably attracted the deputy chief's attention. And, as Weber was not compelled to take the same precautions as Don Luis, and seemed to be breaking down the panel without delaying to look for the mechanism, the danger was close at hand.

"Oh, hang it all!" muttered Don Luis. "This is too silly. What shall I do? Have a dash at them? Ah, if I had all my strength!"

But he was exhausted by want of food. His legs shook beneath him and his brain seemed to lack its usual clearness.

The increasing violence of the blows in the alcove drove him, in spite of all, toward the upper exit; and, as he climbed the ladder, he moved his electric lantern over the stones of the wall and the wood of the trapdoor. He even tried to lift the door with his shoulder. But he again heard a sound of footsteps above his head. The men were still there.

Then, consumed with fury and helpless, he awaited the deputy's coming.

A crash came from below; its echo spread through the tunnel, followed by a tumult of voices.

"That's it," he said to himself. "The handcuffs, the lockup, the cell! Good Lord, what luck—and what nonsense! And Marie Fauville, who's sure to do away with herself. And Florence—Florence—"

Before extinguishing his lantern, he cast its light around him for the last time.

At a couple of yards' distance from the ladder, about three quarters of the way up and set a little way back, there was a big stone missing from the inner wall, leaving a space just large enough to crouch in.

Although the recess did not form much of a hiding-place, it was just possible that they might omit to inspect it. Besides, Don Luis had no choice. At all events, after putting out the light, he leaned toward the edge of the hole, reached it, and managed to scramble in by bending himself in two.

Weber, Mazeroux, and their men were coming along. Don Luis propped himself against the back of his hiding-hole to avoid as far as possible the glare of the lanterns, of which he was beginning to see the gleams. And an amazing thing happened: the stone against which he was pushing toppled over slowly, as though moving on a pivot, and he fell backward into a second cavity situated behind it.

He quickly drew his legs after him and the stone swung back as slowly as before, not, however, without sending down a quantity of small stones, crumbling from the wall and half covering his legs.

"Well, well!" he chuckled. "Can Providence be siding with virtue and righteousness?"

He heard Mazeroux's voice saying:

"Nobody! And here's the end of the passage. Unless he ran away as we came—look, through the trapdoor at the top of this ladder."

Weber replied:

"Considering the slope by which we've come, it's certain that the trapdoor is on a level with the second floor. Well, the other little cross ought to mark the boudoir on the second floor, next to Don Luis's bedroom. That's what I supposed, and why I posted three of our men there. If he's tried to get out on that side, he's caught."

"We've only got to knock," said Mazeroux. "Our men will find the trapdoor and let us out. If not, we will break it down."

More blows echoed down the passage. Fifteen or twenty minutes after, the trapdoor gave way, and other voices now mingled with Weber's and Mazeroux's.

During this time, Don Luis examined his domain and perceived how extremely small it was. The most that he could do was to sit in it. It was a gallery, or, rather, a sort of gut, a yard and a half long and ending in an orifice, narrower still, heaped up with bricks. The walls, besides, were formed of bricks, some of which were lacking; and the building-stones which these should have kept in place crumbled at the least touch. The ground was strewn with them.

"By Jove!" thought Lupin. "I must not wriggle about too much, or I shall risk being buried alive! A pleasant prospect!"

Not only this, but the fear of making a noise kept him motionless. As a matter of fact, he was close to two rooms occupied by the detectives, first the boudoir and then the study, for the boudoir, as he knew, was over that part of his study which included the telephone box.

The thought of this suggested another. On reflection, remembering that he used sometimes to wonder how Count Malonyi's ancestress had managed to keep alive behind the curtain on the days when she had to hide there, he realized that there must have been a communication between the secret passage and what was now the telephone box, a communication too narrow to admit a person's body, but serving as a ventilating shaft.

As a precaution, in case the secret passage was discovered, a stone concealed the upper aperture of this shaft. Count Malonyi must have closed up the lower end when he restored the wainscoting of the study.

So there he was, imprisoned in the thickness of the walls, with no very definite intention beyond that of escaping from the clutches of the police. More hours passed.

Gradually, tortured with hunger and thirst, he fell into a heavy sleep, disturbed by painful nightmares which he would have given much to be able to throw off. But he slept too deeply to recover consciousness until eight o'clock in the evening.

When he woke up, feeling very tired, he saw his position in an unexpectedly hideous light and, at the same time, so accurately that, yielding to a sudden change of opinion marked by no little fear, he resolved to leave his hiding-place and give himself up. Anything was better than the torture which he was enduring and the dangers to which longer waiting exposed him.

But, on turning round to reach the entrance to his hole, he perceived first that the stone did not swing over when merely pushed, and, next, after several attempts, that he could not manage to find the mechanism which no doubt worked the stone. He persisted. His exertions were all in vain. The stone did not budge. Only, at each exertion, a few bits of stone came crumbling from the upper part of the wall and still further narrowed the space in which he was able to move.

It cost him a considerable effort to master his excitement and to say, jokingly:

"That's capital! I shall be reduced now to calling for help. I, Arsène Lupin! Yes, to call in the help of those gentlemen of the police. Otherwise, the odds on my being buried alive will increase every minute. They're ten to one as it is!"

He clenched his fists.

"Hang it! I'll get out of this scrape by myself! Call for help? Not if I know it!"

He summoned up all his energies to think, but his jaded brain gave him none but confused and disconnected ideas. He was haunted by Florence's image and by Marie Fauville's as well.

"It's tonight that I'm to save them," he said to himself. "And I certainly will save them, as they are not guilty and as I know the real criminal. But how shall I set about it to succeed?"

He thought of the Prefect of Police, of the meeting that was to take place at Fauville's house on the Boulevard Suchet. The meeting had begun. The police were watching the house. And this reminded him of the sheet of paper found by Weber in the eighth volume of Shakespeare's plays, and of the sentence written on it, which the Prefect had read out:

"Bear in mind that the explosion is independent of the letters, and that it will take place at three o'clock in the morning."

"Yes," thought Don Luis, accepting M. Desmalions's reasoning, "yes, in ten days' time. As there have been only three letters, the fourth will appear tonight; and the explosion will not take place until the fifth letter appears — that is in ten days from now."

He repeated:

"In ten days — with the fifth letter — in ten days —"

And suddenly he gave a start of fright. A horrible vision had flashed across his mind, a vision only too real. The explosion was to occur that very night! And all at once, knowing that he knew the truth, all at once, in a revival of his usual clear-sightedness, he accepted the theory as certain.

No doubt only three letters had appeared out of the mysterious darkness, but four letters ought to have appeared, because one of them had appeared not on the date fixed, but ten days later; and this for a reason which Don Luis knew. Besides, it was not a question of all this. It was not a question of seeking the truth amid this confusion of dates and letters, amid this intricate tangle in which no one could lay claim to any certainty,

No; one thing alone stood out above the situation: the sentence, "Bear in mind that the explosion is independent of the letters." And, as the explosion was put down for the night of the twenty-fifth of May, it would occur that very night, at three o'clock in the morning!

"Help! Help!" he cried.

This time he did not hesitate. So far, he had had the courage to remain huddled in his prison and to wait for the miracle that might come to his assistance; but he preferred to face every danger and undergo every penalty rather than abandon the Prefect of Police, Weber, Mazeroux, and their companions to the death that threatened them.

"Help! Help!"

Fauville's house would be blown up in three or four hours. That he knew with the greatest certainty. Just as punctually as the mysterious letters had reached their destination in spite of all the obstacles in the way, so the explosion would occur at the hour named. The infernal artificer of the accursed work had wished it so. At three o'clock in the morning there would be nothing left of the Fauvilles' house.

"Help! Help!"

He recovered enough strength to raise desperate shouts and to make his voice carry beyond the stones and beyond the wainscoting.

Then, when there seemed to be no answer to his call, he stopped and listened for a long time. There was not a sound. The silence was absolute.

Thereupon a terrible anguish covered him with a cold sweat. Supposing the detectives had ceased to watch the upper floors and confined themselves to spending the night in the rooms on the ground floor?

He madly took a brick and struck it repeatedly against the stone that closed the entrance, hoping that the noise would spread through the house. But an avalanche of small stones, loosened by the blows, at once fell upon him, knocking him down again and fixing him where he lay.

"Help! Help!"

More silence — a great, ruthless silence.

"Help! Help!"

He felt that his shouts did not penetrate the walls that stifled him. Besides, his voice was growing fainter and fainter, producing a hoarse groan that died away in his strained throat.

He ceased his cries and again listened, with all his anxious attention, to the great silence that surrounded as with layers of lead the stone coffin in which he lay imprisoned. Still nothing, not a sound. No one would come, no one could come to his assistance.

He continued to be haunted by Florence's name and image. And he thought also of Marie Fauville, whom he had promised to save. But Marie would die of starvation. And, like her, like Gaston Sauverand and so many others, he in his turn was the victim of this monstrous horror.

An incident occurred to increase his dismay. All of a sudden his electric lantern, which he had left alight to dispel the terrors of the darkness, went out. It was eleven o'clock at night.

He was overcome with a fit of giddiness. He could hardly breathe in the close and vitiated air. His brain suffered, as it were, a physical and exceedingly painful ailment, from the repetition of images that seemed to encrust themselves there; and it was always Florence's beautiful features or Marie's livid face. And, in his distraught brain, while Marie lay dying, he heard the explosion at the Fauvilles' house and saw the Prefect of Police and Mazeroux lying hideously mutilated, dead.

A numbness crept over him. He fell into a sort of swoon, in which he continued to stammer confused syllables:

"Florence—Marie—Marie—"

13

THE EXPLOSION

The fourth mysterious letter! The fourth of those letters "posted by the devil and delivered by the devil," as one of the newspapers expressed it!

We all of us remember the really extraordinary agitation of the public as the night of the twenty-fifth of May drew near. And fresh news increased this interest to a yet higher degree.

People heard in quick succession of the arrest of Sauverand, the flight of his accomplice, Florence Levasseur, Don Luis Perenna's secretary, and the inexplicable disappearance of Perenna himself, whom they insisted, for the best of reasons, on identifying with Arsène Lupin.

The police, assured from this moment of victory and having nearly all the actors in the tragedy in their power, had gradually given way to indiscretion; and, thanks to the particulars revealed to this or that journalist, the public knew of Don Luis's change of attitude, suspected his passion for Florence Levasseur and the real cause of his right-about-face, and thrilled with excitement as they saw that astonishing figure enter upon a fresh struggle.

What was he going to do? If he wanted to save the woman he loved from prosecution and to release Marie and Sauverand from prison, he would have to intervene sometime that night, to take part, somehow or other, in the event at hand, and to prove the innocence of the three accomplices, either by arresting the invisible bearer of the fourth letter or by suggesting some plausible explanation. In short, he would have to be there; and that was interesting indeed!

And then the news of Marie Fauville was not good. With unwavering obstinacy she persisted in her suicidal plans. She had to be artificially fed; and the doctors in the infirmary at Saint-Lazare did not conceal their anxiety. Would Don Luis Perenna arrive in time?

Lastly, there was that one other thing, the threat of an explosion which was to blow up Hippolyte Fauville's house ten days after the delivery of the fourth letter, a really impressive threat when it was remembered that the enemy had never announced anything that did not take place at the stated hour. And, although it was still ten days—at least, so people thought—from the date fixed for the catastrophe, the threat made the whole business look more and more sinister.

That evening, therefore, a great crowd made its way, through La Muette and Auteuil, to the Boulevard Suchet, a crowd coming not only from Paris, but also from the suburbs and the provinces. The spectacle was exciting, and people wanted to see.

They saw only from a distance, for the police had barred the approaches a hundred yards from either side of the house and were driving into the ditches of the fortifications all those who managed to climb the opposite slope.

The sky was stormy, with heavy clouds revealed at intervals by the light of a silver moon. There were lightning-flashes and peals of distant thunder. Men sang. Street-boys imitated the noises of animals. People formed themselves into groups on the benches and pavements and ate and drank while discussing the matter.

A part of the night was spent in this way and nothing happened to reward the patience of the crowd, who began to wonder, somewhat wearily, if they would not do better to go home, seeing that Sauverand was in prison and that there was every chance that the fourth letter would not appear in the same mysterious way as the others.

And yet they did not go: Don Luis Perenna was due to come!

From ten o'clock in the evening the Prefect of Police and his secretary general, the chief detective and Weber, his deputy, Sergeant Mazeroux, and two detectives were gathered in the large room in which Fauville had been murdered. Fifteen more detectives occupied the remaining rooms, while some twenty others watched the roofs, the outside of the house, and the garden.

Once again a thorough search had been made during the afternoon, with no better results than before. But it was decided that all the men should keep awake. If the letter was delivered anywhere in the big room, they wanted to know and they meant to know who brought it. The police do not recognize miracles.

At twelve o'clock M. Desmalions had coffee served to his subordinates. He himself took two cups and never ceased walking from one end to the other of the room, or climbing the staircase that led to the attic, or going through the passage and hall. Preferring that the watch should be maintained under the most favourable conditions, he left all the doors opened and all the electric lights on.

Mazeroux objected:

"It has to be dark for the letter to come. You will remember, Monsieur le Préfet, that the other experiment was tried before and the letter was not delivered."

"We will try it again," replied M. Desmalions, who, in spite of everything, was really afraid of Don Luis's interference, and increased his measures to make it impossible.

Meanwhile, as the night wore on, the minds of all those present became impatient. Prepared for the angry struggle as they were, they longed for the opportunity to show their strength. They made desperate use of their ears and eyes.

At one o'clock there was an alarm that showed the pitch which the nervous tension had reached. A shot was fired on the first floor, followed by shouts. On inquiry, it was found that two detectives, meeting in the course of a round, had not recognized each other, and one of them had discharged his revolver in the air to inform his comrades.

In the meantime the crowd outside had diminished, as M. Desmalions perceived on opening the garden gate. The orders had been relaxed and sightseers were allowed to come nearer, though they were still kept at a distance from the pavement.

Mazeroux said:

"It is a good thing that the explosion is due in ten days' time and not tonight, Monsieur le Préfet; otherwise, all those good people would be in danger as well as ourselves."

"There will be no explosion in ten days' time, any more than there will be a letter tonight," said M. Desmalions, shrugging his shoulders. And he added, "Besides, on that day, the orders will be strict."

It was now ten minutes past two.

At twenty-five minutes past, as the Prefect was lighting a cigar, the chief detective ventured to joke:

"That's something you will have to do without, next time, Monsieur le Préfet. It would be too risky."

"Next time," said M. Desmalions, "I shall not waste time in keeping watch. For I really begin to think that all this business with the letters is over."

"You can never tell," suggested Mazeroux.

A few minutes more passed. M. Desmalions had sat down. The others also were seated. No one spoke.

And suddenly they all sprang up, with one movement, and the same expression of surprise.

A bell had rung.

They at once heard where the sound came from.

"The telephone," M. Desmalions muttered.

He took down the receiver.

"Hullo! Who are you?"

A voice answered, but so distant and so faint that he could only catch an incoherent noise and exclaimed:

"Speak louder! What is it? Who are you?"

The voice spluttered out a few syllables that seemed to astound him.

"Hullo!" he said. "I don't understand. Please repeat what you said. Who is it speaking?"

"Don Luis Perenna," was the answer, more distinctly this time.

The Prefect made as though to hang up the receiver; and he growled:

"It's a hoax. Some rotter amusing himself at our expense." Nevertheless, in spite of himself, he went on in a gruff voice: "Look here, what is it? You say you're Don Luis Perenna?"

"Yes."

"What do you want?"

"What's the time?"

"What's the time!"

The Prefect made an angry gesture, not so much because of the ridiculous question as because he had really recognized Don Luis's voice beyond mistake.

"Well?" he said, controlling himself. "What's all this about? Where are you?"

"At my house, above the iron curtain, in the ceiling of my study."

"In the ceiling!" repeated the Prefect, not knowing what to think.

"Yes; and more or less done for, I confess."

"We'll send and help you out," said M. Desmalions, who was beginning to enjoy himself.

"Later on, Monsieur le Préfet. First answer me. Quickly! If not, I don't know that I shall have the strength. What's the time?"

"Oh, look here!"

"I beg of you—"

"It's twenty minutes to three."

"Twenty minutes to three!"

It was as though Don Luis found renewed strength in a sudden fit of fear. His weak voice recovered its emphasis, and, by turns imperious, despairing, and beseeching, full of a conviction which he did his utmost to impart to M. Desmalions, he said:

"Go away, Monsieur le Préfet! Go, all of you; leave the house. The house will be blown up at three o'clock. Yes, yes, I swear it will. Ten days after the fourth letter means now, because there has been a ten days' delay in the delivery of the letters. It means now, at three o'clock in the morning. Remember what was written on the sheet which Deputy Chief Weber handed you this morning: 'The explosion is independent of the letters. It will take place at three o'clock in the morning.' At three o'clock in the morning, today, Monsieur le Préfet!" The voice faltered and then continued:

"Go away, please. Let no one remain in the house. You must believe me. I know everything about the business. And nothing can prevent the threat from being executed. Go, go, go! This is horrible; I feel that you do not believe me—and I have no strength left. Go away, every one of you!"

He said a few more words which M. Desmalions could not make out. Then the voice ceased; and, though the Prefect still heard cries, it seemed to him that those cries were distant, as though the instrument were no longer within the reach of the mouth that uttered them.

He hung up the receiver.

"Gentlemen," he said, with a smile, "it is seventeen to three. In seventeen minutes we shall all be blown up together. At least, that is what our good friend Don Luis Perenna declares."

In spite of the jokes with which this threat was met, there was a general feeling of uneasiness. Weber asked:

"Was it really Don Luis, Monsieur le Préfet?"

"Don Luis in person. He has gone to earth in some hiding-hole in his house, above the study; and his fatigue and privations seem to have unsettled him a little. Mazeroux, go and ferret him out—unless this is just some fresh trick on his part. You have your warrant."

Sergeant Mazeroux went up to M. Desmalions. His face was pallid.

"Monsieur le Préfet, did *he* tell you that we were going to be blown up?"

"He did. He relies on the note which M. Weber found in a volume of Shakespeare. The explosion is to take place tonight."

"At three o'clock in the morning?"

"At three o'clock in the morning—that is to say, in less than a quarter of an hour."

"And do you propose to remain, Monsieur le Préfet?"

"What next, Sergeant? Do you imagine that we are going to obey that gentleman's fancies?"

Mazeroux staggered, hesitated, and then, despite all his natural deference, unable to contain himself, exclaimed:

"Monsieur le Préfet, it's not a fancy. I have worked with Don Luis. I know the man. If he tells you that something is going to happen, it's because he has his reasons."

"Absurd reasons."

"No, no. Monsieur le Préfet," Mazeroux pleaded, growing more and more excited. "I swear that you must listen to him. The house will be blown up—he said so—at three o'clock. We have a few minutes left. Let us go. I entreat you, Monsieur le Préfet."

"In other words, you want us to run away."

"But it's not running away, Monsieur le Préfet. It's a simple precaution. After all, we can't risk—You, yourself, Monsieur le Préfet—"

"That will do."

"But, Monsieur le Préfet, as Don Luis said—"

"That will do, I say!" repeated the Prefect harshly. "If you're afraid, you can take advantage of the order which I gave you and go off after Don Luis."

Mazeroux clicked his heels together and, old soldier that he was, saluted:

"I shall stay here, Monsieur le Préfet."

And he turned and went back to his place at a distance.

Silence followed. M. Desmalions began to walk up and down the room, with his hands behind his back. Then, addressing the chief detective and the secretary general:

"You are of my opinion, I hope?" he said.

"Why, yes, Monsieur le Préfet."

"Well, of course! To begin with, that supposition is based on nothing serious. And, besides, we are guarded, aren't we? Bombs don't come tumbling on one's head like that. It takes someone to throw them. Well, how are they to come? By what way?"

"Same way as the letters," the secretary general ventured to suggest.

"What's that? Then you admit—?"

The secretary general did not reply and M. Desmalions did not complete his sentence. He himself, like the others, experienced that same feeling of uneasiness which gradually, as the seconds sped past, was becoming almost intolerably painful.

Three o'clock in the morning!... The words kept on recurring to his mind. Twice he looked at his watch. There was twelve minutes left. There was ten minutes. Was the house really going to be blown up, by the mere effect of an infernal and all-powerful will?

"It's senseless, absolutely senseless!" he cried, stamping his foot.

But, on looking at his companions, he was amazed to see how drawn their faces were; and he felt his courage sink in a strange way. He was certainly not afraid; and the others were no more afraid than he. But all of them, from the chiefs to the simple detectives, were under the influence of that Don Luis Perenna whom they had seen accomplishing such extraordinary feats, and who had shown such wonderful ability throughout this mysterious adventure.

Consciously or unconsciously, whether they wished it or no, they looked upon him as an exceptional being endowed with special faculties, a being of whom they could not think without conjuring up the image of the amazing Arsène Lupin, with his legend of daring, genius, and superhuman insight.

And Lupin was telling them to fly. Pursued and hunted as he was, he voluntarily gave himself up to warn them of their danger. And the danger was immediate. Seven minutes more, six minutes more — and the house would be blown up.

With great simplicity, Mazeroux went on his knees, made the sign of the cross, and said his prayers in a low voice. The action was so impressive that the secretary general and the chief detective made a movement as though to go toward the Prefect of Police.

M. Desmalions turned away his head and continued his walk up and down the room. But his anguish increased; and the words which he had heard over the telephone rang in his ears; and all Perenna's authority, his ardent entreaties, his frenzied conviction — all this upset him. He had seen Perenna at work. He felt it borne in upon him that he had no right, in the present circumstances, to neglect the man's warning.

"Let's go," he said.

The words were spoken in the calmest manner; and it really seemed as if those who heard them regarded them merely as the sensible conclusion of a very ordinary state of affairs. They

THE EXPLOSION

went away without hurry or disorder, not as fugitives, but as men deliberately obeying the dictates of prudence.

They stood back at the door to let the Prefect go first.

"No," he said, "go on; I'll follow you."

He was the last out, leaving the electric light full on.

In the hall he asked the chief detective to blow his whistle. When all the plain-clothesmen had assembled, he sent them out of the house together with the porter, and shut the door behind him. Then, calling the detectives who were watching the boulevard, he said:

"Let everybody stand a good distance away; push the crowd as far back as you can; and be quick about it. We shall enter the house again in half an hour."

"And you, Monsieur le Préfet?" whispered Mazeroux, "You won't remain here, I hope?"

"No, that I shan't!" he said, laughing. "If I take our friend Perenna's advice at all, I may as well take it thoroughly!"

"There is only two minutes left."

"Our friend Perenna spoke of three o'clock, not of two minutes to three. So—"

He crossed the boulevard, accompanied by his secretary general, the chief detective, and Mazeroux, and clambered up the slope of the fortifications opposite the house.

"Perhaps we ought to stoop down," suggested Mazeroux.

"Let's stoop, by all means," said the Prefect, still in a good humour. "But, honestly, if there's no explosion, I shall send a bullet through my head. I could not go on living after making myself look so ridiculous."

"There will be an explosion, Monsieur le Préfet," declared Mazeroux.

"What confidence you must have in our friend Don Luis!"

"You have just the same confidence, Monsieur le Préfet."

They were silent, irritated by the wait, and struggling with the absurd anxiety that oppressed them. They counted the seconds singly, by the beating of their hearts. It was interminable.

Three o'clock sounded from somewhere.

"You see," grinned M. Desmalions, in an altered voice, "you see! There's nothing, thank goodness!"

And he growled:

"It's idiotic, perfectly idiotic! How could anyone imagine such nonsense!"

Another clock struck, farther away. Then the hour also rang from the roof of a neighbouring building.

Before the third stroke had sounded they heard a kind of cracking, and, the next moment, came the terrible blast, complete, but so brief that they had only, so to speak, a vision of an immense sheaf of flames and smoke shooting forth enormous stones and pieces of wall, something like the grand finale of a fireworks display. And it was all over. The volcano had erupted.

"Look sharp!" shouted the Prefect of Police, darting forward. "Telephone for the engines, quick, in case of fire!"

He caught Mazeroux by the arm:

"Run to my motor; you'll see her a hundred yards down the boulevard. Tell the man to drive you to Don Luis, and, if you find him, release him and bring him here."

"Under arrest, Monsieur le Préfet?"

"Under arrest? You're mad!"

"But, if the deputy chief—"

"The deputy chief will keep his mouth shut. I'll see to that. Be off!"

Mazeroux fulfilled his mission, not with greater speed than if he had been sent to arrest Don Luis, for Mazeroux was a conscientious man, but with extraordinary pleasure. The fight which he had been obliged to wage against the man whom he still called "the chief" had often distressed him to the point of tears. This time he was coming to help him, perhaps to save his life.

That afternoon the deputy chief had ceased his search of the house, by M. Desmalions's orders, as Don Luis's escape seemed certain, and left only three men on duty. Mazeroux found them in a room on the ground floor, where they were sitting up in turns. In reply to his questions, they declared that they had not heard a sound.

He went upstairs alone, so as to have no witnesses to his interview with the governor, passed through the drawing-room and entered the study.

Here he was overcome with anxiety, for, after turning on the light, the first glance revealed nothing to his eyes.

"Chief!" he cried, repeatedly. "Where are you, Chief?"

No answer.

"And yet," thought Mazeroux, "as he telephoned, he can't be far away."

In fact, he saw from where he stood that the receiver was hanging from its cord; and, going on to the telephone box, he stumbled over bits of brick and plaster that strewed the carpet. He then switched on the light in the box as well and saw a hand and arm hanging from the ceiling above him. The ceiling was broken up all around that arm. But the shoulder had not been able to pass through; and Mazeroux could not see the captive's head.

He sprang on to a chair and reached the hand. He felt it and was reassured by the warmth of its touch.

"Is that you, Mazeroux?" asked a voice that seemed to the sergeant to come from very far away.

"Yes, it's I. You're not wounded, are you? Nothing serious?"

"No, only stunned—and a bit faint—from hunger... Listen to me."

"I'm listening."

"Open the second drawer on the left in my writing-desk... You'll find—"

"Yes, Chief?"

"An old stick of chocolate."

"But—"

"Do as I tell you, Alexandre; I'm famished."

Indeed, Don Luis recovered after a moment or two and said, in a gayer voice:

"That's better. I can wait now. Go to the kitchen and fetch me some bread and some water."

"I'll be back at once, Chief."

"Not this way. Come back by Florence Levasseur's room and the secret passage to the ladder which leads to the trapdoor at the top."

And he told him how to make the stone swing out and how to enter the hollow in which he had expected to meet with such a tragic end.

The thing was done in ten minutes. Mazeroux cleared the opening, caught hold of Don Luis by the legs and pulled him out of his hole.

"Oh, dear, oh dear!" he moaned, in a voice full of pity. "What a position, Chief! How did you manage it all? Yes, I see: you must have dug down, where you lay, and gone on digging—for more than a yard! And it took some pluck, I expect, on an empty stomach!"

When Don Luis was seated in his bedroom and had swallowed a few bits of bread and drunk what he wanted, he told his story:

"Yes, it took the devil's own pluck, old man. By Jingo! When a chap's ideas are whirling in his head and he can't use his brain, upon my word, all he asks is to die? And then there was no air, you see. I couldn't breathe. I went on digging, however, as you saw, went on digging while I was half asleep, in a sort of nightmare. Just look: my fingers are in a jelly. But there, I was thinking of that confounded business of the explosion and I wanted to warn you at all costs, and I dug away at my tunnel. What a job! And then, oof! I felt space at last!

"I got my hand through and next my arm. Where was I? Why, over the telephone, of course! I knew that at once by feeling the wall and finding the wires. Then it took me quite half an hour to get hold of the instrument. I couldn't reach it with my arm.

"I managed at last with a piece of string and a slip-knot to fish up the receiver and hold it near my mouth, or, say, at ten inches from my mouth. And then I shouted and roared to make my voice carry; and, all the time, I was in pain. And then, at last, my string broke... And then—and then—I hadn't an ounce of strength left in my body. Besides, you fellows had been warned; and it was for you to get yourselves out of the mess."

He looked at Mazeroux and asked him, as though certain of the reply:

"The explosion took place, didn't it?"

"Yes, Chief."

"At three o'clock exactly?"

"Yes."

"And of course M. Desmalions had the house cleared?"

"Yes."

"At the last minute?"

"At the last minute."

Don Luis laughed and said:

"I knew he would wait about and not give way until the crucial moment. You must have had a bad time of it, my poor Mazeroux, for of course you agreed with me from the start."

He kept on eating while he talked; and each mouthful seemed to bring back a little of his usual animation.

"Funny thing, hunger!" he said. "Makes you feel so light-headed. I must practise getting used to it, however."

"At any rate, Chief, no one would believe that you have been fasting for nearly forty-eight hours."

"Ah, that comes of having a sound constitution, with something to fall back upon! I shall be a different man in half an hour. Just give me time to shave and have a bath."

When he had finished dressing, he sat down to the breakfast of eggs and cold meat which Mazeroux had prepared for him; and then, getting up, said:

"Now, let's be off."

"But there's no hurry, Chief. Why don't you lie down for a few hours? The Prefect can wait."

"You're mad! What about Marie Fauville?"

"Marie Fauville?"

"Why, of course! Do you think I'm going to leave her in prison, or Sauverand, either? There's not a second to lose, old chap."

Mazeroux thought to himself that the chief had not quite recovered his wits yet. What? Release Marie Fauville and Sauverand, one, two, three, just like that! No, no, it was going a bit too far.

However, he took down to the Prefect's car a new Perenna, merry, brisk, and as fresh as though he had just got out of bed.

"Very flattering to my pride," said Don Luis to Mazeroux, "most flattering, that hesitation of the Prefect's, after I had warned him over the telephone, followed by his submission at the decisive moment. What a hold I must have on all those jokers, to make them sit up at a sign from little me! 'Beware, gentlemen!' I telephone to them from the bottomless pit. 'Beware! At three o'clock, a bomb!' 'Nonsense!' say they. 'Not a bit of it!' say I. 'How do you know?' 'Because I do.' 'But what proof have you?' 'What proof? That I say so.' 'Oh, well, of course, if you say so!' And, at five minutes to three, out they march. Ah, if I wasn't built up of modesty—"

They came to the Boulevard Suchet, where the crowd was so dense that they had to alight from the car. Mazeroux passed through the cordon of police protecting the approaches to the house and took Don Luis to the slope across the road.

"Wait for me here, Chief. I'll tell the Prefect of Police."

THE EXPLOSION

On the other side of the boulevard, under the pale morning sky in which a few black clouds still lingered, Don Luis saw the havoc wrought by the explosion. It was apparently not so great as he had expected. Some of the ceilings had fallen in and their rubbish showed through the yawning cavities of the windows; but the house remained standing. Even Fauville's built-out annex had not suffered overmuch, and, strange to say, the electric light, which the Prefect had left burning on his departure, had not gone out. The garden and the road were covered with stacks of furniture, over which a number of soldiers and police kept watch.

"Come with me, Chief," said Mazeroux, as he fetched Don Luis and led him toward the engineer's workroom.

A part of the floor was demolished. The outer walls on the left, near the passage, were cracked; and two workmen were fixing up beams, brought from the nearest timber yard, to support the ceiling. But, on the whole, the explosion had not had the results which the man who prepared it must have anticipated.

M. Desmalions was there, together with all the men who had spent the night in the room and several important persons from the public prosecutor's office. Weber, the deputy chief detective, alone had gone, refusing to meet his enemy.

Don Luis's arrival caused great excitement. The Prefect at once came up to him and said:

"All our thanks, Monsieur. Your insight is above praise. You have saved our lives; and these gentlemen and I wish to tell you so most emphatically. In my case, it is the second time that I have to thank you."

"There is a very simple way of thanking me, Monsieur le Préfet," said Don Luis, "and that is to allow me to carry out my task to the end."

"Your task?"

"Yes, Monsieur le Préfet. My action of last night is only the beginning. The conclusion is the release of Marie Fauville and Gaston Sauverand."

M. Desmalions smiled.

"Oh!"

"Am I asking too much, Monsieur le Préfet?"

"One can always ask, but the request should be reasonable. And the innocence of those people does not depend on me."

"No; but it depends on you, Monsieur le Préfet, to let them know if I prove their innocence to you."

"Yes, I agree, if you prove it beyond dispute."

"Just so."

Don Luis's calm assurance impressed M. Desmalions in spite of everything and even more than on the former occasions; and he suggested:

"The results of the hasty inspection which we have made will perhaps help you. For instance, we are certain that the bomb was placed by the entrance to the passage and probably under the boards of the floor."

"Please do not trouble, Monsieur le Préfet. These are only secondary details. The great thing now is that you should know the whole truth, and that not only through words."

The Prefect had come closer. The magistrate and detectives were standing round Don Luis, watching his lips and movements with feverish impatience. Was it possible that that truth, as yet so remote and vague, in spite of all the importance which they attached to the arrests already effected, was known at last?

It was a solemn moment. Everyone was on tenterhooks. The manner in which Don Luis had foretold the explosion lent the value of an accomplished fact to his predictions; and the men whom he had saved from the terrible catastrophe were almost ready to accept as certainties the most improbable statements which a man of his stamp might make.

"Monsieur le Préfet," he said, "you waited in vain last night for the fourth letter to make its appearance. We shall now be able, by an unexpected miracle of chance, to be present at the delivery of the letter. You will then know that it was the same hand that committed all the crimes—and you will know whose hand that was."

And, turning to Mazeroux:

"Sergeant, will you please make the room as dark as you can? The shutters are gone; but you might draw the curtains across the windows and close the doors. Monsieur le Préfet, is it by accident that the electric light is on?"

"Yes, by accident. We will have it turned out."

"One moment. Have any of you gentlemen a pocket lantern about you? Or, no, it doesn't matter. This will do."

There was a candle in a sconce. He took it and lit it.

Then he switched off the electric light.

There was a half darkness, amid which the flame of the candle flickered in the draught from the windows. Don Luis protected the flame with his hand and moved to the table.

"I do not think that we shall be kept waiting long," he said. "As I foresee it, there will be only a few seconds before the facts speak for themselves and better than I could do."

Those few seconds, during which no one broke the silence, were unforgettable. M. Desmalions has since declared, in an interview in which he ridicules himself very cleverly, that his brain, over-stimulated by the fatigues of the night and by the whole scene before him, imagined the most unlikely events, such as an invasion of the house by armed assailants, or the apparition of ghosts and spirits.

He had the curiosity, however, he said, to watch Don Luis. Sitting on the edge of the table, with his head thrown a little back and his eyes roaming over the ceiling, Don Luis was eating a piece of bread and nibbling at a cake of chocolate. He seemed very hungry, but quite at his ease.

The others maintained that tense attitude which we put on at moments of great physical effort. Their faces were distorted with a sort of grimace. They were haunted by the memory of the explosion as well as obsessed by what was going to happen. The flame of the candle cast shadows on the wall.

More seconds elapsed than Don Luis Perenna had said, thirty or forty seconds, perhaps, that seemed endless. Then Perenna lifted the candle a little and said:

"There you are."

They had all seen what they now saw almost as soon as he spoke. A letter was descending from the ceiling. It spun round slowly, like a leaf falling from a tree without being driven by the wind. It just touched Don Luis and alighted on the floor between two legs of the table.

Picking up the paper and handing it to M. Desmalions, Don Luis said:

"There you are, Monsieur le Préfet. This is the fourth letter, due last night."

14

THE "HATER"

M. Desmalions looked at him without understanding, and looked from him to the ceiling. Perenna said:

"Oh, there's no witchcraft about it; and, though no one has thrown that letter from above, though there is not the smallest hole in the ceiling, the explanation is quite simple!"

"Quite simple, is it?" said M. Desmalions.

"Yes, Monsieur le Préfet. It all looks like an extremely complicated conjuring trick, done almost for fun. Well, I say that it is quite simple—and, at the same time, terribly tragic. Sergeant Mazeroux, would you mind drawing back the curtains and giving us as much light as possible?"

While Mazeroux was executing his orders and M. Desmalions glancing at the fourth letter, the contents of which were unimportant and merely confirmed the previous ones, Don Luis took a pair of steps which the workmen had left in the corner, set it up in the middle of the room and climbed to the top, where, seated astride, he was able to reach the electric chandelier.

It consisted of a broad, circular band in brass, beneath which was a festoon of crystal pendants. Inside were three lamps placed at the corners of a brass triangle concealing the wires.

He uncovered the wires and cut them. Then he began to take the whole fitting to pieces. To hasten matters, he asked for a hammer and broke up the plaster all round the clamps that held the chandelier in position.

"Lend me a hand, please," he said to Mazeroux.

Mazeroux went up the steps; and between them they took hold of the chandelier and let it slide down the uprights. The detectives caught it and placed it on the table with some difficulty, for it was much heavier than it looked.

On inspection, it proved to be surmounted by a cubical metal box, measuring about eight inches square, which box, being fastened inside the ceiling between the iron clamps, had obliged Don Luis to knock away the plaster that concealed it.

"What the devil's this?" exclaimed M. Desmalions.

"Open it for yourself, Monsieur le Préfet: there's a lid to it," said Perenna.

M. Desmalions raised the lid. The box was filled with springs and wheels, a whole complicated and detailed mechanism resembling a piece of clockwork.

"By your leave, Monsieur le Préfet," said Don Luis.

He took out one piece of machinery and discovered another beneath it, joined to the first by the gearing of two wheels; and the second was more like one of those automatic apparatuses which turn out printed slips.

Right at the bottom of the box, just where the box touched the ceiling, was a semi circular groove, and at the edge of it was a letter ready for delivery.

"The last of the five letters," said Don Luis, "doubtless continuing the series of denunciations. You will notice, Monsieur le Préfet, that the chandelier originally had a fourth lamp in the centre. It was obviously removed when the chandelier was altered, so as to make room for the letters to pass."

He continued his detailed explanations:

"So the whole set of letters was placed here, at the bottom. A clever piece of machinery, controlled by clockwork, took them one by one at the appointed time, pushed them to the edge of the groove concealed between the lamps and the pendants, and projected them into space."

None of those standing around Don Luis spoke, and all of them seemed perhaps a little disappointed. The whole thing was certainly very clever; but they had expected something better than a trick of springs and wheels, however surprising.

"Have patience, gentlemen," said Don Luis. "I promised you something ghastly; and you shall have it."

"Well, I agree," said the Prefect of Police, "that this is where the letters started from. But a good many points remain obscure; and, apart from this, there is one fact in particular which it seems impossible to understand. How were the criminals able to adapt the chandelier in this way? And, in a house guarded by the police, in a room watched night and day, how were they able to carry out such a piece of work without being seen or heard?"

"The answer is quite easy, Monsieur le Préfet: the work was done before the house was guarded by the police."

"Before the murder was committed, therefore?"

"Before the murder was committed."

"And what is to prove to me that that is so?"

"You have said so yourself, Monsieur le Préfet: because it could not have been otherwise."

"But do explain yourself, Monsieur!" cried M. Desmalions, with a gesture of irritation. "If you have important things to tell us, why delay?"

"It is better, Monsieur le Préfet, that you should arrive at the truth in the same way as I did. When you know the secret of the letters, the truth is much nearer than you think; and you would have already named the criminal if the horror of his crime had not been so great as to divert all suspicion from him."

M. Desmalions looked at him attentively. He felt the importance of Perenna's every word and he was really anxious.

"Then, according to you," he said, "those letters accusing Madame Fauville and Gaston Sauverand were placed there with the sole object of ruining both of them?"

"Yes, Monsieur le Préfet."

"And, as they were placed there before the crime, the plot must have been schemed before the murder?"

"Yes, Monsieur le Préfet, before the murder. From the moment that we admit the innocence of Mme. Fauville and Gaston Sauverand, we are obliged to conclude that, as everything accuses them, this is due to a series of deliberate acts. Mme. Fauville was out on the night of the murder: a plot! She was unable to say how she spent her time while the murder was being committed: a plot! Her inexplicable drive in the direction of La Muette and her cousin Sauverand's walk in the neighbourhood of the house: plots! The marks left in the apple by those teeth, by Mme. Fauville's own teeth: a plot and the most infernal of all!

"I tell you, everything is plotted beforehand, everything is, so to speak, prepared, measured out, labelled, and numbered. Everything takes place at the appointed time. Nothing is left to chance. It is a work very nicely pieced together, worthy of the most skilful artisan, so solidly constructed that outside happenings have not been able to throw it out of gear; and that the scheme works exactly, precisely, imperturbably, like the clockwork in this box, which is a perfect symbol of the whole business and, at the same time, gives a most accurate explanation of it, because the letters denouncing the murderers were duly posted before the crime and delivered after the crime on the dates and at the hours foreseen."

M. Desmalions remained thinking for a time and then objected:

"Still, in the letters which he wrote, M. Fauville accuses his wife."

"He does."

"We must therefore admit either that he was right in accusing her or that the letters are forged?"

"They are not forged. All the experts have recognized M. Fauville's handwriting."

"Then?"

"Then—"

Don Luis did not finish his sentence; and M. Desmalions felt the breath of the truth fluttering still nearer round him.

The others, one and all as anxious as himself, were silent. He muttered:

"I do not understand—"

"Yes, Monsieur le Préfet, you do. You understand that, if the sending of those letters forms an integrate part of the plot hatched against Mme. Fauville and Gaston Sauverand, it is because their contents were prepared in such a way as to be the undoing of the victims."

"What! What! What are you saying?"

"I am saying what I said before. Once they are innocent, everything that tells against them is part of the plot."

Again there was a long silence. The Prefect of Police did not conceal his agitation. Speaking very slowly, with his eyes fixed on Don Luis's eyes, he said:

"Whoever the culprit may be, I know nothing more terrible than this work of hatred."

"It is an even more improbable work than you can imagine, Monsieur le Préfet," said Perenna, with growing animation, "and it is a hatred of which you, who do not know Sauverand's confession, cannot yet estimate the violence. I understood it completely as I listened to the man; and, since then, all my thoughts have been overpowered by the dominant idea of that hatred. Who could hate like that? To whose loathing had

Marie Fauville and Sauverand been sacrificed? Who was the inconceivable person whose perverted genius had surrounded his two victims with chains so powerfully forged?

"And another idea came to my mind, an earlier idea which had already struck me several times and to which I have already referred in Sergeant Mazeroux's presence: I mean the really mathematical character of the appearance of the letters. I said to myself that such grave documents could not be introduced into the case at fixed dates unless some primary reason demanded that those dates should absolutely be fixed. What reason? If a *human* agency had been at work each time, there would surely have been some irregularity dependent on this especially after the police had become cognizant of the matter and were present at the delivery of the letters.

"Well," Perenna continued, "in spite of every obstacle, the letters continued to come, as though they could not help it. And thus the reason of their coming gradually dawned upon me: they came mechanically, by some invisible process set going once and for all and working with the blind certainty of a physical law. This was a case not of a conscious intelligence and will, but just of material necessity... It was the clash of these two ideas—the idea of the hatred pursuing the innocent and the idea of that machinery serving the schemes of the 'hater'— it was their clash that gave birth to the little spark of light. When brought into contact, the two ideas combined in my mind and suggested the recollection that Hippolyte Fauville was an engineer by profession!"

The others listened to him with a sort of uneasy oppression. What was gradually being revealed of the tragedy, instead of relieving the anxiety, increased it until it became absolutely painful.

M. Desmalions objected:

"Granting that the letters arrived on the dates named, you will nevertheless have noted that the hour varied on each occasion.

"That is to say, it varied according as we watched in the dark or not, and that is just the detail which supplied me with the key to the riddle. If the letters—and this was an indispensable precaution, which we are now able to understand—were delivered only under cover of the darkness, it must be because a contrivance of some kind prevented them from appearing when the electric light was on, and because that contrivance was controlled by a switch inside the room. There is no other explanation possible.

"We have to do with an automatic distributor that delivers the incriminating letters which it contains by clockwork, releasing them only between this hour and that on such and such a night fixed in advance and only at times when the electric light is off. You have the apparatus before you. No doubt the experts will admire its ingenuity and confirm my assertions. But, given the fact that it was found in the ceiling of this room, given the fact that it contained letters written by M. Fauville, am I not entitled to say that it was constructed by M. Fauville, the electrical engineer?"

Once more the name of M. Fauville returned, like an obsession; and each time the name stood more clearly defined. It was first M. Fauville; then M. Fauville, the engineer; then M. Fauville, the electrical engineer. And thus the picture of the "hater," as Don Luis said, appeared in its accurate outlines, giving those men, used though they were to the strangest criminal monstrosities, a thrill of terror. The truth was now no longer prowling around them. They were already fighting with it, as you fight with an adversary whom you do not see but who clutches you by the throat and brings you to the ground.

And the Prefect of Police, summing up all his impressions, said, in a strained voice:

"So M. Fauville wrote those letters in order to ruin his wife and the man who was in love with her?"

"Yes."

"In that case—"

"What?"

"Knowing, at the same time, that he was threatened with death, he wished, if ever the threat was realized, that his death should be laid to the charge of his wife and her friend?"

"Yes."

"And, in order to avenge himself on their love for each other and to gratify his hatred of them both, he wanted the whole set of facts to point to them as guilty of the murder of which he would be the victim?"

"Yes."

"So that—so that M. Fauville, in one part of his accursed work, was—what shall I say?—the accomplice of his own murder. He dreaded death. He struggled against it. But he arranged that his hatred should gain by it. That's it, isn't it? That's how it is?"

"Almost, Monsieur le Préfet. You are following the same stages by which I travelled and, like myself, you are hesitating before the last truth, before the truth which gives the tragedy its sinister character and deprives it of all human proportions."

The Prefect struck the table with his two fists and, in a sudden fit of revolt, cried:

"It's ridiculous! It's a perfectly preposterous theory! M. Fauville threatened with death and contriving his wife's ruin with that Machiavellian perseverance? Absurd! The man who came to my office, the man whom you saw, was thinking of only one thing: how to escape dying! He was obsessed by one dread alone, the dread of death.

"It is not at such moments," the Prefect emphasized, "that a man fits up clockwork and lays traps, especially when those traps cannot take effect unless he dies by foul play. Can you see M. Fauville working at his automatic machine, putting in with his own hands letters which he has taken the pains to write to a friend three months before and intercept, arranging events so that his wife shall appear guilty and saying, 'There! If I die murdered, I'm easy in my mind: the person to be arrested will be Marie!'

"No, you must confess, men don't take these gruesome precautions. Or, if they do—if they do, it means that they're sure of being murdered. It means that they agree to be murdered. It means that they are at one with the murderer, so to speak, and meet him halfway. In short, it means—"

He interrupted himself, as if the sentences which he had spoken had surprised him. And the others seemed equally disconcerted. And all of them unconsciously drew from those sentences the conclusions which they implied, and which they themselves did not yet fully perceive.

Don Luis did not remove his eyes from the Prefect, and awaited the inevitable words.

M. Desmalions muttered:

"Come, come, you are not going to suggest that he had agreed—"

"I suggest nothing, Monsieur le Préfet," said Don Luis. "So far, you have followed the logical and natural trend of your thoughts; and that brings you to your present position."

"Yes, yes, I know, but I am showing you the absurdity of your theory. It can't be correct, and we can't believe in Marie Fauville's innocence unless we are prepared to suppose an unheard-of thing, that M. Fauville took part in his own murder. Why, it's laughable!"

And he gave a laugh; but it was a forced laugh and did not ring true.

"For, after all," he added, "you can't deny that that is where we stand."

"I don't deny it."

"Well?"

"Well, M. Fauville, as you say, took part in his own murder."

This was said in the quietest possible fashion, but with an air of such certainty that no one dreamed of protesting. After the work of deduction and supposition which Don Luis had compelled his hearers to undertake, they found themselves in a corner which it was impossible for them to leave without stumbling against unanswerable objections.

There was no longer any doubt about M. Fauville's share in his own death. But of what did that share consist? What part had he played in the tragedy of hatred and murder? Had he played that part, which ended in the sacrifice of his life, voluntarily or under compulsion? Who, when all was said and done, had served as his accomplice or his executioner?

All these questions came crowding upon the minds of M. Desmalions and the others. They thought of nothing but of how to solve them, and Don Luis could feel certain that his solution was accepted beforehand. From that moment he had but to tell his story of what had happened without fear of contradiction. He did so briefly, after the manner of a succinct report limited to essentials:

"Three months before the crime, M. Fauville wrote a series of letters to one of his friends, M. Langernault, who, as Sergeant Mazeroux will have told you, Monsieur le Préfet, had been dead for several years, a fact of which M. Fauville cannot have been ignorant. These letters were posted, but were intercepted by some means which it is not necessary that we should know for the moment. M. Fauville erased the postmarks and the addresses and inserted the letters in a machine constructed for the purpose, of which he regulated the works so that the first letter should be delivered a fortnight after his death and the others at intervals of ten days.

"At this moment it is certain that his plan was concerted down to the smallest detail. Knowing that Sauverand was in love with his wife, watching Sauverand's movements, he must obviously have noticed that his detested rival used to pass under the windows of the house every Wednesday and that Marie Fauville would go to her window.

"This is a fact of the first importance, one which was exceedingly valuable to me; and it will impress you as being equal to a material proof. Every Wednesday evening, I repeat, Sauverand used to wander round the house. Now note this: first, the crime prepared by M. Fauville was committed on a Wednesday evening; secondly, it was at her husband's express request that Mme. Fauville went out that evening to go to the opera and to Mme. d'Ersinger's."

Don Luis stopped for a few seconds and then continued:

"Consequently, on the morning of that Wednesday, everything was ready, the fatal clock was wound up, the incriminating machinery was working to perfection, and the proofs to come would confirm the immediate proofs which M. Fauville held in reserve. Better still, Monsieur le Préfet, you had received from him a letter in which he told you of the plot hatched against him, and he implored your assistance for the morning of the next day—that is to say, *after his death!*

"Everything, in short, led him to think that things would go according to the 'hater's' wishes, when something occurred that nearly upset his schemes: the appearance of Inspector Vérot, who had been sent by you, Monsieur le Préfet, to collect particulars about the Mornington heirs. What happened between the two men? Probably no one will ever know. Both are dead; and their secret will not come to life again. But we can at least say for certain that Inspector Vérot was here and took away with him the cake of chocolate on which the teeth of the tiger were seen for the first time, and also that Inspector Vérot succeeded, thanks to circumstances with which we are unacquainted, in discovering M. Fauville's projects.

"This we know," explained Don Luis, "because Inspector Vérot said so in his own agonizing words; because it was through him that we learned that the crime was to take place on the following night; and because he had set down his discoveries in a letter which was stolen from him.

"And Fauville knew it also, because, to get rid of the formidable enemy who was thwarting his designs, he poisoned him; because, when the poison was slow in acting, he had the audacity, under a disguise which made him look like Sauverand and which was one day to turn suspicion against Sauverand, he had the audacity and the presence of mind to follow Inspector Vérot to the Café du Pont-Neuf, to purloin the letter of explanation which Inspector Vérot wrote you, to substitute a blank sheet of paper for it, and then to ask a passer-by, who might become a witness against Sauverand, the way to the nearest underground station for Neuilly, where Sauverand lived! There's your man, Monsieur le Préfet."

Don Luis spoke with increasing force, with the ardour that springs from conviction; and his logical and closely argued speech seemed to conjure up the actual truth,

"There's your man, Monsieur le Préfet," he repeated. "There's your scoundrel. And the situation in which he found himself was such, the fear inspired by Inspector Vérot's possible revelations was such, that, before putting into execution the horrible deed which he had planned, he came to the police office to make sure that his victim was no longer alive and had not been able to denounce him.

"You remember the scene, Monsieur le Préfet, the fellow's agitation and fright: 'Tomorrow evening,' he said. Yes, it was for the morrow that he asked for your help, because he knew that everything would be over that same evening and that next day the police would be confronted with a murder, with the two culprits against whom he himself had heaped up the charges, with Marie Fauville, whom he had, so to speak, accused in advance...

"That was why Sergeant Mazeroux's visit and mine to his house, at nine o'clock in the evening, embarrassed him so obviously. Who were those intruders? Would they not succeed in shattering his plan? Reflection reassured him, even as we, by our insistence, compelled him to give way."

"After all, what he did care?" asked Perenna.

"His measures were so well taken that no amount of watching could destroy them or even make the watchers aware of them. What was to happen would happen in our presence and unknown to us. Death, summoned by him, would do its work... And the comedy, the tragedy, rather, ran its course. Mme. Fauville, whom he was sending to the opera, came to say goodnight. Then his servant brought him something to eat, including a dish of apples. Then followed a fit of rage, the agony of the man who is about to die and who fears death and a whole scene of deceit, in which he showed us his safe and the drab-cloth diary which was supposed to contain the story of the plot... That ended matters.

"Mazeroux and I retired to the hall passage, closing the door after us; and M. Fauville remained alone and free to act. Nothing now could prevent the fulfilment of his wishes. At eleven o'clock in the evening, Mme. Fauville—to whom no doubt, in the course of the day, imitating Sauverand's handwriting, he had sent a letter—one of those letters which are always torn up at once, in which Sauverand entreated the poor woman to grant him an interview at the Ranelagh—Mme. Fauville would leave the opera and, before going to Mme. d'Ersinger's party, would spend an hour not far from the house.

"On the other hand, Sauverand would be performing his usual Wednesday pilgrimage less than half a mile away, in the opposite direction. During this time the crime would be committed.

"Both of them would come under the notice of the police, either by M. Fauville's allusions or by the incident at the Café du Pont-Neuf; both of them, moreover, would be incapable either of providing an alibi or of explaining their presence so near the house: were not both of them bound to be accused and convicted of the crime?... In the most unlikely event that some chance should protect them, there was an undeniable proof lying ready to hand in the shape of the apple containing the very marks of Marie Fauville's teeth! And then, a few weeks later, the last and decisive trick, the mysterious arrival at intervals of ten days, of the letters denouncing the pair. So everything was settled.

"The smallest details were foreseen with infernal clearness. You remember, Monsieur le Préfet, that turquoise which dropped out of my ring and was found in the safe? There were only four persons who could have seen it and picked it up. M. Fauville was one of them. Well, he was just the one, whom we all excepted; and yet it was he who, to cast suspicion upon me and to forestall an interference which he felt would be dangerous, seized the opportunity and placed the turquoise in the safe!...

"This time the work was completed. Fate was about to be fulfilled. Between the 'hater' and his victims there was but the distance of one act. The act was performed. M. Fauville died."

Don Luis ceased. His words were followed by a long silence; and he felt certain that the extraordinary story which he had just finished telling met with the absolute approval of his hearers. They did not discuss, they believed. And yet it was the most incredible truth that he was asking them to believe.

M. Desmalions asked one last question.

"You were in that passage with Sergeant Mazeroux. There were detectives outside the house. Admitting that M. Fauville knew that he was to be killed that night and at that very hour of the night, who can have killed him and who can have killed his son? There was no one within these four walls."

"There was M. Fauville."

A sudden clamour of protests arose. The veil was promptly torn; and the spectacle revealed by Don Luis provoked, in addition to horror, an unforeseen outburst of incredulity and a sort of revolt against the too kindly attention which had been accorded to those explanations. The Prefect of Police expressed the general feeling by exclaiming:

"Enough of words! Enough of theories! However logical they may seem, they lead to absurd conclusions."

"Absurd in appearance, Monsieur le Préfet; but how do we know that M. Fauville's unheard-of conduct is not explained by very natural reasons? Of course, no one dies with a light heart for the mere pleasure of revenge. But how do we know that M. Fauville, whose extreme emaciation and pallor you must have noted as I did, was not stricken by some mortal illness and that, knowing himself doomed—"

"I repeat, enough of words!" cried the Prefect. "You go only by suppositions. What I want is proofs, a proof, only one. And we are still waiting for it."

"Here it is, Monsieur le Préfet."

"Eh? What's that you say?"

"Monsieur le Préfet, when I removed the chandelier from the plaster that supported it, I found, outside the upper surface of the metal box, a sealed envelope. As the chandelier was placed under the attic occupied by M. Fauville's son, it is evident that M. Fauville was able, by lifting the boards of the floor in his son's room, to reach the top of the machine which he had contrived. This was how, during that last night, he placed this sealed envelope in position, after writing on it the date of the murder, '31 March, 11 P.M.,' and his signature, 'Hippolyte Fauville.'"

M. Desmalions opened the envelope with an eager hand. His first glance at the pages of writing which it contained made him give a start.

"Oh, the villain, the villain!" he said. "How was it possible for such a monster to exist? What a loathsome brute!"

In a jerky voice, which became almost inaudible at times owing to his amazement, he read:

"The end is reached. My hour is striking. Put to sleep by me, Edmond is dead without having been roused from his unconsciousness by the fire of the poison. My own death-agony is beginning. I am suffering all the tortures of hell. My hand can hardly write these last lines. I suffer, how I suffer! And yet my happiness is unspeakable.

"This happiness dates back to my visit to London, with Edmond, four months ago. Until then, I was dragging on the most hideous existence, hiding my hatred of the woman who detested me and who loved another, broken down in health, feeling myself already eaten up with an unrelenting disease, and seeing my son grow daily more weak and languid.

"In the afternoon I consulted a great physician and I no longer had the least doubt left: the malady that was eating into me was cancer. And I knew besides that, like myself, my son Edmond was on the road to the grave, incurably stricken with consumption.

"That same evening I conceived the magnificent idea of revenge. And such a revenge! The most dreadful of accusations made against a man and a woman in love with each other! Prison! The assizes! Penal servitude! The scaffold! And no assistance possible, not a struggle, not a hope! Accumulated proofs, proofs so formidable as to make the innocent themselves doubt their own innocence and remain hopelessly and helplessly dumb. What a revenge!... And what a punishment! To be innocent and to struggle vainly against the very facts that accuse you, the very certainty that proclaims you guilty.

"And I prepared everything with a glad heart. Each happy thought, each invention made me shout with laughter. Lord, how merry I was! You would think that cancer hurts: not a bit of it! How can you suffer physical pain when your soul is quivering with delight? Do you think I feel the hideous burning of the poison at this moment?

"I am happy. The death which I have inflicted on myself is the beginning of their torment. Then why live and wait for a natural death which to them would mean the beginning of their happiness? And as Edmond had to die, why not save him a lingering illness and give him a death which would double the crime of Marie and Sauverand?

"The end is coming. I had to break off: the pain was too much for me. Now to pull myself together... How silent everything is! Outside the house and in the house are emissaries of the police watching over my crime. At no great distance, Marie, in obedience to my letter, is hurrying to the trysting place, where her beloved will not come. And the beloved is roaming under the windows where his darling will not appear.

"Oh, the dear little puppets whose string I pull! Dance! Jump! Skip! Lord, what fun they are! A rope round your neck, sir; and, madam, a rope round yours. Was it not you, sir, who poisoned Inspector Vérot this morning and followed him to the Café du Pont-Neuf, with your grand ebony walking-stick? Why, of course it was! And at night the pretty lady poisons me and poisons her stepson. Prove it? Well, what about this apple, madam, this apple which you did *not* bite into and which all the same will be found to bear the marks of your teeth? What fun! Dance! Jump! Skip!

"And the letters! The trick of my letters to the late lamented Langernault! That was my crowning triumph. Oh, the joy of it, when I invented and constructed my little mechanical toy! Wasn't it nicely thought out? Isn't it wonderfully neat and accurate? On the appointed day, click, the first letter! And, ten days after, click, the second letter! Come, there's no hope for you, my poor friends, you're nicely done for. Dance! Jump! Skip!

"And what amuses me—for I am laughing now—is to think that nobody will know what to make of it. Marie and Sauverand guilty: of that there is not the least doubt. But, outside that, absolute mystery.

"Nobody will know nor ever will know anything. In a few weeks' time, when the two criminals are irrevocably doomed, when the letters are in the hands of the police, on the 25th, or, rather, at 3 o'clock on the morning of the 26th of May, an explosion will destroy every trace of my work. The bomb is in its place. A movement entirely independent of the chandelier will explode it at the hour aforesaid.

"I have just laid beside it the drab-cloth manuscript book in which I pretended that I wrote my diary, the phials containing the poison, the needles which I used, an ebony walking-stick, two letters from Inspector Vérot, in short, anything that might save the culprits. Then how can anyone know? No, nobody will know nor ever will know anything.

"Unless—unless some miracle happens—unless the bomb leaves the walls standing and the ceiling intact. Unless, by some marvel of intelligence and intuition, a man of genius, unravelling the threads which I have tangled, should penetrate to the very heart of the riddle and succeed, after a search lasting for months and months, in discovering this final letter.

"It is for this man that I write, well knowing that he cannot exist. But, after all, what do I care? Marie and Sauverand will be at the bottom of the abyss by then, dead no doubt, or in any case separated forever. And I risk nothing by leaving this evidence of my hatred in the hands of chance.

"There, that's finished. I have only to sign. My hand shakes more and more. The sweat is pouring from my forehead in great drops. I am suffering the tortures of the damned and I am divinely happy! Aha, my friends, you were waiting for my death!

"You, Marie, imprudently let me read in your eyes, which watched me stealthily, all your delight at seeing me so ill! And you were both of you so sure of the future that you had the courage to wait patiently for my death! Well, here it is, my death! Here it is and there are you, united above my grave, linked together with the handcuffs. Marie, be the wife of my friend Sauverand. Sauverand, I bestow my spouse upon you. Be joined together in holy matrimony. Bless you, my children!

"The examining magistrate will draw up the contract and the executioner will read the marriage service. Oh, the delight of it! I suffer agonies—but oh, the delight! What a fine thing is hatred, when it makes death a joy! I am happy in dying. Marie is in prison. Sauverand is weeping in the condemned man's cell. The door opens...

"Oh, horror! The men in black! They walk up to the bed: 'Gaston Sauverand, your appeal is rejected. Courage! Be a man!' Oh, the cold, dark morning—the scaffold! It's your turn, Marie, your turn! Would you survive your lover? Sauverand is dead: it's your turn. See, here's a rope for you. Or would you rather have poison? Die, will you, you hussy! Die with your veins on fire—as I am doing, I who hate you—hate you—hate you!"

M. Desmalions ceased, amid the silent astonishment of all those present. He had great difficulty in reading the concluding lines, the writing having become almost wholly shapeless and illegible.

He said, in a low voice, as he stared at the paper: "'Hippolyte Fauville.' The signature is there. The scoundrel found a last remnant of strength to sign his name clearly. He feared that a doubt might be entertained of his villainy. And indeed how could anyone have suspected it?"

And, looking at Don Luis, he added:

"It needed, to solve the mystery, a really exceptional power of insight and gifts to which we must all do homage, to which I do homage. All the explanations which that madman gave have been anticipated in the most accurate and bewildering fashion."

Don Luis bowed and, without replying to the praise bestowed upon him, said:

"You are right, Monsieur le Préfet; he was a madman, and one of the most dangerous kind, the lucid madman who pursues an idea from which nothing will make him turn aside. He pursued it with superhuman tenacity and with all the resources of his fastidious mind, enslaved by the laws of mechanics.

"Another would have killed his victims frankly and brutally. He set his wits to work to kill at a long date, like an experimenter who leaves to time the duty of proving the excellence of his invention. And he succeeded only too well, because the police fell into the trap and because Mme. Fauville is perhaps going to die."

M. Desmalions made a gesture of decision. The whole business, in fact, was past history, on which the police proceedings would throw the necessary light. One fact alone was of importance to the present: the saving of Marie Fauville's life.

"It's true," he said, "we have not a minute to lose. Mme. Fauville must be told without delay. At the same time, I will send for the examining magistrate; and the case against her is sure to be dismissed at once."

He swiftly gave orders for continuing the investigations and verifying Don Luis's theories. Then, turning to Perenna:

"Come, Monsieur," he said. "It is right that Mme. Fauville should thank her rescuer. Mazeroux, you come, too."

* * *

The meeting was over, that meeting in the course of which Don Luis had given the most striking proofs of his genius. Waging war, so to speak, upon the powers beyond the grave, he had forced the dead man to reveal his secret. He disclosed, as though he had been present throughout, the hateful vengeance conceived in the darkness and carried out in the tomb.

M. Desmalions showed all his admiration by his silence and by certain movements of his head. And Perenna took a keen enjoyment in the strange fact that he, who was being hunted down by the police a few hours ago, should now be sitting in a motor car beside the head of that same force.

Nothing threw into greater relief the masterly manner in which he had conducted the business and the importance which the police attached to the results obtained. The value of his collaboration was such that they were willing to forget the incidents of the last two days. The grudge which Weber bore him was now of no avail against Don Luis Perenna.

M. Desmalions, meanwhile, began briefly to review the new solutions, and he concluded by still discussing certain points.

"Yes, that's it... there is not the least shadow of a doubt... We agree... It's that and nothing else. Still, one or two things remain obscure. First of all, the mark of the teeth. This, notwithstanding the husband's admission, is a fact which we cannot neglect."

"I believe that the explanation is a very simple one, Monsieur le Préfet. I will give it to you as soon as I am able to support it with the necessary proofs."

"Very well. But another question: how is it that Weber, yesterday morning, found that sheet of paper relating to the explosion in Mlle. Levasseur's room?"

"And how was it," added Don Luis, laughing, "that I found there the list of the five dates corresponding with the delivery of the letters?"

"So you are of my opinion?" said M. Desmalions. "The part played by Mlle. Levasseur is at least suspicious."

"I believe that everything will be cleared up, Monsieur le Préfet, and that you need now only question Mme. Fauville and Gaston Sauverand in order to dispel these last obscurities and remove all suspicion from Mlle. Levasseur."

"And then," insisted M. Desmalions, "there is one more fact that strikes me as odd. Hippolyte Fauville does not once mention the Mornington inheritance in his confession. Why? Did he not know of it? Are we to suppose that there is no connection, beyond a mere casual coincidence, between the series of crimes and that bequest?"

"There, I am entirely of your opinion, Monsieur le Préfet. Hippolyte Fauville's silence as to that bequest perplexes me a little, I confess. But all the same I look upon it as comparatively unimportant. The main thing is Fauville's guilt and the prisoners' innocence."

Don Luis's delight was pure and unbounded. From his point of view, the sinister tragedy was at an end with the discovery of the confession written by Hippolyte Fauville. Anything not explained in those lines would be explained by the details to be supplied by Mme. Fauville, Florence Levasseur, and Gaston Sauverand. He himself had lost all interest in the matter.

The car drew up at Saint-Lazare, the wretched, sordid old prison which is still waiting to be pulled down.

The Prefect jumped out. The door was opened at once.

"Is the prison governor there?" he asked. "Quick! Send for him, it's urgent."

Then, unable to wait, he at once hastened toward the corridors leading to the infirmary and, as he reached the first-floor landing, came up against the governor himself.

"Mme. Fauville," he said, without waste of time. "I want to see her—"

But he stopped short when he saw the expression of consternation on the prison governor's face.

"Well, what is it?" he asked. "What's the matter?"

"Why, haven't you heard, Monsieur le Préfet?" stammered the governor. "I telephoned to the office, you know—"

"Speak! What is it?"

"Mme. Fauville died this morning. She managed somehow to take poison."

M. Desmalions seized the governor by the arm and ran to the infirmary, followed by Perenna and Mazeroux.

He saw Marie Fauville lying on a bed in one of the rooms. Her pale face and her shoulders were stained with brown patches, similar to those which had marked the bodies of Inspector Vérot, Hippolyte Fauville, and his son Edmond.

Greatly upset, the Prefect murmured:

"But the poison—where did it come from?"

"This phial and syringe were found under her pillow, Monsieur le Préfet."

"Under her pillow? But how did they get there? How did they reach her? Who gave them to her?"

"We don't know yet, Monsieur le Préfet."

M. Desmalions looked at Don Luis. So Hippolyte Fauville's suicide had not put an end to the series of crimes! His action had done more than aim at Marie's death by the hand of the law: it had now driven her to take poison! Was it possible? Was it admissible that the dead man's revenge should still continue in the same automatic and anonymous manner?

Or rather—or rather, was there not some other mysterious will which was secretly and as audaciously carrying on Hippolyte Fauville's diabolical work?

***

Two days later came a fresh sensation: Gaston Sauverand was found dying in his cell. He had had the courage to strangle himself with his bedsheet. All efforts to restore him to life were vain.

On the table near him lay a half-dozen newspaper cuttings, which had been passed to him by an unknown hand. All of them told the news of Marie Fauville's death.

15

THE HEIR TO THE HUNDRED MILLIONS

On the fourth evening after the tragic events related, an old cab-driver, almost entirely hidden in a huge great-coat, rang at Perenna's door and sent up a letter to Don Luis. He was at once shown into the study on the first floor. Hardly taking time to throw off his great-coat, he rushed at Don Luis:

"It's all up with you this time, Chief!" he exclaimed. "This is no moment for joking: pack up your trunks and be off as quick as you can!"

Don Luis, who sat quietly smoking in an easy chair, answered:
"Which will you have, Mazeroux? A cigar or a cigarette?"
Mazeroux at once grew indignant.
"But look here, Chief, don't you read the papers?"
"Worse luck!"

"In that case, the situation must appear as clear to you as it does to me and everybody else. During the last three days, since the double suicide, or, rather, the double murder of Marie Fauville and her cousin Gaston Sauvrand, there hasn't been a newspaper but has said this kind of thing: 'And, now that M. Fauville, his son, his wife, and his cousin Gaston Sauverand are dead, there's nothing standing between Don Luis Perenna and the Mornington inheritance!'

"Do you understand what that means? Of course, people speak of the explosion on the Boulevard Suchet and of Fauville's posthumous revelations; and they are disgusted with that dirty brute of a Fauville; and they don't know how to praise your cleverness enough. But there is one fact that forms the main subject of every conversation and every discussion.

"Now that the three branches of the Roussel family are extinct, who remains? Don Luis Perenna. In default of the natural heirs, who inherits the property? Don Luis Perenna."

"Lucky dog!"

"That's what people are saying, Chief. They say that this series of murders and atrocities cannot be the effort of chance coincidences, but, on the contrary, points to the existence of an all-powerful will which began with the murder of Cosmo Mornington and ended with the capture of the hundred million. And to give a name to that will, they pitch on the nearest, that of the extraordinary, glorious, ill-famed, bewildering, mysterious, omnipotent, and ubiquitous person who was Cosmo Mornington's intimate friend and who, from the beginning, has controlled events and pieced them together, accusing and acquitting people, getting them arrested, and helping them to escape.

"They say," he went on hurriedly, "that he manages the whole business and that, if he works it in accordance with his interests, there are a hundred million waiting for him at the finish. And this person is Don Luis Perenna, in other words, Arsène Lupin, the man with the unsavoury reputation whom it would be madness not to think of in connection with so colossal a job."

"Thank you!"

"That's what they say, Chief; I'm only telling you. As long as Mme. Fauville and Gaston Sauverand were alive, people did not give much thought to your claims as residuary legatee. But both of them died. Then, you see, people can't help remarking the really surprising persistence with which luck looks after Don Luis Perenna's interests. You know the legal maxim: *fecit cuiprodest.* Who benefits by the disappearance of all the Roussel heirs? Don Luis Perenna."

"The scoundrel!"

"The scoundrel: that's the word which Weber goes roaring out all along the passages of the police office and the criminal investigation department. You are the scoundrel and Florence Levasseur is your accomplice. And hardly anyone dares protest.

"The Prefect of Police? What is the use of his defending you, of his remembering that you have saved his life twice over and rendered invaluable services to the police which he is the first to appreciate? What is the use of his going to the Prime Minister, though we all know that Valenglay protects you?

"There are others besides the Prefect of Police! There are others besides the Prime Minister! There's the whole of the detective office, there's the public prosecutor's staff, there's the examining magistrate, the press and, above all, public opinion, which has to be satisfied and which calls for and expects a culprit. That culprit is yourself or Florence Levasseur. Or, rather, it's you and Florence Levasseur."

Don Luis did not move a muscle of his face. Mazeroux waited a moment longer. Then, receiving no reply, he made a gesture of despair.

"Chief, do you know what you are compelling me to do? To betray my duty. Well, let me tell you this: tomorrow morning you will receive a summons to appear before the examining magistrate. At the end of your examination, whatever questions may have been put to you and whatever you may have answered, you will be taken straight to the lockup. The warrant is signed. That is what your enemies have done."

"The devil!"

"And that's not all. Weber, who is burning to take his revenge, has asked for permission to watch your house from this day onward, so that you may not slip away as Florence Levasseur did. He will be here with his men in an hour's time. What do you say to that, Chief?"

Without abandoning his careless attitude, Don Luis beckoned to Mazeroux.

"Sergeant, just look under that sofa between the windows."

Don Luis was serious. Mazeroux instinctively obeyed. Under the sofa was a portmanteau.

"Sergeant, in ten minutes, when I have told my servants to go to bed, carry the portmanteau to 143 *bis* Rue de Rivoli, where I have taken a small flat under the name of M. Lecocq."

"What for, Chief? What does it mean?"

"It means that, having no trustworthy person to carry that portmanteau for me, I have been waiting for your visit for the last three days."

"Why, but—" stammered Mazeroux, in his confusion.

"Why but what?"

"Had you made up your mind to clear out?"

"Of course I had! But why hurry? The reason I placed you in the detective office was that I might know what was being plotted against me. Since you tell me that I'm in danger, I shall cut my stick."

And, as Mazeroux looked at him with increasing bewilderment, he tapped him on the shoulder and said severely:

"You see, Sergeant, that it was not worthwhile to disguise yourself as a cab-driver and betray your duty. You should never betray your duty, Sergeant. Ask your own conscience: I am sure that it will judge you according to your desserts."

Don Luis had spoken the truth. Recognizing how greatly the deaths of Marie Fauville and Sauverand had altered the situation, he considered it wise to move to a place of safety. His excuse for not doing so before was that he hoped to receive news of Florence Levasseur either by letter or by telephone. As the girl persisted in keeping silence, there was no reason why Don Luis should risk an arrest which the course of events made extremely probable.

And in fact his anticipations were correct. Next morning Mazeroux came to the little flat in the Rue de Rivoli looking very spry.

"You've had a narrow escape, Chief. Weber heard this morning that the bird had flown. He's simply furious! And you must confess that the tangle is getting worse and worse. They're utterly at a loss at headquarters. They don't even know how to set about prosecuting Florence Levasseur.

"You must have read about it in the papers. The examining magistrate maintains that, as Fauville committed suicide and killed his son Edmond, Florence Levasseur has nothing to do with the matter. In his opinion the case is closed on that side. Well, he's a good one, the examining magistrate! What about Gaston Sauverand's death? Isn't it as clear as daylight that Florence had a hand in it, as well as in all the rest?

"Wasn't it in her room, in a volume of Shakespeare, that documents were found relating to M. Fauville's arrangements about the letters and the explosion? And then—"

Mazeroux interrupted himself, frightened by the look in Don Luis's eyes and realizing that the chief was fonder of the girl than ever. Guilty or not, she inspired him with the same passion.

"All right," said Mazeroux, "we'll say no more about it. The future will bear me out, you'll see."

***

The days passed. Mazeroux called as often as possible, or else telephoned to Don Luis all the details of the two inquiries that were being pursued at Saint-Lazare and at the Santé Prison.

Vain inquiries, as we know. While Don Luis's statements relating to the electric chandelier and the automatic distribution of the mysterious letters were found to be correct, the investigation failed to reveal anything about the two suicides.

At most, it was ascertained that, before his arrest, Sauverand had tried to enter into correspondence with Marie through one of the tradesmen supplying the infirmary. Were they to suppose that the phial of poison and the hypodermic syringe had been introduced by the same means? It was impossible to prove; and, on the other hand, it was impossible to discover how the newspaper cuttings telling of Marie's suicide had found their way into Gaston Sauverand's cell.

And then the original mystery still remained, the unfathomable mystery of the marks of teeth in the apple. M. Fauville's posthumous confession acquitted Marie. And yet it was undoubtedly Marie's teeth that had marked the apple. The teeth that had been called the teeth of the tiger were certainly hers. Well, then!

In short, as Mazeroux said, everybody was groping in the dark, so much so that the Prefect, who was called upon by the will to assemble the Mornington heirs at a date not less than three nor more than four months after the testator's decease, suddenly decided that the meeting should take place in the course of the following week and fixed it for the ninth of June.

He hoped in this way to put an end to an exasperating case in which the police displayed nothing but uncertainty and confusion. They would decide about the inheritance according to circumstances and then close the proceedings. And gradually people would cease to talk about the wholesale slaughter of the Mornington heirs; and the mystery of the teeth of the tiger would be gradually forgotten.

It was strange, but these last days, which were restless and feverish like all the days that come before great battles—and everyone felt that this last meeting meant a great battle—were spent by Don Luis in an armchair on his balcony in the Rue de Rivoli, where he sat quietly smoking cigarettes, or blowing soap-bubbles which the wind carried toward the garden of the Tuileries.

Mazeroux could not get over it.

"Chief, you astound me! How calm and careless you look!"

"I am calm and careless, Alexandre."

"But what do you mean? Doesn't the case interest you? Don't you intend to avenge Mme. Fauville and Sauverand? You are openly accused and you sit here blowing soap-bubbles!"

"There's no more delightful pastime, Alexandre."

"Shall I tell you what I think, Chief? You've discovered the solution of the mystery!"

"Perhaps I have, Alexandre, and perhaps I haven't."

Nothing seemed to excite Don Luis. Hours and hours passed; and he did not stir from his balcony. The sparrows now came and ate the crumbs which he threw to them. It really seemed as if the case was coming to an end for him and as if everything was turning out perfectly.

But, on the day of the meeting, Mazeroux entered with a letter in his hand and a scared look on his face.

"This is for you, Chief. It was addressed to me, but with an envelope inside it in your name. How do you explain that?"

"Quite easily, Alexandre. The enemy is aware of our cordial relations; and, as he does not know where I am staying—"

"What enemy?"

"I'll tell you tomorrow evening."

Don Luis opened the envelope and read the following words, written in red ink:

"There's still time, Lupin. Retire from the contest. If not, it means your death, too. When you think that your object is attained, when your hand is raised against me and you utter words of triumph, at that same moment the ground will open beneath your feet. The place of your death is chosen. The snare is laid. Beware, Lupin."

Don Luis smiled.

"Good," he said. "Things are taking shape,"

"Do you think so, Chief?"

"I do. And who gave you the letter?"

"Ah, we've been lucky for once, Chief! The policeman to whom it was handed happened to live at Les Ternes, next door to the bearer of the letter. He knows the fellow well. It was a stroke of luck, wasn't it?"

Don Luis sprang from his seat, radiant with delight.

"What do you mean? Out with it! You know who it is?"

"The chap's an indoor servant employed at a nursing-home in the Avenue des Ternes."

"Let's go there. We've no time to lose."

"Splendid, Chief! You're yourself again."

"Well, of course! As long as there was nothing to do I was waiting for this evening and resting, for I can see that the fight will be tremendous. But, as the enemy has blundered at last, as he's given me a trail to go upon, there's no need to wait, and I'll get ahead of him. Have at the tiger, Mazeroux!"

***

It was one o'clock in the afternoon when Don Luis and Mazeroux arrived at the nursing-home in the Avenue des Ternes. A manservant opened the door. Mazeroux nudged Don Luis. The man was doubtless the bearer of the letter. And, in reply to the sergeant's questions, he made no difficulty about saying that he had been to the police office that morning.

"By whose orders?" asked Mazeroux.

"The mother superior's."

"The mother superior?"

"Yes, the home includes a private hospital, which is managed by nuns."

"Could we speak to the superior?"

"Certainly, but not now: she has gone out."

"When will she be in?"

"Oh, she may be back at any time!"

The man showed them into the waiting-room, where they spent over an hour. They were greatly puzzled. What did the intervention of that nun mean? What part was she playing in the case?

People came in and were taken to the patients whom they had called to see. Others went out. There were also sisters moving silently to and fro and nurses dressed in their long white overalls belted at the waist.

"We're not doing any good here, Chief," whispered Mazeroux.

"What's your hurry? Is your sweetheart waiting for you?"

"We're wasting our time."

"I'm not wasting mine. The meeting at the Prefect's is not till five."

"What did you say? You're joking, Chief! You surely don't intend to go to it."

"Why not?"

"Why not? Well, the warrant—"

"The warrant? A scrap of paper!"

"A scrap of paper which will become a serious matter if you force the police to act. Your presence will be looked upon as a provocation—"

"And my absence as a confession. A gentleman who comes into a hundred million does not lie low on the day of the windfall. So I must attend that meeting, lest I should forfeit my claim. And attend it I will."

"Chief."

A stifled cry was heard in front of them; and a woman, a nurse, who was passing through the room, at once started running, lifted a curtain, and disappeared.

Don Luis rose, hesitating, not knowing what to do. Then, after four or five seconds of indecision, he suddenly rushed to the curtain and down a corridor, came up against a large, leather-padded door which had just closed, and wasted more time in stupidly fumbling at it with shaking hands.

When he had opened it, he found himself at the foot of a back staircase. Should he go up it? On the right, the same staircase ran down to the basement. He went down it, entered a kitchen and, seizing hold of the cook, said to her, in an angry voice:

"Has a nurse just gone out this way?"

"Do you mean Nurse Gertrude, the new one?"

"Yes, yes, quick! She's wanted upstairs."

"Who wants her?"

"Oh, hang it all, can't you tell me which way she went?"

"Through that door over there."

Don Luis darted away, crossed a little hall, and rushed out on to the Avenue des Ternes.

"Well, here's a pretty race!" cried Mazeroux, joining him.

Don Luis stood scanning the avenue. A motor bus was starting on the little square hard by, the Place Saint-Ferdinand.

"She's inside it," he declared. "This time, I shan't let her go."

He hailed a taxi.

"Follow that motor bus, driver, at fifty yards' distance."

"Is it Florence Levasseur?" asked Mazeroux.

"Yes."

"A nice thing!" growled the sergeant. And, yielding to a sudden outburst: "But, look here, Chief, don't you see? Surely you're not as blind as all that!"

Don Luis made no reply.

"But, Chief, Florence Levasseur's presence in the nursing-home proves as clearly as A B C that it was she who told the manservant to bring me that threatening letter for you! There's not a doubt about it: Florence Levasseur is managing the whole business.

"You know it as well as I do. Confess! It's possible that, during the last ten days, you've brought yourself, for love of that woman, to look upon her as innocent in spite of the overwhelming proofs against her. But today the truth hits you in the eye. I feel it, I'm sure of it. Isn't it so, Chief? I'm right, am I not? You see it for yourself?"

This time Don Luis did not protest. With a drawn face and set eyes he watched the motor bus, which at that moment was standing still at the corner of the Boulevard Haussmann.

"Stop!" he shouted to the driver.

The girl alighted. It was easy to recognize Florence Levasseur under her nurse's uniform. She cast round her eyes as if to make sure that she was not being followed, and then took a cab and drove down the boulevard and the Rue de la Pépinière, to the Gare Saint-Lazare.

Don Luis saw her from a distance climbing the steps that run up from the Cour de Rome; and, on following her, caught sight of her again at the ticket office at the end of the waiting hall.

"Quick, Mazeroux!" he said. "Get out your detective card and ask the clerk what ticket she's taken. Run, before another passenger comes."

Mazeroux hurried and questioned the ticket clerk and returned:

"Second class for Rouen."

"Take one for yourself."

Mazeroux did so. They found that there was an express due to start in a minute. When they reached the platform Florence was stepping into a compartment in the middle of the train.

The engine whistled.

"Get in," said Don Luis, hiding himself as best he could. "Telegraph to me from Rouen; and I'll join you this evening. Above all, keep your eyes on her. Don't let her slip between your fingers. She's very clever, you know."

"But why don't you come yourself, Chief? It would be much better—"

"Out of the question. The train doesn't stop before Rouen; and I couldn't be back till this evening. The meeting at the Prefect's is at five o'clock."

"And you insist on going?"

"More than ever. There, jump in!"

He pushed him into one of the end carriages. The train started and soon disappeared in the tunnel.

Then Don Luis flung himself on a bench in a waiting room and remained there for two hours, pretending to read the newspapers. But his eyes wandered and his mind was haunted by the agonizing question that once more forced itself upon him: was Florence guilty or not?

***

It was five o'clock exactly when Major Comte d'Astrignac, Maitre Lepertuis, and the secretary of the American Embassy were shown into M. Desmalions's office. At the same moment someone entered the messengers' room and handed in his card.

The messenger on duty glanced at the pasteboard, turned his head quickly toward a group of men talking in a corner, and then asked the newcomer:

"Have you an appointment, sir?"

"It's not necessary. Just say that I'm here: Don Luis Perenna."

A kind of electric shock ran through the little group in the corner; and one of the persons forming it came forward. It was Weber, the deputy chief detective.

The two men looked each other straight in the eyes. Don Luis smiled amiably. Weber was livid; he shook in every limb and was plainly striving to contain himself.

Near him stood a couple of journalists and four detectives.

"By Jove! The beggars are there for me!" thought Don Luis. "But their confusion shows that they did not believe that I should have the cheek to come. Are they going to arrest me?"

Weber did not move, but in the end his face expressed a certain satisfaction as though he were saying:

"I've got you this time, my fine fellow, and you shan't escape me."

The office messenger returned and, without a word, led the way for Don Luis. Perenna passed in front of Weber with the politest of bows, bestowed a friendly little nod on the detectives, and entered.

The Comte d'Astrignac hurried up to him at once, with hands outstretched, thus showing that all the tittle-tattle in no way affected the esteem in which he continued to hold Private Perenna of the Foreign Legion. But the Prefect of Police maintained an attitude of reserve which was very significant. He went on turning over the papers which he was examining and conversed in a low voice with the solicitor and the American Secretary of Embassy.

Don Luis thought to himself:

"My dear Lupin, there's someone going to leave this room with the bracelets on his wrists. If it's not the real culprit, it'll be you, my poor old chap."

And he remembered the early part of the case, when he was in the workroom at Fauville's house, before the magistrates, and had either to deliver the criminal to justice or to incur the penalty of immediate arrest. In the same way, from the start to the finish of the struggle, he had been obliged, while fighting the invisible enemy, to expose himself to the attacks of the law with no means of defending himself except by indispensable victories.

Harassed by constant onslaughts, never out of danger, he had successively hurried to their deaths Marie Fauville and Gaston Sauverand, two innocent people sacrificed to the cruel laws of war. Was he at last about to fight the real enemy, or would he himself succumb at the decisive moment?

He rubbed his hands with such a cheerful gesture that M. Desmalions could not help looking at him. Don Luis wore the radiant air of a man who is experiencing a pure joy and who is preparing to taste others even greater.

The Prefect of Police remained silent for a moment, as though asking himself what that devil of a fellow could be so pleased with; then he fumbled through his papers once more and, in the end, said:

"We have met again, gentlemen, as we did two months ago, to come to a definite conclusion about the Mornington inheritance. Señor Caceres, the attaché of the Peruvian legation, will not be here. I have received a telegram from Italy to tell me that Señor Caceres is seriously ill. However, his presence was not indispensable. There is no one lacking, therefore—except those, alas, whose claims this meeting would gladly have sanctioned, that is to say, Cosmo Mornington's heirs."

"There is one other person absent, Monsieur le Préfet." M. Desmalions looked up. The speaker was Don Luis. The Prefect hesitated and then decided to ask him to explain.

"Whom do you mean? What person?"

"The murderer of the Mornington heirs."

This time again Don Luis compelled attention and, in spite of the resistance which he encountered, obliged the others to take notice of his presence and to yield to his ascendancy. Whatever happened, they had to listen to him. Whatever happened, they had to discuss with him things which seemed incredible, but which were possible because he put them into words.

"Monsieur le Préfet," he asked, "will you allow me to set forth the facts of the matter as it now stands? They will form a natural sequel and conclusion of the interview which we had after the explosion on the Boulevard Suchet."

M. Desmalions's silence gave Don Luis leave to speak. He at once continued:

"It will not take long, Monsieur le Préfet. It will not take long for two reasons: first, because M. Fauville's confessions remain at our disposal and we know definitely the monstrous part which he played; and, secondly, because, after all, the truth, however complicated it may seem, is really very simple.

"It all lies in the objection which you, Monsieur le Préfet, made to me on leaving the wrecked house on the Boulevard Suchet: 'How is it,' you asked, 'that the Mornington inheritance is not once mentioned in Hippolyte Fauville's confession?' It all lies in that, Monsieur le Préfet. Hippolyte Fauville did not say a word about the inheritance; and the reason evidently is that he did not know of it.

"And the reason why Gaston Sauverand was able to tell me his whole sensational story without making the least allusion to the inheritance was that the inheritance played no sort of part in Gaston Sauverand's story. He, too, knew nothing of it before those events, any more than Marie Fauville did, or Florence Levasseur. There is no denying the fact: Hippolyte Fauville was guided by revenge and by revenge alone. If not, why should he have acted as he did, seeing that Cosmo Mornington's millions reverted to him by the fullest of rights? Besides, if he had wished to enjoy those millions, he would not have begun by killing himself.

"One thing, therefore, is certain: the inheritance in no way affected Hippolyte Fauville's resolves or actions. And, nevertheless, one after the other, with inflexible regularity, as if they had been struck down in the very order called for by the terms of the Mornington inheritance, they all disappeared: Cosmo Mornington, then Hippolyte Fauville, then Edmond Fauville, then Marie Fauville, then Gaston Sauverand. First, the possessor of the fortune; next, all those whom he had appointed his legatees; and, I repeat, in the very order in which the will enabled them to lay claim to the fortune!

"Is it not strange?" asked Perenna, "and are we not bound to suppose that there was a controlling mind at the back of it all? Are we not bound to admit that the formidable contest was influenced by that inheritance, and that, above the hatred and jealousy of the loathsome Fauville, there loomed a being endowed with even more tremendous energy, pursuing a tangible aim and driving to their deaths, one by one, like so many numbered victims, all the unconscious actors in the tragedy of which he tied and of which he is now untying the threads?"

Don Luis leaned forward and continued earnestly:

"Monsieur le Préfet, the public instinct so thoroughly agrees with me, a section of the police, with M. Weber, the deputy chief detective at its head, argues in a manner so exactly identical with my own, that the existence of that being is at once confirmed in every mind. There had to be someone to act as the controlling brain, to provide the will and the energy. That someone was myself. After all, why not? Did not I possess the condition which was indispensable to make anyone interested in the murders? Was I not Cosmo Mornington's heir?

"I will not defend myself. It may be that outside interference, it may be that circumstances, will oblige you, Monsieur le Préfet, to take unjustifiable measures against me; but I will not insult you by believing for one second that you can imagine the man whose acts you have been able to judge for the last two months capable of such crimes. And yet the public instinct is right in accusing me.

"Apart from Hippolyte Fauville, there is necessarily a criminal; and that criminal is necessarily Cosmo Mornington's heir. As I am not the man, another heir of Cosmo Mornington exists. It is he whom I accuse, Monsieur le Préfet.

"There is something more than a dead man's will in the wicked business that is being enacted before us. We thought for a time that there was only that; but there is something more. I have not been fighting a dead man all the time; more than once I have felt the very breath of life strike against my face. More than once I have felt the teeth of the tiger seeking to tear me.

"The dead man did much, but he did not do everything. And, even then, was he alone in doing what he did? Was the being of whom I speak merely one who executed his orders? Or was he also the accomplice who helped him in his scheme? I do not know. But he certainly continued a work which he perhaps began by inspiring and which, in any case, he turned to his own profit, resolutely completed and carried out to the very end. And he did so because he knew of Cosmo Mornington's will. It is he whom I accuse, Monsieur le Préfet.

"I accuse him at the very least of that part of the crimes and felonies which cannot be attributed to Hippolyte Fauville. I accuse him of breaking open the drawer of the desk in which Maitre Lepertuis, Cosmo Mornington's solicitor, had put his client's will. I accuse him of entering Cosmo Mornington's room and substituting a phial containing a toxic fluid for one of the phials of glycero-phosphate which Cosmo Mornington used for his hypodermic injections. I accuse him of playing the part of a doctor who came to certify Cosmo Mornington's death and of delivering a false certificate. I accuse him of supplying Hippolyte Fauville with the poison which killed successively Inspector Vérot, Edmond Fauville, and Hippolyte Fauville himself. I accuse him of arming and turning against me the hand of Gaston Sauverand, who, acting under his advice and his instructions, tried three times to take my life and ended by causing the death of my chauffeur. I accuse him of profiting by the relations which Gaston Sauverand had established with the infirmary in order to communicate with Marie Fauville, and of arranging for Marie Fauville to receive the hypodermic syringe and the phial of poison with which the poor woman was able to carry out her plans of suicide."

Perenna paused to note the effect of these charges. Then he went on:

"I accuse him of conveying to Gaston Sauverand, by some unknown means, the newspaper cuttings about Marie Fauville's death and, at the same time, foreseeing the inevitable results of his act. To sum up, therefore, without mentioning his share in the other crimes—the death of Inspector Vérot, the death of my chauffeur—I accuse him of killing Cosmo Mornington, Edmond Fauville, Hippolyte Fauville, Marie Fauville, and Gaston Sauverand; in plain words, of killing all those who stood between the millions and himself. These last words, Monsieur le Préfet, will tell you clearly what I have in my mind.

"When a man does away with five of his fellow creatures in order to secure a certain number of millions, it means that he is convinced that this proceeding will positively and mathematically insure his entering into possession of the millions. In short, when a man does away with a millionaire and his four successive heirs, it means that he himself is the millionaire's fifth heir. The man will be here in a moment."

"What!"

It was a spontaneous exclamation on the part of the Prefect of Police, who was forgetting the whole of Don Luis Perenna's powerful and closely reasoned argument, and thinking only of the stupefying apparition which Don Luis announced. Don Luis replied:

"Monsieur le Préfet, his visit is the logical outcome of my accusations. Remember that Cosmo Mornington's will explicitly states that no heir's claim will be valid unless he is present at today's meeting."

"And suppose he does not come?" asked the Prefect, thus showing that Don Luis's conviction had gradually got the better of his doubts.

"He will come, Monsieur le Préfet. If not, there would have been no sense in all this business. Limited to the crimes and other actions of Hippolyte Fauville, it could be looked upon as the preposterous work of a madman. Continued to the deaths of Marie Fauville and Gaston Sauverand, it demands, as its inevitable outcome, the appearance of a person who, as the last descendant of the Roussels of Saint-Etienne and consequently as Cosmo Mornington's absolute heir, taking precedence of myself, will come to claim the hundred million which he has won by means of his incredible audacity."

"And suppose he does not come?" M. Desmalions once more exclaimed, in a more vehement tone.

"Then, Monsieur le Préfet, you may take it that I am the culprit; and you have only to arrest me. This day, between five and six o'clock, you will see before you, in this room, the person who killed the Mornington heirs. It is, humanly speaking, impossible that this should not be so. Consequently, the law will be satisfied in any circumstances. He or I: the position is quite simple."

M. Desmalions was silent. He gnawed his moustache thoughtfully and walked round and round the table, within the narrow circle formed by the others. It was obvious that objections to the supposition were springing up in his mind. In the end, he muttered, as though speaking to himself:

"No, no. For, after all, how are we to explain that the man should have waited until now to claim his rights?"

"An accident, perhaps, Monsieur le Préfet, an obstacle of some kind. Or else—one can never tell—the perverse longing for a more striking sensation. And remember, Monsieur le

Préfet, how minutely and subtly the whole business was worked. Each event took place at the very moment fixed by Hippolyte Fauville. Cannot we take it that his accomplice is pursuing this method to the end and that he will not reveal himself until the last minute?"

M. Desmalions exclaimed, with a sort of anger:

"No, no, and again no! It is not possible. If a creature monstrous enough to commit such a series of murders exists, he will not be such a fool as to deliver himself into our hands."

"Monsieur le Préfet, he does not know the danger that threatens him if he comes here, because no one has even contemplated the theory of his existence. Besides, what risk does he run?"

"What risk? Why, if he has really committed those murders—"

"He has committed them, Monsieur le Préfet. He has *caused* them to be committed, which is a different thing. And you now see where the man's unsuspected strength lies! He does not act in person. From the day when the truth appeared to me, I have succeeded in gradually discovering his means of action, in laying bare the machinery which he controls, the tricks which he employs. He does not act in person. There you have his method. You will find that it is the same throughout the series of murders.

"In appearance, Cosmo Mornington died of the results of a carelessly administered injection. In reality, it was this man who caused the injection to prove fatal. In appearance, Inspector Vérot was killed by Hippolyte Fauville. In reality, it must have been this man who contrived the murder by pointing out the necessity to Fauville and, so to speak, guiding his hand. And, in the same way, in appearance, Fauville killed his son and committed suicide; Marie Fauville committed suicide; Gaston Sauverand committed suicide. In reality, it was this man who wanted them dead, who prompted them to commit suicide, and who supplied them with the means of death.

"There you have the method, and there, Monsieur le Préfet, you have the man." And, in a lower voice, that contained a sort of apprehension, he added, "I confess that never before, in the course of a life that has been full of strange meetings, have I encountered a more terrifying person, acting with more devilish ability or greater psychological insight."

His words created an ever-increasing sensation among his hearers. They really saw that invisible being. He took shape in their imaginations. They waited for him to arrive. Twice Don Luis had turned to the door and listened. And his action did more than anything else to conjure up the image of the man who was coming.

M. Desmalions said:

"Whether he acted in person or caused others to act, the law, once it has hold of him, will know how to—"

"The law will find it no easy matter, Monsieur le Préfet! A man of his powers and resource must have foreseen everything, even his arrest, even the accusation of which he would be the subject; and there is little to be brought against him but moral charges without proofs."

"Then you think—"

"I think, Monsieur le Préfet, that the thing will be to accept his explanations as quite natural and not to show any distrust. What you want is to know who he is. Later on, before long, you will be able to unmask him."

The Prefect of Police continued to walk round the table. Major d'Astrignac kept his eyes fixed on Perenna, whose coolness amazed him. The solicitor and the secretary of Embassy seemed greatly excited. In fact nothing could be more sensational than the thought that filled all their minds. Was the abominable murderer about to appear before them?

"Silence!" said the Prefect, stopping his walk.

Someone had crossed the anteroom.

There was a knock at the door.

"Come in!"

The office messenger entered, carrying a card-tray. On the tray was a letter; and in addition there was one of those printed slips on which callers write their name and the object of their visit.

M. Desmalions hastened toward the messenger. He hesitated a moment before taking up the slip. He was very pale. Then he glanced at it quickly.

"Oh!" he said, with a start.

He looked toward Don Luis, reflected, and then, taking the letter, he said to the messenger:

"Is the bearer outside?"

"In the anteroom, Monsieur le Préfet."

"Show the person in when I ring."

The messenger left the room.

M. Desmalions stood in front of his desk, without moving. For the second time Don Luis met his eyes; and a feeling of perturbation came over him. What was happening?

With a sharp movement the Prefect of Police opened the envelope which he held in his hand, unfolded the letter and began to read it.

The others watched his every gesture, watched the least change of expression on his face. Were Perenna's predictions about to be fulfilled? Was a fifth heir putting in his claim?

The moment he had read the first lines, M. Desmalions looked up and, addressing Don Luis, murmured:

"You were right, Monsieur. This is a claim."

"On whose part, Monsieur le Préfet?" Don Luis could not help asking.

M. Desmalions did not reply. He finished reading the letter. Then he read it again, with the attention of a man weighing every word. Lastly, he read aloud:

"MONSIEUR LE PRÉFET:

"A chance correspondence has revealed to me the existence of an unknown heir of the Roussel family. It was only today that I was able to procure the documents necessary for identifying this heir; and, owing to unforeseen obstacles, it is only at the last moment that I am able to send them to you *by the person whom they concern*. Respecting a secret which is not mine and wishing, as a woman, to remain outside a business in which I have been only accidentally involved, I beg you, Monsieur le Préfet, to excuse me if I do not feel called upon to sign my name to this letter."

So Perenna had seen rightly and events were justifying his forecast. Someone was putting in an appearance within the period indicated. The claim was made in good time. And the very way in which things were happening at the exact moment was curiously suggestive of the mechanical exactness that had governed the whole business.

The last question still remained: who was this unknown person, the possible heir, and therefore the five or six-fold murderer? He was waiting in the next room. There was nothing but a wall between him and the others. He was coming in. They would see him. They would know who he was.

The Prefect suddenly rang the bell.

A few tense seconds elapsed. Oddly enough, M. Desmalions did not remove his eyes from Perenna. Don Luis remained quite master of himself, but restless and uneasy at heart.

The door opened. The messenger showed someone in.

It was Florence Levasseur.

16

WEBER TAKES HIS REVENGE

Don Luis was for one moment amazed. Florence Levasseur here! Florence, whom he had left in the train under Mazeroux's supervision and for whom it was physically impossible to be back in Paris before eight o'clock in the evening!

Then, despite his bewilderment, he at once understood. Florence, knowing that she was being followed, had drawn them after her to the Gare Saint-Lazare and simply walked through the railway carriage, getting out on the other platform, while the worthy Mazeroux went on in the train to keep his eye on the traveller who was not there.

But suddenly the full horror of the situation struck him. Florence was here to claim the inheritance; and her claim, as he himself had said, was a proof of the most terrible guilt.

Acting on an irresistible impulse, Don Luis leaped to the girl's side, seized her by the arm and said, with almost malevolent force:

"What are you doing here? What have you come for? Why did you not let me know?"

M. Desmalions stepped between them. But Don Luis, without letting go of the girl's arm, exclaimed:

"Oh, Monsieur le Préfet, don't you see that this is all a mistake? The person whom we are expecting, about whom

I told you, is not this one. The other is keeping in the background, as usual. Why it's impossible that Florence Levasseur—"

"I have no preconceived opinion on the subject of this young lady," said the Prefect of Police, in an authoritative voice. "But it is my duty to question her about the circumstances that brought her here; and I shall certainly do so."

He released the girl from Don Luis's grasp and made her take a seat. He himself sat down at his desk; and it was easy to see how great an impression the girl's presence made upon him. It afforded so to speak an illustration of Don Luis's argument.

The appearance on the scene of a new person, laying claim to the inheritance, was undeniably, to any logical mind, the appearance on the scene of a criminal who herself brought with her the proofs of her crimes. Don Luis felt this clearly and, from that moment, did not take his eyes off the Prefect of Police.

Florence looked at them by turns as though the whole thing was the most insoluble mystery to her. Her beautiful dark eyes retained their customary serenity. She no longer wore her nurse's uniform; and her gray gown, very simply cut and devoid of ornaments, showed her graceful figure. She was grave and unemotional as usual.

M. Desmalions said:

"Explain yourself, Mademoiselle."

She answered:

"I have nothing to explain, Monsieur le Préfet. I have come to you on an errand which I am fulfilling without knowing exactly what it is about."

"What do you mean? Without knowing what it is about?"

"I will tell you, Monsieur le Préfet. Someone in whom I have every confidence and for whom I entertain the greatest respect asked me to hand you certain papers. They appear to concern the question which is the object of your meeting today."

"The question of awarding the Mornington inheritance?"

"Yes."

"You know that, if this claim had not been made in the course of the present sitting, it would have had no effect?"

"I came as soon as the papers were handed to me."

"Why were they not handed to you an hour or two earlier?"

"I was not there. I had to leave the house where I am staying, in a hurry."

Perenna did not doubt that it was his intervention that upset the enemy's plans by causing Florence to take to flight.

The Prefect continued:

"So you are ignorant of the reasons why you received the papers?"

"Yes, Monsieur le Préfet."

"And evidently you are also ignorant of how far they concern you?"

"They do not concern me, Monsieur le Préfet."

M. Desmalions smiled and, looking into Florence's eyes, said, plainly:

"According to the letter that accompanies them, they concern you intimately. It seems that they prove, in the most positive manner, that you are descended from the Roussel family and that you consequently have every right to the Mornington inheritance."

"I?"

The cry was a spontaneous exclamation of astonishment and protest.

And she at once went on, insistently:

"I, a right to the inheritance? I have none at all, Monsieur le Préfet, none at all. I never knew Mr Mornington. What is this story? There is some mistake."

She spoke with great animation and with an apparent frankness that would have impressed any other man than the Prefect of Police. But how could he forget Don Luis's arguments and the accusation made beforehand against the person who would arrive at the meeting?

"Give me the papers," he said.

She took from her handbag a blue envelope which was not fastened down and which he found to contain a number of faded documents, damaged at the folds and torn in different places.

He examined them amid perfect silence, read them through, studied them thoroughly, inspected the signatures and the seals through a magnifying glass, and said:

"They bear every sign of being genuine. The seals are official."

"Then, Monsieur le Préfet—?" said Florence, in a trembling voice.

"Then, Mademoiselle, let me tell you that your ignorance strikes me as most incredible."

And, turning to the solicitor, he said:

"Listen briefly to what these documents contain and prove. Gaston Sauverand, Cosmo Mornington's heir in the fourth line, had, as you know, an elder brother, called Raoul, who lived in the Argentine Republic. This brother, before his death, sent to Europe, in the charge of an old nurse, a child of five who was none other than his daughter, a natural but legally recognized daughter whom he had had by Mlle. Levasseur, a French teacher at Buenos Aires.

"Here is the birth certificate. Here is the signed declaration written entirely in the father's hand. Here is the affidavit signed by the old nurse. Here are the depositions of three friends, merchants or solicitors at Buenos Aires. And here are the death certificates of the father and mother.

"All these documents have been legalized and bear the seals of the French consulate. For the present, I have no reason to doubt them; and I am bound to look upon Florence Levasseur as Raoul Sauverand's daughter and Gaston Sauverand's niece."

"Gaston Sauvarand's niece?... His niece?" stammered Florence.

The mention of a father whom she had, so to speak, never known, left her unmoved. But she began to weep at the recollection of Gaston Sauverand, whom she loved so fondly and to whom she found herself linked by such a close relationship.

Were her tears sincere? Or were they the tears of an actress able to play her part down to the slightest details? Were those facts really revealed to her for the first time? Or was she acting the emotions which the revelation of those facts would produce in her under natural conditions?

Don Luis observed M. Desmalions even more narrowly than he did the girl, and tried to read the secret thoughts of the man with whom the decision lay. And suddenly he became certain that Florence's arrest was a matter resolved upon as definitely as the arrest of the most monstrous criminal. Then he went up to her and said:

"Florence."

She looked at him with her tear-dimmed eyes and made no reply.

Slowly, he said:

"To defend yourself, Florence—for, though I am sure you do not know it, you are under that obligation—you must understand the terrible position in which events have placed you.

"Florence, the Prefect of Police has been led by the logical outcome of those events to come to the final conclusion that the person entering this room with an evident claim to the inheritance is the person who killed the Mornington heirs. You entered the room, Florence, and you are undoubtedly Cosmo Mornington's heir."

He saw her shake from head to foot and turn as pale as death. Nevertheless, she uttered no word and made no gesture of protest.

He went on:

"It is a formal accusation. Do you say nothing in reply?"

She waited some time and then declared:

"I have nothing to say. The whole thing is a mystery. What would you have me reply? I do not understand!"

Don Luis stood quivering with anguish in front of her. He stammered:

"Is that all? Do you accept?"

After a second, she said, in an undertone:

"Explain yourself, I beg of you. What you mean, I suppose, is that, if I do not reply, I accept the accusation?"

"Yes."

"And then?"

"Arrest—prison—"

"Prison!"

She seemed to be suffering hideously. Her beautiful features were distorted with fear. To her mind, prison evidently represented the torments undergone by Marie and Sauverand. It must mean despair, shame, death, all those horrors which Marie and Sauverand had been unable to avoid and of which she in her turn would become the victim.

An awful sense of hopelessness overcame her, and she moaned:

"How tired I am! I feel that there is nothing to be done! I am stifled by the mystery around me! Oh, if I could only see and understand!"

There was another long pause. Leaning over her, M. Desmalions studied her face with concentrated attention. Then, as she did not speak, he put his hand to the bell on his table and struck it three times.

Don Luis did not stir from where he stood, with his eyes despairingly fixed on Florence. A battle was raging within him between his love and generosity, which led him to believe the girl, and his reason, which obliged him to suspect her. Was she innocent or guilty? He did not know. Everything was against her. And yet why had he never ceased to love her?

Weber entered, followed by his men. M. Desmalions spoke to him and pointed to Florence. Weber went up to her.

"Florence!" said Don Luis.

She looked at him and looked at Weber and his men; and, suddenly, realizing what was coming, she retreated, staggered for a moment, bewildered and fainting, and fell back in Don Luis's arms:

"Oh, save me, save me! Do save me!"

The action was so natural and unconstrained, the cry of distress so clearly denoted the alarm which only the innocent can feel, that Don Luis was promptly convinced. A fervent belief in her lightened his heart. His doubts, his caution, his hesitation, his anguish: all these vanished before a certainty that dashed upon him like an irresistible wave. And he cried:

"No, no, that must not be! Monsieur le Préfet, there are things that cannot be permitted—"

He stooped over Florence, whom he was holding so firmly in his arms that nobody could have taken her from him. Their eyes met. His face was close to the girl's. He quivered with emotion at feeling her throbbing, so weak, so utterly helpless; and he said to her passionately, in a voice too low for any but her to hear:

"I love you, I love you... Ah, Florence, if you only knew what I feel: how I suffer and how happy I am! Oh, Florence, I love you, I love you—"

Weber had stood aside, at a sign from the Prefect, who wanted to witness the unexpected conflict between those two mysterious beings, Don Luis Perenna and Florence Levasseur.

Don Luis unloosed his arms and placed the girl in a chair. Then, putting his two hands on her shoulders, face to face with her, he said:

"Though you do not understand, Florence, I am beginning to understand a good deal; and I can already almost see my way in the mystery that terrifies you. Florence, listen to me. It is not you who are doing all this, is it? There is somebody else behind you, above you—somebody who gives you your instructions, isn't there, while you yourself don't know where he is leading you?"

"Nobody is instructing me. What do you mean? Explain."

"Yes, you are not alone in your life. There are many things which you do because you are told to do them and because you think them right and because you do not know their consequences or even that they can have any consequences. Answer my question: are you absolutely free? Are you not yielding to some influence?"

The girl seemed to have come to herself, and her face recovered some of its usual calmness. Nevertheless, it seemed as if Don Luis's question made an impression on her.

"No," she said, "there is no influence—none at all—I'm sure of it."

He insisted, with growing eagerness:

"No, you are not sure; don't say that. Someone is dominating you without your knowing it. Think for a moment. You are Cosmo Mornington's heir, heir to a fortune which you don't care about, I know, I swear! Well, if you don't want that fortune, to whom will it belong? Answer me. Is there anyone who is interested or believes himself interested in seeing you rich? The whole question lies in that. Is your life linked with that of someone else? Is he a friend of yours? Are you engaged to him?"

She gave a start of revolt.

"Oh, never! The man of whom you speak is incapable—"

"Ah," he cried, overcome with jealousy, "you confess it! So the man of whom I speak exists! I swear that the villain—"

He turned toward M. Desmalions, his face convulsed with hatred. He made no further effort to contain himself:

"Monsieur le Préfet, we are in sight of the goal. I know the road that will lead us to it. The wild beast shall be hunted down tonight, or tomorrow at least. Monsieur le Préfet, the letter that accompanied those documents, the unsigned letter which this young lady handed you, was written by the mother superior who manages a nursing-home in the Avenue des Ternes.

"By making immediate inquiries at that nursing-home, by questioning the superior and confronting her with Mlle. Levasseur, we shall discover the identity of the criminal himself. But we must not lose a minute, or we shall be too late and the wild beast will have fled."

His outburst was irresistible. There was no fighting against the violence of his conviction. Still, M. Desmalions objected:

"Mlle. Levasseur could tell us—"

"She will not speak, or at least not till later, when the man has been unmasked in her presence. Monsieur le Préfet, I entreat you to have the same confidence in me as before. Have not all my promises been fulfilled? Have confidence, Monsieur le Préfet; cast aside your doubts. Remember how Marie Fauville and Gaston Sauverand were overwhelmed with charges, the most serious charges, and how they succumbed in spite of their innocence.

"Does the law wish to see Florence Levasseur sacrificed as the two others were? And, besides, what I ask for is not her release, but the means to defend her—that is to say, an hour or two's delay. Let Deputy Chief Weber be responsible for her safe custody. Let your detectives go with us: these and more as well, for we cannot have too many to capture the loathsome brute in his lair."

M. Desmalions did not reply. After a brief moment he took Weber aside and talked to him for some minutes. M.

Desmalions did not seem very favourably disposed toward Don Luis's request. But Weber was heard to say:

"You need have no fear, Monsieur le Préfet. We run no risk."

And M. Desmalions yielded.

A few moments later Don Luis Perenna and Florence Levasseur took their seats in a motor car with Weber and two inspectors. Another car, filled with detectives, followed.

The hospital was literally invested by the police force and Weber neglected none of the precautions of a regular siege.

The Prefect of Police, who arrived in his own car, was shown by the manservant into the waiting-room and then into the parlour, where the mother superior came to him at once. Without delay or preamble of any sort he put his questions to her, in the presence of Don Luis, Weber, and Florence:

"Reverend mother," he said, "I have a letter here which was brought to me at headquarters and which tells me of the existence of certain documents concerning a legacy. According to my information, this letter, which is unsigned and which is in a disguised hand, was written by you. Is that so?"

The mother superior, a woman with a powerful face and a determined air, replied, without embarrassment:

"That is so, Monsieur le Préfet. As I had the honour to tell you in my letter, I would have preferred, for obvious reasons, that my name should not be mentioned. Besides, the delivery of the documents was all that mattered. However, since you know that I am the writer, I am prepared to answer your questions."

M. Desmalions continued, with a glance at Florence:

"I will first ask you, Reverend Mother, if you know this young lady?"

"Yes, Monsieur le Préfet. Florence was with us for six months as a nurse, a few years ago. She gave such satisfaction that I was glad to take her back this day fortnight. As I had read her story in the papers, I simply asked her to change her name. We had a new staff at the hospital, and it was therefore a safe refuge for her."

"But, as you have read the papers, you must be aware of the accusations against her?"

"Those accusations have no weight, Monsieur le Préfet, with anyone who knows Florence. She has one of the noblest characters and one of the strictest consciences that I have ever met with."

The Prefect continued:

"Let us speak of the documents, Reverend Mother. Where do they come from?"

"Yesterday, Monsieur le Préfet, I found in my room a communication in which the writer proposed to send me some papers that interested Florence Levasseur—"

"How did anyone know that she was here?" asked M. Desmalions, interrupting her.

"I can't tell you. The letter simply said that the papers would be at Versailles, at the *poste restante*, in my name, on a certain day—that is to say, this morning. I was also asked not to mention them to anybody and to hand them at three o'clock this afternoon to Florence Levasseur, with instructions to take them to the Prefect of Police at once. I was also requested to have a letter conveyed to Sergeant Mazeroux."

"To Sergeant Mazeroux! That's odd."

"That letter appeared to have to do with the same business. Now, I am very fond of Florence. So I sent the letter, and this morning went to Versailles and found the papers there, as stated. When I got back, Florence was out. I was not able to hand them to her until her return, at about four o'clock."

"Where were the papers posted?"

"In Paris. The postmark on the envelope was that of the Avenue Niel, which happens to be the nearest office to this."

"And did not the fact of finding that letter in your room strike you as strange?"

"Certainly, Monsieur le Préfet, but no stranger than all the other incidents in the matter."

"Nevertheless," continued M. Desmalions, who was watching Florence's pale face, "nevertheless, when you saw that the instructions which you received came from this house and that they concerned a person living in this house, did you not entertain the idea that that person—"

"The idea that Florence had entered the room, unknown to me, for such a purpose?" cried the superior. "Oh, Monsieur le Préfet, Florence is incapable of doing such a thing!"

The girl was silent, but her drawn features betrayed the feelings of alarm that upset her.

Don Luis went up to her and said:

"The mystery is clearing, Florence, isn't it? And you are suffering in consequence. Who put the letter in Mother Superior's room? You know, don't you? And you know who is conducting all this plot?"

She did not answer. Then, turning to the deputy chief, the Prefect said:

"Weber, please go and search the room which Mlle. Levasseur occupied."

And, in reply to the nun's protest:

"It is indispensable," he declared, "that we should know the reasons why Mlle. Levasseur preserves such an obstinate silence."

Florence herself led the way. But, as Weber was leaving the room, Don Luis exclaimed:

"Take care, Deputy Chief!"

"Take care? Why?"

"I don't know," said Don Luis, who really could not have said why Florence's behaviour was making him uneasy. "I don't know. Still, I warn you—"

Weber shrugged his shoulders and, accompanied by the superior, moved away. In the hall he took two men with him.

Florence walked ahead. She went up a flight of stairs and turned down a long corridor, with rooms on either side of it, which, after turning a corner, led to a short and very narrow passage ending in a door.

This was her room. The door opened not inward, into the room, but outward, into the passage. Florence therefore drew it to her, stepping back as she did so, which obliged Weber to do likewise. She took advantage of this to rush in and close the door behind her so quickly that the deputy chief, when he tried to grasp the handle, merely struck the air.

He made an angry gesture:

"The baggage! She means to burn some papers!"

And, turning to the superior:

"Is there another exit to the room?"

"No, Monsieur."

He tried to open the door, but she had locked and bolted it. Then he stood aside to make way for one of his men, a giant, who, with one blow of his fist, smashed a panel.

Weber pushed by him, put his arm through the opening, drew the bolt, turned the key, pulled open the door and entered.

Florence was no longer in her room. A little open window opposite showed the way she had taken.

"Oh, curse my luck!" he shouted. "She's cut off!"

And, hurrying back to the staircase, he roared over the balusters:

"Watch all the doors! She's got away! Collar her!"

M. Desmalions came hurrying up. Meeting the deputy, he received his explanations and then went on to Florence's room. The open window looked out on a small inner yard, a sort of well which served to ventilate a part of the house. Some rain-pipes ran down the wall. Florence must have let herself down by them. But what coolness and what an indomitable will she must have displayed to make her escape in this manner!

The detectives had already distributed themselves on every side to bar the fugitive's road. It soon became manifest that Florence, for whom they were hunting on the ground floor and in the basement, had gone from the yard into the room underneath her own, which happened to be the mother superior's; that she had put on a nun's habit; and that, thus disguised, she had passed unnoticed through the very men who were pursuing her.

They rushed outside. But it was now dark; and every search was bound to be vain in so populous a quarter.

The Prefect of Police made no effort to conceal his displeasure. Don Luis was also greatly disappointed at this flight, which thwarted his plans, and enlarged openly upon Weber's lack of skill.

"I told you so, Deputy Chief! You should have taken your precautions. Mlle. Levasseur's attitude ought to have warned you. She evidently knows the criminal and wanted to go to him, ask him for explanations and, for all we can tell, save him, if he managed to convince her. And what will happen between them? When the villain sees that he is discovered, he will be capable of anything."

M. Desmalions again questioned the mother superior and soon learned that Florence, before taking refuge in the nursing-home, had spent forty-eight hours in some furnished apartments on the Ile Saint-Louis.

The clue was not worth much, but they could not neglect it. The Prefect of Police, who retained all his doubts with regard to Florence and attached extreme importance to the girl's capture, ordered Weber and his men to follow up this trail without delay. Don Luis accompanied the deputy chief.

Events at once showed that the Prefect of Police was right. Florence had taken refuge in the lodging-house on the Ile Saint-Louis, where she had engaged a room under an assumed name. But she had no sooner arrived than a small boy called at the house, asked for her, and went away with her.

They went up to her room and found a parcel done up in a newspaper, containing a nun's habit. The thing was obvious.

Later, in the course of the evening, Weber succeeded in discovering the small boy. He was the son of the porter of one of the houses in the neighbourhood. Where could he have taken Florence? When questioned, he definitely refused to betray the lady who had trusted him and who had cried when she kissed him. His mother entreated him. His father boxed his ears. He was inflexible.

In any case, it was not unreasonable to conclude that Florence had not left the Ile Saint-Louis or its immediate vicinity. The detectives persisted in their search all the evening. Weber established his headquarters in a tap room where every scrap of information was brought to him and where his men returned from time to time to receive his orders. He also remained in constant communication with the Prefect's office.

At half-past ten a squad of detectives, sent by the Prefect, placed themselves at the deputy chief's disposal. Mazeroux, newly arrived from Rouen and furious with Florence, joined them.

The search continued. Don Luis had gradually assumed its management; and it was he who, so to speak, inspired Weber to ring at this or that door and to question this or that person.

At eleven o'clock the hunt still remained fruitless; and Don Luis was the victim of an increasing and irritating restlessness. But, shortly after midnight, a shrill whistle drew all the men to the eastern extremity of the island, at the end of the Quai d' Anjou.

Two detectives stood waiting for them, surrounded by a small crowd of onlookers. They had just learned that, some distance farther away, on the Quai Henri IV, which does not form part of the island, a motor car had pulled up outside a house, that there was the noise of a dispute, and that the cab had subsequently driven off in the direction of Vincennes.

They hastened to the Quai Henri IV and at once found the house. There was a door on the ground floor opening straight on the pavement. The taxi had stopped for a few minutes in front of this door. Two persons, a woman and a man leading her along, had left the ground floor flat. When the door of the taxi was shut, a man's voice had shouted from the inside:

"Drive down the Boulevard Saint-Germain and along the quays. Then take the Versailles Road."

But the porter's wife was able to furnish more precise particulars. Puzzled by the tenant of the ground floor, whom she had only seen once, in the evening, who paid his rent by checks signed in the name of Charles and who but very seldom came to his apartment, she had taken advantage of the fact that her lodge was next to the flat to listen to the sound of voices. The man and the woman were arguing. At one moment the man cried, in a louder tone:

"Come with me, Florence. I insist upon it; and I will give you every proof of my innocence tomorrow morning. And, if you nevertheless refuse to become my wife, I shall leave the country. All my preparations are made."

A little later he began to laugh and, again raising his voice, said:

"Afraid of what, Florence? That I shall kill you perhaps? No, no, have no fear—"

The portress had heard nothing more. But was this not enough to justify every alarm?

Don Luis caught hold of the deputy chief:

"Come along! I knew it: the man is capable of anything. It's the tiger! He means to kill her!"

He rushed outside, dragging the deputy toward the two police motors waiting five hundred yards down. Meanwhile, Mazeroux was trying to protest:

"It would be better to search the house, to pick up some clues—"

"Oh," shouted Don Luis, increasing his pace, "the house and the clues will keep!... But he's gaining ground, the ruffian—and he has Florence with him—and he's going to kill her! It's a trap!... I'm sure of it—"

He was shouting in the dark, dragging the two men along with irresistible force.

They neared the motors.

"Get ready!" he ordered as soon as he was in sight. "I'll drive myself."

He tried to get into the driver's seat. But Weber objected and pushed him inside, saying:

"Don't trouble—the chauffeur knows his business. He'll drive faster than you would."

Don Luis, the deputy chief, and two detectives crowded into the cab; Mazeroux took his seat beside the chauffeur.

"Versailles Road!" roared Don Luis.

The car started; and he continued:

"We've got him! You see, it's a magnificent opportunity. He must be going pretty fast, but without forcing the pace, because he doesn't think we're after him. Oh, the villain, we'll make him sit up! Quicker, driver! But what the devil are we loaded up like this for? You and I, Deputy Chief, would have been enough. Hi, Mazeroux, get down and jump into the other car! That'll be better, won't it, Deputy? It's absurd—"

He interrupted himself; and, as he was sitting on the back seat, between the deputy chief and a detective, he rose toward the window and muttered:

"Why, look here, what's the idiot doing? That's not the road! I say, what does this mean?"

A roar of laughter was the only answer. It came from Weber, who was shaking with delight. Don Luis stifled an oath and, making a tremendous effort, tried to leap from the car. Six hands fell upon him and held him motionless. The deputy chief had him by the throat. The detectives clutched his arms. There was no room for him to struggle within the restricted space of the small car; and he felt the cold iron of a revolver on his temple.

"None of your nonsense," growled Weber, "or I'll blow out your brains, my boy! Aha! You didn't expect this! It's Weber's revenge, eh?"

And, when Perenna continued to wriggle, he went on, in a threatening tone:

"You'll have only yourself to blame, mind!... I'm going to count three: one, two—"

"But what's it all about?" bellowed Don Luis.

"Prefect's orders, received just now."

"What orders?"

"To take you to the lockup if the Florence girl escaped us again."

"Have you a warrant?"

"I have."

"And what next?"

"What next? Nothing: the Sante—the examining magistrate—"

"But, hang it all, the tiger's making tracks meanwhile! Oh, rot! Is it possible to be so dense? What mugs those fellows are! Oh, dash it!"

He was fuming with rage, and when he saw that they were driving into the prison yard, he gathered all his strength, knocked the revolver out of the deputy's hand, and stunned one of the detectives with a blow of his fist.

But ten men came crowding round the doors. Resistance was useless. He understood this, and his rage increased.

"The idiots!" he shouted, while they surrounded him and searched him at the door of the office. "The rotters! The bunglers! To go mucking up a job like that! They can lay hands on the villain if they want to, and they lock up the honest man—while the villain makes himself scarce! And he'll do more murder yet! Florence! Florence..."

Under the lamp light, in the midst of the detectives holding him, he was magnificent in his helpless violence.

They dragged him away. With an unparalleled display of strength, he drew himself up, shook off the men who were hanging on to him like a pack of hounds worrying some animal at bay, got rid of Weber, and accosted Mazeroux in familiar tones. He was gloriously masterful, almost calm, so wholly did he appear to control his seething rage. He gave his orders in breathless little sentences, curt as words of command.

"Mazeroux, run around to the Prefect's. Ask him to ring up Valenglay: yes, the Prime Minister. I want to see him. Have him informed. Ask the Prefect to say it's I: the man who made the German Emperor play his game. My name? He knows. Or, if he forgets, the Prefect can tell him my name."

He paused for a second or two; and then, calmer still, he declared:

"Arsène Lupin! Telephone those two words to him and just say this: 'Arsène Lupin wishes to speak to the Prime Minister on very important business.' Get that through to him at once. The Prime Minister would be very angry if he heard afterward that they had neglected to communicate my request. Go, Mazeroux, and then find the villain's tracks again."

The governor of the prison had opened the jail book.

"You can enter my name, Monsieur le Directeur," said Don Luis. "Put down 'Arsène Lupin.'"

The governor smiled and said:

"I should find a difficulty in putting down any other. It's on the warrant: 'Arsène Lupin, alias Don Luis Perenna.'"

Don Luis felt a little shudder pass through him at the sound of those words. The fact that he was arrested under the name of Arsène Lupin made his position doubly dangerous.

"Ah," he said, "so they've resolved—"

"I should think so!" said Weber, in a tone of triumph. "We've resolved to take the bull by the horns and to go straight for Lupin. Plucky of us, eh? Never fear, we'll show you something better than that!"

Don Luis did not flinch. Turning to Mazeroux again, he said:

"Don't forget my instructions, Mazeroux."

But there was a fresh blow in store for him. The sergeant did not answer his remark. Don Luis watched him closely and once more gave a start. He had just perceived that Mazeroux also was surrounded by men who were holding him tight. And the poor sergeant stood silently shedding tears.

Weber's liveliness increased.

"You'll have to excuse him, Lupin. Sergeant Mazeroux accompanies you to prison, though not in the same cell."

"Ah!" said Don Luis, drawing himself up. "Is Mazeroux put into jail?"

"Prefect's orders, warrant duly executed."

"And on what charge?"

"Accomplice of Arsène Lupin."

"Mazeroux my accomplice? Get out! Mazeroux? The most honest man that ever lived!"

"The most honest man that ever lived, as you say. That didn't prevent people from going to him when they wanted to write to you or prevent him from bringing you the letters. Which proves that he knew where you were hanging out. And there's a good deal more which we'll explain to you, Lupin, in good time. You'll have plenty of fun, I assure you."

Don Luis murmured:

"My poor Mazeroux!"

Then, raising his voice, he said:

"Don't cry, old chap. It's just a matter of the remainder of the night. Yes, I'll share my cards with you and we'll turn the king and mark game in a very few hours. Don't cry. I've got a much finer berth waiting for you, a more honourable and above all a more lucrative position. I have just what you want.

"You don't imagine, surely, that I wasn't prepared for this! Why, you know me! Take it from me: I shall be at liberty tomorrow, and the government, after setting you free, will pitch you into a colonelcy or something, with a marshal's pay attached to it. So don't cry, Mazeroux."

Then, addressing Weber, he said to him in the voice of a principal giving an order, and knowing that the order will be executed without discussion:

"Monsieur, I will ask you to fulfil the confidential mission which I was entrusting to Mazeroux. First, inform the Prefect of Police that I have a communication of the very highest importance to make to the Prime Minister. Next, discover the tiger's tracks at Versailles before the night is over. I know your merit, Monsieur, and I rely entirely upon your diligence and your zeal. Meet me at twelve o'clock tomorrow."

And, still maintaining his attitude of a principal who has given his instructions, he allowed himself to be taken to his cell.

It was ten to one. For the last fifty minutes the enemy had been bowling along the highroad, carrying off Florence like a prey which it now seemed impossible to snatch from him.

The door was locked and bolted.

Don Luis reflected:

"Even presuming that Monsieur le Prefect consents to ring up Valenglay, he won't do so before the morning. So they've given the villain eight hours' start before I'm free. Eight hours! Curse it!"

He thought a little longer, then shrugged his shoulders with the air of one who, for the moment, has nothing better to do than wait, and flung himself on his mattress, murmuring:

"Hushaby, Lupin!"

17

OPEN SESAME!

In spite of his usual facility for sleep, Don Luis slept for three hours at most. He was racked with too much anxiety; and, though his plan of conduct was worked out mathematically, he could not help foreseeing all the obstacles which were likely to frustrate that plan. Of course, Weber would speak to M. Desmalions. But would M. Desmalions telephone to Valenglay?

"He is sure to telephone," Don Luis declared, stamping his foot. "It doesn't let him in for anything. And at the same time, he would be running a big risk if he refused, especially as Valenglay must have been consulted about my arrest and is obviously kept informed of all that happens."

He next asked himself what exactly Valenglay could do, once he was told. For, after all, was it not too much to expect that the head of the government, that the Prime Minister, should put himself out to obey the injunctions and assist the schemes of M. Arsène Lupin?

"He will come!" he cried, with the same persistent confidence. "Valenglay doesn't care a hang for form and ceremony and all that nonsense. He will come, even if it is only out of curiosity, to learn what the Kaiser's friend can have to say to him. Besides, he knows me! I am not one of those beggars who inconvenience people for nothing. There's always something to be gained by meeting me. He'll come!"

But another question at once presented itself to his mind. Valenglay's coming in no way implied his consent to the bargain which Perenna meant to propose to him. And even if Don Luis succeeded in convincing him, what risks remained! How many doubtful points to overcome! And then the possibilities of failure!

Would Weber pursue the fugitive's motor car with the necessary decision and boldness? Would he get on the track again? And, having got on the track, would he be certain not to lose it?

And then—and then, even supposing that all the chances were favourable, was it not too late? Taking for granted that they hunted down the wild beast, that they drove him to bay, would he not meanwhile have killed his prey? Knowing himself beaten, would a monster of that kind hesitate to add one more murder to the long list of his crimes?

And this, to Don Luis, was the crowning terror. After all the difficulties which, in his stubbornly confident imagination, he had managed to surmount, he was brought face to face with the horrible vision of Florence being sacrificed, of Florence dead!

"Oh, the torture of it!" he stammered. "I alone could have succeeded; and they shut me up!"

He hardly put himself out to inquire into the reasons for which M. Desmalions, suddenly changing his mind, had consented to his arrest, thus bringing back to life that troublesome Arsène Lupin with whom the police had not hitherto cared to hamper themselves. No, that did not interest him. Florence alone mattered. And the minutes passed; and each minute wasted brought Florence nearer to her doom.

He remembered a similar occasion when, some years before, he waited in the same way for the door of his cell to open and the German Emperor to appear. But how much greater was the solemnity of the present moment! Before, it was at the very most his liberty that was at stake. This time it was Florence's life which fate was about to offer or refuse him.

"Florence! Florence!" he kept repeating, in his despair.

He no longer had a doubt of her innocence. Nor did he doubt that the other loved her and had carried her off not so much for the hostage of a coveted fortune as for a love spoil, which a man destroys if he cannot keep it.

"Florence! Florence!"

He was suffering from an extraordinary fit of depression. His defeat seemed irretrievable. There was no question of hastening after Florence, of catching the murderer. Don Luis was in prison under his own name of Arsène Lupin; and the whole problem lay in knowing how long he would remain there, for months or for years!

It was then that he fully realized what his love for Florence meant. He perceived that it took the place in his life of his former passions, his craving for luxury, his desire for mastery, his pleasure in fighting, his ambition, his revenge. For two months he had been struggling to win her and for nothing else. The search after the truth and the punishment of the criminal were to him no more than means of saving Florence from the dangers that threatened her.

If Florence had to die, if it was too late to snatch her from the enemy, in that case he might as well remain in prison. Arsène Lupin spending the rest of his days in a convict settlement was a fitting end to the spoilt life of a man who had not even been able to win the love of the only woman he had really loved.

It was a passing mood and, being totally opposed to Don Luis's nature, finished abruptly in a state of utter confidence which no longer admitted the least particle of anxiety or doubt. The sun had risen. The cell gradually became filled with daylight. And Don Luis remembered that Valenglay reached his office on the Place Beauveau at seven o'clock in the morning.

From this moment he felt absolutely calm. Coming events presented an entirely different aspect to him, as though they had, so to speak, turned right round. The contest seemed to him easy, the facts free from complications. He understood as clearly as if the actions had been performed that his will could not but be obeyed. The deputy chief must inevitably have made a faithful report to the Prefect of Police. The Prefect of Police must inevitably that morning have transmitted Arsène Lupin's request to Valenglay.

Valenglay would inevitably give himself the pleasure of an interview with Arsène Lupin. Arsène Lupin would inevitably, in the course of that interview, obtain Valenglay's consent. These were not suppositions, but certainties; not problems awaiting solution, but problems already solved. Starting from A and continuing along B and C, you arrive, whether you wish it or not, at D.

Don Luis began to laugh:

"Come, come, Arsène, old chap, remember that you brought Mr Hohenzollern all the way from his Brandenburg Marches. Valenglay does not live as far as that, by Jove! And, if necessary, you can put yourself out a little... That's it: I'll consent to take the first step. I will go and call on M. de Beauveau. M. Valenglay, it is a pleasure to see you."

He went gayly to the door, pretending that it was open and that he had only to walk through to be received when his turn came.

He repeated this child's play three times, bowing low and long, as though holding a plumed hat in his hand, and murmuring:

"Open sesame!"

At the fourth time, the door opened, and a warder appeared.

Don Luis said, in a ceremonious tone:

"I hope I have not kept the Prime Minister waiting?"

There were four inspectors in the corridor.

"Are these gentlemen my escort?" he asked. "That's right. Announce Arsène Lupin, grandee of Spain, his most Catholic Majesty's cousin. My lords, I follow you. Turnkey, here are twenty crowns for your pains, my friend."

He stopped in the corridor.

"By Jupiter, no gloves; and I haven't shaved since yesterday!"

The inspectors had surrounded him and were pushing him a little roughly. He seized two of them by the arm. They groaned.

"That'll teach you," he said. "You've no orders to thrash me, have you? Nor even to handcuff me? That being so, young fellows, behave!"

The prison governor was standing in the hall.

"I've had a capital night, my dear governor," said Don "Your C.T.C. rooms are the very acme of comfort. I'll see that the Lockup Arms receives a star in the 'Baedeker.' Would you like me to write you a testimonial in your jail book? You wouldn't? Perhaps you hope to see me again? Sorry, my dear governor, but it's impossible. I have other things to do."

A motor car was waiting in the yard. Don Luis stepped in with the four detectives:

"Place Beauveau," he said to the driver.

"No, Rue Vineuse," said one of the detectives, correcting him.

"Oho!" said Don Luis. "His Excellency's private residence! His Excellency prefers that my visit should be kept secret. That's a good sign. By the way, dear friends, what's the time?"

His question remained unanswered. And as the detectives had drawn the blinds, he was unable to consult the clocks in the street.

* * *

It was not until he was at Valenglay's, in the Prime Minister's little ground-floor flat near the Trocadero, that he saw a clock on the mantelpiece:

"A quarter to seven!" he exclaimed. "Good! There's not been much time lost."

Valenglay's study opened on a flight of steps that ran down to a garden filled with aviaries. The room itself was crammed with books and pictures.

A bell rang, and the detectives went out, following the old maidservant who had shown them in. Don Luis was left alone.

He was still calm, but nevertheless felt a certain uneasiness, a longing to be up and doing, to throw himself into the fray; and his eyes kept on involuntarily returning to the face of the clock. The minute hand seemed endowed with extraordinary speed.

At last someone entered, ushering in a second person. Don Luis recognized Valenglay and the Prefect of Police.

"That's it," he thought. "I've got him."

He saw this by the sort of vague sympathy perceptible on the old Premier's lean and bony face. There was not a sign of arrogance, nothing to raise a barrier between the Minister and the suspicious individual whom he was receiving: just a manifest, playful curiosity and sympathy. It was a sympathy which Valenglay had never concealed, and of which he even boasted when, after Arsène Lupin's sham death, he spoke of the adventurer and the strange relations between them.

"You have not changed," he said, after looking at him for some time. "Complexion a little darker, a trifle grayer over the temples, that's all."

And putting on a blunt tone, he asked:

"And what is it you want?"

"An answer first of all, Monsieur le Président du Conseil. Has Deputy Chief Weber, who took me to the lockup last night, traced the motor cab in which Florence Levasseur was carried off?"

"Yes, the motor stopped at Versailles. The persons inside it hired another cab which is to take them to Nantes. What else do you ask for, besides that answer?"

"My liberty, Monsieur le Président."

"At once, of course?" said Valenglay, beginning to laugh.

"In thirty or thirty-five minutes at most."

"At half-past seven, eh?"

"Half-past seven at latest, Monsieur le Président."

"And why your liberty?"

"To catch the murderer of Cosmo Mornington, of Inspector Vérot, and of the Roussel family."

"Are you the only one that can catch him?"

"Yes."

"Still, the police are moving. The wires are at work. The murderer will not leave France. He shan't escape us."

"You can't find him."

"Yes, we can."

"In that case he will kill Florence Levasseur. She will be the scoundrel's seventh victim. And it will be your doing."

Valenglay paused for a moment and then resumed:

"According to you, contrary to all appearances, and contrary to the well-grounded suspicions of Monsieur le Préfet de Police, Florence Levasseur is innocent?"

"Oh, absolutely, Monsieur le Président!"

"And you believe her to be in danger of death?"

"She is in danger of death."

"Are you in love with her?"

"I am."

Valenglay experienced a little thrill of enjoyment. Lupin in love! Lupin acting through love and confessing his love! But how exciting!

He said:

"I have followed the Mornington case from day to day and I know every detail of it. You have done wonders, Monsieur. It is evident that, but for you, the case would never have emerged from the mystery that surrounded it at the start. But I cannot help noticing that there are certain flaws in it.

"These flaws, which astonished me on your part, are more easy to understand when we know that love was the primary motive and the object of your actions. On the other hand, and in spite of what you say, Florence Levasseur's conduct, her claims as the heiress, her unexpected escape from the hospital, leave little doubt in our minds as to the part which she is playing."

Don Luis pointed to the clock:

"Monsieur le Ministre, it is getting late."

Valenglay burst out laughing.

"I never met anyone like you! Don Luis Perenna, I am sorry that I am not some absolute monarch. I should make you the head of my secret police."

"A post which the German Emperor has already offered me."

"Oh, nonsense!"

"And I refused it."

Valenglay laughed heartily; but the clock struck seven. Don Luis began to grow anxious. Valenglay sat down and, coming straight to the point, said, in a serious voice:

"Don Luis Perenna, on the first day of your reappearance— that is to say, at the very moment of the murders on the Boulevard Suchet—Monsieur le Préfet de Police and I made up our minds as to your identity. Perenna was Lupin.

"I have no doubt that you understood the reason why we did not wish to bring back to life the dead man that you were, and why we granted you a sort of protection. Monsieur le Préfet de Police was entirely of my opinion. The work which you were pursuing was a salutary work of justice; and your assistance was so valuable to us that we strove to spare you any sort of annoyance. As Don Luis Perenna was fighting the good fight, we left Arsène Lupin in the background. Unfortunately—"

Valenglay paused again and declared:

"Unfortunately, Monsieur le Préfet de Police last night received a denunciation, supported by detailed proofs, accusing you of being Arsène Lupin."

"Impossible!" cried Don Luis. "That is a statement which no one is able to prove by material evidence. Arsène Lupin is dead."

"If you like," Valenglay agreed. "But that does not show that Don Luis Perenna is alive."

"Don Luis Perenna has a duly legalized existence, Monsieur le Président."

"Perhaps. But it is disputed."

"By whom? There is only one man who would have the right; and to accuse me would be his own undoing. I cannot believe him to be stupid enough—"

"Stupid enough, no; but crafty enough, yes."

"You mean Caceres, the Peruvian attaché?"

"Yes."

"But he is abroad!"

"More than that: he is a fugitive from justice, after embezzling the funds of his legation. But before leaving the country he signed a statement that reached us yesterday evening, declaring that he faked up a complete record for you under the name of Don Luis Perenna. Here is your correspondence with him and here are all the papers establishing the truth of his allegations. Anyone will be convinced, on examining them, first, that you are not Don Luis Perenna, and, secondly, that you are Arsène Lupin."

Don Luis made an angry gesture.

"That blackguard of a Caceres is a mere tool," he snarled. "The other man's behind him, has paid him, and is controlling his actions. It's the scoundrel himself; I recognize his touch. He has once more tried to get rid of me at the decisive moment."

"I am quite willing to believe it," said the Prime Minister. "But as all these documents, according to the letter that came with them, are only photographs, and as, if you are not arrested this morning, the originals are to be handed to a leading Paris newspaper tonight, we are obliged to take note of the accusation."

"But, Monsieur le Président," exclaimed Don Luis, "as Caceres is abroad and as the scoundrel who bought the papers of him was also obliged to take to flight before he was able to execute his threats, there is no fear now that the documents will be handed to the press."

"How do we know? The enemy must have taken his precautions. He may have accomplices."

"He has none."

"How do we know?"

Don Luis looked at Valenglay and said:

"What is it that you really wish to say, Monsieur le Président?"

"I will tell you. Although pressure was brought to bear upon us by Caceres's threats, Monsieur le Préfet de Police, anxious to see all possible light shed on the plot played by Florence Levasseur, did not interfere with your last night's expedition. As that expedition led to nothing, he determined, at any rate, to profit by the fact that Don Luis had placed himself at our disposal and to arrest Arsène Lupin.

"If we now let him go the documents will certainly be published; and you can see the absurd and ridiculous position in which that will place us in the eyes of the public. Well, at this very moment, you ask for the release of Arsène Lupin, a release which would be illegal, uncalled for, and inexcusable. I am obliged, therefore, to refuse it, and I do refuse it."

He ceased; and then, after a few seconds, he added:

"Unless—"

"Unless?" asked Don Luis.

"Unless—and this is what I wanted to say—unless you offer me in exchange something so extraordinary and so tremendous that I could consent to risk the annoyance which the absurd release of Arsène Lupin would bring down upon my head."

"But, Monsieur le Président, surely, if I bring you the real criminal, the murderer of—"

"I don't need your assistance for that."

"And if I give you my word of honour, Monsieur le Président, to return the moment my task is done and give myself up?"

Valenglay struck the table with his fist and, raising his voice, addressed Don Luis with a certain genial familiarity:

"Come, Arsène Lupin," he said, "play the game! If you really want to have your way, pay for it! Hang it all, remember that after all this business, and especially after the incidents of last night, you and Florence Levasseur will be to the public what you already are: the responsible actors in the tragedy; nay, more, the real and only criminals. And it is now, when Florence Levasseur has taken to her heels, that you come and ask me for your liberty! Very well, but damn it, set a price to it and don't haggle with me!"

"I am not haggling, Monsieur le Président," declared Don Luis, in a very straightforward manner and tone. "What I have to offer you is certainly much more extraordinary and tremendous than you imagine. But if it were twice as extraordinary and twice as tremendous, it would not count once Florence Levasseur's life is in danger. Nevertheless, I was entitled to try for a less expensive transaction. Of this your words remove all hope. I will therefore lay my cards upon the table, as you demand, and as I had made up my mind to do."

He sat down opposite Valenglay, in the attitude of a man treating with another on equal terms.

"I shall not be long. A single sentence, Monsieur le Président, will express the bargain which I am proposing to the Prime Minister of my country."

And, looking Valenglay straight in the eyes, he said slowly, syllable by syllable:

"In exchange for twenty-four hours' liberty and no more, undertaking on my honour to return here tomorrow morning and to return here either with Florence, to give you every proof of her innocence, or without her, to constitute myself a prisoner, I offer you—"

He took his time and, in a serious voice, concluded:

"I offer you a kingdom, Monsieur le Président du Conseil"

The sentence sounded bombastic and ludicrous, sounded silly enough to provoke a shrug of the shoulders, sounded like one of those sentences which only an imbecile or a lunatic could utter. And yet Valenglay remained impassive. He knew that, in such circumstances as the present, the man before him was not the man to indulge in jesting.

And he knew it so fully that, instinctively, accustomed as he was to momentous political questions in which secrecy is of the utmost importance, he cast a glance toward the Prefect of Police, as though M. Desmalions's presence in the room hindered him.

"I positively insist," said Don Luis, "that Monsieur le Préfet de Police shall stay and hear what I have to say. He is better able than anyone else to appreciate the value of it; and he will bear witness to its correctness in certain particulars."

"Speak!" said Valenglay.

His curiosity knew no bounds. He did not much care whether Don Luis's proposal could have any practical results. In his heart he did not believe in it. But what he wanted to know was the lengths to which that demon of audacity was prepared to go, and on what new prodigious adventure he based the pretensions which he was putting forward so calmly and frankly.

Don Luis smiled:

"Will you allow me?" he asked.

Rising and going to the mantelpiece, he took down from the wall a small map representing Northwest Africa. He spread it on the table, placed different objects on the four corners to hold it in position, and resumed:

"There is one matter, Monsieur le Président, which puzzled Monsieur le Préfet de Police and about which I know that he caused inquiries to be made; and that matter is how I employed my time, or, rather, how Arsène Lupin employed his time during the last three years of his service with the Foreign Legion."

"Those inquiries were made by my orders," said Valenglay.

"And they led—?"

"To nothing."

"So that you do not know what I did during my captivity?"

"Just so."

"I will tell you, Monsieur le Président. It will not take me long."

Don Luis pointed with a pencil to a spot in Morocco marked on the map.

"It was here that I was taken prisoner on the twenty-fourth of July. My capture seemed queer to Monsieur le Préfet de Police and to all who subsequently heard the details of the incident. They were astonished that I should have been foolish enough to get caught in ambush and to allow myself to be trapped by a troop of forty Berber horse. Their surprise is justified. My capture was a deliberate move on my part.

"You will perhaps remember, Monsieur le Président, that I enlisted in the Foreign Legion after making a fruitless attempt to kill myself in consequence of some really terrible private disasters. I wanted to die, and I thought that a Moorish bullet would give me the final rest for which I longed.

"Fortune did not permit it. My destiny, it seemed, was not yet fulfilled. Then what had to be was. Little by little, unknown to myself, the thought of death vanished and I recovered my love of life. A few rather striking feats of arms had given me back all my self-confidence and all my desire for action.

"New dreams seized hold of me. I fell a victim to a new ideal. From day to day I needed more space, greater independence, wider horizons, more unforeseen and personal sensations. The Legion, great as my affection was for the plucky fellows who had welcomed me so cordially, was no longer enough to satisfy my craving for activity.

"One day, without thinking much about it, in a blind prompting of my whole being toward a great adventure which I did not clearly see, but which attracted me in a mysterious fashion, one day, finding myself surrounded by a band of the enemy, though still in a position to fight, I allowed myself to be captured.

"That is the whole story, Monsieur le Président. As a prisoner, I was free. A new life opened before me. However, the incident nearly turned out badly. My three dozen Berbers, a troop detached from an important nomad tribe that used to pillage and put to ransom the districts lying on the middle chains of the Atlas Range, first galloped back to the little cluster of tents where the wives of their chiefs were encamped under the guard of some ten men. They packed off at once; and, after a week's march which I found pretty arduous, for I was on foot, with my hands tied behind my back, following a mounted party, they stopped on a narrow upland commanded by rocky slopes and covered with skeletons mouldering among the stones and with remains of French swords and other weapons.

"Here they planted a stake in the ground and fastened me to it. I gathered from the behaviour of my captors and from a few words which I overheard that my death was decided on. They meant to cut off my ears, nose, and tongue, and then my head.

"However, they began by preparing their repast. They went to a well close by, ate and drank and took no further notice of me except to laugh at me and describe the various treats they held in store for me... Another night passed. The torture was postponed until the morning, a time that suited them better. At break of day they crowded round me, uttering yells and shouts with which were mingled the shrill cries of the women.

"When my shadow covered a line which they had marked on the sand the night before, they ceased their din, and one of them, who was to perform the surgical operations prescribed for me, stepped forward and ordered me to put out my tongue. I did so. He took hold of it with a corner of his burnous and, with his other hand, drew his dagger from its sheath.

"I shall never forget the ferocity, coupled with ingenuous delight, of his expression, which was like that of a mischievous boy amusing himself by breaking a bird's wings and legs. Nor shall I ever forget the man's stupefaction when he saw that his dagger no longer consisted of anything but the pommel and a harmless and ridiculously small stump of the blade, just long enough to keep it in its sheath. His fury was revealed by a splutter of curses and he at once rushed at one of his friends and snatched his dagger from him.

"The same stupefaction followed: this dagger was also broken off at the hilt. The next thing was a general tumult, in which one and all brandished their knives. But all of them uttered howls of rage.

"There were forty-five men there; and their forty-five knives were smashed... The chief flew at me as if holding me responsible for this incomprehensible phenomenon. He was a tall, lean old man, slightly hunchbacked, blind of one eye, hideous to look upon. He aimed a huge pistol point blank at my head and he struck me as so ugly that I burst out laughing in his face. He pulled the trigger. The pistol missed fire. He pulled it again. The pistol again missed fire...

"All of them at once began to dance around the stake to which I was fastened. Gesticulating wildly, hustling one another and roaring like thunder, they levelled their various firearms at me: muskets, pistols, carbines, old Spanish blunderbusses. The hammers clicked. But the muskets, pistols, carbines, and blunderbusses did not go off!

"It was a regular miracle. You should have seen their faces. I never laughed so much in my life; and this completed their bewilderment.

"Some ran to the tents for more powder. Others hurriedly reloaded their arms, only to meet with fresh failure, while I did nothing but laugh and laugh! The thing could not go on indefinitely. There were plenty of other means of doing away with me. They had their hands to strangle me with, the butt ends of their muskets to smash my head with, pebbles to stone me with. And there were over forty of them!

"The old chief picked up a bulky stone and stepped toward me, his features distorted with hatred. He raised himself to his full height, lifted the huge block, with the assistance of two of his men, above my head and dropped it—in front of me, on the stake! It was a staggering sight for the poor old man. I had, in one second, unfastened my bonds and sprung backward; and I was standing at three paces from him, with my hands outstretched before me, and holding in those outstretched hands the two revolvers which had been taken from me on the day of my capture!

"What followed was the business of a few seconds. The chief now began to laugh as I had laughed, sarcastically. To his mind, in the disorder of his brain, those two revolvers with which I threatened him could have no more effect than the useless weapons which had spared my life. He took up a large pebble and raised his hand to hurl it at my face. His two assistants did the same. And all the others were prepared to follow his example.

"'Hands down!' I cried, 'or I fire!' The chief let fly his stone. At the same moment three shots rang out. The chief and his two men fell dead to the ground. 'Who's next?' I asked, looking round the band.

"Forty-two Moors remained. I had eleven bullets left. As none of the men budged, I slipped one of my revolvers under my arm and took from my pocket two small boxes of cartridges containing fifty more bullets. And from my belt I drew three great knives, all of them nicely tapering and pointed. Half of the troop made signs of submission and drew up in line behind me. The other half capitulated a moment after. The battle was over. It had not lasted four minutes."

18

ARSÈNE I EMPEROR OF MAURETANIA

Don Luis ceased. A smile of amusement played round his lips. The recollection of those four minutes seemed to divert him immensely.

Valenglay and the Prefect of Police, who were neither of them men to be unduly surprised at courage and coolness, had listened to him, nevertheless, and were now looking at him in bewildered silence. Was it possible for a human being to carry heroism to such unlikely lengths?

Meanwhile, he went up to the other side of the chimney and pointed to a larger map, representing the French roads.

"You told me, Monsieur le Président, that the scoundrel's motor car had left Versailles and was going toward Nantes?"

"Yes; and all our arrangements are made to arrest him either on the way, or else at Nantes or at Saint-Nazaire, where he may intend to take ship."

Don Luis Perenna followed with his forefinger the road across France, stopping here and there, marking successive stages. And nothing could have been more impressive than this dumb show.

The man that he was, preserving his composure amid the overthrow of all that he had most at heart, seemed by his calmness to dominate time and circumstances. It was as though the murderer were running away at one end of an unbreakable thread of which Don Luis held the other, and as though Don Luis could stop his flight at any time by a mere movement of his finger and thumb.

As he studied the map, the master seemed to command not only a sheet of cardboard, but also the highroad on which a motor car was spinning along, subject to his despotic will.

He went back to the table and continued:

"The battle was over. And there was no question of its being resumed. My forty-two worthies found themselves face to face with a conqueror, against whom revenge is always possible, by fair means or foul, but with one who had subjugated them in a supernatural manner. There was no other explanation of the inexplicable facts which they had witnessed. I was a sorcerer, a kind of marabout, a direct emissary of the Prophet."

Valenglay laughed and said:

"Their interpretation was not so very unreasonable, for, after all, you must have performed a sleight-of-hand trick which strikes me also as being little less than miraculous."

"Monsieur le Président, do you know a curious short story of Balzac's called 'A Passion in the Desert?'"

"Yes."

"Well, the key to the riddle lies in that."

"Does it? I don't quite see. You were not under the claws of a tigress. There was no tigress to tame in this instance."

"No, but there were women."

"Eh? How do you mean?"

"Upon my word, Monsieur le Président," said Don Luis gayly, "I should not like to shock you. But I repeat that the troop which carried me off on that week's march included women; and women are a little like Balzac's tigress, creatures whom it is not impossible to tame, to charm, to break in, until you make friends of them."

"Yes, yes," muttered the Premier, madly puzzled, "but that needs time."

"I had a week."

"And complete liberty of action."

"No, no, Monsieur le Président. The eyes are enough to start with. The eyes give rise to sympathy, interest, affection, curiosity, a wish to know you better. After that, the merest opportunity—"

"And did an opportunity offer?"

"Yes, one night. I was fastened up, or at least they thought I was. I knew that the chief's favourite was alone in her tent close by. I went there. I left her an hour afterward."

"And the tigress was tamed?"

"Yes, as thoroughly as Balzac's: tamed and blindly submissive."

"But there were several of them?"

"I know, Monsieur le Président, and that was the difficulty. I was afraid of rivalry. But all went well: the favourite was not jealous, far from it. And then, as I have told you, her submission was absolute. In short, I had five staunch, invisible friends, resolved to do anything I wanted and suspected by nobody.

"My plan was being carried out before we reached the last halting-place. My five secret agents collected all the arms during the night. They dashed the daggers to the ground and broke them. They removed the bullets from the pistols. They damped the powder. Everything was ready for ringing up the curtain."

Valenglay bowed.

"My compliments! You are a man of resource. And your scheme was not lacking in charm. For I take it that your five ladies were pretty?"

Don Luis put on a bantering expression. He closed his eyes, as if to recall his bliss, and let fall the one word:

"Hags!"

The epithet gave rise to a burst of merriment. But Don Luis, as though in a hurry to finish his story, at once went on:

"In any case, they saved my life, the hussies, and their aid never failed me. My forty-two watch dogs, deprived of their arms and shaking with fear in those solitudes where everything is a trap and where death lies in wait for you at any minute, gathered round me as their real protector. When we joined the great tribe to which they belonged I was their actual chief. And it took me less than three months of dangers faced in common, of ambushes defeated under my advice, of raids and pillages effected by my direction, to become the chief also of the whole tribe.

"I spoke their language, I practised their religion, I wore their dress, I conformed to their customs: alas! had I not five wives? Henceforward, my dream, which had gradually taken definite shape in my mind, became possible.

"I sent one of my most faithful adherents to France, with sixty letters to hand to sixty men whose names and addresses he learned by heart. Those sixty men were sixty associates whom Arsène Lupin had disbanded before he threw himself from the Capri cliffs. All had retired from business, with a hundred thousand francs apiece in ready money and a small trade or public post to keep them occupied. I had provided one with a tobacconist's shop, another with a job as a park-keeper, others with sinecures in the government offices. In short, they were respectable citizens.

"To all of them—whether public servants, farmers, municipal councillors, grocers, sacristans, or what not—I wrote the same letter, made the same offer, and gave the same instructions in case they should accept... Monsieur le Président, I thought that, of the sixty, ten or fifteen at most would come and join me: sixty came, Monsieur le Président, sixty, and not one less! Sixty men punctually arrived at the appointed place.

"On the day fixed, at the hour named, my old armed cruiser, the *Ascendant*, which they had brought back, anchored in the mouth of the Wady Draa, on the Atlantic coast, between Cape Nun and Cape Juby. Two longboats plied to and fro and landed my friends and the munitions of war which they had brought with them: camp furniture, quick-firing guns, ammunition, motor-boats, stores and provisions, trading wares, glass beads, and cases of gold as well, for my sixty good men and true had insisted on turning their share of the old profits into cash and on putting into the new venture the six million francs which they had received from their governor...

"Need I say more, Monsieur le Président? Must I tell you what a chief like Arsène Lupin was able to attempt seconded by sixty fine fellows of that stamp and backed by an army of ten thousand well-armed and well-trained Moorish fanatics? He attempted it; and his success was unparalleled.

"I do not think that there has ever been an idyll like that through which we lived during those fifteen months, first on the heights of the Atlas range and then in the infernal plains of the Sahara: an idyll of heroism, of privation, of superhuman torture and superhuman joy; an idyll of hunger and thirst, of total defeat and dazzling victory...

"My sixty trusty followers threw themselves into their work with might and main. Oh, what men! You know them, Monsieur le Président du Conseil! You've had them to deal with, Monsieur le Préfet de Police! The beggars! Tears come to my eyes when I think of some of them.

"There were Charolais and his son, who distinguished themselves in the case of the Princesse de Lamballe's tiara. There were Marco, who owed his fame to the Kesselbach case, and Auguste, who was your chief messenger, Monsieur le Président. There were the Growler and the Masher, who achieved such glory in the hunt for the crystal stopper. There were the brothers Beuzeville, whom I used to call the two

Ajaxes. There were Philippe d'Antrac, who was better born than any Bourbon, and Pierre Le Grand and Tristan Le Roux and Joseph Le Jeune."

"And there was Arsène Lupin," said Valenglay, roused to enthusiasm by this list of Homeric heroes.

"And there was Arsène Lupin," repeated Don Luis.

He nodded his head, smiled, and continued, in a very quiet voice:

"I will not speak of him, Monsieur le Président. I will not speak of him, for the simple reason that you would not believe my story. What they tell about him when he was with the Foreign Legion is mere child's play beside what was to come later. Lupin was only a private soldier. In South Morocco he was a general. Not till then did Arsène Lupin really show what he could do. And, I say it without pride, not even I foresaw what that was. The Achilles of the legend performed no greater feats. Hannibal and Caesar achieved no more striking results.

"All I need tell you is that, in fifteen months, Arsène Lupin conquered a kingdom twice the size of France. From the Berbers of Morocco, from the indomitable Tuaregs, from the Arabs of the extreme south of Algeria, from the negroes who overrun Senegal, from the Moors along the Atlantic coast, under the blazing sun, in the flames of hell, he conquered half the Sahara and what we may call ancient Mauretania.

"A kingdom of deserts and swamps? Partly, but a kingdom all the same, with oases, wells, rivers, forests, and incalculable riches, a kingdom with ten million men and a hundred thousand warriors. This is the kingdom which I offer to France, Monsieur le Président du Conseil."

Valenglay did not conceal his amazement. Greatly excited and even perturbed by what he had learned, looking over his extraordinary visitor, with his hands clutching at the map of Africa, he whispered:

"Explain yourself; be more precise."

Don Luis answered:

"Monsieur le Président du Conseil, I will not remind you of the events of the last few years. France, resolving to pursue a splendid dream of dominion over North Africa, has had to part with a portion of the Congo. I propose to heal the painful wound by giving her thirty times as much as she has lost. And I turn the magnificent and distant dream into an immediate certainty by joining the small slice of Morocco which you have conquered to Senegal at one blow.

"Today, Greater France in Africa exists. Thanks to me, it is a solid and compact expanse. Millions of square miles of territory and a coastline stretching for several thousand miles from Tunis to the Congo, save for a few insignificant interruptions."

"It's a Utopia," Valenglay protested.

"It's a reality."

"Nonsense! It will take us twenty years' fighting to achieve."

"It will take you exactly five minutes!" cried Don Luis, with irresistible enthusiasm. "What I offer you is not the conquest of an empire, but a conquered empire, duly pacified and administered, in full working order and full of life. My gift is a present, not a future gift.

"I, too, Monsieur le Président du Conseil, I, Arsène Lupin, had cherished a splendid dream. After toiling and moiling all my life, after knowing all the ups and downs of existence, richer than Croesus, because all the wealth of the world was mine, and poorer than Job, because I had distributed all my treasures, surfeited with everything, tired of unhappiness, and more tired still of happiness, sick of pleasure, of passion, of excitement, I wanted to do something that is incredible in the present day: to reign!

"And a still more incredible phenomenon: when this thing was accomplished, when the dead Arsène Lupin had come to life again as a sultan out of the Arabian Nights, as a reigning, governing, law-giving Arsène Lupin, head of the state and head of the church, I determined, in a few years, at one stroke, to tear down the screen of rebel tribes against which you were waging a desultory and tiresome war in the north of Morocco, while I was quietly and silently building up my kingdom at the back of it.

"Then, face to face with France and as powerful as herself, like a neighbour treating on equal terms, I would have cried to her, 'It's I, Arsène Lupin! Behold the former swindler and gentleman burglar! The Sultan of Adrar, the Sultan of Iguidi, the Sultan of El Djouf, the Sultan of the Tuaregs, the Sultan of Aubata, the Sultan of Brakna and Frerzon, all these am I, the Sultan of Sultans, grandson of Mahomet, son of Allah, I, I, I, Arsène Lupin!'

"And, before taking the little grain of poison that sets one free — for a man like Arsène Lupin has no right to grow old — I should have signed the treaty of peace, the deed of gift in which I bestowed a kingdom on France, signed it, below the flourishes of my grand dignitaries, kaids, pashas, and marabouts, with my lawful signature, the signature to which I am fully entitled, which I conquered at the point of my sword and by my all-powerful will: 'Arsène I, Emperor of Mauretania!'"

Don Luis uttered all these words in a strong voice, but without emphasis, with the very simple emotion and pride of a man who has done much and who knows the value of what he has done. There were but two ways of replying to him: by a shrug of the shoulders, as one replies to a madman, or by the silence that expresses reflection and approval.

The Prime Minister and the Prefect of Police said nothing, but their looks betrayed their secret thoughts. And deep down within themselves they felt that they were in the presence of an absolutely exceptional specimen of mankind, created to perform immoderate actions and fashioned by his own hand for a superhuman destiny.

Don Luis continued:

"It was a fine curtain, was it not, Monsieur le Président du Conseil? And the end was worthy of the work. I should have been happy to have had it so. Arsène Lupin dying on a throne, sceptre in hand, would have been a spectacle not devoid of glamour. Arsène Lupin dying with his title of Arsène I, Emperor of Mauretania and benefactor of France: what an apotheosis! The gods have willed it otherwise. Jealous, no doubt, they are lowering me to the level of my cousins of the old world and turning me into that absurd creature, a king in exile. Their will be done! Peace to the late Emperor of Mauretania. He has strutted and fretted his hour upon the stage.

"Arsène I is dead: long live France! Monsieur le Président du Conseil, I repeat my offer. Florence Levasseur is in danger. I alone can rescue her from the monster who is carrying her away. It will take me twenty-four hours. In return for twenty-four hours' liberty I will give you the Mauretanian Empire. Do you accept, Monsieur le Président du Conseil?"

"Well, certainly, I accept," said Valenglay, laughing. "What do you say, my dear Desmalions? The whole thing may not be very orthodox, but, hang it! Paris is worth a mass and the Kingdom of Mauretania is a tempting morsel. We'll risk the experiment."

Don Luis's face expressed so sincere a joy that one might have thought that he had just achieved the most brilliant victory instead of sacrificing a crown and flinging into the gutter the most fantastic dream that mortal man had ever conceived and realized.

He asked:

"What guarantees do you require, Monsieur le Président?"

"None."

"I can show you treaties, documents to prove—"

"Don't trouble. We'll talk about all that tomorrow. Meanwhile, go ahead. You are free."

The essential word, the incredible word, was spoken.

Don Luis took a few steps toward the door.

"One word more, Monsieur le Président," he said, stopping. "Among my former companions is one for whom I procured a post suited to his inclinations and his desserts. This man I did not send for to come to Africa, thinking that someday or other he might be of use to me through the position which he occupied. I am speaking of Mazeroux, a sergeant in the detective service."

"Sergeant Mazeroux, whom Caceres denounced, with corroborating evidence, as an accomplice of Arsène Lupin, is in prison."

"Sergeant Mazeroux is a model of professional honour, Monsieur le Président. I owed his assistance only to the fact that I was helping the police. I was accepted as an auxiliary and more or less patronized by Monsieur le Préfet. Mazeroux thwarted me in anything I tried to do that was at all illegal. And he would have been the first to take me by the collar if he had been so instructed. I ask for his release."

"Oho!"

"Monsieur le Président, your consent will be an act of justice and I beg you to grant it. Sergeant Mazeroux shall leave France. He can be charged by the government with a secret mission in the south of Morocco, with the rank of colonial inspector."

"Agreed," said Valenglay, laughing heartily. And he added, "My dear Prefect, once we depart from the strictly lawful path, there's no saying where we come to. But the end justifies the means; and the end which we have in view is to have done with this loathsome Mornington case."

"This evening everything will be settled," said Don Luis.

"I hope so. Our men are on the track."

"They are on the track, but they have to check that track at every town, at every village, by inquiries made of every peasant they meet; they have to find out if the motor has not branched off somewhere; and they are wasting time. I shall go straight for the scoundrel."

"By what miracle?"

"That must be my secret for the present, Monsieur le Président."

"Very well. Is there anything you want?"

"This map of France."

"Take it."

"And a couple of revolvers."

"Monsieur le Préfet will be good enough to ask his inspectors for two revolvers and to give them to you. Is that all? Any money?"

"No, thank you, Monsieur le Président. I always carry a useful fifty thousand francs in my pocketbook, in case of need."

"In that case," said the Prefect of Police, "I shall have to send someone with you to the lockup. I presume your pocketbook was among the things taken from you."

Don Luis smiled:

"Monsieur le Préfet, the things that people can take from me are never of the least importance. My pocketbook is at the lockup, as you say. But the money—"

He raised his left leg, took his boot in his hands and gave a slight twist to the heel. There was a little click, and a sort of double drawer shot out of the front of the sole. It contained two sheafs of bank notes and a number of diminutive articles, such as a gimlet, a watch spring, and some pills.

"The wherewithal to escape," he said, "to live and—to die. Goodbye, Monsieur le Président."

In the hall M. Desmalions told the inspectors to let their prisoner go free. Don Luis asked:

"Monsieur le Préfet, did Deputy Chief Weber give you any particulars about the brute's car?"

"Yes, he telephoned from Versailles. It's a deep-yellow car, belonging to the Compagnie des Comètes. The driver's seat is on the left. He's wearing a gray cloth cap with a black leather peak."

"Thank you, Monsieur le Préfet."

And he left the house.

***

An inconceivable thing had happened. Don Luis was free. Half an hour's conversation had given him the power of acting and of fighting the decisive battle.

He went off at a run. At the Trocadero he jumped into a taxi.

"Go to Issy-les-Moulineaux!" he cried. "Full speed! Forty francs!"

The cab flew through Passy, crossed the Seine and reached the Issy-les-Moulineaux aviation ground in ten minutes.

None of the aeroplanes was out, for there was a stiff breeze blowing. Don Luis ran to the sheds. The owners' names were written over the doors.

"Davanne," he muttered. "That's the man I want."

The door of the shed was open. A short, stoutish man, with a long red face, was smoking a cigarette and watching some mechanics working at a monoplane. The little man was Davanne himself, the famous airman.

Don Luis took him aside and, knowing from the papers the sort of man that he was, opened the conversation so as to surprise him from the start:

"Monsieur," he said, unfolding his map of France, "I want to catch up someone who has carried off the woman I love and is making for Nantes by motor. The abduction took place at midnight. It is now about eight o'clock. Suppose that the motor, which is just a hired taxi with a driver who has no inducement to break his neck, does an average of twenty miles an hour, including stoppages—in twelve hours' time—that is to say, at twelve o'clock—our man will have covered two hundred and forty miles and reached a spot between Angers and Nantes, at this point on the map."

"Les Ponts-de-Drive," agreed Davanne, who was quietly listening.

"Very well. Suppose, on the other hand, that an aeroplane were to start from Issy-les-Moulineaux at eight o'clock in the morning and travel at the rate of sixty miles an hour, without stopping—in four hours' time—that is to say, at twelve o'clock—it would reach Les Ponts-de-Drive at the exact same moment as the motor. Am I right?"

"Perfectly."

"In that case, if we agree, all is well. Does your machine carry a passenger?"

"Sometimes she does."

"We'll start at once. What are your terms?"

"It depends. Who are you?"

"Arsène Lupin."

"The devil you are!" exclaimed Davanne, a little taken aback.

"I am Arsène Lupin. You must know the best part of what has happened from reading about it in the papers. Well, Florence Levasseur was kidnapped last night. I want to save her. What's your price?"

"Nothing."

"That's too much!"

"Perhaps, but the adventure amuses me. It will be an advertisement."

"Very well. But your silence is necessary until tomorrow. I'll buy it. Here's twenty thousand francs."

Ten minutes later Don Luis was dressed in an airman's suit, cap, and goggles; and an aeroplane rose to a height of two thousand five hundred feet to avoid the air currents, flew above the Seine, and darted due west across France.

Versailles, Maintenon, Chartres...

Don Luis had never been up in an aeroplane. France had achieved the conquest of the air while he was fighting with the Legion and in the plains of the Sahara. Nevertheless, sensitive though he was to new impressions—and what more exciting impression could he have than this?—he did not experience the heavenly delight of the man who for the first time soars above the earth. What monopolized his thoughts, strained his nerves, and excited his whole being to an exquisite degree was the as yet impossible but inevitable sight of the motor which they were pursuing.

Amid the tremendous swarm of things beneath them, amid the unexpected din of the wings and the engine, in the immensity of the sky, in the infinity of the horizon, his eyes sought nothing but that, and his ears admitted no other sound than the hum of the invisible car. His were the mighty and brutal sensations of the hunter chasing his game. He was the bird of prey whom the distraught quarry has no chance of escaping.

Nogent-le-Rotrou, La Ferte-Bemard, Le Mans...

The two companions did not exchange a single word. Before him Perenna saw Davanne's broad back and powerful neck and shoulders. But, by bending his head a little, he saw the boundless space beneath him; and nothing interested him but the white ribbon of road that ran from town to town and from village to village, at times quite straight, as though a hand had stretched it, and at others lazily winding, broken by a river or a church.

On this ribbon, at some place always closer and closer, were Florence and her abductor!

He never doubted it! The yellow taxi was continuing its patient and plucky little effort. Mile after mile, through plains and villages, fields and forests, it was making Angers, with Les Ponts-de-Drive after, and, right at the end of the ribbon, the unattainable goal: Nantes, Saint-Nazaire, the steamer ready to start, and victory for the scoundrel...

He laughed at the idea. As if there could be a question of any victory but his, the victory of the falcon over its prey, the victory of the flying bird over the game that runs afoot! Not for a second did he entertain the thought that the enemy might have slunk away by taking another road.

There are some certainties that are equivalent to facts. And this one was so great that it seemed to him that his adversaries were obliged to comply with it. The car was travelling along the road to Nantes. It would cover an average of twenty miles an hour. And as he himself was travelling at the rate of sixty miles, the encounter would take place at the spot named, Les Ponts-de-Drive, and at the hour named, twelve o'clock.

A cluster of houses, a huge castle, towers, steeples: Angers...

Don Luis asked Davanne the time. It was ten minutes to twelve.

Already Angers was a vanished vision. Once more the open country, broken up with many-coloured fields. Through it all, a road.

And, on that road, a yellow motor.

The yellow motor! The brute's motor! The motor with Florence Levasseur!

Don Luis's joy contained no surprise. He knew so well that this was bound to happen!

Davanne turned round and cried:

"That's the one, isn't it?"

"Yes, go straight for them."

The airship dipped through space and caught up the car almost at once. Then Davanne slowed his engine and kept at six hundred feet above the car and a little way behind.

From here they made out all the details. The driver was seated on the left. He wore a gray cap with a black peak. It was one of the deep-yellow taxis of the Compagnie des Comètes. It was the taxi which they were pursuing. And Florence was inside with her abductor.

"At last," thought Don Luis, "I have them!"

They flew for some time, keeping the same distance.

Davanne waited for a signal which Don Luis was in no hurry to give. He was revelling in the sensation of his power, with a force made up of mingled pride, hatred, and cruelty. He was indeed the eagle hovering overhead with its talons itching to rend live flesh. Escaped from the cage in which he had been imprisoned, released from the bonds that fastened him, he had come all the way at full flight and was ready to swoop upon the helpless prey.

He lifted himself in his seat and gave Davanne his instructions:

"Be careful," he said, "not to brush too close by them. They might put a bullet into us."

Another minute passed.

Suddenly they saw that, half a mile ahead, the road divided into three, thus forming a very wide-open space which was still further extended by two triangular patches of grass where the three roads met.

"Now?" asked Davanne, turning to Don Luis.

The surrounding country was deserted.

"Off you go!" cried Don Luis.

The aeroplane seemed to shoot down suddenly, as though driven by an irresistible force, which sent it flying like an arrow toward the mark. It passed at three hundred feet above the car, and then, all at once, checking its career, choosing the spot at which it meant to hit the target, calmly, silently, like a nightbird, steering clear of the trees and sign-posts, it alighted softly on the grass of the crossroads.

Don Luis sprang out and ran toward the motor, which was coming along at a rapid pace. He stood in the middle of the road, levelled his two revolvers, and shouted:

"Stop, or I fire!"

The terrified driver put on both brakes. The car pulled up.

Don Luis rushed to one of the doors.

"Thunder!" he roared, discharging one of his revolvers for no reason and smashing a window-pane.

There was no one in the car.

19

"THE SNARE IS LAID. BEWARE, LUPIN!"

The power that had impelled Don Luis to battle and victory was so intense that it suffered, so to speak, no check. Disappointment, rage, humiliation, torture, were all swallowed up in an immediate desire for action and information, together with a longing to continue the chase. The rest was but an incident of no importance, which would soon be very simply explained.

The petrified taxi-driver was gazing wildly at the peasants coming from the distant farms, attracted by the sound of the aeroplane. Don Luis took him by the throat and put the barrel of his revolver to the man's temple:

"Tell me what you know—or you're a dead man."

And when the unhappy wretch began to stammer out entreaties:

"It's no use moaning, no use hoping for assistance... Those people won't get here in time. So there's only one way of saving yourself: speak! Last night a gentleman came to Versailles from Paris in a taxi, left it and took yours: is that it?"

"Yes."

"The gentleman had a lady with him?"

"Yes."

"And he engaged you to take him to Nantes?"

"Yes."

"But he changed his mind on the way and told you to put him down?"

"Yes."

"Where?"

"Before we got to Mans, in a little road on the right, with a sort of coach-house, looking like a shed, a hundred yards down it. They both got out there."

"And you went on?"

"He paid me to."

"How much?"

"Five hundred francs. And there was another fare waiting at Nantes that I was to pick up and bring back to Paris for a thousand francs more."

"Do you believe in that other fare?"

"No. I think he wanted to put people off the scent by sending them after me to Nantes while he branched off. Still, I had my money."

"And, when you left them, weren't you curious to see what happened?"

"No."

"Take care! A movement of my finger and I blow out your brains. Speak!"

"Well, yes, then. I went back on foot, behind a bank covered with trees. The man had opened the coach-house and was starting a small limousine car. The lady did not want to get in. They argued pretty fiercely. He threatened and begged by turns. But I could not hear what they said. She seemed very tired. He gave her a glass of water, which he drew from a tap in the wall. Then she consented. He closed the door on her and took his seat at the wheel."

"A glass of water!" cried Don Luis. "Are you sure he put nothing else into the glass?"

The driver seemed surprised at the question and then answered:

"Yes, I think he did. He took something from his pocket."

"Without the lady's knowledge?"

"Yes, she didn't see."

Don Luis mastered his horror. After all it was impossible that the villain had poisoned Florence in that way, at that place, without anything to warrant so great a hurry. No, it was more likely that he had employed a narcotic, a drug of some sort which would dull Florence's brain and make her incapable of noticing by what new roads and through what towns he was taking her.

"And then," he repeated, "she decided to step in?"

"Yes; and he shut the door and got into the driver's seat. I went away then."

"Before knowing which direction they took?"

"Yes."

"Did you suspect on the way that they thought that they were being followed?"

"Certainly. He did nothing but put his head out of the window."

"Did the lady cry out at all?"

"No."

"Would you know him again if you saw him?"

"No, I'm sure I shouldn't. At Versailles it was dark. And this morning I was too far away. Besides, it's curious, but the first time he struck me as very tall, and this morning, on the contrary, he looked quite a short man, as though bent in two. I can't understand it at all."

Don Luis reflected. It seemed to him that he had asked all the necessary questions. Moreover, a gig drawn by a quick-trotting horse was approaching the crossroads. There were two others behind it. And the groups of peasants were now quite near. He must finish the business.

He said to the chauffeur:

"I can see by your face that you intend to talk about me. Don't do that, my man: it would be foolish of you. Here's a thousand franc note for you. Only, if you blab, I'll make you repent it. That's all I have to say to you."

He turned to Davanne, whose machine was beginning to block the traffic, and asked:

"Can we start?"

"Whenever you like. Where are we going?"

Paying no attention to the movements of the people coming from every side, Don Luis unfolded his map of France and spread it out before him. He experienced a few seconds of anxiety at seeing the complicated tangle of roads and picturing the infinite number of places to which the villain might carry Florence. But he pulled himself together. He did not allow himself to hesitate. He refused even to reflect.

He was determined to find out, and to find out everything, at once, without clues, without useless consideration, simply by the marvellous intuition which invariably guided him at any crisis in his life.

And his self-respect also required that he should give Davanne his answer without delay, and that the disappearance of those whom he was pursuing should not seem to embarrass him. With his eyes glued to the map, he placed one finger on Paris and another on Le Mans and, even before he had asked himself why the scoundrel had chosen that Paris-Le Mans-Angers route, he knew the answer to the question.

The name of a town had struck him and made the truth appear like a flash of lightning: Alençon! Then and there, by the light of his memory, he penetrated the mystery.

He repeated:

"Where are we going? Back again, bearing to the left."

"Any particular place?"

"Alençon."

"All right," said Davanne. "Lend a hand, some of you. I can make an easy start from that field just there."

Don Luis and a few others helped him, and the preparations were soon made. Davanne tested his engine. Everything was in perfect order.

At that moment a powerful racing car, with a siren yelling like a vicious animal, came tearing along the Angers Road and promptly stopped. Three men got out and rushed up to the driver of the yellow taxicab. Don Luis recognized them. They were Weber, the deputy chief, and the men who had taken him to the lockup the night before, sent by the Prefect of Police to follow up the scoundrel's tracks.

They had a brief interchange of words with the cab-driver, which seemed to put them out; and they kept on gesticulating and plying him with fresh questions while looking at their watches and consulting their road maps.

Don Luis went up to them. He was unrecognizable, with his head wrapped in his aviation cap and his face concealed by his goggles. Changing his voice:

"The birds have flown, Mr Deputy Chief," he said.

Weber looked at him in utter amazement,

Don Luis grinned.

"Yes, flown. Our friend from the Ile Saint Louis is an artful dodger, you know. My lord's in his third motor. After the yellow car of which you heard at Versailles last night, he took another at Le Mans—destination unknown."

The deputy chief opened his eyes in amazement. Who was this person who was mentioning facts that had been telephoned to police headquarters only at two o'clock that morning? He gasped:

"But who are you, Monsieur?"

"What? Don't you know me? What's the good of making appointments with people? You strain every nerve to be punctual, and then they ask you who you are! Come, Weber, confess that you're doing it to annoy me. Must you gaze on my features in broad daylight? Here goes!"

He raised his mask.

"Arsène Lupin!" spluttered the detective.

"At your service, young fellow: on foot, in the saddle, and in mid-air. That's where I'm going now. Goodbye."

And so great was Weber's astonishment at seeing Arsène Lupin, whom he had taken to the lockup twelve hours before, standing in front of him, free, at two hundred and forty miles from Paris, that Don Luis, as he went back to Davanne, thought:

"What a crusher! I've knocked him out in one round. There's no hurry. The referee will count ten at least three times before Weber can say 'Mother!'"

***

Davanne was ready. Don Luis climbed into the monoplane. The peasants pushed at the wheels. The machine started.

"North-northeast," Don Luis ordered. "Ninety miles an hour. Ten thousand francs."

"We've the wind against us," said Davanne.

"Five thousand francs extra for the wind," shouted Don Luis.

He admitted no obstacle in his haste to reach Damigni. He now understood the whole thing and, harking back to the very beginning, he was surprised that his mind had never perceived the connection between the two skeletons hanging in the barn and the series of crimes resulting from the Mornington inheritance. Stranger still, how was it that the almost certain murder of Langernault, Hippolyte Fauville's old friend, had not afforded him all the clues which it contained? The crux of the sinister plot lay in that.

Who could have intercepted, on Fauville's behalf, the letters of accusation which Fauville was supposed to write to his old friend Langernault, except someone in the village or someone who had lived in the village?

And now everything was clear. It was the nameless scoundrel who had started his career of crime by killing old Langernault and then the Dedessuslamare couple. The method was the same as later on: it was not direct murder, but anonymous murder, murder by suggestion. Like Mornington the American, like Fauville the engineer, like Marie, like Gaston Sauverand, old Langernault had been craftily done away with and the Dedessuslamare couple driven to commit suicide in the barn.

It was from there that the tiger had come to Paris, where later he was to find Fauville and Cosmo Mornington and plot the tragic affair of the inheritance.

And it was there that he was now returning!

There was no doubt about that. To begin with, the fact that he had administered a narcotic to Florence constituted an indisputable proof. Was he not obliged to put Florence to sleep in order to prevent her from recognizing the landscape at Alençon and Damigni, or the Old Castle, which she had explored with Gaston Sauverand?

On the other hand, the Le Mans-Angers-Nantes route, which had been taken to put the police on a false track, meant only an extra hour or two, at most, for anyone motoring to Alençon. Lastly, that coach-house near a big town, that limousine waiting, ready charged with petrol, showed that the villain, when he intended to visit his retreat, took the precaution of stopping at Le Mans, in order to go from there, in his limousine, to Langernault's deserted estate.

He would therefore reach his lair at ten o'clock that morning. And he would arrive there with Florence Levasseur dead asleep!

The question forced itself upon him, the terrible persistent question—what did he mean to do with Florence Levasseur?

"Faster! Faster!" cried Don Luis.

Now that he knew the scoundrel's haunt, the man's scheme became hideously evident to him. Feeling himself hunted down, lost, an object of hatred and terror to Florence, whose eyes were now opened to the true state of things, what plan could he have in mind except his invariable plan of murder?

"Faster!" cried Don Luis. "We're making no headway. Go faster, can't you?"

Florence murdered! Perhaps the crime was not yet accomplished. No, it could not be! Killing takes time. It is preceded by words, by the offer of a bargain, by threats, by entreaties, by a wholly unspeakable scene. But the thing was being prepared, Florence was going to die!

Florence was going to die by the hand of the brute who loved her. For he loved her: Don Luis had an intuition of that monstrous love; and he was bound to believe that such a love could only end in torture and bloodshed.

Sablé... Sillé-le-Guillaume...

The earth sped beneath them. The trees and houses glided by like shadows.

And then Alençon.

It was hardly more than a quarter to two when they landed in a meadow between the town and Damigni. Don Luis made inquiries. A number of motor cars had passed along the road to Damigni, including a small limousine driven by a gentleman who had turned down a crossroad. And this crossroad led to the woods at the back of Langernault's estate, the Old Castle.

Don Luis's conviction was so firm that, after taking leave of Davanne, he helped him to start on his homeward flight. He had no further need of him. He needed nobody. The final duel was at hand.

He ran along, guided by the tracks of the tires in the dust, and followed the crossroad. To his great surprise this road went nowhere near the wall behind the barn from which he had jumped a few weeks before. After clearing the woods, Don Luis came out into a large unfilled space where the road turned back toward the estate and ended at an old two-winged gate protected with iron sheets and bars.

The limousine had gone in that way.

"And I must get in this way, too," thought Don Luis. "I must get in at all costs and immediately, without wasting time in looking for an opening or a handy tree."

Now the wall was thirteen feet high at this spot. Don Luis got in. How he managed it, by what superhuman effort, he himself could not have said after he had done it.

Somehow or other, by hanging on to invisible projections, by digging a knife which he had borrowed from Davanne into the interstices between the stones, he managed it.

And when he was on the other side he discovered the tracks of the tires running to the left, toward a part of the grounds which he did not know, more undulating than the other and broken up with little hills and ruined buildings covered with thick curtains of ivy.

Deserted though the rest of the park was, this portion seemed much more uncivilized, in spite of the ragged remains of box and laurel hedges that stood here and there amidst the nettles and brambles, and the luxuriant swarm of tall wild-flowers, valerian, mullein, hemlock, foxglove, and angelica.

Suddenly, on turning the corner of an old hedge of clipped yews, Don Luis saw the limousine, which had been left, or, rather, hidden there in a hollow. The door was open. The disorder of the inside of the car, the rug hanging over the footboard, a broken window, a cushion on the floor, all bore witness to a struggle. The scoundrel had no doubt taken advantage of the fact that Florence was asleep to tie her up; and on arriving, when he tried to take her out of the car, Florence must have clutched at everything that offered.

Don Luis at once verified the correctness of his theory. As he went along the very narrow, grass-grown path that led up the slope, he saw that the grass was uniformly pressed down.

"THE SNARE IS LAID. BEWARE, LUPIN!" 375

"Oh, the villain!" he thought. "The villain! He doesn't carry his victim, he drags her!"

If he had listened only to his instinct, he would have rushed to Florence's rescue. But his profound sense of what to do and what to avoid saved him from committing any such imprudence. At the first alarm, at the least sound, the tiger would have throttled his prey. To escape this hideous catastrophe, Don Luis must take him by surprise and then and there deprive him of his power of action. He controlled himself, therefore, and slowly and cautiously mounted the incline.

The path ran upward between heaps of stones and fallen buildings, and among clumps of shrubs overtopped by beeches and oaks. The place was evidently the site of the old feudal castle which had given the estate its name; and it was here, near the top, that the scoundrel had selected one of his retreats.

The trail continued over the trampled herbage. And Don Luis even caught sight of something shining on the ground, in a tuft of grass. It was a ring, a tiny and very simple ring, consisting of a gold circlet and two small pearls, which he had often noticed on Florence's finger. And the fact that caught his attention was that a blade of grass passed and repassed and passed a third time through the inside of the ring, like a ribbon that had been rolled round it deliberately.

"It's a clear signal," said Perenna to himself. "The villain probably stopped here to rest; and Florence, bound up; but with her fingers free, was able to leave this evidence of her passage."

So the girl still hoped. She expected assistance. And Don Luis reflected with emotion that it was perhaps to him that this last desperate appeal was addressed.

Fifty steps farther—and this detail pointed to the rather curious fatigue experienced by the scoundrel—there was a second halt and a second clue, a flower, a field-sage, which the poor little hand had picked and plucked of its petals. Next came the print of the five fingers dug into the ground, and next a cross drawn with a pebble. And in this way he was able to follow, minute by minute, all the successive stages of the horrible journey.

The last stopping-place was near. The climb became steeper and rougher. The fallen stones occasioned more frequent obstacles. On the right the Gothic arches, the remains of a chapel, stood out against the blue sky. On the left was a strip of wall with a mantelpiece still clinging to it.

Twenty steps farther Don Luis stopped. He seemed to hear something.

He listened. He was not mistaken. The sound was repeated, and it was the sound of laughter. But such an awful laugh! A strident laugh, evil as the laughter of a devil, and so shrill! It was more like the laugh of a woman, of a madwoman.

Again silence. Then another noise, the noise of an implement striking the ground, then silence again.

And this was happening at a distance which Don Luis estimated at a hundred yards.

The path ended in three steps cut in the earth. At the top was a fairly large plateau, also encumbered with rubbish and ruins. In the centre, opposite Don Luis, stood a screen of immense laurels planted in a semicircle. The marks of trodden grass led up to it.

Don Luis was a little surprised, for the screen presented an impenetrable outline. He walked on and found that there had once been a cutting, and that the branches had ended by meeting again. They were easy to push aside; and it was through here that the scoundrel must have passed. To all appearances he was there now, at the end of his journey, not far away, occupied in some sinister task.

Indeed the air was rent by a chuckle, so close by that Don Luis gave a start and felt as if the scoundrel were laughing beforehand at his intervention. He remembered the letter with the words written in red ink:

There's still time, Lupin. Retire from the contest. If not, it means your death, too. When you think that your object is attained, when your hand is raised against me and you utter words of triumph, at the same moment the ground will open beneath your feet. The place of your death is chosen. The snare is laid. Beware, Lupin!

The whole letter passed through his brain, with its formidable threat. And he felt a shiver of fear. But no fear could stay the man that he was. He had already taken hold of the branches with his hands and was clearing a way for himself.

He stopped. A last bulwark of leaves hid him from sight. He pulled some of them aside at the level of his eyes.

And he saw...

First of all, he saw Florence, alone at this moment, lying on the ground, bound, at thirty yards in front of him; and he at once perceived, to his intense delight, from certain movements of her head that she was still alive. He had come in time. Florence was not dead. She would not die. That was a certainty against which nothing could prevail. Florence would not die.

Then he examined the things around. To the right and left of where he stood the screen of laurels curved and embraced a sort of arena in which, among yews that had once been clipped into cones, lay capitals, columns, broken pieces of arches and vaults, obviously placed there to adorn the formal garden that had been laid out on the ruins of the ancient donjon-keep.

In the middle was a small circular space reached by two narrow paths, one of which presented the same traces of trodden grass and was a continuation of that by which Don Luis had come, while the other intersected the first at right angles and joined the two ends of the screen of shrubs.

Opposite was a confused heap of broken stones and natural rocks, cemented with clay, bound together by the roots of gnarled trees, the whole forming at the back of the picture a small, shallow grotto, full of crevices that admitted the light.

The floor, which Don Luis could easily distinguish, consisted of three or four flagstones.

Florence Levasseur lay inside this grotto, bound hand and foot, looking like the victim of some mysterious sacrifice about to be performed on the altar of the grotto, in the amphitheatre of this old garden closed by the wall of tall laurels and overlooked by a pile of ancestral ruins.

In spite of the distance, Don Luis was able to make out every detail of her pale face. Though convulsed with anguish, it still retained a certain serenity, an expression of waiting and even of expectancy, as if Florence, believing, until the last moment, in the possibility of a miracle, had not yet relinquished all hope of life.

Nevertheless, though she was not gagged, she did not call for help. Perhaps she thought that it was useless, and that the road which she had strewn with the marks of her passing was more likely to bring assistance to her side than cries, which the villain would soon have stifled. Strange to say, it seemed to Don Luis as if the girl's eyes were obstinately fixed on the very spot where he was hiding. Possibly she suspected his presence. Possibly she foresaw his help.

Suddenly Don Luis clutched one of his revolvers and half raised his arm, ready to take aim. The sacrificer, the butcher, had just appeared, not far from the altar on which the victim lay.

He came from between two rocks, of which a bush marked the intervening space, which apparently afforded but a very low outlet, for he still walked as though bent double, with his head bowed and his long arms swinging so low as to touch the ground.

He went to the grotto and gave his horrible chuckle:

"You're still there, I see," he said. "No sign of the rescuer? Perseus is a little late, I fear. He'd better hurry!"

The tone of his voice was so shrill that Don Luis heard every word, and so odd, so unhuman, that it gave him a feeling of physical discomfort. He gripped his revolver tightly, prepared to shoot at the first suspicious movement.

"He'd better hurry!" repeated the scoundrel, with a laugh. "If not, all will be over in five minutes. You see that I'm a man of method, eh, Florence, my darling?"

He picked up something from the ground. It was a stick shaped like a crutch. He put it under his left arm and, still bent in two, began to walk like a man who has not the strength to stand erect. Then suddenly and with no apparent cause to explain his change of attitude, he drew himself up and used his crutch as he would a cane. He then walked round the outside of the grotto, making a careful inspection, the meaning of which escaped Don Luis for the time.

He was of a good height in this position; and Don Luis easily understood why the driver of the yellow taxi, who had seen him under two such different aspects, was unable to say whether he was very tall or very short.

But his legs, slack and unsteady, gave way beneath him, as if any prolonged exertion were beyond his power. He relapsed into his first attitude.

The man was a cripple, smitten with some disease that affected his powers of locomotion. He was excessively thin. Don Luis also saw his pallid face, his cavernous cheeks, his hollow temples, his skin the colour of parchment: the face of a sufferer from consumption, a bloodless face.

When he had finished his inspection, he came up to Florence and said:

"Though you've been very good, baby, and haven't screamed so far, we'd better take our precautions and remove any possibility of a surprise by giving you a nice little gag to wear, don't you think?"

He stooped over her and wound a large handkerchief round the lower part of her face. Then, bending still farther down, he began to speak to her in a very low voice, talking almost into her ear. But wild bursts of laughter, horrible to hear, interrupted this whispering.

Feeling the imminence of the danger, dreading some movement on the wretch's part, a sudden murderous attack, the prompt prick of a poisoned needle, Don Luis had levelled his revolver and, confident of his skill, waited events.

What was happening over there? What were the words spoken? What infamous bargain was the villain proposing to Florence? At what shameful price could she obtain her release?

The cripple stepped back angrily, shouting in furious accents:

"But don't you understand that you are done for? Now that I have nothing more to fear, now that you have been silly enough to come with me and place yourself in my power, what hope have you left? To move me, perhaps: is that it? Because I'm burning with passion, you imagine—? Oh, you never made a greater mistake, my pet! I don't care a fig if you do die. Once dead, you cease to count...

"What else? Perhaps you consider that, being crippled, I shall not have the strength to kill you? But there's no question of my killing you, Florence. Have you ever known me kill people? Never! I'm much too big a coward, I should be frightened, I should shake all over. No, no, Florence, I shan't touch you, and yet—

"Here, look what's going to happen, see for yourself. I tell you the thing's managed in my own style... And, whatever you do, don't be afraid. It's only a preliminary warning."

He had moved away and, helping himself with his hands, holding on to the branches of a tree, he climbed up the first layers of rock that formed the grotto on the right. Here he knelt down. There was a small pickaxe lying beside him. He took it and gave three blows to the nearest heap of stones. They came tumbling down in front of the grotto.

"THE SNARE IS LAID. BEWARE, LUPIN!"

Don Luis sprang from his hiding-place with a roar of terror. He had suddenly realized the position: The grotto, the accumulation of boulders, the piles of granite, everything was so placed that its equilibrium could be shattered at any moment, and that Florence ran the risk of being buried under the rubbish. It was not a question, therefore, of slaying the villain, but of saving Florence on the spot.

He was halfway across in two or three seconds. But here, in one of those mental flashes which are even quicker than the maddest rush, he became aware that the tracks of trampled grass did not cross the central circus and that the scoundrel had gone round it. Why? That was one of the questions which instinct, ever suspicious, puts, but which reason has not the time to answer. Don Luis went straight ahead. And he had no sooner set foot on the place than the catastrophe occurred.

It all happened with incredible suddenness, as though he had tried to walk on space and found himself hurled into it. The ground gave way beneath him. The clods of grass separated, and he fell.

He fell down a hole which was none other than the mouth of a well four feet wide at most, the curb of which had been cut down level with the ground. Only this was what took place: as he was running very fast, his impetus flung him against the opposite wall in such a way that his forearms lay on the outer ledge and his hands were able to clutch at the roots of plants.

So great was his strength that he might just have been able to drag himself up by his wrists. But responding to the attack, the scoundrel had at once hurried to meet his assailant and was now standing at ten paces from Don Luis, threatening him with his revolver:

"Don't move!" he cried, "or I'll smash you!"

Don Luis was thus reduced to helplessness, at the risk of receiving the enemy's fire.

Their eyes met for a few seconds. The cripple's were burning with fever, like the eyes of a sick man.

Crawling along, watching Don Luis's slightest movement, he came and squatted beside the well. The revolver was levelled in his outstretched hand. And his infernal chuckle rang out again:

"Lupin! Lupin! That's done it! Lupin's dive!... What a mug you must be! I warned you, you know, warned you in blood-red ink. Remember my words: 'The place of your death is chosen. The snare is laid. Beware, Lupin!' And here you are! So you're not in prison? You warded off that stroke, you rogue, you! Fortunately, I foresaw events and took my precautions. What do you say to it? What do you think of my little scheme? I said to myself, 'All the police will come rushing at my heels. But there's only one who's capable of catching me, and that's Lupin. So we'll show him the way, we'll lead him on the leash all along a little path scraped clean by the victim's body.'

"And then a few landmarks, scattered here and there. First, the fair damsel's ring, with a blade of grass twisted round it; farther on a flower without its petals; farther on the marks of five fingers in the ground; next, the sign of the cross.' No mistaking them, was there? Once you thought me fool enough to give Florence time to play Hop-o'-my-Thumb's game, it was bound to lead you straight to the mouth of the well, to the clods of turf which I dabbed across it, last month, in anticipation of this windfall.

"Remember: 'The snare is laid.' And a snare after my own style, Lupin; one of the best! Oh, I love getting rid of people with their kind assistance. We work together like friends and partners. You've caught the notion, haven't you?

"I don't do my own job. The others do it for me, hanging themselves or giving themselves careless injections—unless they prefer the mouth of a well, as you seem to do, Lupin. My poor old chap, what a sticky mess you're in! I never saw such a

"THE SNARE IS LAID. BEWARE, LUPIN!"

face, never, on my word! Florence, do look at the expression on your swain's mobile features!"

He broke off, seized with a fit of laughter that shook his outstretched arm, imparted the most savage look to his face, and set his legs jerking under his body like the legs of a dancing doll. His enemy was growing weaker before his eyes. Don Luis's fingers, which had first gripped the roots of the grass, were now vainly clutching the stones of the wall. And his shoulders were sinking lower and lower into the well.

"We've done it!" spluttered the villain, in the midst of his convulsions of merriment. "Lord, how good it is to laugh! Especially when one so seldom does. Yes, I'm a wet blanket, I am; a first-rate man at a funeral! You've never seen me laugh, Florence, have you? But this time it's really too amusing. Lupin in his hole and Florence in her grotto; one dancing a jig above the abyss and the other at her last gasp under her mountain. What a sight!

"Come, Lupin, don't tire yourself! What's the use of those grimaces? You're not afraid of eternity, are you? A good man like you, the Don Quixote of modem times! Come, let yourself go. There's not even any water in the well to splash about in. No, it's just a nice little slide into infinity. You can't so much as hear the sound of a pebble when you drop it in; and just now I threw a piece of lighted paper down and lost sight of it in the dark. Brrrr! It sent a cold shiver down my back!

"Come, be a man. It'll only take a moment; and you've been through worse than that!... Good, you nearly did it then. You're making up your mind to it... I say, Lupin!... Lupin!... Aren't you going to say goodbye? Not a smile, not a word of thanks? Au revoir, Lupin, au revoir—"

He ceased. He watched for the appalling end which he had so cleverly prepared and of which all the incidents were following close on one another in accordance with his inflexible will.

It did not take long. The shoulders had gone down; the chin; and then the mouth convulsed with the death-grin; and then the eyes, drunk with terror; and then the forehead and the hair: the whole head, in short, had disappeared.

The cripple sat gazing wildly, as though in ecstasy, motionless, with an expression of fierce delight, and without a word that could trouble the silence and interrupt his hatred.

At the edge of the abyss nothing remained but the hands, the obstinate, stubborn, desperate, heroic hands, the poor, helpless hands which alone still lived, and which, gradually, retreating toward death, yielded and fell back and let go.

The hands had slipped. For a moment the fingers held on like claws. So natural was the effort which they made that it looked as if they did not even yet despair, unaided, of resuscitating and bringing back to the light of day the corpse already entombed in the darkness. And then they in their turn gave way. And then—and then, suddenly, there was nothing more to be seen and nothing more to be heard.

The cripple started to his feet, as though released by a spring, and yelled with delight:

"Oof! That's done it! Lupin in the bottomless pit! One more adventure finished! Oof!"

Turning in Florence's direction, he once more danced his dance of death. He raised himself to his full height and then suddenly crouched down again, throwing about his legs like the grotesque, ragged limbs of a scarecrow. And he sang and whistled and belched forth insults and hideous blasphemies.

Then he came back to the yawning mouth of the well and, standing some way off, as if still afraid to come nearer, he spat into it three times.

Nor was this enough for his hatred. There were some broken pieces of statuary on the ground. He took a carved head, rolled it along the grass, and sent it crashing down the well. A little farther away was a stack of old, rusty cannon balls. These also he rolled to the edge and pushed in. Five, ten, fifteen cannon balls went scooting down, one after the other, banging against the walls with a loud and sinister noise which the echo swelled into the angry roar of distant thunder.

"There, take that, Lupin! I'm sick of you, you dirty cad! That's for the spokes you put in my wheel, over that damned inheritance!... Here, take this, too!... And this!... And this!... Here's a chocolate for you in case you're hungry... Do you want another? Here you are, old chap! catch!"

He staggered, seized with a sort of giddiness, and had to squat on his haunches. He was utterly spent. However, obeying a last convulsion, he still found the strength to kneel down by the well, and leaning over the darkness, he stammered, breathlessly:

"Hi! I say! Corpse! Don't go knocking at the gate of hell at once!... The little girl's joining you in twenty minutes... Yes, that's it, at four o'clock... You know I'm a punctual man and keep my appointments to the minute... She'll be with you at four o'clock exactly.

"By the way, I was almost forgetting: the inheritance—you know, Mornington's hundred million—well, that's mine. Why, of course! You can't doubt that I took all my precautions! Florence will explain everything presently... It's very well thought out—you'll see—you'll see—"

He could not get out another word. The last syllables sounded more like hiccoughs. The sweat poured from his hair and his forehead, and he sank to the ground, moaning like a dying man tortured by the last throes of death.

He remained like that for some minutes, with his head in his hands, shivering all over his body. He appeared to be suffering everywhere, in each anguished muscle, in each sick nerve. Then, under the influence of a thought that seemed to make him act unconsciously, one of his hands crept spasmodically down his side, and, groping, uttering hoarse cries of pain, he managed to take from his pocket and put to his lips a phial out of which he greedily drank two or three mouthfuls.

He at once revived, as though he had swallowed warmth and strength. His eyes grew calmer, his mouth shaped itself into a horrible smile. He turned to Florence and said:

"Don't flatter yourself, pretty one; I'm not gone yet, and I've plenty of time to attend to you. And then, after that, there'll be no more worries, no more of that scheming and fighting that wears one out. A nice, quiet, uneventful life for me!... With a hundred million one can afford to take life easy, eh, little girl?... Come on, I'm feeling much better!"

20

FLORENCE'S SECRET

It was time for the second act of the tragedy. Don Luis Perenna's death was to be followed by that of Florence. Like some monstrous butcher, the cripple passed from one to the other with no more compassion than if he were dealing with the oxen in a slaughter-house.

Still weak in his limbs, he dragged himself to where the girl lay, took a cigarette from a gun-metal case, and, with a final touch of cruelty, said:

"When this cigarette is quite burnt out, Florence, it will be your turn. Keep your eyes on it. It represents the last minutes of your life reduced to ashes. Keep your eyes on it, Florence, and think.

"I want you to understand this: all the owners of the estate, and old Langernault in particular, have always considered that the heap of rocks and stones overhanging your head was bound to fall to pieces sooner or later. And I myself, for years, with untiring patience, believing in a favourable opportunity, have amused myself by making it crumble away still more, by undermining it with the rain water, in short, by working at it in such a way that, upon my word, I can't make out how the thing keeps standing at all. Or, rather, I do understand.

"The few strokes with the pickaxe which I gave it just now were merely intended for a warning. But I have only to give one more stroke in the right place, and knock out a little brick wedged in between two lumps of stone, for the whole thing to tumble to the ground like a house of cards.

"A little brick, Florence," he chuckled, "a tiny little brick which chance placed there, between two blocks of stone, and has kept in position until now. Out comes the brick, down come the blocks, and there's your catastrophe!"

He took breath and continued:

"After that? After that, Florence, this: either the smash will take place in such a way that your body will not even be in sight, if anyone should dream of coming here to look for you, or else it will be partly visible, in which case I shall at once cut and destroy the cords with which you are tied.

"What will the law think then? Simply that Florence Levasseur, a fugitive from justice, hid herself in a grotto which fell upon her and crushed her. That's all. A few prayers for the rash creature's soul, and not another word.

"As for me—as for me, when my work is done and my sweetheart dead—I shall pack my traps, carefully remove all the traces of my coming, smooth every inch of the trampled grass, jump into my motor car, sham death for a little while, and then put in a sensational claim for the hundred million."

He gave a little chuckle, took two or three puffs at his cigarette, and added, calmly:

"I shall claim the hundred million and I shall get them. That's the prettiest part of it. I shall claim them because I'm entitled to them; and I explained to you just now before Master Lupin came interfering, how, from the moment that you were dead, I had the most undeniable legal right to them. And I shall get them, because it is physically impossible to bring up the least sort of proof against me."

He moved closer.

"There's not a charge that can hurt me. Suspicions, yes, moral presumptions, clues, anything you like, but not a scrap of material evidence. Nobody knows me. One person has seen me as a tall man, another as a short man. My very name is unknown. All my murders have been committed anonymously. All my murders are more like suicides, or can be explained as suicides.

"I tell you the law is powerless. With Lupin dead, and Florence Levasseur dead, there's no one to bear witness against me. Even if they arrested me, they would have to discharge me in the end for lack of evidence. I shall be branded, execrated, hated, and cursed; my name will stink in people's nostrils, as if I were the greatest of malefactors. But I shall possess the hundred million; and with that, pretty one, I shall possess the friendship of all decent men!

"I tell you again, with Lupin and you gone, it's all over. There's nothing left, nothing but some papers and a few little things which I have been weak enough to keep until now, in this pocketbook here, and which would be enough and more than enough to cost me my head, if I did not intend to burn them in a few minutes and send the ashes to the bottom of the well.

"So you see, Florence, all my measures are taken. You need not hope for compassion from me, nor for help from anywhere else, since no one knows where I have brought you, and Arsène Lupin is no longer alive. Under these conditions, Florence, make your choice. The ending is in your own hands: either you die, absolutely and irrevocably, or you accept my love."

There was a moment of silence, then:

"Answer me yes or no. A movement of your head will decide your fate. If it's no, you die. If it's yes, I shall release you. We will go from here and, later, when your innocence is proved—and I'll see to that—you shall become my wife. Is the answer yes, Florence?"

He put the question to her with real anxiety and with a restrained passion that set his voice trembling. His knees dragged over the flagstones. He begged and threatened, hungering to be entreated and, at the same time, almost eager for a refusal, so great was his natural murderous impulse.

"Is it yes, Florence? A nod, the least little nod, and I shall believe you implicitly, for you never lie and your promise is sacred. Is it yes, Florence? Oh, Florence, answer me! It is madness to hesitate. Your life depends on a fresh outburst of my anger. Answer me! Here, look, my cigarette is out. I'm throwing it away, Florence. A sign of your head: is the answer yes or no?"

He bent over her and shook her by the shoulders, as if to force her to make the sign which he asked for. But suddenly seized with a sort of frenzy, he rose to his feet and exclaimed:

"She's crying! She's crying! She dares to weep! But, wretched girl, do you think that I don't know what you're crying for? I know your secret, pretty one, and I know that your tears do not come from any fear of dying. You? Why, you fear nothing! No, it's something else! Shall I tell you your secret? Oh, I can't, I can't—though the words scorch my lips. Oh, cursed woman, you've brought it on yourself! You yourself want to die, Florence, as you're crying—you yourself want to die—"

While he was speaking he hastened to get to work and prepare the horrible tragedy. The leather pocketbook which he had mentioned as containing the papers was lying on the ground; he put it in his pocket. Then, still trembling, he pulled off his jacket and threw it on the nearest bush. Next, he took up the pickaxe and climbed the lower stones, stamping with rage and shouting:

"It's you who have asked to die, Florence! Nothing can prevent it now. I can't even see your head, if you make a sign. It's too late! You asked for it and you've got it! Ah, you're crying! You dare to cry! What madness!"

He was standing almost above the grotto, on the right. His anger made him draw himself to his full height. He looked horrible, hideous, atrocious. His eyes filled with blood as he inserted the bar of the pickaxe between the two blocks of granite, at the spot where the brick was wedged in. Then, standing on one side, in a place of safety, he struck the brick, struck it again. At the third stroke the brick flew out.

What happened was so sudden, the pyramid of stones and rubbish came crashing with such violence into the hollow of the grotto and in front of the grotto, that the cripple himself, in spite of his precautions, was dragged down by the avalanche and thrown upon the grass. It was not a serious fall, however, and he picked himself up at once, stammering:

"Florence! Florence!"

Though he had so carefully prepared the catastrophe, and brought it about with such determination, its results seemed suddenly to stagger him. He hunted for the girl with terrified eyes. He stooped down and crawled round the chaos shrouded in clouds of dust. He looked through the interstices. He saw nothing.

Florence was buried under the ruins, dead, invisible, as he had anticipated.

"Dead!" he said, with staring eyes and a look of stupor on his face. "Dead! Florence is dead!"

Once again he lapsed into a state of absolute prostration, which gradually slackened his legs, brought him to the ground and paralyzed him. His two efforts, following so close upon each other and ending in disasters of which he had been the immediate witness, seemed to have robbed him of all his remaining energy.

With no hatred in him, since Arsène Lupin no longer lived, with no love, since Florence was no more, he looked like a man who has lost his last motive for existence.

Twice his lips uttered the name of Florence. Was he regretting his friend? Having reached the last of that appalling series of crimes, was he imagining the several stages, each marked with a corpse? Was something like a conscience making itself felt deep down in that brute? Or was it not rather the sort of physical torpor that numbs the sated beast of prey, glutted with flesh, drunk with blood, a torpor that is almost voluptuousness?

Nevertheless, he once more repeated Florence's name, and tears rolled down his cheeks.

He lay long in this condition, gloomy and motionless; and when, after again taking a few sips of his medicine, he went back to his work, he did so mechanically, with none of that gayety which had made him hop on his legs and set about his murder as though he were going to a pleasure party.

He began by returning to the bush from which Lupin had seen him emerge. Behind this bush, between two trees, was a shelter containing tools and arms, spades, rakes, guns, and rolls of wire and rope.

Making several journeys, he carried them to the well, intending to throw them down it before he went away. He next examined every particle of the little mound up which he had climbed, in order to make sure that he was not leaving the least trace of his passage.

He made a similar examination of those parts of the lawn on which he had stepped, except the path leading to the well, the inspection of which he kept for the last. He brushed up the trodden grass and carefully smoothed the trampled earth.

He was obviously anxious and seemed to be thinking of other things, while at the same time mechanically doing those things which a murderer knows by force of habit that it is wise to do.

One little incident seemed to wake him up. A wounded swallow fell to the ground close by where he stood. He stooped, caught it, and crushed it in his hands, kneading it like a scrap of crumpled paper. And his eyes shone with a savage delight as he gazed at the blood that trickled from the poor bird and reddened his hands.

But, when he flung the shapeless little body into a furze bush, he saw on the spikes in the bush a hair, a long, fair hair; and all his depression returned at the memory of Florence.

He knelt in front of the ruined grotto. Then, breaking two sticks of wood, he placed the pieces in the form of a cross under one of the stones.

As he was bending over, a little looking-glass slipped from his waistcoat pocket and, striking a pebble, broke. This sign of ill luck made a great impression on him, He cast a suspicious look around him and, shivering with nervousness, as though he felt threatened by the invisible powers, he muttered:

"I'm afraid—I'm afraid. Let's go away—"

His watch now marked half-past four. He took his jacket from the shrub on which he had hung it, slipped his arms into the sleeves, and put his hand in the right-hand outside pocket, where he had placed the pocketbook containing his papers:

"Hullo!" he said, in great surprise. "I was sure I had—"

He felt in the left outside pocket, then in the handkerchief pocket, then, with feverish excitement, in both the inside pockets. The pocketbook was not there. And, to his extreme amazement, all the other things which he was absolutely certain that he had left in the pockets of his jacket were gone: his cigarette-case, his box of matches, his notebook.

He was flabbergasted. His features became distorted. He spluttered incomprehensible words, while the most terrible thought took hold of his mind so forcibly as to become a reality: there was someone within the precincts of the Old Castle.

There was someone within the precincts of the Old Castle! And this someone was now hiding near the ruins, in the ruins perhaps! And this someone had seen him! And this someone had witnessed the death of Arsène Lupin and the death of Florence Levasseur! And this someone, taking advantage of his heedlessness and knowing from his words that the papers existed, had searched his jacket and rifled the pockets!

His eyes expressed the alarm of a man accustomed to work in the darkness unperceived, and who suddenly becomes aware that another's eyes have surprised him at his hateful task and that he is being watched in every movement for the first time in his life.

Whence did that look come that troubled him as the daylight troubles a bird of the night? Was it an intruder hiding there by accident, or an enemy bent upon his destruction? Was it an accomplice of Arsène Lupin, a friend of Florence, one of the police? And was this adversary satisfied with his stolen booty, or was he preparing to attack him?

The cripple dared not stir. He was there, exposed to assault, on open ground, with nothing to protect him against the blows that might come before he even knew where the adversary was.

At last, however, the imminence of the danger gave him back some of his strength. Still motionless, he inspected his surroundings with an attention so keen that it seemed as if no detail could escape him. He would have sighted the most indistinct shape among the stones of the ruined pile, or in the bushes, or behind the tall laurel screen.

Seeing nobody, he came along, supporting himself on his crutch. He walked without the least sound of his feet or of the crutch, which probably had a rubber shoe at the end of it. His raised right hand held a revolver. His finger was on the trigger. The least effort of his will, or even less than that, a spontaneous injunction of his instinct, was enough to put a bullet into the enemy.

He turned to the left. On this side, between the extreme end of the laurels and the first fallen rocks, there was a little brick path which was more likely the top of a buried wall. The cripple followed this path, by which the enemy might have reached the shrub on which the jacket hung without leaving any traces.

The last branches of the laurels were in his way, and he pushed them aside. There was a tangled mass of bushes. To avoid this, he skirted the foot of the mound, after which he took a few more steps, going round a huge rock. And then, suddenly, he started back and almost lost his balance, while his crutch fell to the ground and his revolver slipped from his hand.

What he had seen, what he saw, was certainly the most terrifying sight that he could possibly have beheld. Opposite him, at ten paces distance, with his hands in his pockets, his feet crossed, and one shoulder resting lightly against the rocky wall, stood not a man: it was not a man, and could not be a man, for this man, as the cripple knew, was dead, had died the death from which there is no recovery. It was therefore a ghost; and this apparition from the tomb raised the cripple's terror to its highest pitch.

He shivered, seized with a fresh attack of fever and weakness. His dilated pupils stared at the extraordinary phenomenon. His whole being, filled with demoniacal superstition and dread, crumpled up under the vision to which each second lent an added horror.

Incapable of flight, incapable of defence, he dropped upon his knees. And he could not take his eyes from that dead man, whom hardly an hour before he had buried in the depths of a well, under a shroud of iron and granite.

Arsène Lupin's ghost!

A man you take aim at, you fire at, you kill. But a ghost! A thing which no longer exists and which nevertheless disposes of all the supernatural powers! What was the use of struggling against the infernal machinations of that which is no more? What was the use of picking up the fallen revolver and levelling it at the intangible spirit of Arsène Lupin?

And he saw an incomprehensible thing occur: the ghost took its hands out of its pockets. One of them held a cigarette-case; and the cripple recognized the same gun-metal case for which he had hunted in vain. There was therefore not a doubt left that the creature who had ransacked the jacket was the very same who now opened the case, picked out a cigarette and struck a match taken from a box which also belonged to the cripple!

O miracle! A real flame came from the match! O incomparable marvel! Clouds of smoke rose from the cigarette, real smoke, of which the cripple at once knew the particular smell!

He hid his head in his hands. He refused to see more. Whether ghost or optical illusion, an emanation from another world, or an image born of his remorse and proceeding from himself, it should torture his eyes no longer.

But he heard the sound of a step approaching him, growing more and more distinct as it came closer! He felt a strange presence moving near him! An arm was stretched out! A hand fell on his shoulder! That hand clutched his flesh with an irresistible grip! And he heard words spoken by a voice which, beyond mistake, was the human and living voice of Arsène Lupin!

"Why, my dear sir, what a state we're getting ourselves into! Of course, I understand that my sudden return seems an unusual and even an inconvenient proceeding, but still it does not do to be so uncontrollably impressed. Men have seen much more extraordinary things than that, such as Joshua staying the sun, and more sensational disasters, such as the Lisbon earthquake of 1755.

"The wise man reduces events to their proper proportions and judges them, not by their action upon his own destiny, but by the way in which they influence the fortunes of the world. Now confess that your little mishap is purely individual and does not affect the equilibrium of the solar system. You know what Marcus Aurelius says, on page 84, of Charpentier's edition—"

The cripple had plucked up courage to raise his head; and the real state of things now became so obviously apparent that he could no longer get away from the undeniable fact: Arsène Lupin was not dead! Arsène Lupin whom he had hurled into the bowels of the earth and crushed as surely as an insect is crushed with a hammer; Arsène Lupin was not dead!

How to explain so astounding a mystery the cripple did not even stop to wonder. One thing alone mattered: Arsène Lupin was not dead. Arsène Lupin looked and spoke as a living man does. Arsène Lupin was not dead. He breathed, he smiled, he talked, he lived!

And it was so certainly life that the scoundrel saw before him that, obeying a sudden impulse of his nature and of his hatred for life, he flattened himself to his full length, reached his revolver, seized it, and fired.

He fired; but it was too late. Don Luis had caused the weapon to swerve with a kick of his boot. Another kick sent it flying out of the cripple's hand.

The villain ground his teeth with fury and at once began hurriedly to fumble in his pockets.

"Is this what you're looking for, sir?" asked Don Luis, holding up a hypodermic syringe filled with a yellow fluid. "Excuse me, but I was afraid lest you should prick yourself by mistake. That would have been a fatal prick, would it not? And I should never have forgiven myself."

The cripple was disarmed. He hesitated for a moment, surprised that the enemy did not attack him more violently, and sought to profit by the delay. His small, blinking eyes wandered around him, looking for something to throw. But an idea seemed to strike him and to restore his confidence little by little; and, in a new and really unexpected fit of delight, he indulged in one of his loudest chuckles:

"And what about Florence?" he shouted. "Don't forget Florence! For I've got you there! I can miss you with my revolver and you can steal my poison; but I have another means of hitting you, right in the heart. You can't live without

Florence, can you? Florence's death means your own sentence, doesn't it? If Florence is dead, you'll put the rope round your own neck, won't you, won't you, won't you?"

"Yes. If Florence were to die, I could not survive her!"

"She is dead!" cried the scoundrel, with a renewed burst of merriment, hopping about on his knees. "She's dead, quite, quite dead! What am I saying? She's more than dead! A dead person retains the appearance of a live one for a time; but this is much better: there's no corpse here, Lupin; just a mess of flesh and bone!

"The whole scaffolding of rocks has come down on top of her! You can picture it, eh? What a sight! Come, quick, it's your turn to kick the bucket. Would you like a length of rope? Ha, ha, ha! It's enough to make one die with laughing. Didn't I say that you'd meet at the gates of hell? Quick, your sweetheart's waiting for you. Do you hesitate? Where's your old French politeness? You can't keep a lady waiting, you know. Hurry up, Lupin! Florence is dead!"

He said this with real enjoyment, as though the mere word of death appeared to him delicious.

Don Luis had not moved a muscle. He simply nodded his head and said:

"What a pity!"

The cripple seemed petrified. All his joyous contortions, all his triumphal pantomime, stopped short. He blurted out:

"Eh? What did you say?"

"I say," declared Don Luis, preserving his calm and courteous demeanour and refraining from echoing the cripple's familiarity, "I say, my dear sir, that you have done very wrong. I never met a finer nature nor one more worthy of esteem than that of Mlle. Levasseur. The incomparable beauty of her face and figure, her youth, her charm, all these deserved a better treatment. It would indeed be a matter for regret if such a masterpiece of womankind had ceased to be."

The cripple remained astounded. Don Luis's serene manner dismayed him. He said, in a blank voice:

"I tell you, she has ceased to be. Haven't you seen the grotto? Florence no longer exists!"

"I refuse to believe it," said Don Luis quietly. "If that were so, everything would look different. The sky would be clouded; the birds would not be singing; and nature would wear her mourning garb. But the birds are singing, the sky is blue, everything is as it should be: the honest man is alive; and the rascal is crawling at his feet. How could Florence be dead?"

A long silence followed upon these words. The two enemies, at three paces distance, looked into each other's eyes: Don Luis still as cool as ever, the cripple a prey to the maddest anguish. The monster understood. Obscure as the truth was, it shone forth before him with all the light of a blinding certainty: Florence also was alive! Humanly and physically speaking, the thing was not possible; but the resurrection of Don Luis was likewise an impossibility; and yet Don Luis was alive, with not a scratch on his face, with not a speck of dust on his clothes.

The monster felt himself lost. The man who held him in the hollow of his implacable hand was one of those men whose power knows no bounds. He was one of those men who escape from the jaws of death and who triumphantly snatch from death those of whom they have taken charge.

The monster retreated, dragging himself slowly backward on his knees along the little brick path.

He retreated. He passed by the confused heap of stones that covered the place where the grotto had been, and did not turn his eyes in that direction, as if he were definitely convinced that Florence had come forth safe and sound from the appalling sepulchre.

He retreated. Don Luis, who no longer had his eyes fixed on him, was busy unwinding a coil of rope which he had picked up, and seemed to pay no further attention to him.

He retreated.

And suddenly, after a glance at his enemy, he spun round, drew himself up on his slack legs with an effort, and started running toward the well.

He was twenty paces from it. He covered one half, three quarters of the distance. Already the mouth opened before him. He put out his arms, with the movement of a man about to dive, and shot forward.

His rush was stopped. He rolled over on the ground, dragged back violently, with his arms fixed so firmly to his body that he was unable to stir.

It was Don Luis, who had never wholly lost sight of him, who had made a slip-knot to his rope and who had lassoed the cripple at the moment when he was going to fling himself down the abyss. The cripple struggled for a few moments. But the slip-knot bit into his flesh. He ceased moving. Everything was over.

Then Don Luis Perenna, holding the other end of the lasso, came up to him and bound him hand and foot with what remained of the rope. The operation was carefully performed. Don Luis repeated it time after time, using the coils of rope which the cripple had brought to the well and gagging him with a handkerchief. And, while applying himself to his work, he explained, with affected politeness:

"You see, sir, people always come to grief through excessive self-confidence. They never imagine that their adversaries can have resources which they themselves do not possess. For instance, when you got me to fall into your trap, how could you have supposed, my dear sir, that a man like myself, a man like Arsène Lupin, hanging on the brim of a well, with his arms resting on the brim and his feet against the inner wall, would allow himself to drop down it like the first silly fool that comes along?

"Look here: you were fifteen or twenty yards away; and do you think that I had not the strength to leap out nor the courage to face the bullets of your revolver, when it was a question of saving Florence Levasseur's life and my own? Why, my poor sir, the tiniest effort would have been enough, believe me!

"My reason for not making the effort was that I had something better to do, something infinitely better. I will tell you why, that is, if you care to know. Do you?

"Well, then, at the very first moment, my knees and feet, propped against the inner wall, had smashed in a thick layer of plaster which closed up an old excavation in the well; and this I at once perceived. It was a stroke of luck, wasn't it? And it changed the whole situation. My plan was settled at once. While I went on acting my little part of the gentleman about to tumble down an abyss, putting on the most scared face, the most staring eyes, the most hideous grin, I enlarged that excavation, taking care to throw the chunks of plaster in front of me in such a way that their fall made no noise. When the moment came, at the very second when my swooning features vanished before your eyes, I simply jumped into my retreat, thanks to a rather plucky little wriggle of the loins.

"I was saved, because the retreat was dug out on the side where you were moving and because, being dark itself, it cast no light. All that I now had to do was to wait.

"I listened quietly to your threatening speeches. I let the things you flung down the well go past me. And, when I thought you had gone back to Florence, I was preparing to leave my refuge, to return to the light of day, and to fall upon you from behind, when—"

Don Luis turned the cripple over, as though he were a parcel which he was tying up with string, and continued:

"Have you ever been to Tancarville, the old feudal castle in Normandy, on the banks of the Seine? Haven't you? Well, you must know that, outside the ruins of the keep, there is an old well which, like many other wells of the period, possesses the peculiarity of having two openings, one at the top, facing the sky, and the other a little lower down, hollowed out sideways in the wall and leading to one of the rooms of the keep.

"At Tancarville this second opening is nowadays closed with a grating. Here it was walled up with a layer of small stones and plaster. And it was just the recollection of Tancarville that made me stay, all the more as there was no hurry, since you had had the kindness to inform me that Florence would not join me in the next world until four o'clock. I therefore inspected my refuge and soon realized that, as I had already felt by intuition, it was the foundation of a building which was now demolished and which had the garden laid out on its ruins.

"Well, I went on, groping my way and following the direction which, above ground, would have taken me to the grotto. My presentiments were not deceived. A gleam of daylight made its way at the top of a staircase of which I had struck the bottom step. I went up it and heard the sound of your voice."

Don Luis turned the cripple over and over and was pretty rough about it. Then he resumed:

"I wish to impress upon you, my dear sir, that the upshot would have been exactly similar if I had attacked you directly and from the start in the open air. But, having said this, I confess that chance favoured me to some purpose. It has often failed me, in the course of our struggle, but this time I had no cause to complain.

"I felt myself in such luck that I never doubted for a second that, having found the entrance to the subterranean passage, I should also find the way out. As a matter of fact, I had only to pull gently at the slight obstacle of a few stacked bricks which hid the opening in order to make my exit amid the remains of the castle keep.

"Guided by the sound of your voice, I slipped through the stones and thus reached the back of the grotto in which Florence lay. Amusing, wasn't it?

"You can imagine what fun it was to hear you make your little speeches: 'Answer me, yes or no, Florence. A movement of your head will decide your fate. If it's yes, I shall release you. If it's no, you die. Answer me, Florence! A sign of your head: is the answer yes or no?' And the end, above all, was delicious, when you scrambled to the top of the grotto and started roaring from up there: 'It's you who have asked to die, Florence. You asked for it and you've got it!'

"Just think what a joke it was: at that moment there was no one in the grotto! Not a soul! With one effort, I had drawn Florence toward me and put her under shelter. And all that you were able to crush with your avalanche of rocks was one or two spiders, perhaps, and a few flies dozing on the flagstones.

"The trick was done and the farce was nearly finished. Act first: Arsène Lupin saved. Act second: Florence Levasseur saved. Act third and last: the monster vanquished... absolutely and with a vengeance!"

Don Luis stood up and contemplated his work with a satisfied eye.

"You look like a sausage, my son!" he cried, yielding at last to his sarcastic nature and his habit of treating his enemies familiarly. "A regular sausage! A bit on the thin side, perhaps: a saveloy for poor people! But there, you don't much care what you look like, I suppose? Besides, you're rather like that at all times; and, in any case, you're just the thing for the little display of indoor gymnastics which I have in mind for you. You'll see: it's an idea of my own, a really original idea. Don't be impatient: we shan't be long."

He took one of the guns which the cripple had brought to the well and tied to the middle of the gun the end of a twelve- or fifteen-yards' length of rope, fastening the other end to the cords with which the cripple was bound, just behind his back. He next took his captive round the body and held him over the well:

"Shut your eyes, if you feel at all giddy. And don't be frightened. I'll be very careful. Ready?"

He put the cripple down the yawning hole and next took hold of the rope which he had just fastened. Then, little by little, inch by inch, cautiously, so that it should not knock against the sides of the well, the bundle was let down at arm's length.

When it reached a depth of twelve yards or so, the gun stopped its further descent and there it remained, slung in the dark and in the exact centre of the narrow circumference.

Don Luis set light to a number of pieces of paper, which went whirling down, shedding their sinister gleams upon the walls. Then, unable to resist the craving for a last speech, he leaned over, as the scoundrel had done, and grinned:

"I selected the place with care, so that you shouldn't catch cold. I'm bound to look after you, you see. I promised Florence that I wouldn't kill you; and I promised the French Government to hand you over alive as soon as possible. Only, as I didn't know what to do with you until tomorrow morning, I've hung you up in the air.

"It's a pretty trick, isn't it? And you ought to appreciate it, for it's so like your own way of doing things. Just think: the gun is resting on its two ends, with hardly an inch to spare. So, if you start wriggling, or moving, or even breathing too hard, either the barrel or the butt end'll give way; and down you go! As for me, I've nothing to do with it!

"If you die, it'll be a pretty little case of suicide. All you've got to do, old chap, is to keep quiet. And the beauty of my little contrivance is that it will give you a foretaste of the few nights that will precede your last hour, when they cut off your head. From this moment forward you are alone with your conscience, face to face with what you perhaps call your soul, without anything to disturb your silent soliloquy. It's nice and thoughtful of me, isn't it?...

"Well, I'll leave you. And remember: not a movement, not a sigh, not a wink, not a throb of the heart! And, above all, no larks! If you start larking, you're in the soup. Meditate: that's the best thing you can do. Meditate and wait. Goodbye, for the present!"

And Don Luis, satisfied with his homily, went off, muttering:

"That's all right. I won't go so far as Eugene Sue, who says that great criminals should have their eyes put out. But, all the same, a little corporal punishment, nicely seasoned with fear, is right and proper and good for the health and morals."

Don Luis walked away and, taking the brick path round the ruins, turned down a little road, which ran along the outer wall to a clump of fir trees, where he had brought Florence for shelter.

She was waiting for him, still aching from the horrible suffering which she had endured, but already in full possession of her pluck, mistress of herself, and apparently rid of all anxiety as to the issue of the fight between Don Luis and the cripple.

"It's finished," he said, simply. "Tomorrow I will hand him over to the police."

She shuddered. But she did not speak; and he observed her in silence.

It was the first time that they were alone together since they had been separated by so many tragedies, and next hurled against each other like sworn enemies. Don Luis was so greatly excited that, in the end, he could utter only insignificant sentences, having no connection with the thoughts that came rushing through his mind.

"We shall find the motor car if we follow this wall and then strike off to the left... Do you think you can manage to walk so far?... When we're in the car, we'll go to Alençon. There's a quiet hotel close to the chief square. You can wait there until things take a more favourable turn for you—and that won't be long, as the criminal is caught."

"Let's go," she said.

He dared not offer to help her. For that matter, she stepped out firmly and her graceful body swung from her hips with the same even rhythm as usual. Don Luis once again felt all his old admiration and all his ardent love for her. And yet that had never seemed more remote than at this moment when he had saved her life by untold miracles of energy.

She had not vouchsafed him a word of thanks nor yet one of those milder glances which reward an effort made; and she remained the same as on the first day, the mysterious creature whose secret soul he had never understood, and upon whom not even the storm of terrible events had cast the faintest light.

What were her thoughts? What were her wishes? What aim was she pursuing? These were obscure problems which he could no longer hope to solve. Henceforth each of them must go his own way in life and each of them could only remember the other with feelings of anger and spite.

"No!" he said to himself, as she took her place in the limousine. "No! The separation shall not take place like that. The words that have to be spoken between us shall be spoken; and, whether she wishes or not, I will tear the veil that hides her."

***

The journey did not take long. At Alençon Don Luis entered Florence in the visitors' book under the first name that occurred to him and left her to herself. An hour later he came and knocked at her door.

This time again he had not the courage at once to ask her the question which he had made up his mind to put to her. Besides, there were other points which he wished to clear up.

"Florence," he said, "before I hand over that man, I should like to know what he was to you."

"A friend, an unhappy friend, for whom I felt pity," she declared. "I find it difficult today to understand my compassion for such a monster. But, some years ago, when I first met him, I became attached to him because of his wretchedness, his physical weakness, and all the symptoms of death which he bore upon him even then. He had the opportunity of doing me a few services; and, though he led a hidden life, which worried me in certain respects, he gradually and without my knowing it acquired a considerable influence over me.

"I believed in his insight, in his will, in his absolute devotion; and, when the Mornington case started, it was he, as I now realize, who guided my actions and, later, those of Gaston Sauverand. It was he who compelled me to practise lying and deceit, persuading me that he was working for Marie Fauville's safety. It was he who inspired us with such suspicion of yourself and who taught us to be so silent, where he and his affairs were concerned, that Gaston Sauverand did not even dare mention him in his interview with you.

"I don't know how I can have been so blind. But it was so. Nothing opened my eyes. Nothing made me suspect for a moment that harmless, ailing creature, who spent half his life in hospitals or nursing-homes, who underwent every possible sort of operation, and who, if he did sometimes speak to me of his love, must have known that he could not hope to—"

Florence did not finish her sentence. Her eyes had encountered Don Luis's eyes; and she received a deep impression that he was not listening to what she said. He was looking at her; and that was all. The words she uttered passed unheard.

To Don Luis any explanation concerning the tragedy itself mattered nothing, so long as he was not enlightened on the one point that interested him, on Florence's private thoughts about himself, thoughts of aversion, of contempt. Outside that, anything that she could say was vain and tedious.

He went up to her and, in a low voice, said:

"Florence, you know what I feel for you, do you not?"

She blushed, taken aback, as though the question was the very last that she expected to hear. Nevertheless, she did not lower her eyes, and she answered frankly:

"Yes, I know."

"But, perhaps," he continued, more eagerly, "you do not know how deeply I feel it? Perhaps you do not know that my life has no other aim but you?"

"I know that also," she said.

"Then, if you know it," he said, "I must conclude that it was just that which caused your hostility to me. From the beginning I tried to be your friend and I tried only to defend you. And yet from the beginning I felt that for you I was the object of an aversion that was both instinctive and deliberate. Never did I see in your eyes anything but coldness, dislike, contempt, and even repulsion.

"At moments of danger, when your life or your liberty was at stake, you risked committing any imprudence rather than accept my assistance. I was the enemy, the man to be distrusted, the man capable of every infamy, the man to be avoided, and to be thought of only with a sort of dread. Isn't that hatred? Is there anything but hatred to explain such an attitude?"

Florence did not answer at once. She seemed to be putting off the moment at which to speak the words that rose to her lips. Her face, thin and drawn with weariness and pain, was gentler than usual.

"Yes," she said, "there are other things than hatred to explain that attitude."

Don Luis was dumfounded. He did not quite understand the meaning of the reply; but Florence's tone of voice disconcerted him beyond measure, and he also saw that Florence's eyes no longer wore their usual scornful expression and that they were filled with smiling charm. And it was the first time that Florence had smiled in his presence.

"Speak, speak, I entreat you!" he stammered.

"I mean to say that there is another feeling which explains coldness, mistrust, fear, and hostility. It is not always those whom we detest that we avoid with the greatest fear; and, if we avoid them, it is often because we are afraid of ourselves, because we are ashamed, because we rebel and want to resist and want to forget and cannot—"

She stopped; and, when he wildly stretched out his arms to her, as if beseeching her to say more and still more, she nodded her head, thus telling him that she need not go on speaking for him to read to the very bottom of her soul and discover the secret of love which she kept hidden there.

Don Luis staggered on his feet. He was intoxicated with happiness, almost suffered physical pain from that unexpected happiness. After the horrible minutes through which he had passed amid the impressive surroundings of the Old Castle, it appeared to him madness to admit that such extraordinary bliss could suddenly blossom forth in the commonplace setting of that room at a hotel.

He could have longed for space around him, forest, mountains, moonlight, a radiant sunset, all the beauty and all the poetry of the earth. With one rush, he had reached the very acme of happiness. Florence's very life came before him, from the instant of their meeting to the tragic moment when the cripple, bending over her and seeing her eyes filled with tears, had shouted:

"She's crying! She's crying! What madness! But I know your secret, Florence! And you're crying! Florence, Florence, you yourself want to die!"

It was a secret of love, a passionate impulse which, from the first day, had driven her all trembling toward Don Luis. Then it had bewildered her, filled her with fear, appeared to her as a betrayal of Marie and Sauverand and, by turns urging her toward and drawing her away from the man whom she loved and whom she admired for his heroism and loyalty, rending her with remorse and overwhelming her as though it were a crime, had ended by delivering her, feeble and disabled, to the diabolical influence of the villain who coveted her.

Don Luis did not know what to do, did not know in what words to express his rapture. His lips trembled. His eyes filled with tears. His nature prompted him to take her in his arms, to kiss her as a child kisses, full on the lips, with a full heart. But a feeling of intense respect paralyzed his yearning. And, overcome with emotion, he fell at Florence's feet, stammering words of love and adoration.

21

LUPIN'S LUPINS

Next morning, a little before eight o'clock, Valenglay was talking in his own flat to the Prefect of Police, and asked:

"So you think as I do, my dear Prefect? He'll come?"

"I haven't the least doubt of it, Monsieur le Président. And he will come with the same punctuality that has been shown throughout this business. He will come, for pride's sake, at the last stroke of eight."

"You think so?"

"Monsieur le Président, I have been studying the man for months. As things now stand, with Florence Levasseur's life in the balance, if he has not smashed the villain whom he is hunting down, if he does not bring him back bound hand and foot, it will mean that Florence Levasseur is dead and that he, Arsène Lupin, is dead."

"Whereas Lupin is immortal," said Valenglay, laughing. "You're right. Besides, I agree with you entirely. No one would be more astonished than I if our good friend was not here to the minute. You say you were rung up from Angers yesterday?"

"Yes, Monsieur le Président. My men had just seen Don Luis Perenna. He had gone in front of them, in an aeroplane. After that, they telephoned to me again from Le Mans, where they had been searching a deserted coach-house.

"You may be sure that the search had already been made by Lupin, and that we shall know the results. Listen: eight o'clock!"

At the same moment they heard the throbbing of a motor car. It stopped outside the house; and the bell rang almost immediately after. Orders had been given beforehand. The door opened and Don Luis Perenna was shown in.

To Valenglay and the Prefect of Police his arrival was certainly not unexpected, for they had just been saying that they would have been surprised if he had not come. Nevertheless, their attitude showed that astonishment which we all experience in the face of events that seem to pass the bounds of human possibility.

"Well?" cried the Prime Minister eagerly.

"It's done, Monsieur le Président."

"Have you collared the scoundrel?"

"Yes."

"By Jove!" said Valenglay. "You're a fine fellow!" And he went on to ask, "An ogre, of course? An evil, undaunted brute?—"

"No, Monsieur le Président, a cripple, a degenerate, responsible for his actions, certainly, but a man in whom the doctors will find every form of wasting illness: disease of the spinal cord, tuberculosis, and all the rest of it."

"And is that the man whom Florence Levasseur loved?"

"Monsieur le Président!" Don Luis violently protested. "Florence never loved that wretch! She felt sorry for him, as anyone would for a fellow-creature doomed to an early death; and it was out of pity that she allowed him to hope that she might marry him later, at some time in the vague future."

"Are you sure of that?"

"Yes, Monsieur le Président, of that and of a good deal more besides, for I have the proofs in my hands." Without further preamble, he continued: "Monsieur le Président, now that the man is caught, it will be easy for the police to find out every detail of his life. But meanwhile I can sum up that monstrous life for you, looking only at the criminal side of it, and passing briefly over three murders which have nothing to do with the story of the Mornington case.

"Jean Vernocq was born at Alençon and brought up at old M. Langernault's expense. He got to know the Dedessuslamare couple, robbed them of their money and, before they had time to lodge a complaint against the unknown thief, took them to a barn in the village of Damigni, where, in their despair, stupefied and besotted with drugs, they hanged themselves.

"This barn stood in a property called the Old Castle, belonging to M. Langernault, Jean Vernocq's protector, who was ill at the time. After his recovery, as he was cleaning his gun, he received a full charge of shot in the abdomen. The gun had been loaded without the old fellow's knowledge. By whom? By Jean Vernocq, who had also emptied his patron's cash box the night before...

"In Paris, where he went to enjoy the little fortune which he had thus amassed, Jean Vernocq bought from some rogue of his acquaintance papers containing evidence of Florence Levasseur's birth and of her right to all the inheritance of the Roussel family and Victor Sauverand, papers which the friend in question had purloined from the old nurse who brought Florence over from America. By hunting around, Jean Vernocq ended by discovering first a photograph of Florence and then Florence herself.

"He made himself useful to her and pretended to be devoted to her, giving up his whole life to her service. At that time he did not yet know what profit he could derive from the papers stolen from the girl or from his relations with her.

"Suddenly everything became different. An indiscreet word let fall by a solicitor's clerk told him of a will in Maitre Lepertuis's drawer which would be interesting to look at. He obtained a sight of it by bribing the clerk, who has since disappeared, with a thousand-franc note. The will, as it happened, was Cosmo Mornington's; and in it Cosmo Mornington bequeathed his immense wealth to the heirs of the Roussel sisters and of Victor Sauverand...

"Jean Vernocq saw his chance. A hundred million francs! To get hold of that sum, to obtain riches, luxury, power, and the means of buying health and strength from the world's great healers, all that he had to do was first to put away the different persons who stood between the inheritance and Florence, and then, when all the obstacles were overcome, to make Florence his wife.

"Jean Vernocq went to work. He had found among the papers of Hippolyte Fauville's old friend Langernault particulars relating to the Roussel family and to the discord that reigned in the Fauville household. Five persons, all told, were in his way: first, of course, Cosmo Mornington; next, in the order of their claims, Hippolyte Fauville, his son Edmond, his wife Marie, and his cousin Gaston Sauverand.

"With Cosmo Mornington, the thing was easy enough. Introducing himself to the American as a doctor, Jean Vernocq put poison into one of the phials which Mornington used for his hypodermic injections.

"But in the case of Hippolyte Fauville, whose goodwill he had secured through his acquaintance with old Langernault, and over whose mind he soon obtained an extraordinary influence, he had a greater difficulty to contend with. Knowing on the one hand that the engineer hated his wife and on the other that he was stricken with a fatal disease, he took occasion, after the consultation with the specialist in London, to suggest to Fauville's terrified brain the incredible plan of suicide of which you were subsequently able to trace the Machiavellian execution.

"In this way and with a single effort, anonymously, so to speak, and without appearing in the business, without Fauville's even suspecting the action brought to bear upon him, Jean Vernocq procured the deaths of Fauville and his son, and got rid of Marie and Sauverand by the devilish expedient of causing the charge of murder, of which no one could accuse him, to fall upon them. The plan succeeded.

"There was only one hitch at the present time: the intervention of Inspector Vérot. Inspector Vérot died. And there was only one danger in the future: the intervention of myself, Don Luis Perenna, whose conduct Vernocq was bound to foresee, as I was the residuary legatee by the terms of Cosmo Mornington's will. This danger Vernocq tried to avert first by giving me the house on the Place du Palais-Bourbon to live in and Florence Levasseur as a secretary, and next by making four attempts to have me assassinated by Gaston Sauverand.

"He therefore held all the threads of the tragedy in his hands. Able to come and go as he pleased in my house, enforcing himself upon Florence and later upon Gaston Sauverand by the strength of his will and the cunning of his character, he was within sight of the goal.

"When my efforts succeeded in proving the innocence of Marie Fauville and Gaston Sauverand, he did not hesitate: Marie Fauville died; Gaston Sauverand died.

"So everything was going well for him. The police pursued me. The police pursued Florence. No one suspected him. And the date fixed for the payment of the inheritance was at hand.

"This was two days ago. At that time, Jean Vernocq was in the midst of the fray. He was ill and had obtained admission to the nursing-home in the Avenue des Ternes. From there he conducted his operations, thanks to his influence over Florence Levasseur and to the letters addressed to the mother superior from Versailles. Acting under the superior's orders and ignorant of the meaning of the step which she was taking, Florence went to the meeting at the Prefect's office, and herself brought the documents relating to her.

"Meanwhile, Jean Vernocq left the private hospital and took refuge near the Ile Saint-Louis, where he awaited the result of an enterprise which, at the worst, might tell against Florence, but which did not seem able to compromise him in any case.

"You know the rest, Monsieur le Président," said Don Luis, concluding his statement. "Florence, staggered by the sudden revelation of the part which she had unconsciously taken in the matter, and especially by the terrible part played by Jean Vernocq, ran away from the nursing-home where the Prefect had brought her at my request. She had but one thought: to see Jean Vernocq, demand an explanation of him, and hear what he had to say in his defence. That same evening he carried her away by motor, on the pretence of giving her proofs of his innocence. That is all, Monsieur le Président."

Valenglay had listened with growing interest to this gruesome story of the most malevolent genius conceivable to the mind of man. And he heard it perhaps without too great disgust, because of the light which it threw by contrast upon the bright, easy, happy, and spontaneous genius of the man who had fought for the good cause.

"And you found them?" he asked.

"At three o'clock yesterday afternoon, Monsieur le Président. It was time. I might even say that it was too late, for Jean Vernocq began by sending me to the bottom of a well, and by crushing Florence under a block of stone."

"Oh, so you're dead, are you?"

"Yes, Monsieur le Président."

"But why did that villain want to do away with Florence Levasseur? Her death destroyed his indispensable scheme of matrimony."

"It takes two to get married, Monsieur le Président, and Florence refused."

"Well—"

"Some time ago Jean Vernocq wrote a letter leaving all that he possessed to Florence Levasseur. Florence, moved by pity for him, and not realizing the importance of what she was doing, wrote a similar letter leaving her property to him. This letter constitutes a genuine and indisputable will in favour of Jean Vernocq.

"As Florence was Cosmo Mornington's legal and settled heiress by the mere fact of her presence at yesterday's meeting with the documents proving her descent from the Roussel family, her death caused her rights to pass to her own legal and settled heir.

"Jean Vernocq would have come into the money without the possibility of any litigation. And, as you would have been obliged to discharge him after his arrest, for lack of evidence against him, he would have led a quiet life, with fourteen murders on his conscience—I have added them up—but with a hundred million francs in his pocket. To a monster of his stamp, the one made up for the other."

"But do you possess all the proofs?" asked Valenglay eagerly.

"Here they are," said Perenna, producing the pocketbook which he had taken out of the cripple's jacket. "Here are letters and documents which the villain preserved, owing to a mental aberration common to all great criminals. Here, by good luck, is his correspondence with Hippolyte Fauville. Here is the original of the prospectus from which I learned that the house on the Place du Palais-Bourbon was for sale. Here is a memorandum of Jean Vernocq's journeys to Alençon to intercept Fauville's letters to old Langernault.

"Here is another memorandum showing that Inspector Vérot overheard a conversation between Fauville and his accomplice, that he shadowed Vernocq and robbed him of Florence Levasseur's photograph, and that Vernocq sent Fauville in pursuit of him. Here is a third memorandum, which is just a copy of the two found in the eighth volume of Shakespeare and which proves that Jean Vernocq, to whom that set of Shakespeare belonged, knew all about Fauville's machination. Here is his correspondence with Caceres, the Peruvian attaché, and the letters denouncing myself and Sergeant Mazeroux, which he intended to send to the press. Here—

"But need I say more, Monsieur le Président? You have the complete evidence in your hands. The magistrates will find that all the accusations which I made yesterday, before the Prefect of Police, were strictly true."

"And he?" cried Valenglay. "The criminal? Where is he?"

"Outside, in a motor car, in his motor car, rather."

"Have you told my men?" asked M. Desmalions anxiously.

"Yes, Monsieur le Préfet. Besides, the fellow is carefully tied up. Don't be alarmed. He won't escape."

"Well, you've foreseen every contingency," said Valenglay, "and the business seems to me to be finished. But there's one problem that remains unexplained, the one perhaps that interested the public most. I mean the marks of the teeth in the apple, the teeth of the tiger, as they have been called, which were certainly Mme. Fauville's teeth, innocent though she was. Monsieur le Préfet declares that you have solved this problem."

"Yes, Monsieur le Président, and Jean Vernocq's papers prove that I was right. Besides, the problem is quite simple. The apple was marked with Mme. Fauville's teeth, but Mme. Fauville never bit the apple."

"Come, come!"

"Monsieur le Président, Hippolyte Fauville very nearly said as much when he mentioned this mystery in his posthumous confession."

"Hippolyte Fauville was a madman."

"Yes, but a lucid madman and capable of reasoning with the most appalling logic. Some years ago, at Palermo, Mme. Fauville had a very bad fall, hitting her mouth against the marble top of a table, with the result that a number of her teeth, in both the upper and the lower jaw, were loosened. To repair the damage and to make the gold plate intended to strengthen the teeth, a plate which Mme. Fauville wore for several months, the dentist, as usual, took an impression of her mouth.

"M. Fauville happened to have kept the mould; and he used it to print the marks of his wife's teeth in the cake of chocolate shortly before his death and in the apple on the night of his death. When this was done, he put the mould with the other things which the explosion was meant to, and did, destroy."

Don Luis's explanation was followed by a silence. The thing was so simple that the Prime Minister was quite astonished. The whole tragedy, the whole charge, everything that had caused Marie's despair and death and the death of Gaston Sauverand: all this rested on an infinitely small detail which had occurred to none of the millions and millions of people who had interested themselves so enthusiastically in the mystery of the teeth of the tiger.

The teeth of the tiger! Everybody had clung stubbornly to an apparently invincible argument. As the marks on the apple and the print of Mme. Fauville's teeth were identical, and as no two persons in the world were able, in theory or practice, to produce the same print with their teeth, Mme. Fauville must needs be guilty.

Nay, more, the argument seemed so absolute that, from the day on which Mme. Fauville's innocence became known, the problem had remained unsolved, while no one seemed capable of conceiving the one paltry idea: that it was possible to obtain the print of a tooth in another way than by a live bite of that same tooth!

"It's like the egg of Columbus," said Valenglay, laughing. "It had to be thought of."

"You are right, Monsieur le Président. People don't think of those things. Here is another instance: may I remind you that during the period when Arsène Lupin was known at the same time as M. Lenormand and as Prince Paul Sernine, no one noticed that the name Paul Sernine was merely an anagram of Arsène Lupin? Well, it's just the same today: Luis Perenna also is an anagram of Arsène Lupin. The two names are composed of the same eleven letters, neither more nor less. And yet, although it was the second time, nobody thought of making that little comparison. The egg of Columbus again! It had to be thought of!"

Valenglay was a little surprised at the revelation. It seemed as if that devil of a man had sworn to puzzle him up to the last moment and to bewilder him by the most unexpected sensational news. And how well this last detail depicted the fellow, a queer mixture of dignity and impudence, of mischief and simplicity, of smiling chaff and disconcerting charm, a sort of hero who, while conquering kingdoms by most incredible adventures, amused himself by mixing up the letters on his name so as to catch the public napping!

The interview was nearly at an end. Valenglay said to Perenna:

"Monsieur, you have done wonders in this business and ended by keeping your word and handing over the criminal. I also will keep my word. You are free."

"I thank you, Monsieur le Président. But what about Sergeant Mazeroux?"

"He will be released this morning. Monsieur le Préfet de Police has arranged matters so that the public do not know of the arrest of either of you. You are Don Luis Perenna. There is no reason why you should not remain Don Luis Perenna."

"And Florence Levasseur, Monsieur le Président?"

"Let her go before the examining magistrate of her own accord. He is bound to discharge her. Once free and acquitted of any charge or even suspicion, she will certainly be recognized as Cosmo Mornington's legal heiress and will receive the hundred million."

"She will not keep it, Monsieur le Président."

"How do you mean?"

"Florence Levasseur doesn't want the money. It has been the cause of unspeakably awful crimes. She hates the very thought of it."

"What then?"

"Cosmo Mornington's hundred million will be wholly devoted to making roads and building schools in the south of Morocco and the northern Congo."

"In the Mauretanian Empire which you are giving us?" said Valenglay, laughing. "By Jove, it's a fine work and I second it with all my heart. An empire and an imperial budget to keep it up with! Upon my word, Don Luis has behaved well to his country, and has handsomely paid the debts—of Arsène Lupin!"

A month later Don Luis Perenna and Mazeroux embarked in the yacht which had brought Don Luis to France. Florence was with them. Before sailing they heard of the death of Jean Vernocq, who had managed to poison himself in spite of all the precautions taken to prevent him.

On his arrival in Africa, Don Luis Perenna, Sultan of Mauretania, found his old associates and accredited Mazeroux to them and to his grand dignitaries. He organized the government to follow on his abdication and precede the annexation of the new empire by France, and he had several secret interviews on the Moorish border with General Léauty, commanding the French troops, interviews in the course of which they thought out all the measures to be executed in succession so as to lend to the conquest of Morocco an appearance of facility which would otherwise be difficult to explain.

The future was now assured. Soon the thin screen of rebellious tribes standing between the French and the pacified districts would fall to pieces, revealing an orderly empire, provided with a regular constitution, with good roads, schools, and courts of law, a flourishing empire in full working order.

Then, when his task was done, Don Luis abdicated.

※ ※ ※

He has now been back for over two years. Everyone remembers the stir caused by his marriage with Florence Levasseur. The controversy was renewed; and many of the newspapers clamoured for Arsène Lupin's arrest. But what could the authorities do?

Although nobody doubted who he really was, although the name of Arsène Lupin and the name of Don Luis Perenna consisted of the same letters, and people ended by remarking the coincidence, legally speaking, Arsène Lupin was dead and Don Luis Perenna was alive; and there was no possibility of bringing Arsène Lupin back to life or of killing Don Luis Perenna.

He is today living in the village of Saint-Maclou, among those charming valleys which run down to the Oise. Who does not know his modest little pink-washed house, with its green shutters and its garden filled with bright flowers? People make up parties to go there from Paris on Sundays, in the hope of catching a sight, through the elder hedges, of the man who was Arsène Lupin, or of meeting him in the village square.

He is there, with his hair just touched with gray, his still youthful features, and a young man's bearing; and Florence is there, too, with her pretty figure and the halo of fair hair around her happy face, unclouded by even the shadow of an unpleasant recollection.

Very often visitors come and knock at the little wooden gate. They are unfortunate people imploring the master's aid, victims of oppression, weaklings who have gone under in the struggle, reckless persons who have been ruined by their passions.

For all these Don Luis is full of pity. He gives them his full attention, the help of his far-seeing advice, his experience, his strength, and even his time, disappearing for days and weeks to fight the good fight once more.

And sometimes also it is an emissary from the Prefect's office or some subordinate of the police who comes to submit a complex case to his judgment. Here again Don Luis applies the whole of his wonderful mind to the business.

In addition to this, in addition to his old books on ethics and philosophy, to which he has returned with such pleasure, he cultivates his garden. He dotes on his flowers. He is proud of them. He takes prizes at the shows; and the success is still remembered of the treble carnation, streaked red and yellow, which he exhibited as the "Arsène carnation."

But he works hardest at certain large flowers that blossom in summer. During July and the first half of August they fill two thirds of his lawn and all the borders of his kitchen-garden. Beautiful, decorative plants, standing erect like flag-staffs, they proudly raise their spiky heads of all colours: blue, violet, mauve, pink, white.

They are lupins and include every variety: Cruikshank's lupin, the two-coloured lupin, the scented lupin, and the last to appear, Lupin's lupin. They are all there, resplendent, in serried ranks like an army of soldiers, each striving to outstrip the others and to hold up the thickest and gaudiest spike to the sun. They are all there; and, at the entrance to the walk that leads to their motley beds, is a streamer with this device, taken from an exquisite sonnet of Jose Maria de Heredia:

"And in my kitchen-garden lupins grow."

You will say that this is a confession. But why not?

In the evening, when a few privileged neighbours meet at his house—the justice of the peace, the notary, Major Comte d'Astrignac, who has also gone to live at Saint-Maclou—Don Luis is not afraid to speak of Arsène Lupin.

"I used to see a great deal of him," he says. "He was not a bad man. I will not go so far as to compare him with the Seven Sages, or even to hold him up as an example to future generations, but still we must judge him with a certain indulgence.

"He did a vast amount of good and a moderate amount of harm. Those who suffered through him deserved what they got; and fate would have punished them sooner or later if he had not forestalled her. Between a Lupin who selected his victims among the ruck of wicked rich men and some big company promoter who deliberately ruins numbers of poor people, would you hesitate for a moment? Does not Lupin come out best?

"And, on the other hand, what a host of good actions! What countless proofs of disinterested generosity! A burglar? I admit it. A swindler? I don't deny it. He was all that. But he was something more than that. And, while he amused the gallery with his skill and ingenuity, he roused the general enthusiasm in other ways.

"People laughed at his practical jokes, but they loved his pluck, his courage, his adventurous spirit, his contempt for danger, his shrewd insight, his unfailing good humour, his reckless energy: all qualities that stood out at a period when the most active virtues of our race had reached their zenith, the period of the motor car and the aeroplane...

"One day," he said, as a joke, "I should like my epitaph to read, 'Here lies Arsène Lupin, adventurer.' That was quite correct. He was a master of adventure.

"And, if the spirit of adventure led him too often to put his hand in other people's pockets, it also led him to battlefields where it gives those who are worthy opportunity to fight and win titles of distinction which are not within reach of all. It was there that he gained his. It is there that you should see him at work, spending his strength braving death, and defying destiny. And it is because of this that you must forgive him, even if he did sometimes get the better of a commissary of police or steal the watch of an examining magistrate. Let us show some indulgence to our professors of energy."

And, nodding his head, Don Luis concludes:

"Then, you see, he had another virtue which is not to be despised. It is a virtue for which we should be grateful to him in these gray days of ours: he knew how to smile!"

Assembling the greatest detectives all together

Covering the full range and history of detective fiction.
From Zadig, *The Moonstone*, and Dupin through Sherlock Holmes, Loveday Brooke, Montague Egg, Lord Peter Wimsey, *The Thinking Machine*, Father Brown down to Solar Pons.

Voltaire/Beckford	Wilkie Collins	Edgar Allan Poe	Catherine Pirkis	G.K. Chesterton
ZADIG AND VATHEK	THE MOONSTONE	THE COMPLETE DUPIN	THE EXPERIENCES OF LOVEDAY BROOKE, LADY DETECTIVE	THE COMPLETE FATHER BROWN VOLUME 1
Jacques Futrelle	**Dorothy L. Sayers**	**Baroness Orczy**	**Dorothy L. Sayers**	**August Derleth**
THE COMPLETE THINKING MACHINE VOLUME 2	THE COMPLETE MONTAGUE EGG	LADY MOLLY OF SCOTLAND YARD	A PETER WIMSEY OMNIBUS	THE MEMOIRS OF SOLAR PONS
Sax Rohmer	**Edgar Wallace**	**Émile Gaboriau**	**Ernest Bramah**	**Freeman Wills Crofts**
THE FU MANCHU OMNIBUS	THE COMPLETE J.G. REEDER STORIES	MONSIEUR LECOQ	THE COMPLETE MAX CARRADOS VOLUME 1	INSPECTOR FRENCH'S GREATEST CASE

John P. Marquand MR. MOTO VOLUME 1	**Louis Joseph Vance** THE LONE WOLF	**Maurice LeBlanc** ARSÈNE LUPIN VS. HERLOCK SHOLMES	**Melville Davisson Post** MASTER OF MYSTERIES THE COMPLETE UNCLE ABNER COLLECTION	**M.P. Shiel** PRINCE ZALESKI AND CUMMING'S KING MONK
Gaston Leroux THE ROULETABILLE OMNIBUS	**R. Austin Freeman** THE EYE OF OSIRIS	**A. E. W. Mason** AT THE VILLA ROSE	**Aleister Crowley** THE COMPLETE SIMON IFF STORIES	**Algernon Blackwood** THE JOHN SILENCE COLLECTION
Peter Cheyney THE SLIM CALLAGHAN OMNIBUS	**Baroness Orczy** THE OLD MAN IN THE CORNER	**Patricia Wentworth** GREY MASK	**Raymond Chandler** THE PHILIP MARLOWE OMNIBUS	**H.C. Bailey** CALL MR. FORTUNE
Josephine Tey THE DAUGHTER OF TIME	**Anna Katherine Green** THAT AFFAIR NEXT DOOR	**Sexton Blake** THE SEXTON BLAKE COLLECTION VOLUME 1	**S. S. Van Dine** THE BENSON MURDER CASE	**Freeman Wills Crofts** THE CASK

For more details and a full list of titles:
visit https://www.hachetteindia.com/home/yellowbacks

WELCOME BACK TO THE GOLDEN AGE